DESPERATE HEARTS

"Highly recommended!"
—*Manderley*

A TASTE OF HEAVEN

"Charming, warm-hearted."
—*Romantic Times*

"A TASTE OF HEAVEN is everything its name has promised."
—*Affaire de Coeur*

A LIGHT FOR MY LOVE

"A very special love story between two unforgettable characters."
—*Affaire de Coeur*

HOMEWARD HEARTS

"A very special work by a talented author."
—*Affaire de Coeur*

"This book is a real triumph!"
—*Rendezvous*

ALLIE'S MOON

Alexis Harrington

St. Martin's Paperbacks

ALLIE'S MOON

Copyright © 2000 by Alexis Harrington.

All rights reserved. No part of this book may be used or reproduced in any manner whatsoever without written permission except in the case of brief quotations embodied in critical articles or reviews. For information address St. Martin's Press, 175 Fifth Avenue, New York, N.Y. 10010.

ISBN: 0-312-97307-1

Printed in the United States of America

St. Martin's Paperbacks edition / April 2000

10 9 8 7 6 5 4 3 2 1

My sincere gratitude to my best friends and confidantes, Catherine Anderson, Susan Lisa Jackson, Margaret Vajdos, and my mom, Nikki Harrington. You give me strength and joy, every single day.

To KMC and KEW,
thanks for being Jeff Hicks and Allie Ford.

ALLIE'S
MOON

Chapter One

Decker Prairie, Oregon
May, 1880

ALTHEA FORD NEEDED A MAN AND SHE'D WALKED ALL the way to town to find one.

His looks didn't matter and neither did his age. But he'd better be good with his hands and possess physical stamina because she planned to keep him busy from early morning until sundown.

Coming to town—that was something she tried to avoid. Decker Prairie was a quiet, slow-moving place. That tended to give its residents long memories for the rare sensational event, and curiosity that bordered on rudeness. To hide her self-consciousness, she moved along the sidewalk with a purposeful stride, looking neither right nor left. But she was aware of people staring at her as she passed, and whispering behind their hands. She knew they had forgotten nothing about the Ford family.

Worse than being the subject of scrutiny and gossip was the errand that brought her here today. It wasn't one that she looked forward to. In fact, only desperation drove her to it. It seemed a crime to ruin such a beautiful spring afternoon with a disagreeable task.

As she rounded the corner, the Liberal Saloon came into

view. Even from here she could smell the warm, yeasty
scent of beer and stale cigar smoke. That a man should
waste his time in a place like that, she thought with her lips
pursed. She lifted her nose a notch. Why, there was one
now, just hanging around outside the door, and a pitiful-
looking specimen he was, too, with his slouched shoulders
and dog-eared appearance. He probably smelled as bad as
he looked.

Just as she came abreast of him and was about to step
off the sidewalk to give him a wide berth, the man looked
up at her. Their eyes met for a breathless instant, and Althea's train of thought jumped the track. Leaning against
the doorjamb that way, he seemed familiar but she couldn't
place him. She thought he rather resembled Jefferson Hicks,
Decker Prairie's former sheriff. But this couldn't be him.
She swallowed. Surely she would remember a man with
eyes that color—green, like fields of ripe cornstalks. Inten-
sity burned in them, as if trouble and danger were his in-
timates. His gaze swept over her, searching, speculative, but
what he sought she couldn't guess. It wasn't like the rude,
furtive looks she got from other people. In fact, he gave no
indication of recognizing her. No man had ever looked at
her that way. For a moment, she thought he might even
speak to her, but he didn't. An odd thrill of fear and curiosity rushed through her, stiffening her spine and hurrying
her steps. After she passed him, an irresistible urge made
her glance back at him over her shoulder. But he was no
longer watching her, and she felt an unbelievable twinge
of disappointment.

Whatever was she thinking of? she wondered. With all
the trouble she had facing her, why on earth was she curious about that dirty, ill-kempt man?

Althea tightened her shawl around her shoulders and
sped on to Kincade's Livery. It was with a different sort of

trepidation that she approached. Stepping from bright sun-light into large, gloomy enclosures like stables and barns always made her hands feel a little clammy.

And Cooper Matthews was a man of such low degree and reputation, some might say that no decent woman should have any dealings with him. But necessity left her with no choice.

She lingered in the big doorway, hoping to spot him without having to actually go in search of him. Without having to go into this dark, cavernous building. Cooper did odd jobs around the livery to earn his keep, and this was where he ought to be. She knew that he lived in a shack behind the stables, but it would hardly be proper—or safe, in her opinion—to look for him back there.

Though her trips to Decker Prairie were rare, Althea had been privy to enough gossip to know that with the possible exception of his crony Floyd Endicott, no one in town re-ally liked Cooper. The boy who delivered groceries out to the Ford place was a busybody who'd told Althea that Coo-per was a bully who drank too much, and that since his youth his cruel streak had shown itself time and again. Pull-ing the wings off flies and making fun of others' debilities or differences were great sport to him. For women, Cooper reputedly had no respect at all.

Taking one step inside the stables, Althea peered into the dim interior. The pungent smells of horses and hay struck her, along with the faint musty odor that seemed to lurk in all barns. She swallowed and closed her hands into fists, pressing them to her chest.

"Mr. Matthews?" she called. "Mr. Matthews, are you here?"

Only soft nickering answered her.

She took another careful step deeper into the stables. A glance at the rafters overhead made her heart beat heavily, and she immediately dropped her gaze to the hard-packed dirt floor. After having worked up the courage and determination to come in search of him, Althea didn't know if she could bring herself to return later if he wasn't here now. She backed up and looked over her shoulder to see if he was in the corral. "Mr. Matth—"

"Quit your yellin', lady. I ain't deef."

Althea jumped and turned her head so quickly, a joint in her neck made a soft popping sound. A wiry man of medium height emerged from the shadows of the back stalls. He walked with a cocky nonchalance that made her wish again for some other option. But there was none.

"Mr. Matthews," she repeated. Although his battered hat hid part of his features, she recognized him.

"Yeah, that's me. What do you want?"

She felt slightly winded, as if she needed to take a breath between each word. "I'm Althea Ford. I live on the north edge of town."

"So? Got a horse you want tended or what?" His voice had a coarse, nasal quality. Bib overalls hung like a grimy bag on his frame, as though they were never taken off, never washed. The undershirt beneath might have been white at one time. Now it was various shades of sweat-stained ecru. In all, he was filthy and unpleasant and dangerous, even more so than the man outside the saloon.

Althea did her best to look him in the face while she spoke, but it was difficult. She saw a cold, intimidating appraisal in his dark eyes that made her chest feel tight. "I have a house—" She drew another breath. "That is, I need a lot of work done around my house. The roof leaks and my kitchen garden hasn't been planted yet. The gutters are overflowing and the whole place needs painting. I hoped you might—I was wondering if you'd be interested in the job."

He scrutinized her with a suspicious gaze. "Yeah? How much are you payin'?"

"I'll give you good wages if the work is completed to my satisfaction."

Finally a glimmer of recognition crossed his long face, and he hooked his thumbs in the suspenders of his overalls. "Oh, yeah, I heard about you. You're one of them crazy Ford women, ain'tcha? Your mama strung herself up."

Althea swallowed against the lump beginning to form in her throat but said nothing.

"You've been goin' around town, beggin' to hire someone. Since you're here, I guess you ain't found any takers. Huh, nobody wants to work for a persnickety woman. I'd just as soon do chores for those old Pratt women."

Decker Prairie talked as much about Mary and Louise Pratt as they did the Fords. A pair of cantankerous, demanding old crones, Mary and Louise Pratt were sisters-in-law who lived in town and didn't have one good word to say about anything or anyone. So disagreeable were they that children were warned the Pratts would "get them" if they misbehaved.

Begging? Persnickety! She felt her face color hotly. "If you mean that I want an honest day's labor for the money I'm paying—"

"Sounds more like slave labor to hear tell at the Liberal Saloon. Last spring Heck Germaine had to paint your damned fence twice before you'd pay him. And Floyd Endicott had a try at it before that, and you didn't pay him at all."

Feeling obliged to defend herself, she replied, "I asked Hector Germaine to put two coats of paint on the fence so that it would weather well. As for Mr. Endicott, no, I would not give good money to someone who left the barn door open and spent the day napping under my pear tree."

Cooper shook his arrow-shaped head. "I don't like takin' orders from a woman anytime, but a picky one—hell, lady, for all that you're a tolerable-lookin' female"—he leaned over slightly and shot a stream of tobacco juice into the dirt, barely missing her skirts—"you just don't know your place. I guess you ain't found a man willin' to teach it to you, neither."

Althea's face flamed hotter. She had never suffered so many insults in the space of five minutes. She'd done nothing to warrant them, and she could not bear to stand here and take them any longer. "I see I've made a mistake," she replied coolly and turned to walk away.

"Yeah, with them other boys you did," he agreed, obviously misunderstanding her. "I'll do the work, but we're gonna get a few things straight."

Astounded, she stopped in her tracks and faced him. He dragged his gray-brown sleeve across his mouth. The man's insolent self-assurance nearly took her breath. But the malevolence she saw in his face made her bite back the hot reply that sprang to her mind. Oh, what a stupid thing to do, coming here to talk to him. Stupid. She felt defenseless and knew that he sensed it, the way a vicious dog smelled fear.

"No, thank you, Mr. Matthews. I'm no longer interested."

He raked her with those cold narrow eyes again, considering her slender form in a way that was both profane and derisive at the same time. Finally, a cruel smirk split his face, revealing oddly tiny, tobacco-stained teeth. "Y'ain't, huh? Are *you* gonna climb up to the roof to patch it? Steer the plow yourself?"

Althea took a deep breath and forced back the tears she felt gathering under her eyelids. How could this obnoxious, rude man who smelled of stale beer, horse manure, and old sweat make her cry? He was no one to her. Less than no one.

But he was right about one thing—over the past few weeks she had asked every available man in town before she'd come here. And she'd heard as many excuses as a dog had fleas why they couldn't do the job. Though no one had come out and said so, their meaning was plain enough: they didn't want to work for her. And her advertisements at Wickwire's General Merchandise and the Decker Prairie Grange had gone unanswered. Despite that, she would walk away from Cooper Matthews this minute if she could.

Then in her memory rose the picture of all the basins and pans she'd had to put out during the winter and spring rains to catch the drips. Night and day, the steady *plink-plink* could be heard throughout the house.

The roof had to be fixed this year. It leaked over almost every room, and mildew was sure to follow. The gutters were sprouting weeds. The paint was peeling off the house in blistered sheets. The garden had to be planted. She might be able to do that much if she had just a little help. But there was no one.

"All right, then, Mr. Matthews," she resolved, regaining control of herself and, she hoped, the situation. "I'll pay you ten cents an hour plus the cost of supplies. I'd like you to get started after lunch."

He rubbed his stubbled jaw with a dirty hand and grinned again. "We'll see about all that, too, now, won't we?"

In the end, the handyman had demanded and gotten the outrageous wage of thirteen cents an hour, plus his meals. He also announced that he would start in the morning, not that afternoon. There was no point in protesting—he had Althea over a barrel and he knew it.

After a brief stop at Wickwire's to get a little gift for Olivia, Althea trudged the mile back home, feeling like a mouse worn out by its struggle with a dirty feral cat. Her reclusive life had not prepared her to deal with men like Cooper Matthews. In fact, it hadn't prepared her to deal with men much at all.

Although the late May afternoon was clear and bright and filled with the promise of spring, she found only worry in it as she walked along the road that led out of town. The sight of pretty wildflowers lifting their heads to the sun reminded her how overgrown her own yard was. The light, clean breeze brought to mind the peeling paint, the loose front step, the rotting roof—everything that was wrong with her house.

She glanced at a green field stretching out to her right, dotted with sheep and wobbly-limbed new lambs. Persnickety, was she? So Cooper Matthews had called her. He'd made it sound like the most loathsome of characteristics, worse than any of the seven deadly sins. She couldn't think of anyone who would pay a man for sleeping instead of working. If that was persnickety, so be it. Was it asking so much that things be done the way she wanted? Why should she accept a fence painted once when she'd asked for two coats?

And it seemed a simple enough request that the barn door be kept closed, so that she wouldn't have to see inside the dark, gaping maw. Wouldn't have to see inside and remember what had happened in there. Even now, eighteen years later, it gave her shudders to think about it.

Even now.

"Olivia? I'm home," Althea called from the kitchen. From the parlor she could hear the high, sweet notes of "Für Elise" and knew that her sister was in the same place she

had left her. Following the sound of the melody, she saw
Olivia sitting at her rosewood grand piano, the one Father
had given her for her tenth birthday. The instrument nearly
overpowered their small neat parlor, but when she'd expressed the desire to play, of course Amos Ford had wanted
her to have the very best.

Although she had the talent to play beautifully, at that
moment Olivia thumped out the Beethoven piece with more
force than it called for. The notes ricocheted off the walls
in a way that surely would have outraged the late maestro.

Althea sighed. Though Olivia gave no other sign of it,
obviously her younger sister was still in a sulk. "Were you
all right while I was gone?" she asked, trying again for a
response.

Finally Olivia broke off the tortured melody and lifted
her hazel eyes. Her pale blue dress was the perfect com-
plement to her coloring. With hair the color of corn silk,
and a smooth, translucent complexion like fine china, she
looked as delicate and ethereal as an angel. Like their
mother, or at least what Althea could remember of her.
Althea had been told she herself favored a distant aunt
whom she'd never met, but she thought that she resembled
no one else in the family. In fact, at moments of her greatest
self-doubt, when things had been the darkest, she'd wondered if Olivia had been the Fords' only true child. Perhaps
Althea had been a foundling.

"Yes, I was fine. But I still wish I could have come with
you. You know I'm feeling much stronger these days."

Althea reached up to pull the pins out of her straw hat.
"I know you are and I'm glad for that. It just wasn't a good
time for you to go with me today."

"Well, I would've liked to have pie and tea at Elmira's
Café." Her sister's soft, clear voice carried just the edge of
a pout.

Althea pushed aside the lace curtain and glanced through the front door glass at the ratty yard. She thought she had explained her town trip plainly enough, but as was her way, Olivia didn't always listen very closely. Facing her, Althea said, "I didn't go to have pie at the café or do anything else that was fun, Olivia. I hired a man to repair the roof and plant our garden. So many things need to be fixed around here. Anyway, you didn't miss much. Decker Prairie doesn't change."

Olivia said nothing but her face betrayed a shadow of moping disbelief. Clearly she thought she'd missed having a grand time.

"I'll fix us an early supper," Althea said with forced brightness. "I left a kettle of soup simmering on the stove." It was a challenge to get Olivia to do more than pick at her food, especially if it was something she didn't care for— and that seemed to be just about everything. "Are you feeling hungry?"

She shrugged. "I guess. But pie and tea would've tasted better."

"We'll go another time." Then, remembering her stop at the general store, she tantalized, "I brought you a surprise."

Immediately Olivia perked up, and her hazel eyes widened like a child's. "What?"

Sometimes it was difficult for Althea to remember that her sister was twenty years old. She seemed more like a young girl, one whose mind was incapable of a grave or dark thought. Unless a bad case of the "mopes" was upon her, of course. Then she could be downright gloomy.

Olivia rose from the bench and clasped her hands at her waist. "Oh, did you bring a music box, or maybe those garnet eardrops in the jeweler's display window?"

"Good heavens, Olivia!" Althea said, and laughed.

"Those are the kinds of gifts people give for birthdays or at Christmas. It's just a *little* surprise."

She sank back to the piano bench with a rustle of her blue skirts. "Oh. Yes, of course, you're right."

Althea searched her dress pocket and withdrew a pair of bone hairpins. "I got these at Wickwire's. You're always losing yours and I thought you could use them."

She took them from Althea's outstretched hand and put them on top of the piano. "Thank you."

"Maybe we can go into town next week, after the repairs are started. We can shop and have lunch at the café," Althea offered.

Olivia nodded, her face still reflecting her disappointment.

Althea made her exit to the kitchen, anxious to get away. After tying on her apron, she went to the table and began cutting careful slices from a loaf of fresh bread. The rich smell of simmering beef soup filled the room.

Olivia followed her to the stove and lifted the lid on the pot of soup Althea had made. "We could have a picnic on the grass tomorrow. Wouldn't that be fun?" She looked up at Althea, her face suddenly full of excitement. "You could make little sandwiches with the crusts cut off, and potato salad and cake. Then afterward you could read aloud to me, just like when I was little, remember?"

Althea walked to the stove and spooned some of the soup into a flowered tureen. "Not tomorrow, Olivia, maybe the day after. And I remember very well. But we'll probably have to sit on the back porch." She nodded in the general direction of the yard. "The grass is too tall and still too wet to sit on."

"Oh, is it? I hadn't noticed." Olivia glanced outside, and her face fell into sullen lines again. "Maybe the man you hired will cut it down for us when he comes out."

It didn't happen all that often, but when Olivia got into the mopes she could be so trying. Of course, Althea supposed she couldn't blame her sister; she had suffered from frail health off and on since her childhood. Father's death had sent her into a frightening decline in which she had lingered for almost three years. Despite the fact that Dr. Brewster had never found a medical reason for what he dismissed as Olivia's hysterical convulsions, Althea had not completely abandoned the hope that her sister might some-day grow well enough to marry and lead an independent life. But deep in her heart, Althea didn't believe that was likely to happen.

Lane Smithfield hadn't understood the depth of her de-votion to Olivia when he'd come courting Althea. In fact, he'd once even confided to her that he doubted the seri-ousness of Olivia's condition. Then one Saturday evening while the three of them sat at the dinner table, as if to prove him wrong, Olivia had suffered one of her spells. It had been a particularly severe and frightening event during which several dishes were broken and food was splattered on the walls.

Althea never saw Lane again. Three months later she received an invitation to his wedding to Sarah Wilcott. Looking at the careful script that told the day and time, she felt her throat grow tight with discouragement.

It hadn't been that she cared about Lane. She hadn't had a chance to begin caring about him. Their courtship had been so brief she wasn't certain she could even call it a "court-ship."

But what he had kindled in her heart was hope. Hope for a life beyond this crumbling house—hope to be some-one other than Amos Ford's daughter and Olivia Ford's sister. He'd even brought her a small bouquet of wildflow-ers that she had later pressed in a book. It had very likely

been the only bouquet she'd ever receive, and she wanted
to remember it always.

When she'd read the invitation, a part of her slipped
away and she'd mourned its passing, weeping silently in
the darkest part of the night. Any dreams Althea had held
for herself were put to rest during those sleepless hours.

Olivia had finally begun to improve again over the last
few months, just about the time that Lane stopped courting
Althea. She realized that it was only natural that her sister
would want to get out more often now that she was feeling
better.

As for herself, Althea was grateful for the arrangement
she had with Wickwire's—twice a week Eli Wickwire sent
his son out with deliveries of meat, eggs, milk, and other
groceries. She was spared from having to go into Decker
Prairie, and suffer the prying stares.

She knew why they stared. It had all been her fault, and
now she had Olivia to look after.

Take care of your sister when I'm gone.

Don't let me down again, girl.

Trying to shrug off the indictment that lay on her shoulders as heavy as a millstone, she finished making two small
diamond-shaped sandwiches, mortared with raspberry jam.
She didn't care what other people thought, she told herself.
She didn't have time to worry about it. Her duty and responsibility were right here with Olivia, and Decker Prairie
had done nothing to make her job easier.

Getting the soup bowls from the cupboard, she caught
her reflection in a small mirror that hung next to the back
door. What she saw made her pause. Did her hair seem a
bit more dull than it used to? And when had she lost the
youthful roundness in her cheeks that she'd once had? Time
seemed to have flown by, and yet, here on the Ford farm,
it also had crawled to a stop while life and the rest of the

world had gone about their business and passed her by. She'd had hopes and dreams for herself once, a yearning for a meaningful life. Now, though . . .

Just as Althea put the soup and sandwiches on the dining room table, from the parlor she heard Beethoven's gift to Elise commence again, this time with a much gentler touch. Maybe Olivia's doldrums were gone.

Althea ladled soup into the bowls and sighed.

Long after Althea went to bed that night, she could hear her sister prowling around in her bedroom on the other side of the wall. She heard the sound of bureau drawers being opened and closed. The tread of slippered feet made the floor creak so softly, Althea could barely hear it over the sound of the rain outside. But she was aware of it, just the same.

What Olivia did with her time this late at night, Althea couldn't begin to guess. She had been withdrawn through dinner, but at least her disappointment about not going to town had diminished.

Althea pulled her quilt closer to her chin, as much for comfort as for warmth. Maybe Olivia didn't feel as keenly the curious stares and gossipy murmurs when she and Althea went to Decker Prairie. Even that dreadful Cooper Matthews had identified Althea as "one of them crazy Ford women."

Her hands clenched on the hem of the quilt and she gazed through the bedroom window at the cold, white moon that showed its face from between silver-edged clouds.

Crazy.

She'd heard it before.

Insane.

Not right in the head.

They were nasty little words and phrases that sat like spiders in the corner of people's minds. It had started with her mother, long before that dark day all those years ago. And, of course, there had been speculation about Olivia since then. Why should she, Althea, hope to be excluded?

What was that old saying?

The fruit doesn't fall far from the tree . . .

She rolled over and tried to force the thoughts from her mind. Maybe that was often true, but not about her. She was positive about that.

And it wasn't true about Olivia. Her sister was just— childlike. Frail and childlike. Why couldn't people understand that?

Jefferson Hicks made his way down a rain-slick hillside and approached the split-rail fence surrounding the barn-yard. Although the sky had finally cleared, it was cold and damp. He hunched his shoulders against the night chill, wondering briefly where he'd left his coat. He thought he still owned one, but then again, he couldn't be sure.

Jeff Hicks was never sure of anything anymore.

He proceeded as carefully as a man could who had just emerged from a two-day drunk. The world wasn't quite steady yet, and the darkness didn't help.

When he touched the latch on the henhouse door, he stood there for a moment, gripping it to get his bearings. The wood beneath his fingers was weathered and rough, and his hand trembled, although not from nervousness. He'd done this a dozen times or more over the past two years. He wasn't proud of the fact, but he'd gotten to be fairly good at it. At least he'd never been caught.

Glancing over his shoulder, he looked at the farmhouse windows again. His hand tightened on the latch.

The stink of the chicken coop nearly stifled him, and he

wasn't even inside yet. What was it about those damned birds, anyway? he wondered as he lifted the bar from its notch. Even the cleanest henhouse smelled like a full chamber pot under an August sun. As he inched open the door, the warm, fetid odor poured out and flowed over him. His empty stomach lurched and his aching head throbbed harder. He turned his face away, waiting for his insides to settle down. Then he took a deep breath of clean, cool air and opened the door wide. After he stepped inside, the light breeze pushed it closed behind him.

It was as dark as the east side of midnight in there. Working from memory—and he knew that wasn't very reliable—he reached out and let his hand trail through straw and God knew what else, feeling for a nest box. An angry squawk and a hard, sharp peck on the back of his wrist told him he'd found what he was looking for.

He plunged his fingers under the chicken and she let out a series of outraged clucks while he rooted through feathers and straw in search of his prize.

"Shut up, you old bitch," he whispered irritably. "You're sitting on my breakfast. And quit pecking!" Finally his hand closed around a solitary, warm, wet egg. He withdrew it and put it inside his shirt. After thinking about it for a moment, he stuck two fingers into his tight front pants pocket, pulled out a penny, his last, and shoved it under the chicken. The biddy set up a caterwauling that was loud enough to wake both the living and the dead.

As if someone had rung a fire bell, a dog in the yard began yapping along with the chickens. Farley always kept his dog in the house at night. What was it doing outside? The animal apparently rushed to the henhouse because Jeff could hear the heavy, deep-chested *woofs* just outside, moving around the perimeter. The rest of the hens added their panicky cackling to the racket and flapped blindly around him. He backed up through the coop with his hand out-stretched behind him, groping for the door.

Oh, hell, that dog was probably standing on its hind legs with its front paws and full weight resting on Jeff's only escape route. A clammy sweat broke out all over him that glued his dirty shirt to his body and inched over his scalp. He knew he was trapped. Fast thinking wasn't one of Jeff's more adroit abilities these days, but by God, if he couldn't out-think a dog—

Suddenly, the door flew open and glaring lantern light filled his vision. Jeff found himself staring down the double barrels of a shotgun.

"Just hold it right there, mister!" At the other end of the weapon stood Farley Wright, half of his angry, weather-seamed face covered with shaving soap, the other half scraped clean. One strap of his suspenders looped down next to his leg and brushed against the head of his still-barking black-and-white sheepdog. "You stand right there now so's I can get a look at you before I blow you to kingdom come!"

Jeff took a couple of dragging steps forward, keeping his eyes on the shotgun, while the dog circled him and jumped at his feet. He wasn't afraid to die—in fact, he didn't care one way or the other if he lived. He'd just never expected to be shot for raiding a henhouse.

The farmer raised his lantern and squinted at Jeff. After studying him closely, Farley lowered his shotgun a notch, then scowled.

"*Sheriff* Hicks. I mighta knowed you'd stoop to chicken stealin'." Disgusted, the farmer looked Jeff up and down as though he were lower than a dog's pizzle. Well, the old man was right about that.

Jefferson Hicks had fallen as low as a man could.

Chapter Two

"I CAUGHT HIM RED-HANDED AND I'M PRESSING CHARGES, Will. To the full hilt of the law. I got rights—I can't have this man helping himself to my henhouse whenever the notion strikes him. And I'll warrant it's struck often enough." Farley Wright stood before Sheriff Will Mason's desk, brimming with moral indignation.

"Have you got proof that anything was stolen, Farley?" Will Mason asked. He glanced at Jeff and shifted in his chair, making the badge above his breast pocket flash in the early morning sunlight that came through the window.

"Well, just look at that!" His weathered face vermilion with anger, Farley pointed to a big wet spot on the front of Jeff's shirt, just above his belt. "That's where he hid the egg 'fore it broke. Besides, isn't it enough to catch someone rummaging in my henhouse before dawn? I don't suppose he was there for a social visit!" The picture Farley presented—half shaved, one suspender still dragging around his knee, his hair sticking up like a privet hedge—rather detracted from his oration, but not his vigor.

Jeff Hicks guessed that Farley even fancied himself as something of a hero for bringing in the big, bad egg thief.

His own head already thumping like a hammer on a rock, Jeff shut out the sound of the farmer's voice. He'd had to endure the man's outraged, nonstop monologue all the way into town. Farley had tied Jeff's hands behind his back and forced him at shotgunpoint into the back of his wagon. He hadn't needed to. Jeff had offered no resistance.

In fact, he hadn't felt more than a twinge of self-consciousness when Farley marched him in here, still under cover of his shotgun. At least he kept telling himself that. He'd sensed the curious stares from shopkeepers and people on the street, but what the hell—Decker Prairie had been talking about him for a long time. He'd given them *lots* to talk about.

From his vantage point in the corner by the stove, he let his gaze wander the confines of the sheriff's office. He hadn't seen the inside of this place for more than two years, but it seemed like twenty. Some of it looked familiar—the wall clock, the blue enamel coffeepot on the stove, the rifle rack, the scarred oak desk. With his hands tied with a rope that cut like a saw blade, it was hard for him to recall that he'd once occupied the same swivel desk chair that Will Mason now sat in as he let Farley ramble on. He'd worn the same silver-star badge, and a long-barreled revolver strapped to his thigh. That had been another life. Another Jefferson Hicks.

Finally Sheriff Mason leaned back in his chair and turned a wry gaze on Jeff. "Well? Is this just about the way it happened, Jeff?"

Hearing his name, Jeff dragged his attention back to the moment and shrugged. "I guess. I left a penny in one of the nests to pay for the egg."

"A penny!" Farley exploded. "By God, I don't know where you've been, boy . . . Well, yes I do—you've been chasing the bottom of a whiskey bottle. But I get more than a penny for my eggs, and on market day—"

Sighing, Will lifted his hand and motioned Farley to silence. "Hold on now, let's stick to the subject. Do you want to sign a complaint?"

The farmer drew himself up as straight as a rake handle and adjusted his one suspender strap. "Hell, yes, I'll sign! If that'll ship Jeff Hicks off to Salem, I'll sign a whole pile of complaints."

"Jesus, Farley, we don't send men to the state penitentiary for stealing an egg. I'll just keep him here for a while." Will sat up in his chair and rummaged around in his desk for several moments before bringing out a big key ring. "Come on, Hicks."

While old man Wright grumbled on about justice, Will Mason led Jeff to the back of the building, which contained two jail cells. He unlocked one of the cell doors and opened it.

"Turn around," Will ordered, and Jeff turned his back to him. Following a faint sawing noise and a slight tug, Jeff felt the rope around his wrists fall away. "All right, get in there."

Jeff walked to the bunk and sat down on the same stained tick he remembered from his days on the other side of the desk. Behind him, the door clanged shut.

Will folded his pocket knife and turned it over in his hands while he studied it. Then he gazed at Jeff between the bars. "What the hell are you doing to yourself? You look like something the dog puked up, and you smell just as bad. And *stealing* eggs, for chrissakes?"

Jeff hunched forward, his elbows on his knees, and stared at the gouged plank flooring between his feet. The last thing he wanted to hear today was another lecture. And he sure didn't want to hear one from the man who had succeeded him in his own job.

Apparently realizing that he wasn't going to answer, Will Mason sighed again. "I'm going to let you sit here for a few days to sober up and think about things."

Jeff lifted his head, surprised. "A few days—" His voice came out as a croak. He wouldn't have kept someone longer than a day for such a paltry offense, if he kept him at all.

Will turned to leave, then said over his shoulder, "At least you'll get fed, courtesy of Decker Prairie and Elmira's Café." Then he was gone, pulling closed a heavy oak door that separated the office from the cells.

Jeff stared blankly at the bars and the brick wall beyond. If he'd had any humor left in him, he might have laughed at this turn of events. He could even envision the newspaper headline: *Former Sheriff Jefferson Hicks Jailed for Egg Theft.*

He'd lost count of the number of times he'd cursed himself for taking the damned job in the first place, for coming to this town. Nothing about his life had been the same since. And while the days and weeks now blended together into a dateless, unchanging blur, he remembered with exquisite detail the moment when his life had turned. The fourteen-year-old boy with a gun . . . the deafening blast when he had pulled the trigger . . . the bullet nicking Jeff's chin . . . the following events that had snowballed in a roaring avalanche, engulfing all the good things in his life and finally consuming him . . .

He sighed and cradled his tender head in his hands. A few days in this place? Hell, what did it matter? It wasn't as if he had somewhere important to go.

He didn't have anywhere to go at all.

Althea stood at the kitchen window watching the road. Now and then she looked over her shoulder at the clock in the parlor. She looked again, for what must have been the fiftieth time this morning.

Late. Cooper Matthews was two hours late. He had told her he would arrive at seven o'clock sharp, and now here it was almost nine on the second clear day they'd had in a month. Half the morning was already gone, and still there was no sign of him.

It had been hard enough to get him to agree to do the work. He'd been rude and insulting, and more than a little intimidating. When she thought about talking to him yesterday, her stomach felt icy. All Althea wanted was to get the kitchen garden planted and the roof patched before it rained again.

She paced across the kitchen floor, then stepped out to the back porch and peered down the road. She saw no one coming or going. As her gaze drifted over the property, she noted again how tangled and overgrown it had become. The spring rains had given new life to the grass that she swore grew an inch every hour, and the weeds that threatened to choke out everything else. On the right end of the porch the trellis, bearing the weight of an old climbing rose, sagged alarmingly—a strong wind might send the whole business crashing through the side window.

Almost unwillingly, she turned her eyes to the spot under a solitary ancient oak tree where her parents were buried. It was surrounded by a wrought-iron fence and planted with flowers. Although she hadn't been able to keep up the rest of the yard, this place was as neat as a town square, and Althea tended it zealously. Any weed with the temerity to take root within that enclosure was promptly yanked out. Sometimes she almost feared that Amos Ford would leap from his grave if he realized that the rest of his land was not being properly attended. Just before her father died, he had charged Althea with the care of Olivia and this house.

"Don't let me down again, girl," he'd bade with a rattling breath. Again. Of course, there had been no need to review the time she failed. Her negligence had been horrible, monstrous, and unforgivable. Though they never spoke of it over the years, she had seen his chilly disapproval every time he looked at her for the rest of his life, right up until its last moment. And it had not been until that final moment, while she sat by his deathbed and held his icy hand between her own, that she'd realized how little he cared for her.

In the parlor the clock tolled nine times, bringing Althea back to the present. She looked down the road one last time, then turned to go inside and fetch her shawl.

She had a responsibility to fulfill. And if Cooper Matthews would not come to her, she would go in search of him.

It was hard enough to eat with a headache that would have felled a horse. And the gamy odor drifting up from the stained tick, the only place to sit, didn't help Jeff's stomach, either. It wasn't a bad meal that he held on his knees—a dish of cold, dried-up fried eggs with a biscuit, some limp bacon and coffee. God knew he'd eaten worse. But with Will Mason watching the fork make its shaky trip from his plate to his mouth and back again, Jeff found it nearly impossible to swallow. In the not-so-distant past, he'd had a rock-steady grip.

For just an instant, Jeff stared at his palsied hands and felt humiliation send a flush of heat up his neck. Then sanity returned. That rock-steady grip he'd once prided himself on had enabled him to become one of the fastest and most accurate shots in the territory. That talent had ended up robbing a boy of his life before he'd had a chance to really live. Maybe people did look down on him now, Jeff thought. So what? At least he wasn't hurting anyone but himself.

Mason didn't say anything. He just leaned against the brick wall beyond the cell door, his arms crossed over his chest. His hard gaze assessed, judged. It was very easy to assess and judge from that side of the bars. Oh, and didn't Jeff know that.

Maybe if he didn't look at him, if he kept his eyes on his plate, the sheriff would get bored and go back to his desk. But he didn't. He just leaned against that wall, watching.

"Don't you have something better to do?" Jeff finally asked, throwing down the fork. He couldn't make himself look up into those hard, shadowed eyes. "I'm not planning to try an escape, if that's what you're worried about. Farley caught me in his henhouse fair and square."

Will pushed himself away from the bricks and uncrossed his arms. "Hell, that isn't why I'm keeping you here. If you were any other man, you'd have gotten a sharp talking-to and that would have been the end of it. And you know it."

Now Jeff looked up, wary. "So, what's your grudge against me, Mason?"

Will shook his head. "I don't have a grudge against you, Jeff. But you do raise my dander more than most men. You're drunk half the time and sleeping it off the other half. Cooper Matthews was already the town drunk before you decided to join in. We don't need two of them in Decker Prairie."

Hearing himself compared to Matthews, Jeff felt hot blood rise to his face, partly from shame but mostly from anger. It seemed like all of his troubles could be traced to that bastard. He put the unfinished tray on the floor and stood. "I mind my own business. What do you care how I spend my time? You're a lawman, not a preacher recruiting souls."

"I hate to see a man lie down and wallow in self-pity, that's all. Are you going to spend the rest of your life feeling sorry for yourself? Do nothing more than an odd job here and there for whiskey money? Your hands shake so bad, I'll bet if I gave you a pistol you wouldn't be able to hit the side of a barn. There was a time when no one could hold a candle to your aim."

Smarting from this last comment, Jeff looked at Will Mason's holstered Colt and then turned his eyes away from the sheriff's granite stare. Jeff couldn't tolerate the idea of even *holding* a gun again. The last time he'd tried, when he'd still worn that silver star on his shirt, the palsy in his hands had been worse than now. If his own life depended upon it—and from his viewpoint, that was little reason— Jeff knew he couldn't fire a pistol again. Not to defend himself or anyone else. The knowledge was somehow emasculating, and was a notion that Will seemed to share.

"Being good with a gun never made anyone a man," Jeff muttered, more uncomfortable than ever.

"And sleeping it off in someone's barn does?" Will's gaze did not waver.

"Don't go flapping your gums until you've walked in my boots for a while. Things look a whole lot different from here."

"I remember what happened that night at Wickwire's. It was bum luck, but you don't have to throw everything away trying to forget it."

Will's words hit a little too close to the truth and made Jeff feel even more weary than he had before. "Look, just leave me be, Will. It's none of your business what I do as long as it isn't against the law." Turning, he went back to the cot and lay down with his hands locked beneath his head.

Will shrugged, then walked to the door. "I guess you crossed that line this morning, didn't you?"

The sun angled through the high, barred window above Jeff and caught him in a bright rectangle that threw striped shadows across his torso. He lay on his back, watching a spider weave an intricate web in the corner overhead. The hours dragged on, yet Will Mason hadn't returned. Maybe Mason was sticking with his plan to leave Jeff alone to think. It was the last thing Jeff wanted to do, but the thoughts came anyway.

He'd tried to sleep, but his mind had jumped around from memory to memory as if he'd had a whole pot of coffee instead of one lukewarm cup. With the sun setting against the other side of the wall, it grew warm in the cell. The heat gave a ripe edge to the stink of his own unwashed clothes and body, and the spot where the egg had broken under his shirt was glued stiffly to his skin. Yeah, Will's earlier description of him was probably not far from the truth. Jeff most likely did look like something a dog had puked up.

He didn't care. Absently, he put a hand to his jaw and felt the coarse stubble growing there. He had never been a vain man, and his appearance was just another of the details that no longer mattered to him. His world had become very narrow and simple. His aim was to get from one day to the next, and to find forgetfulness in a drink.

His thoughts continued down the roads of his past until drowsiness moved upon him. Everything—his marriage, the man he'd once been—it all seemed so long ago.

Jeff turned toward the brick wall and drew his arms and

legs close to his chest. Sally had been gone for more than a year now.

That was just as well.

At his feet, Wesley Matthews lay with a bleeding hole in his chest. Blood, there was so much blood. Jeff knew he could save him if he could just reach him. But he stood paralyzed and couldn't move no matter how hard he tried.

Jeff came awake with a jerk. Dreaming . . . he'd been dreaming again. His shirt and the old tick beneath him were drenched with sweat. His eyes focused on Will Mason, who stood in the open doorway to his cell, holding the keys.

"Come on, Jeff. There's some work that needs doing."

Chapter Three

WILL MASON PULLED ON THE REINS OF THE DELIVERY wagon he'd borrowed from Eli Wickwire. Their harnesses and bridles jingling, the horses in the doubletree stopped at the entrance to a road that led to a yellow farmhouse with green shutters. The back of the wagon was loaded with tools, and on the seat next to him Jefferson Hicks rode in silence.

A brilliant noonday sun glared out of the blue sky and pounded down on Jeff's head. He squinted against the brightness. He wasn't accustomed to being out at this hour of the day anymore.

"Okay, there she is," Will said, pointing at the house with the end of one rein.

Jeff peered at the place. Surrounded by unplowed fields punctuated with stands of old oak and fir, it didn't look like anyone lived there. Blackberry brambles grew like tangles of barbed wire, engulfing part of a well house, and forming a thorny crown around the stovepipe of an old smokehouse. The property was so run-down it had to be deserted. "This is a joke, right? You're going to dump me here at this abandoned house and make me walk back to town." He wasn't used to stringing so many words together. There weren't many people he talked to these days.

Will pushed back his hat and snorted. "Nope. It's not abandoned, and I'm not joking. Miss Althea Ford needs some help around the place, and I think you're the man for the job."

Jeff peered at the house again. "Who's Miss Althea?"

"You remember Althea Ford. She lives here with her ailing sister. Their father, old man Amos Ford, died about three–four years ago."

Jeff remembered the name and something about a pair of odd, reclusive sisters but nothing more, and he'd never met either of them. He looked again at the wild shrubbery and decrepit house. "Jesus, Will, how much do you expect me to do here? I took one lousy egg from Farley, not his whole damned farm!"

Will fixed him with a stern look. "Look, the lady said she needs help and I guess even a fool can see that she does. You never really struck me as the lazy type."

Stung, Jeff muttered, "I'm not lazy—I just don't give a damn. And I don't think there's anything you can do to me to change that."

Will slapped the reins on the horses' backs and the wagon lurched forward. As he turned into the road that led to the house, he replied, "That's your problem, not mine. I don't need you to give a damn. As for Miss Althea, she only needs your labor. That'll be enough."

"Why don't you just release me? Then I can go about my business and you won't have to trouble yourself with keeping me busy."

"You know that if I decide to, I have the legal authority to hold you for thirty days for what you did. You can help out here or you can go back to the cell in town and think some more."

Jeff frowned. That wasn't much of an alternative. Yeah, he knew Will could keep him. He just couldn't figure out why he bothered. He didn't remember the sheriff's job being so boring that he needed to hunt around for diversions. He hadn't lied when he said he didn't care. Nothing much mattered to him anymore, and what once *had* mattered was fainter in his mind than winter shadows now. But he supposed that spending the day outdoors in the clean May air beat the hell out of being trapped in the jailhouse with his thoughts and memories for company.

"Since when is it the sheriff's job to provide a handyman for the local spinsters?" he asked.

Will held the reins loosely in his hands, letting the horses pull them along at a slow pace. "Miss Althea came to the office looking for Cooper Matthews. He promised to be here this morning and he didn't show up. So you're taking his place."

Jeff stiffened at the name. "Matthews—how did he get involved?"

"She was desperate." He gestured at the surrounding landscape. "You can see why."

Yes, he could. Nearing the house, Jeff took note of the silver-gray barn that had waist-high grass and weeds growing in front of its doors. Maybe someone really did live here, but he'd bet a dollar that neither of those sisters had set foot in that barn for years. On the house, some of the shutters hung slightly askew and the whole thing needed painting. An ancient farm wagon stood disintegrating in the tall grass, its iron wheel rims rusted and some of the spokes broken. Everywhere he looked—the land, the outbuildings—something needed fixing. Jeff was no stranger to hard work. He'd done his share at the ranch and house when Sally still— But, damn, there was enough here to keep a man busy for months.

"God, I wouldn't even know where to begin," he said, feeling overwhelmed and more than little put upon.

"Don't worry, Althea Ford will tell you exactly what to do," Will replied with a slight smile as he maneuvered the wagon around to the back porch.

Jeff eyed him suspiciously; he thought he heard the hint of satisfied laughter behind his words. He could picture her now, *Miss Althea*. A dry, creaking old maid wrapped up in the depths of a big black shawl, her white hair nailed to her head in a tight bun. She was probably a little dotty, too, living here with her equally dry and dotty sister.

Will set the wagon brake and wound the reins around the handle. "Looks like you might need the tools we brought. It's hard to say what they have here."

Jeff jumped down from the seat and looked around, feeling like a prisoner being put to work on a chain gang. He reached into the back of the wagon and lifted out the shovel, hammer, hoe, and other gear Will had collected for him. If only that one stringy chicken hadn't started squalling the other morning, he would have slipped out of Farley's henhouse undetected, and he wouldn't be faced with the chore before him now.

Will led the way to the back door on the one clear path Jeff could see near the house. When Will knocked, Jeff, keeping his eyes on the worn porch flooring, again pictured a hunched woman as dried up as last year's corn husks.

He heard the door open.

"Miss Althea, I hope we're not late." Will's tone was as pinched and respectful as a schoolboy's.

Oh, brother, Jeff thought, short of rolling his eyes.

"I can certainly overlook fifteen minutes, Sheriff."

The feminine voice was young and clear, Jeff realized, and he let his eyes venture as far as the hem of her apron.

Will continued. "I couldn't find Cooper and I gave my

word that I'd have a man out here. It looks like you've got enough work to keep him busy."

Jeff inched his gaze up higher. The line of her dark blue skirt draped over the modest flare of her hips, ebbing to a small waist that accentuated her full breasts.

She faltered. "Yes, well . . . Yes, I've had some trouble getting anyone to come out here, as I mentioned. I'm afraid things have declined to a pretty bad state."

Jeff lifted his eyes to discover a straight-backed, softly rounded woman in her middle twenties. The sight of her hit him with an impact that startled him. He'd seen her outside the saloon yesterday. He remembered that—he'd almost asked her for money when she'd passed him. But he'd been so taken by the sight of her, his pride had frozen the words in his throat. Her hair, rather than white, was a thick, rich auburn that framed her heart-shaped face with red and amber highlights. She wore it pulled into a knot at the back of her head, but soft, vagrant tendrils had escaped here and there.

In vivid contrast with her surroundings, she was tidy and unrumpled, and beautiful in a way that many women were not: she didn't realize her beauty. How he knew that he had no idea. But those big blue-gray eyes of hers . . . They looked as if they could see into his very soul and read the shame written there, all the doubt and failure and cowardice.

Jeff dropped his gaze to the floorboards again, feeling a flush work its way up his neck and over his face. He couldn't remember the last time he'd done more than rinse his clothes out in a rain barrel or the branch that ran in back of the Liberal Saloon. And baths had become occasional rather than regular events. He reached up to flatten out his hair with his palm, then caught himself. Maybe she hadn't noticed. He had never been as conscious of his own appearance as he was right now, but hell, how was he supposed to look? He'd spent a day and a night in jail, and he'd been drafted to do a job that no one else would take. Little wonder. There was enough work here to overwhelm three men and a small boy.

Althea stared at the two men on the porch. Assuming that Sheriff Mason would find Will Cooper, she'd been surprised to find him standing at her back door with a tall, unkempt stranger. The man looked as if he lived in a hog wallow, and when the breeze eddied around the confines of the porch, she caught an overripe whiff of his unwashed body. His long, sandy hair stuck up in cowlicks all over his head, and his frayed dungarees and shirt were of some undefinable color. He looked even worse than Cooper Matthews had.

"This is Jefferson Hicks. He'll be happy to hire on for a day or two, won't you, Jeff?"

The man grunted without taking his eyes off his feet.

Jefferson Hicks! Althea gaped at him, astounded. He *was* the man she'd seen on the street yesterday. Even as isolated as she and Olivia were, she'd heard talk about the total ruination of Decker Prairie's last sheriff. He'd killed Wesley Matthews, she remembered that much. From then on he'd slid downhill.

Will shifted his weight from one foot to the other and adjusted his hat. "To be honest, I have to tell you that Jeff has been spending a little time in the Decker Prairie jail. Farley Wright caught him in his henhouse taking a couple of eggs. It was a minor charge, but I thought you should know."

"Um, yes—I can't think of—I'm sure—" Althea stumbled along, feeling trapped. She gazed at the top of Jefferson's downturned head and hesitated to commit herself. He was still a young man, if her memory served, but he seemed more dilapidated and rundown than her house. She'd heard that he'd taken to the drink after that incident with Wesley Matthews. But the man looked like a total derelict. How much work could he have left in him? And what kind of a job would a man do who'd squandered his life on alcohol? The calm hand of reality stopped her questions—it wasn't as if she had a lot of choice. "I haven't met many men who were willing to work. What about you, Jefferson Hicks? Are you afraid of work?"

"No, ma'am," he mumbled.

"All right, then. Mr. Hicks, I'll pay you ten cents an hour and I'll give you a meal. That's satisfactory, I hope."

He nodded, although he wouldn't look her in the face. Maybe that was preferable to the insolent, disrespectful gazes Cooper Matthews had directed at her.

Obviously relieved, Will smiled and clapped his hands together once, making both Jeff and Althea jump. "That's fine! I'll be back around sundown to pick him up." He left the porch and clambered up to the wagon seat. Taking up the reins, he turned the horses back toward the road through the tall grass. "Jeff, you mind what the lady says."

Jeff cast what Althea thought was an angry, desperate look in the sheriff's direction, but he remained mute. He followed the wagon with his eyes until it was out of sight, then he turned to her.

A chasm of silence opened between them as he studied her skirt hem and she studied him.

He'd been a very attractive man. Althea remembered that. On one of her rare trips to town, she'd seen him from a distance when he was still sheriff, and had privately admired his tall, long-legged stride as she'd watched him walk down the street.

His shoulders were the same, wide but not bulky. He was more lean now than muscled, and more than a little on the thin side. His face had fallen into gaunt lines, as if he never had a square meal anymore. And she'd remembered him as being taller. Then she realized that he was slouching, the way youngsters did when they felt self-conscious. The ghost of his good looks remained, but if Will hadn't told her his name she wouldn't have recognized the former sheriff. Even so, his rolled-up shirt sleeves revealed sinewed arms that appeared to have strength left in them.

Breaking off her stare, she asked, "Do you know anything about patching a roof? That's what I need done first."

Still not looking at her, he stepped down from the porch and backed up to inspect the top part of the house. "Some."

"Good. You'll find some shingles and nails in—in the— over in there." She pointed at the barn. Its big, sliding door faced the porch. "There's a ladder in there, too. And please don't forget to close the door when you aren't in there. That's very important." From within the house, she heard Olivia call her.

He lowered his gaze from the roof to look at her for an instant, long enough for her to see that his eyes were deep green, like the last leaves of summer, just before they turned.

"If you need anything else I'll be right inside. Just knock."

He nodded and walked across the yard toward the barn. Althea crossed her arms over her chest and watched him go, shaking her head, half in pity, half in irritation.

Some people were prisoners of their own making. They let months and years slip away from them with nothing to show for the passing of time but hearts full of regrets or bitterness. Jefferson Hicks was a champion example of such a man.

Olivia called again, more insistent this time. She turned and went to answer her sister's summons.

*   *   *

Jeff waded through the weeds and grass to reach the barn.
Sharp-spined thistle snagged his jeans and Queen Anne's
lace bobbed in the breeze. He wished Mason had thought
to bring a scythe while he was piling up the tools. Grabbing
the pull, he tried to slide open the barn door but it wouldn't
budge more than six inches. He braced his foot on the jamb
and pulled again with both hands. The door gave way with
a deafening screech of rusted wheels, crashing across the
front of the barn, and Jeff landed on his back in a patch of
thistle. His palms were stabbed in a hundred places with its
needle-like spines. A group of sparrows that had apparently
been nesting under one of the eaves evacuated with alarmed
chirps and resettled in a nearby pear tree.

"Damn it to hell!" Jeff groused. Regaining his feet he
looked at the insides of his hands and saw stickers lodged
in them. He stepped into the cool dimness of the barn,
absently pulling out the spines with his teeth.

The feeling of abandonment was strong here, stronger
than anywhere else on the property. Livestock—a horse or
two, maybe a couple of cows—had once occupied the
stalls. The vague scent of them still lingered. But nothing
lived in here now except the spiders that wove curtains of
webs draping the rafters and probably a lot of mice.

Jeff searched the walls and all the corners, looking for
the materials he needed. He found an old horse harness and
a plow, rusting farm tools, a crate of filberts, a keg of axle
grease, a box of shingle nails, and a few milk cans. He
even found the ladder. But no shingles.

Up in the loft he found the remnants of a hay crop, a
trunk, and some old picture frames, but no shingles.

Exasperated, he stood in the doorway and glanced back
at the house, loath to go up there and ask questions of
Althea Ford. He didn't want to look into those probing

blue-gray eyes again so soon. Even though he'd mostly kept his face lowered, he'd felt the searing touch of her gaze as she examined him.

But where the hell were the shingles?

Jeff went back outside and battled more weeds and blackberries to circle the old building, searching for a shed or a springhouse, anyplace that might have been used for storage.

After he narrowly avoided a hornet's nest, his patience shortened to the quick. He stood in the thin midday shadow of the barn and dragged his arm across his sweating forehead. If he could lay an egg to replace the one he'd taken from Farley, he'd do it or die trying, just to get out of this damned job. Mason had said this sentence wasn't about his pilfering, but that's what had landed him in jail.

Looking at the house again, he searched the windows for a watchful face. Then he scanned the sea of grass surrounding him. If he stayed off the road— Maybe he could cut across the fields and walk back to town. Let Will find Cooper Matthews to come out here. After all, he'd made the promise to Althea Ford, not Jeff.

If he stayed out of sight in Decker Prairie, he could avoid Mason. All he wanted was enough money to buy some whiskey at the Liberal and find forgetfulness. Alcohol offered a kindly oblivion for only the cost of a bottle. For a few hours he wouldn't see a dead boy's face in his mind, or Sally's note. If he had a whale of a headache afterward— well, nothing in life was free. Money . . . he rummaged in his empty pockets. Oh, yeah—he didn't have any. That was how this had all come about to begin with.

But if he lasted the afternoon here, the Ford woman would pay him and he could buy that whiskey.

Just then he noticed a small lean-to addition near the front end of the barn. Slogging back through the grass, he pushed open its door. Amid a jumble of stuff, including the shingles, he found an old iron bed, a table with a bowl and pitcher, and a battered chest of drawers.

Jeff stepped outside and looked at the steep roof again. He only had to last through the rest of the day. When Will came to pick him up he'd tell him he didn't want to come back. Maybe the sheriff would forget about teaching him a lesson, and he could go get that whiskey.

Now if he didn't fall off and break his fool neck—

"Who did you say he is?" Olivia stood at the side window in the parlor and craned her neck, trying to see the top of the ladder that rested against the house on the other side of the glass. With her head tipped back, her long, silky curls brushed her waist.

"His name is Jefferson Hicks," Althea repeated, raising her voice. She sat in her favorite chair, the one with the needlepoint seat and back that she'd stitched herself. In fact, needlepoint was the only diversion she permitted herself. Right now, however, she used her needle and thread to mend one of her chemises. The hammering overhead had begun about two hours earlier, and while she had no idea whether the man knew a thing about roofing, just hearing the noise was a relief. At least *something* was getting done.

"That name sounds familiar, but I don't remember him. Who is he?"

"He was the sheriff in town, Olivia. You remember that."

"Hmm, maybe. Why isn't he the sheriff anymore?"

Why, indeed. "He started drinking. He eventually left his job."

"Is he married?"

"I believe he was. I'm not sure he is now." How could he be? What woman would let her husband deteriorate into the town drunk? Althea wondered. If she were his wife, she certainly wouldn't have allowed that. In Althea's opinion, it was almost sinful to waste a life by frittering it away.

"I didn't see him. Is he handsome?"

"Yes, at least he used to be. The liquor has taken a toll on him." She glanced up from her mending. It wasn't like Olivia to express an interest in any man. But she'd been feeling so much better; perhaps she was coming out of her shell. The hope Althea had nursed in her heart for her sister sparked a little flame. "Why are you so curious?"

Her sister shrugged. "Oh, no reason. He won't do the work as well as Daddy would have liked," she observed with an artless finality.

"I'm sure that's true," Althea said, and bit back a sigh.

"Daddy was very particular about the way things should be done, and he wouldn't have wanted just anyone pounding on his house, Althea." Olivia's slightly imperious tone made Althea clench her back teeth. Their father had been a difficult man to please in all things save one. Olivia had given him as much joy as a joyless man could feel. Althea had given him as much displeasure.

"Then it's a good thing he won't know about this, isn't it?" Althea asked.

Olivia stayed at the window. "I guess. I see your Mr. Jefferson has been in the barn."

"Hicks, dear. His name is Jefferson Hicks. Of course, he's been in the b-barn. That's where the ladder was."

"Well, he's left the door open." She turned then and looked at the clock. "Goodness, it's nearly three. I believe I'll go up and take a nap for a while. That is, if I can sleep with all that hammering." She dropped a light kiss on the top of Althea's head and swept from the parlor.

Althea heard her soft tread on the stairs but remained in the chair. She would not get up and look, she told herself.

She wouldn't go see that open doorway for herself. Perhaps Olivia was mistaken—

Overhead, she heard muted footsteps and supposed that Jefferson Hicks was walking around up there. She put aside the mending, then took it up again. Finally she put it down and rose from her chair.

She approached the window with a sense of dread, and when she looked across the yard her fear was confirmed. The barn door was open, and she saw the black, yawning portal that brought back the horror of that summer afternoon as vividly if it had happened yesterday.

Tucking the hammer into the waistband of his jeans, Jeff kept a tight grip on the rim of the chimney and straddled the peak of the roof to look out across the valley. Somehow up here the world looked different—cleaner and newborn under the afternoon sun. From the roof, Decker Prairie seemed more like a sleepy village instead of a busy town.

A high-pitched call overhead caught Jeff's attention. He shaded his eyes and looked up in time to see a peregrine falcon cross the sky, its wings spread to catch warm drafts of air. Off in the distance, a ribbon of shining creek wound across the Ford land and disappeared into the woods. And even farther away was Mount Hood, a snow-covered giant with miles and miles of fertile farmlands on its western side.

Gazing out at this view, a man could almost forget the heartache and bad luck dogging his past.

"Mr. Hicks!"

Her stern tone cut through his moment of peace, and carried over the stiff breeze rustling the grass and trees. He peered beyond the edge of the roof and saw Althea Ford standing in the yard, her hands on her hips and her face turned up to his. The breeze ruffled the loose tendrils of hair around her face, each curl catching the sunlight and flashing red-gold.

For just an instant, Jeff's masculine nature gained the upper hand, and his gaze swept the length of her pleasing figure. And very pleasing it was. So pleasing, in fact, that Jeff momentarily forgot where he was standing and damned near lost his precarious foothold on the steeply sloped roof. He scrambled for purchase, imagining himself sliding backward and tumbling to the ground. He clenched his jaw to hold back a curse.

He had taken his shirt off and tied it around his waist. Her large eyes were fixed on his chest, her startled expression saying, more clearly than words, that she'd never seen a man's bare torso. Not wishing to offend her maidenly sensibilities—Christ, how did he land himself in these messes?—he fumbled with the knot and hastily shoved his arms into the sleeves, nearly losing his balance again as he shifted his weight.

"Mr. Hicks, you have left the barn door open!"

With the way she was gaping at him, Jeff thought for a horrible moment that his chest wasn't the only body part he was exposing, but a fast downward glance at his fly assured him it was buttoned. He looked across the weed-infested yard at the barn, vaguely recollecting as he did that she'd asked him to keep it closed.

"Um—yes, ma'am."

Even from here he could see the nettled expression on her pretty face. "I believe I asked you to keep that door closed."

"It needs to be fixed—it hangs up."

"It—it—*what h-hangs?*"

"It hangs up—it's stuck."

"Oh. You mean it won't close at all?" He heard a baffling edge of panic in her voice.

"It does but it's hard to work, so I left it open because I've been going in and out for tools. Should I fix it?"

She pressed a hand to her slender waist, something about the gesture making her seem vulnerable. "No! It doesn't need fixing."

"I don't mean to argue, ma'am, but it does."

"But it doesn't matter because I don't use the barn and I want the door shut. It's not much to ask, Mr. Hicks."

It wasn't his place, or even in his nature to pursue it, but he did anyway. Maybe because the whole thing seemed so damned harebrained. "There's nothing in there that can get out. What difference does it make?"

She glanced around, as if she were groping for an answer. "It looks, well, it looks untidy."

Jeff let his gaze drift over the rest of the property, taking note of the jungle-like yard and sagging fences. "Untidy."

Obviously realizing how ridiculous that sounded, she pressed on. "Mr. Hicks, I don't have to explain myself to you. Please, just come down here and do as I asked."

He sighed, wondering if she had any idea how slick a roof was when a man wasn't wearing spiked boots. "Yes, ma'am."

As Jeff worked his way across the steep roof to the ladder, he glanced at the sky again, this time to judge the hour. He figured he had another five to go here.

He hoped to God they'd pass quickly.

Chapter Four

THE SUN CAST LONG SHADOWS THE NEXT TIME ALTHEA emerged from the house to talk to Jeff. Wading through the tall grass, she carried a tray that held a bowl of beef soup, a big chunk of hot, fresh bread, and coffee.

Despite the matter about the barn door, he'd displayed much more industry than she'd expected. The hammering and patching had continued all afternoon, and he deserved a hot meal. She'd also brought with her an old towel, and a piece of soap was tucked in her apron pocket. The meal wasn't fancy, but he'd wash before he ate it, or she'd know the reason why. Setting the tray on a stump, she scanned the roof for him. Oh—there he was, near the chimney.

Althea's breath caught in her throat.

The low, red-gold sun silhouetted Jeff's length, outlining his bare upper torso as he stood watching the western horizon. He studied it the way a ship's captain might, as if he were searching for something. The evening breeze blew back his unkempt hair, revealing his profile. With the haggard lines on his face burnished by the sun, he looked startlingly handsome standing up there, in command, as though he were a natural leader bearing a great responsibility.

Overhead, a pair of meadowlarks winged their way across the darkening blue sky, completing the tableau.

Althea realized she was staring at him again, and this time with more than general curiosity. *Shame*, she scolded herself. She had no business noticing anything about Jefferson Hicks, no business wondering what he was thinking as he stared at the horizon, or what had turned him into the man he was now.

"Mr. Hicks, is the roof finished?" she called up.

Jeff turned at the sound of her voice and put his shirt back on. "I'd say there's another half a day's work to be done on it, ma'am."

Oh, dear. She didn't know if Will Mason would allow him to return to finish the job. She'd certainly abandoned all hope of seeing Cooper Matthews out here. "Well, come down, now, and eat your dinner while it's hot. Cold soup loses its flavor."

Jeff picked up the hammer and tucked the handle back into the waistband of his jeans. Stepping carefully onto the ladder, he worked his way down and crossed the yard. Watching him, Althea couldn't mistake the expression of hunger that crossed his thin face when he saw the tray.

He reached for the bowl with two dirty hands. "It sure smells good." He glanced up, quickly tacking on "ma'am," as if it were an afterthought.

Blocking his reach, Althea thrust the soap and towel into his grasp. A thin medicinal odor blended with that of old sweat, as if alcohol were coming through his pores. "You'll pardon me for saying so, Mr. Hicks, but you do not."

After gazing for a moment at the rectangular bar and folded length of linen he found himself holding, he cast a blank look at her.

Expounding the point, she continued, "I'm sure you'd

like the opportunity to wash up. There's a water trough next to the woodshed."

Crimson highlighted his sharply cut cheekbones. "Yes, ma'am," he said. With his eyes downcast, he disappeared around the corner of the house.

Realizing that she had embarrassed him, Althea caught her lower lip in her teeth. But after this fleeting sense of remorse, she drew herself up and set her chin. The man reeked. If he needed prodding to wash every day, then she would provide the motivation as long as he remained here in her employ. It was either that or wear a clothespin on her nose every time she got near him.

She heard vigorous splashing and when he returned, his hair, hands, and face were clean, even if the rest of him wasn't. His lashes still held droplets of water and formed spiky frames around his striking green eyes. As though still embarrassed, he dropped his gaze from hers again.

"Well—you—that's better," she said, feeling an odd little flutter in her stomach. "You can bring that stool over here from the porch to sit on."

As he went for the stool, Althea heard horses coming down the road to the house. The clatter of their hooves broke the stillness of the countryside. Turning, she saw Will Mason returning with the wagon.

Will brought the conveyance to a stop in front of the porch, and climbed down. "Miss Althea," he acknowledged, touching his hat brim. "How did it go today?"

"Mr. Hicks tells me there's a little work left to be done on the roof, but I believe he's got most of it patched."

Will scanned the yard with a slow perusal that made her fidget. She already knew the property looked horrible. "Well, I'll tell you what, ma'am. I don't suppose it's any secret that Jeff has a little problem with the bottle." Will's voice dropped to a confidential tone. "As matters stand, he's not doing himself or anyone else any good. I think it's time to change that."

Althea nodded, not sure where the sheriff was taking the conversation.

He fished a match out of his shirt pocket and put it in the corner of his mouth. "If you'll have him," he continued, "he can keep working here until he dries out. Or better still, until harvest time. I figure that's about four months from now."

"Do you mean that he would stay here?"

"Believe me, Miss Althea, if you can make up a bed for him in the barn, that will be an improvement over where he sometimes sleeps."

It seemed the sheriff had completely overlooked a very worrisome fact. She glanced back at Jeff Hicks, long-legged and wide-shouldered. He might be too thin, but he was still a big man. If he chose to overpower a woman, to take liberties, like a—a kiss, or God forbid, something more, there would be nothing she could do. The very notion gave Althea a case of the jitters.

With her hand flat against her chest, Althea said in a confidential tone, "Sheriff, I think you've forgotten that my sister and I are *alone* here. I realize that Mr. Hicks once held a position of respect in Decker Prairie, but those days are obviously long past—"

Will shifted the match to the other corner of his mouth. "Now, ma'am, I would never suggest an arrangement like this if I thought that you or your sister would be, um, compromised in any way. That's not something you have to fear. I've known Jeff for a long time, and he sure can be a handful. But he wouldn't harm anyone, especially a lady."

"I remember that he killed a boy—Wesley Matthews, I believe."

Will nodded. "He did, in the line of duty. Maybe you

should ask Jeff about it." He paused and then added, "Of course, it's your decision."

The sincerity in the Will's eyes made her feel guilty for refusing. "Well, if you think . . ." she wavered.

Jeff returned with the stool, and Althea felt him edging closer to her left, apparently trying to hear the conversation.

"My only other choice is to take him back to jail. He's got a four-month term to serve, be it here or behind bars. And I mean to see that he does at least part of his time."

"But, Sheriff, that seems a bit harsh—"

"What?" Jeff demanded, momentarily jolted from his apathy.

Still holding the stool, Jeff moved closer. He wasn't about to stand there and let them discuss their arrangements for him as if he were a mule or a dog and couldn't understand English.

"Now, just a goddamned minute, Mason. You can't seriously intend to hold me for four damned months! Not just for stealing an egg!" He saw the startled look on prissy Miss Althea's face. She probably wasn't accustomed to hearing a gentleman swear. Well, too bad, because he was no damned gentleman.

He'd been sweating up there on that roof all afternoon. The only thing that had made it bearable was looking forward to getting paid so he could head off to the Liberal Saloon and get his hands around his whiskey bottle and drown himself in forgetfulness. Now Will was talking about *leaving* him out here for the whole summer? Not if Jeff had anything to say about it.

Will poked Jeff in the ribs, then seized his arm and drew him away. "Excuse us, won't you, ma'am?" He nudged Jeff toward the back of the wagon.

Jeff jerked his arm from Will's grasp. "What kind of scheme are you cooking up, Will?"

"I didn't want to embarrass you in front of the lady, Hicks, although you managed to do well enough on your own. True, I can't hold you for four months, and I wasn't going to try. But I can keep you for a month. And I'll tell you this—" He took the match out of his mouth and pointed it at Jeff, punctuating each low-spoken word with it. "Every time I see you on the street in town, I'll be keeping an eye you. I won't let you sleep it off in my barn anymore. And Caroline put her foot down a long time ago about bringing you into the house. If you pass out in someone's haystack, or in a doorway in town, I'll arrest you for vagrancy." Will's expression was dead serious, and Jeff knew the threat was, too.

"Getting drunk isn't a crime in Decker Prairie," Jeff mumbled.

"In your case, I'll make it my business to turn it into one."

Jeff snorted. "You can't rewrite the law to suit yourself, Will!"

"Watch me."

Jeff couldn't quite believe this was happening. "You'd actually jail a man for an entire month for taking one lousy egg? Where's the justice in that? Or don't you believe in justice?"

Will's mouth turned down at the corners. "I'll tell you what I believe in—that's the responsibility I have to folks in this town who need a helping hand. You, my friend, are one of them."

"Me?" Jeff asked incredulously. "I don't want or need a helping hand from you or anyone else."

"Have you had a good look at yourself lately? Your hands shake like an old man's and your eyes remind me of my red flannel long johns. Christ, you look ten years older than your age. I'm doing you a favor here, if you'd just realize it."

Jeff couldn't believe his ears. He was also very aware of Althea Ford standing there in her yard while Will gave him this dressing down. Oh, it must have made Will Mason feel high and mighty to stand there in his clean, starched shirt and stoop to save unworthy, unwashed Jefferson Hicks. Mr. High-and-Mighty, who had a wife to go home to every night, a wife who waited with a hot meal, and offered the comfort of her arms and the solace of her bed. "Favor? You'd be doing me a big favor if you'd let me go my way. It's getting harder and harder for me to remember that we were ever friends."

Fleeting images sliced through Jeff's mind: the summer afternoons they fished at the stream, the Saturday night dinners he and Sally spent with Will and his wife, Caroline, the laughter and fun—it had all been part of that other life Jeff had known. And it was as dead as autumn leaves. He regretted that, as much as his sense of insulated detachment would allow, anyway.

Will sighed and pushed his hat off his forehead. "Damn, Jeff, you sure haven't made it easy. I've wanted to turn my back on you lots of times over the past couple of years."

"Then why the hell didn't you?"

Will propped his foot on the wagon wheel hub. "Because *true* friends don't do that. I owe it to the man I used to know and respect—I owe it to him to help you now."

Jeff scuffed at the dirt with his boot but had the grace to keep his mouth shut.

"Well, Jeff, what do you say?"

He jammed his hands in his pockets but wouldn't look Will in the face. What *could* he say? A twinge of sentiment stirred somewhere inside him. "Yeah, I guess I'll stay here," he muttered.

Will lifted his head and called to Althea, "Ma'am, how about it? Can you use the help?"

Jeff chanced a look at her. The sunset gave her heavy auburn hair highlights of fire. She turned and glanced over her shoulder at the house, as if seeking permission. "Yes, I suppose—I suppose it will be all right."

"Good. I'll let you two work out the details." Will hopped up to the wagon seat and took the reins. "I'll drop by sometime next week, just to see how things are going."

Jeff couldn't keep the scowl off his face as he watched Will drive away. After the wagon was out of sight, he looked around him again, remembering what he'd thought just this morning when he first saw this place—there was enough work here to keep a man busy for months. At that moment, he hadn't realized he'd be stranded out here and have the months to give.

He heard Althea approach him; her skirts swished through the tall grass, and the faintest fragrance accompanied her. "I'll warm up your dinner in a minute, Mr. Hicks. But perhaps we should discuss our arrangement."

He faced her and nodded. Her smooth skin was the color of fresh cream, and in keeping with that dark-flame hair she had a spray of pale freckles across her nose and cheeks. But those eyes . . . he felt as if they saw all the secrets, all the hurts.

"Why did you steal those eggs from Farley Wright?"

He pushed his hands into his back pockets. "Because I was hungry." He wished he had a better answer, a more noble answer, but he didn't.

"Are you going to steal from me?"

By God, but she was blunt. Her directness had a way of cutting a man to the bone. "No, ma'am."

"You know if you do, I'll have Sheriff Mason take you back to jail before you can say Sam Hill."

He didn't know why he should care what she thought, but he blurted, "I only took one egg. And I didn't steal it. I left a penny for it."

She nodded again, apparently satisfied. "You won't go hungry here. I'll give you room and board, and pay you a wage—seven cents an hour—provided that you don't drink on my property or on my time. There is no excuse for that sort of behavior, Mr. Hicks. Our years are too precious to waste on self-indulgence."

Keeping his expression carefully blank, in his head Jeff sneered at her self-righteousness. She didn't know what she was talking about, and sounded like someone who'd never had a bad experience in her life. Some things were too horrible to bear, and humming a happy tune or looking on the bright side didn't make them one damn bit easier to live with.

She probably felt sorry for him, too. He wasn't sure which was worse, people's pity or their busybody whispering.

Her eyes touched him here and there, examining his lack of barbering and dirty clothes. "I must also insist that you clean up and let me cut your hair. I think I can find something for you to wear, too. Cleanliness is one of the qualities that raises us above animals."

She was beginning to sound like a missionary. The minute she brought out a Bible, he'd be gone from here, no matter what Will Mason threatened. "I'm no church project, Miss Ford," he warned.

She got a tight look around her mouth, and her nose pinched up, as if she smelled something bad. "This is not Christian charity I'm offering, Mr. Hicks. Even you must agree that your clothes have already seen their best days. And there is nothing wrong with being clean. Soap and water are cheap."

He couldn't deny that. She was the fussy sort, though, and probably hard to please. It showed in everything about her—the way she dressed with her high, tight collar, and the way she wanted things done. Her foolishness about the barn door was a good example.

But he sensed that there was more to her, a femininity that made him remember a time in his life when he could appreciate softness and tender feelings. It made him want to study her when she wasn't looking at him.

"You can stay in that room over there." She pointed to the lean-to where he'd found the shingles. "I'll give you clean linen and a tick. If you do as I ask, we'll get along. Is this agreeable to you?"

Agreeable? What choice did he have? He looked into her eyes. "Well, ma'am, my mother used to say that some people are born with no place to go. I don't think she was talking about me, but I guess that's the way it's turned out."

"Do you mean he's going to live here? A *man*?" Olivia asked, a delicate horror on her delicate face. She buttered a biscuit she'd made herself with dainty strokes and added, "Goodness, Althea, we don't know anything about him. He could murder us in our beds. I saw him from the window— he looks quite disgusting and disreputable."

They were eating dinner later than usual; good Lord, it was nearly eight o'clock, Althea noted when she glanced up at the parlor clock. Getting Jeff Hicks fed and settled were tasks that she hadn't anticipated.

Olivia had made the dinner biscuits in an effort to be helpful, and Althea took one, but eating it was a labor of love. Olivia could try her patience down to its last fiber, and then she'd do something sweet like making these biscuits or ironing. Unfortunately, Olivia had no talent for the domestic arts. Althea owned several chemises with large, iron-shaped scorch marks that Olivia had branded upon them, and her biscuits could be used for cannonballs.

On her plate, Althea mashed a boiled potato with her fork. "We do know something about him. He was the sheriff and he needs the work. We certainly need the help. Anyway, Will Mason recommended him, and I think that counts for something." Althea kept her own misgivings and Will's reasons for the recommendation to herself. Olivia would probably fuss and worry too much if she knew the details. "Besides, he won't look so disreputable after he's cleaned up. I'll give him a haircut and he'll look better."

Her sister dropped her knife on her plate with a clatter. "You're going to *touch* him?" she whispered. "Do you think you should? After all, he's a man—I mean, isn't it indecent?"

Althea didn't know whether to laugh or frown. Olivia was even more innocent than Althea, and her own experience with men was limited to serving dinner to Lane Smithfield. "Cutting a man's hair isn't indecent. I used to cut Father's hair."

"But that was different. He was, well, he was a relative."

Now she did laugh. "Don't worry, Olivia. Cutting Mr. Hicks' hair isn't going to jeopardize my reputation or my immortal soul. If I have to deal with him, I want him to look tidy."

Olivia took a nibble of her biscuit. "Well, I hope he won't be here long. You know how difficult it is for me to adjust to changes." She looked up, her expression emphatic. "We'll still have our picnic, won't we? I mean, we don't have to invite *him*, do we?"

Althea took a sip of her coffee. "Of course not. Jeff Hicks is a handyman, Olivia, not our guest. Except for eating his own lunch, he'll be busy working while we picnic."

Olivia took up her knife again. "All right. You won't

forget to make the tea sandwiches and potato salad, will you?"

A picnic was not something Althea really had time for. She had ironing to do, and the rugs needed to be beaten, aired, and put in storage. The graves needed weeding and that was a task that she could not delegate to Jeff Hicks or anyone else. But to keep Olivia happy, she would set aside her other chores. "No, I won't forget. I'll get up early to fix them."

There would be no needlepoint tonight. By the time the dishes were washed, Althea was ready to fall into bed. It had been a very long day and tomorrow promised to be just as tiring.

But when she turned down the wick on her bedside lamp, Althea found her mind on the man staying in the lean-to. She didn't know what to think of Jefferson Hicks; he wouldn't meet her gaze, he didn't speak unless directly questioned, and then he responded in short, clipped sentences. Although she knew it was none of her business, it bothered her that he was squandering his life on dissolution. Despite his grubby appearance, something about him touched her—he looked as if neither he nor anyone else in the world cared one whit about him.

Althea knew that feeling very well.

Late that night Jeff lay on top of the bed he'd just finished making in the little lean-to. It was only an old corn-husk mattress that Althea had given him, but the sheets were clean and he didn't feel right about crawling between them without a bath. He figured he'd take one at dawn, when he could see his way to the trough.

He'd been lying here a long time watching a moth bump restlessly around the globe of the kerosene lantern hanging on the wall. He knew how that moth felt. It had been many,

many months since he'd had to face silence and his own thoughts without the pleasant blur of a head full of whiskey. He knew it was nearly midnight, and after the hard work he'd put in on that roof, he should be sleeping like the dead. He would need the rest if he meant to put in a full day tomorrow.

Except he couldn't sleep at all. His nerves seemed to be on fire just beneath his skin, and his heart was pounding as if Farley Wright's dog had him trapped in the henhouse again. Once in a while, he'd begin to doze off, only to lurch awake again with a sense of profound panic. He had nothing to be afraid of, exactly, but the feeling wouldn't go away.

He tossed and turned, wishing to God he'd been able to get that whiskey he longed for. Without it, Wes Matthews lay dead before him again, his chest spouting blood like a geyser. Or he'd see Sally's face, cold and shuttered, or worse, he'd hear her voice, sweet and soothing, as it had sounded before she'd turned away from him.

Sometimes even a picture of Althea Ford rose in his mind, and he found that most amazing of all. He hadn't given much thought to having a woman in the last two years, so why he should think of her, he couldn't guess. Miss Fussy Drawers didn't approve of him or what he did with his time. But now he imagined what her softness would feel like under his hands and lips. Would her hair be lush and sweet-smelling when she freed it from its pins? Would her body be as smooth and cream-white as her complexion?

He flopped over on his belly and punched the feather pillow.

The endless night stretched out before him like a dark, twisting path, full of mystery and danger.

Just one drink—if he had just one, it might shut out

those memories and faces. He never should have let Will twist his arm into staying here. If he'd refused, Will would've had to take him back to town and he would have been free a lot sooner than the end of summer. He could have his whiskey, and he wouldn't need to deal with the demanding Miss Althea Ford.

Maybe when Will came back out in a few days, he could weasel out of this deal. Until then, though, he was stuck.

Dawn came sooner than Althea would have liked, but there was no getting around the work she had to do today. After she washed and dressed, she went down the hall to her father's old bedroom. The door was kept closed, and Althea had not willingly set foot inside since his death. She gripped the cold glass knob for a moment, then gave it a twist and pushed. The bedroom looked exactly as it had for as long as she could remember. She hadn't moved or changed a thing.

Running her hand over the already tidy counterpane, Althea stared at the chair next to the bed. She'd spent hours sitting in here toward the end of her father's life. Years of working the land had not made him sturdy and rugged, as it did other men. At the age of fifty, his failing heart had turned him into an invalid. It had been impossible for him to take more than a step or two without becoming winded, and he'd coughed continually.

Olivia had been no help. In a state of nervous exhaustion she'd rarely ventured beyond her own bed. So Althea had shouldered the responsibility of caring for both of them.

But Althea had been dutiful—Amos Ford had not had to so much as ask for a drink of water. She'd anticipated and seen to his every need and want.

Hoping . . . hoping that he would forgive her at last, and not carry his bitterness with him to his grave.

When he'd taken his last strangled breath, it was long past midnight. With Olivia on her knees sobbing hysterically beside the bed, Althea had stood over them, feeling excluded and alone. Finally a welcome sense of detachment numbed her pain and disappointment. As if she'd been watching the scene from some other place, she wondered why people so often went to meet Death in the deepest part of the night.

But no matter whether at dawn or dusk, her father had gone, and the words she'd yearned for since she was seven years old, the absolution, never came and never would.

Forcing her mind back to the present, Althea's gaze fell to the bureau where there lay a razor, a shaving mug and brush, and a comb, the objects of her mission to this place of bad memories. She reached out with a hesitant hand and let her fingertips rest lightly on the ivory-handled blade. Still dutiful, she tended this room the same way she tended her parents' graves. Only at night, while alone with her thoughts, did Althea admit—and then reluctantly—that she was dutiful more out of fear than respect. It was silly, she knew, but even from the grave, her father ruled her life with an iron fist from dawn to dark, just as he had when he was alive, always dangling the hope before her that he might one day forgive her.

If only she pleased him enough.

If only she worked just a little harder.

If only . . .

Ludicrous as it was, she couldn't shake the notion that he'd find a way to punish her if she failed to do things now exactly as he'd demanded when he'd been alive. Before daybreak, she had to be washed and dressed. By dawn, breakfast had to be on the stove. That finished and served to his order at table, she'd been allowed to eat her own meal. Then while he and Olivia had lingered over coffee, it was time to wash the dishes. Then the floors. So it went throughout the day, and even now, when his death should have freed her, she was afraid to break the routine.

That made the idea of loaning her father's razor and shaving mug to Jeff Hicks seem almost sacrilegious. But she had no others to give him, and these were simply sitting in this room, going unused. Olivia wouldn't approve, Althea was sure of that. Fortunately, she probably wouldn't realize they were missing. She never came into this room, either. And maybe she wouldn't recognize the overalls and shirts that Althea lifted out of the bureau drawers to clothe Jeff.

Before a demon of misgivings could change her mind, Althea scooped up the items. She spotted the razor strop hanging next to the door and grabbed that, too. Then she fled the room as if Amos Ford's angry spirit had chased her out and slammed the door behind her.

Chapter Five

ARMED WITH A BASKET THAT HELD A SCISSORS, MIRROR, towel, and the other things she'd collected, Althea took a deep breath and went down the back steps in search of Jeff Hicks. The new day was crowned by a cloudless blue sky, and a light, clean breeze stirred the oak and pear trees with a sound like the faint rustle of silk petticoats. Chickadees and nuthatches were already busy in the branches, pairing off and building nests.

Everywhere Althea looked, life was renewing itself. A funny little flutter skittered through her as she crossed the grass. She'd had the same feeling yesterday when she saw Jeff on the roof staring at the horizon. It felt like anticipation, yearning for something, but for the life of her she couldn't understand what it meant.

Scanning the yard, she didn't see Jeff, and he wasn't on the roof. He was probably still asleep. Well, he'd find out soon enough that days around this farm started early. Shifting the basket to her other arm, she cut a wide path around the barn and avoided looking at it directly.

She approached the lean-to gingerly and stood well back, not knowing what to expect. The door was ajar, but she risked only a quick, furtive peek. Good heavens, for all she knew he could be sleeping nake—without clothing. The very idea brought such heat to her cheeks and neck, she almost turned around and went back to the house. But no—she would see this through.

"Mr. Hicks," she called to the door opening, "the morning is well underway and there is a lot of work to do. I've brought you some clothes and a few other personal items."

Althea waited for a response, but only a noisy crow perched on a nearby fence post answered her.

She tried again, this time with more emphasis in her voice. "Mr. Hicks, lollygagging is not a virtue. The spring rains won't really end until after June, so you must take advantage of every sunny day that we have now. Please make yourself decent and come out here so I can cut your hair. I have my own work to do."

Still she got no answer. She took one step forward.

"Mr. Hicks! If you don't answer me now—"

"Ma'am?"

Althea jumped and whirled to face Jeff Hicks as he rounded the back corner of the barn. He carried his wrung-out shirt in one hand and his towel in the other. His long, wet hair streamed water down his bare chest. Although his thinness threw his ribs into moderate relief, they were criss-crossed with lean, hard muscle that extended into the waist-band of his jeans. His shaggy beard also sparkled with water droplets and made him look not simply disreputable now, but downright dangerous.

And, to Althea's horror, utterly fascinating.

"I-I'm sorry, I thought you were still—" She gestured at the lean-to. "I thought you were in there."

"No, ma'am. I was washing at the trough."

Her eyes followed the trail of another rivulet that snaked over his collarbone and into the hair that spanned his chest.

"Yes, I see—well, I came out to cut your hair and bring you some clothes and things." She indicated the basket.

He nodded. "I'll get that stool."

Following, Althea watched him stride across the yard to get the stool from the back porch. His legs were long and slim, and his shoulders were broader than she'd realized. He set the stool next to the tree stump that had served as his dinner table the evening before. When he sat down with his back to her, she stepped closer and considered the bare breadth of his shoulders.

"I brought a shirt that might fit you," she said, thinking her voice sounded high and very young. "You should probably put it on now."

He turned his head and said over his shoulder, "I'll wait until you're done. If I put it on before you cut my hair, it'll just itch all day."

"Oh, yes, of course," she stumbled, feeling timid. Taking up the comb, her hand remained suspended just above his head. He smelled clean, like the soap she'd given him, but like a man, too. She knew she should work the tangles out of his hair soon; the morning sun was warm and it was already beginning to dry, turning a rich sandy color.

Do it—just do it and get this over with. She sank the comb's teeth into the damp strands at the back of his head.

"Were you comfortable in the lean-to last night?" she asked, desperate to fill the awkward silence.

"Yes, ma'am," Jeff lied. He'd barely slept at all, and this morning his muscles ached in places that he'd forgotten existed. But he'd gladly give up another night's sleep if it meant he could sit here again tomorrow and feel her fiddling with his hair. She worked out the tangles carefully, not pulling or ripping at them as he was inclined to do. The delicious sensation of the comb scraping lightly over his scalp raised goose bumps all over him. He glanced down at the hair on his arms standing on end. He couldn't remember the last time someone had touched him.

"Fine. As soon as you finish the roof and shore up the trellis, I'll need you to start plowing the garden. I'm very late getting it planted this year. I hope you know something about plowing and planting." She talked on about what needed fixing, patching, painting.

"Hmm, yes, ma'am." With her fingers playing in his hair, it was the only response he could make. His eyes crossed slightly as he relaxed, and he heard the blades of the scissors snipping here and there. It was followed by more combing. Hair scraps tumbled down his upper arms to be carried away on the wind. This wasn't like having the barber cut his hair. That felt completely different. Barbers were heavier-handed. They cinched a striped bib around a man's neck and pushed his head this way and that, making quick, decisive moves. This was a woman's touch, lighter and infinitely more gentle. Now and then he felt her clothing brush against his bare back and wondered idly if perhaps it was her breast beneath the fabric. And she smelled good, like starch and clothes hung out to dry in the sun.

"Will anyone in town be missing you while you're here?"

"No, ma'am."

"Your wife knows where you are, then?"

Jeff's eyes snapped back into focus. "I don't have a wife," he answered stiffly, his muscles tensing again. Was it clever sarcasm that she aimed at him? Nobody in town could have missed Sally's desertion.

"Oh, that's good—" The teeth of the comb paused on his scalp. "I mean, it's good that you haven't left anyone alone." Jeff couldn't see her face, but her voice sounded unsure and as innocent as a girl's. He relaxed again.

"Who looks after your stock?" He thought it wise to change the subject just in case she got curious and wanted to ask more questions.

"We don't have animals anymore. After my father took sick, and with my sister Olivia to see to, tending the stock was more than I could handle alone. And I wouldn't go into the b-barn anyway."

"Why not?"

Her hands fell still. "I-I haven't been in there in years. I'll never go in there—I can't—" She broke off so abruptly that he turned to look at her. She suddenly looked very young and very frightened.

"Ma'am?"

She took a deep breath and made a circular motion with her hand to turn him back to his original position. The snipping started again. "I sold the livestock a few years ago."

"What do you do for meat and butter and such?" he asked.

"I made an arrangement with Wickwire's to have fresh provisions sent out a couple of times a week. I used to buy from the Smithfields' farm but, well, that was a while back. At any rate, Mr. Wickwire has my standing order in his store. I imagine I'll have to send him a note to increase our order while you're here. Of course, I put up my own vegetables and fruit. The pear tree always gives me a good crop." She went on cutting his hair without another word. Finally she ran the comb over his whole head with light strokes, then walked a slow circle around him to survey her handiwork. "That's much better. You can finish up with the razor I brought you. Then you can get on with patching the roof."

Disappointed that the barbering session was over, Jeff stood up. "I don't think I'm ready to shave—"

Althea Ford drew herself to her full height—all of five feet and maybe three or four inches at most, Jeff figured—all businessy and bossy again. "I'll be having none of that, Mr. Hicks. Believe me, you are *more* than ready. We agreed yesterday that you would clean up, and so you will. In the meantime, I'll fix your breakfast. It will be ready by the time you're finished."

She walked back to the house, her auburn head held high, and her skirts swaying as she went. Goddamn it, but she was a fussy, demanding woman. And she had a way of saying "Mr. Hicks" that sounded as if she'd been sucking a lemon. Jeff glanced at the contents of the basket she'd left for him. An old ivory-handled razor lay in the bottom and he stretched out a shaking hand to pick it up.

He could buck her and refuse to do her bidding. It was a tantalizing idea. Or he could do as she asked and show her the result.

He swung open the razor. The shiny blade caught the morning sun and gleamed like a cavalry saber. He looked up at the house again, just in time to see the screen door slam behind Althea.

Breakfast actually sounded good—his stomach wasn't as jumpy as it had been yesterday. He supposed if his shaky hand didn't cut his throat with the razor, he'd survive to eat.

"Althea, I thought you'd never finish with that man." Olivia met her in the kitchen. Her baby-fine, uncurled hair hung loosely around her waist, and she wore only her shift and an old shawl. Her feet were bare.

Startled, Althea demanded, "What on earth are you doing up at this hour? It isn't even eight o'clock yet."

"I couldn't sleep so I came downstairs looking for you, and I saw you outside with him, that—that handyman. You

were there for an hour. You *touched* him." Olivia's eyes
had a distraught look to them that made Althea wary. She'd
seen that look in her sister's eyes many times before—it
signaled an upsurge of emotions that nearly always led to
one of her spells. It might not happen right away; sometimes days might pass.

Anxious to soothe Olivia, Althea immediately changed
her tone. "Remember, dear? Last night I mentioned that I
was going to cut Mr. Hicks' hair this morning."

"Yes, I remember. But Althea, I saw your face. You
looked as if you were enjoying it."

Althea dropped her gaze to the scissors she still held.
Enjoyed cutting Jeff's hair, the feel of the clean, wet strands
in her fingers? And the warmth that radiated from his big
frame while she stood behind him?

"Nonsense, Olivia. It was just another job to do, like the
laundry or the cooking." Was that why she'd asked him
about a wife, double-checking what she already knew?

"But you weren't here. And I wanted to help with the
picnic food."

It didn't sound rational to Althea, but when Olivia got
this way she *didn't* sound rational. Althea's stomach sank
to her knees. *Oh, please,* she thought, *please don't let her
go into the declines again.*

"That's fine, I'd love your help. But don't you want to
wash and get dressed first? I haven't even cooked breakfast
yet. We have plenty of time to fix lunch."

Olivia glanced out the window again, and Althea followed the path of her gaze. His face covered with white
lather, Jeff Hicks stood outside the lean-to, staring into the
mirror she'd given him. He'd hung it on a nail next to the
door.

"I don't think he should be here," Olivia murmured. "I
don't think any good will come of it."

"He's just helping us. You go on, and I'll have pancakes ready for you when you come down again."

Finally Olivia nodded and padded to the back stairway.

Althea watched her sister climb the steps and released the breath she'd been holding. Olivia hadn't suffered from a convulsion in months. Althea hoped with all her heart that she wasn't going to begin having them again. Maybe she hadn't slept enough, or perhaps the change of having Jeff on the property had upset her a little. She'd be fine, Althea assured herself. She just had to be.

Turning, she began to gather flour, eggs, and the other necessary ingredients to make pancakes. With an extra mouth to feed, she'd have to remember to tell Mr. Wickwire to send more food out.

An extra mouth.

. . . you were enjoying it.

Oh, well, maybe she had found satisfaction in cutting Jeff Hicks' shaggy mop, she admitted to herself, but only because it gave her a sense of accomplishment and order. She cracked the eggs into a bowl and whisked them with a fork. Revealing the shape of his head hiding beneath almost made him look younger. Now his hair just brushed his collar—or where she'd estimated that his collar would reach. He'd been wearing no shirt, after all. Although she'd tried, she couldn't ignore the sharp-edged wings of his shoulder blades, or the shadowed hollows they created. His skin had been cool and damp from his bath, but it soon warmed under the sun. And he'd smelled good—different from her father or Lane.

Glancing at the eggs again, she realized she'd whipped them into a high, pale-yellow froth. "For heaven's sakes," she muttered. She measured flour, baking powder, and a little milk into the bowl.

Soon she had bacon and eggs frying while she poured

pancake batter onto the cast iron griddle. It was a working man's kind of breakfast, she realized. Neither she nor Olivia ate this much in the morning. But Jeff was too thin—who knew when he'd eaten his last decent meal before last night?—and she had hard work planned for him. He'd need a big meal to sustain him until lunch.

She assembled a tray for him: a stack of four fluffy pancakes dotted with butter, two fried eggs, three slices of bacon, and coffee. When she pushed open the screen door, she spotted him still at the lean-to, just finishing with the razor.

"Mr. Hicks," she called. He looked up and she lifted the tray slightly. He hurried into the shirt she'd given him. The sleeves were a bit too short, so he folded them back to his elbows, exposing sturdy forearms dusted with blond hair. Then he jammed the short tails into the waist of his jeans. Well, she supposed the shirt didn't really fit—at least it was clean and whole, even if his jeans were not. But as he neared her she saw that he still looked worn out, although his eyes were not as red as they had been the day before. The most striking feature at the moment, though, were a dozen or more nicks on his face. Some of them slowly oozed blood, others were drying.

"Goodness, Mr. Hicks! What have you done to yourself?"

"It's nothing, ma'am." He reached up and pressed his thumb to a particularly nasty cut on his chin. Then he shrugged like a self-conscious youth, and turned his profile to her.

But he wasn't a youth. He was a man, and his hand shook as if he had Saint Vitus' dance.

Guilt skittered through Althea. *That* was why he hadn't wanted to use the razor, because his hands trembled, not because he was being stubborn.

And she had insisted.

She put the tray down on the tree stump and searched her apron pocket for her clean handkerchief. "Here," she said quietly, pulling it out, "wet this at the pump. The cold water will help stop the bleeding."

He took a step backward. "No, ma'am, I'll ruin it."

She was beginning to wish that he'd stop calling her "ma'am." "You won't ruin it. It's just an ordinary square of linen." Olivia's things were lacy and furbelowed. Althea's were plain and serviceable. She held out the handkerchief for several moments, feeling as if she were waving it at a passing train. "Go on, now." Finally he took it from her.

"Thanks."

"I'll leave your breakfast here. Just put the hanky on the tray when you're finished with it. I can find some other ones for you to use." Knowing where those handkerchiefs would come from, Althea's gaze strayed briefly to the grave site, half expecting to see the earth swell and buckle as Amos Ford rolled over.

"Thanks again, ma'am."

Althea nearly cringed. "Mr. Hicks, it isn't necessary to call me 'ma'am.' "

He grinned at her suddenly, briefly. It was the first real smile she'd seen on his face. His eyes crinkled at the outer corners and another five years came off his appearance. She marveled at this attractive man who'd been hiding under the shaggy hair and straggling beard. The funny flutter in her stomach came back.

"All right, Allie. I'm not real partial to 'Mr. Hicks,' either. My name is Jeff."

Allie! She had not given him permission to address her so informally. "*My* name is Althea, but you may call me

Miss Ford. Anyway, a woman my age can't be called a name that sounds so—so girlish."

He considered her with a slight squint. "You don't look like an Althea."

"No? And what does an Althea look like?"

He pulled his thumb away from his chin to check the blood there. "I'm not sure. But not like you."

She couldn't believe that she lingered with this silly conversation—she had work to do, a picnic to get ready for, and a sister to mollify. Maybe it was the ache she saw in his green eyes that kept her there. Or the way the sun glinted off the gold strands in his hair. But she had to end it.

"You clean up your face and then eat your breakfast, Mr. Hicks." She couldn't bring herself to call him by his first name. "You've got a lot to keep you busy, and I have to look after my sister. She's a bit feeble."

"Yes, *ma'am*." He dropped his gaze and an edge of tired bitterness crept into his voice. Hearing it, Althea knew she'd put it there.

"Well, I—I'll see you at lunch." Althea turned and walked back toward the house, hoping she wouldn't have to see that haunted pain hiding behind his eyes again anytime soon.

The morning went faster than Jeff had expected. The big breakfast Althea had given him saw him through hours of hammering and crab-walking across the steep pitch of the roof. The sun warmed up early on, and sweat trickled over the nicks and razor burn on his face, stinging like witch hazel.

But now, after giving his work a final inspection, he looked over the expanse of shingles and felt satisfaction. That was something Jefferson Hicks hadn't felt in a long time. And he realized that so far this morning, he'd thought about taking a drink only twice. He'd done hard work and he'd done it well. Of course, the next rain would bring the true test.

He was about to step onto the ladder when he heard two female voices outside. Although their words were too faint to catch, one voice he recognized as Althea's. The other, higher and much younger, he assumed belonged to her sister.

"Mr. Hicks, I'm putting your lunch over here," Althea called as she carried a tray to the tree stump. She glanced up briefly, but didn't make eye contact with him. And she was still calling him Mr. Hicks.

She was a fine-looking woman, he thought again, even if she was as stiff as a collar stay. He racked his memory, trying to recall what had been said in town about these two sisters. All he could remember was something about them being crazy, but obviously that hadn't been right. He'd met their father once or twice—he'd been a dour, sour man, one to whom joy had seemed to be an enemy.

Jeff came down the ladder and eyed the tray. It looked like she'd given him a few sandwiches, some potato salad, and a piece of cake with chocolate frosting. The stool was still there by the tree stump, so he sat down. The little sandwiches had their crusts cut off and they were cut in quarters. It made him think of food a person would give to a child. He cast a sidelong glance at the porch, where Althea's sister sat on a blanket. She was slight and fragile-looking, and Jeff guessed her to be about fourteen or fifteen years old. She sat on a blanket with her hands folded in her lap and her skirts arranged around her as if she posed for a portrait. In fact, with her long, light blond hair hanging down her back, she reminded him of an illustration he'd once seen in *Alice's Adventures in Wonderland*.

And she was staring at him.

He gave her a smile and a nod, but she only looked away, and appeared not to have noticed. Althea had told him that her sister was feeble—hell, maybe she'd meant feeble-minded.

Althea came outside again with a plate. "Here, Olivia, take a sandwich and start eating." Then seeing Jeff, she called, "Oh, Mr. Hicks—this is my sister, Olivia."

"Ma'am."

Olivia didn't answer, and then he saw Althea whisper something to her.

"How do you do, Mr. Hicks," Olivia replied woodenly.

"It's such a nice day, we thought we'd have a little picnic here on the porch," Althea added.

Olivia didn't speak to him again, but she began talking to her sister in hushed tones.

Jeff felt like a conspicuous outsider, like a fly on a white tablecloth, with the two of them whispering about him, so he concentrated on his lunch. He examined the sandwiches—he didn't think he'd ever seen ones like these, with the crusts trimmed off. He supposed that a woman as finicky as Althea Ford would hack off any crust that interfered with her sense of order. They were good, though. A couple of them were made with roast beef and some others with blackberry jam that smelled sweet and tart at the same time. Hell, he couldn't remember the last time someone had fixed him a lunch.

This was how people lived, he recalled, even odd ones like the Ford sisters. With scheduled mealtimes and days filled with work and activity. They slept under the same roof every night, and woke up in a familiar place in the morning, not wondering how they'd gotten out of their clothes, or why they'd slept with their clothes on, or where they'd lost their boots. He'd let all of that slip away from him in the past couple of years. But then, it was pretty hard for a man to keep a schedule when he didn't give a damn about what happened to him.

After gobbling down his lunch, Jeff was about to stand up and go investigate the rickety front porch trellis when a voice stopped him.

"I was in discord in Gateshead Hall: I was like nobody there; I had nothing in harmony with Mrs. Reed or her children, or her chosen vassalage. If they did not love me, in fact as little did I love them."

Jeff glanced at the two on the porch and saw that Althea was reading to her sister. He didn't know what book she held on her lap, but with the birds twittering in the oaks and the light breeze ruffling his shirt collar, it seemed right to hear a woman reading aloud on a day like this. Her voice was clear and distinct, and a memory darted through his mind of his mother reading to her boys.

He was glad his mother couldn't see what had happened to him. She hadn't raised him or his brothers to be lazy or dirty. No, ma'am. A tiny, strong-willed widow left with five boys to bring up, Kate Hicks had taught them that hard work, honor, and acceptance of responsibility were their own rewards. He doubted that she would even recognize him now.

He got a letter from her once or twice a year. Kirby Bromfield at the telegraph office would hunt him down and deliver it. Jeff kept the letters with his gear, but he'd stopped opening them. A current of hurt ran through them when she described wondering how he was and asked why he'd stopped writing. They tore at Jeff's heart to read them. He'd tried to write back to her once, to lie and tell her that he was fine, just to give her peace. After all, how could he tell her the truth—that her eldest son, the sheriff of Decker Prairie of whom she'd been so proud—had fallen to such depths? But his hand had trembled so much that he'd splattered ink on the paper, and the few words he'd managed to scratch out had been illegible. He couldn't ask someone else to do the writing—his pride wouldn't permit that. Frustrated, he'd balled up the page and thrown it away.

The last time his mother had seen him was on his wedding day in Klamath Falls five years earlier. With cheering family and old friends waving them on, he and Sally had started out on the three-day trip to Decker Prairie, and his new job, that afternoon. Pretty little Sally, just two weeks older than seventeen, sat on the wagon seat next to him with her hand tucked in the crook of his arm. He thought she was the most beautiful bride he'd ever seen. The thinly veiled eagerness he'd seen in her eyes made him only too happy to escape the inevitable shivaree that would have interrupted their wedding night. He would make love to his new wife slowly and completely, with only the stars and moon to witness their consummation.

He didn't want to think about those days, or the fact that other people lived safe, comfortable lives, untouched by the kind of guilt he dragged around with him. Jefferson Hicks didn't deserve anything more than what he had right now, and that was the way it would stay.

But he supposed it wouldn't hurt to spend a few minutes on a bright spring afternoon, listening to the measured, lulling sweetness of a woman's voice.

Althea sat on an old rocker and held the book on her lap. She had never really enjoyed reading aloud, but at least she didn't stumble over the text as some did.

Sitting across the quilt from her, Olivia selected another jam sandwich from a flowered plate and listened with eyes wide, as if Althea were reading from a lurid dime novel instead of *Jane Eyre*.

Althea felt a kinship with Charlotte Brontë's much-abused heroine, but she kept that fact to herself. And even though Jane triumphed by the last chapter and married the man she loved, she wasn't allowed to have a completely happy ending. No, indeed. For the sin of loving a man with an insane wife, Jane was punished—when she finally won Mr. Rochester he had been stricken blind. For a moment, she imagined Jeff Hicks with a pair of dark spectacles and a white cane, with his hand tucked in her arm. Oh, God, how horrible—

"Altheeeah," Olivia carped, "I know there's more on the page. You've stopped in the middle of a sentence."

Althea was jolted back to the porch. "Oh, dear, I guess my thoughts wandered. We can take this up again later." She laid a tatted bookmark between the pages and closed the volume. "I have chores to get to, and you might want to lie down for a while."

"Oh, all right," Olivia replied with a sigh. She leaned back against a porch upright and closed her eyes dreamily. "I'm so glad we had this little lunch. I know I'm such a pest sometimes, dear Althea. I don't know how you put up with me."

Althea began gathering the tablecloth she'd spread on top of the quilt. "You're my sister, not a pest."

"And all we have is each other, isn't that so? Nothing and no one can come between sisters." Olivia bent a brief, hard look on Jeff, who'd left his seat by the tree stump and appeared to be heading toward the front porch.

Althea noticed the glance, but dismissed it. "Of course not. We're family. No one can break up a family."

Olivia picked herself up with surprising strength and agility, and scampered across the porch toward the screen door. "Do you promise?"

"Promise—" It seemed as if Olivia were asking if her

eyes would always be hazel or if the sky would always be blue. "We'll always be sisters, Olivia. Nothing can change that. We're related by blood."

Olivia lingered with her hand on the screen door pull, digesting her answer. Then she gave Althea a sweet, endearing smile and went into the house.

Chapter Six

"COME ON, YOU SON OF A BITCH." JEFF GROUND OUT MORE epithets through gritted teeth as he worked a saw in short, quick strokes. He'd been struggling with this monster for the better part of an hour, and now he was drenched in sweat and in a lousy mood.

His opponent was an ancient climbing rose. It had grown bigger than its trellis, literally pulling the support out of the ground and loose from the rusty nails that had once held it in place against the porch overhang. It was as if the rosebush had a gray-white, fan-shaped skeleton.

At least he *thought* the trellis itself was generally fan-shaped, but it was hard to see through the foliage and twisting branches that gripped it. The rose encircled every slat and grew through every opening. The thing had branches as big around as his fist and thorns the size of arrowheads. Its pale pink blooms were full of enamored honeybees, further complicating his work.

Jeff's arms bore so many long, red scratches he looked as if he'd been in a saloon fight with a mountain lion, and in several places he'd snagged his shirt on the thorns, ripping holes in the fabric. Branches that had fallen to his saw were in a pile around his feet, their thorns grabbing his pants legs, too. He thought the whole damned business ought to be chopped down with a double-headed axe, but Althea had insisted that he merely trim it. She liked the climbing rose, she said, its flowers were pretty and they smelled sweet.

Pretty. "Well, then let her come out here and argue with this no-good—"

Over the sound of his sawing, swearing, and shrubbery-rustling, Jeff heard the muffled thud of slow hoofbeats in the road that passed the front of the house. Dragging his torn shirtsleeve across his forehead, he looked up to see if Will Mason had come back to deliver him from this miserable job. But when the rider climbed down from his horse and stood back to look at the place, Jeff felt every muscle in his body tense.

It was not Will Mason at the gate. It was Cooper Matthews.

Slowly, Jeff let the saw drop to the floor. He didn't own this property—hell, he hadn't even been here long enough to say he lived here. And he was not related to either of the women who did own this place. But whether or not it was his right, a fierce territorial instinct rushed through his veins, surprising him as much as it incited him to wariness. The general consensus in Decker Prairie was that Cooper Matthews was a no-account scum. There weren't many, though, who knew just how black his heart really was.

Jeff Hicks knew. And there was bad blood between them, as bad as it could get.

He stepped down from the porch, making his presence known, and stood with his arms crossed over his chest. Though it had turned into a hot day, the sun pounding down on Jeff's shoulders did nothing to dispel the icy knot in his stomach.

Matthews saw him, as Jeff had intended, and sauntered forward. As long as he'd known him, Jeff had seen only two expressions on the man's face: a haughty smirk, or a malevolent glare. Right now he wore the smirk.

"What are you doin' out here, Hicks?" He raked Jeff up and down with a venomous, contemptuous look. "You courtin' one of those crazy Ford women?" If it were possible, Jeff thought that Matthews actually smelled worse than he had himself before his dunk in the trough. His clothes were even dirtier, and his teeth looked like short, walnut-dyed pegs in his red, puffy gums. He had the kind of face that made Jeff long to mash his fist into it, just to get rid of that smirk.

"I'm here because you didn't show up yesterday, like you told Miss Ford you would."

"Shee-it, today, yesterday, it don't make any difference." He waved his grimy hand at the house. "This place ain't goin' nowhere, and besides, that woman just don't know her place. Nobody orders Cooper Matthews around. But I guess you know that, don't you, *Sheriff*?"

Jeff had arrested Matthews once or twice, and he'd raised such a ruckus while in custody, Jeff had been sorely tempted to either lynch him or turn him loose.

"Besides, me and Floyd Endicott had somethin' better to do with a couple of gals he knows over in New Era. But I'm here now, so you run along back to what you do best— bein' a coward and shootin' boys."

Jeff clenched his jaw so tightly his head began to throb. He uncrossed his arms and let them hang at his sides, his hands closed into fists. As much as Wesley Matthews' death had tortured his dreams and dogged his waking hours, Jeff believed that the boy's father hadn't been troubled by the loss. Oh, he had vowed revenge against the man who'd shot Wes. But on the afternoon of his son's funeral, while

Wes was buried Cooper Matthews had stood at the bar in the Liberal Saloon, telling all who would listen that now he had one less mouth to worry about feeding. Since then, Jeff had cut a wide path around him and done his best to avoid the man.

"You're a day too late, Matthews. Miss Ford hired me to help out here." Jeff didn't feel an urgent need to reveal just how that had come about.

The smirk on the other man's face turned into a malevolent glower. "The hell she did. You? You're just a sorry-assed wreck." He pushed past Jeff and climbed the front porch steps. "We'll just see who's doin' the work here. It sure *ain't* gonna be you." Matthews pounded on the front door. Palpable unreasoning fury rolled off him in waves that were just as obvious as the body odor he exuded. He was like a vicious dog that barked at anything that moved or came near.

Anger, an emotion that Jeff had long ago abandoned with the rest of his feelings, stirred inside him. He shot up the steps behind Matthews and grabbed the man's arm hard enough to spin him around. "Leave the woman out of this. If you wanted the job so much you should have been here when you promised."

Matthews' glower evolved into a snarl, revealing his brown pegs of teeth. "I'll hear it from her own mouth! You get your hands off me, you goddamn—"

At that moment, Althea opened the door, and found both Jeff and Cooper Matthews standing there. The tension on the front porch was heavy and thick. "What's going on out—?"

With a tremendous yank, Matthews pulled his arm out of Jeff's grip. "Tell him, this bastard that murdered my boy," he demanded, a maniacal look in his eyes. "You hired me to do the work here and he's got to git. *Tell him!*"

No one had ever spoken to Althea like that. In the life she'd known, voices were never raised, anger was never expressed. In fact, no feelings were expressed. Amos Ford had considered emotional outbursts, angry, happy, or sad, to be the sign of a weak character. Well, there had been just that one time he'd gotten angry, with a fury she would remember till her last day on earth, a rage even more frightening than Matthews'—

Althea looked desperately to Jeff, hoping he would intervene, but it seemed that even he waited to hear her decision, as if she might choose Cooper Matthews over him.

Her heart thundering with fear, she laced her hands together to hide their trembling. She wished she could slam the door and put both men on the other side of it. But Althea Ford was no coward, she told herself. "Mr. Matthews, I did hire you, but you didn't keep to our agreement. So I went into town and made other arrangements. Mr. Hicks is going to do the work for me."

Jeff stood aside, clearing the path to the steps. "All right, you heard her. Now you're leaving."

Matthews didn't budge. Instead, his expression grew even wilder, and he unleashed his rage on Althea. "You want a trigger-happy murderer workin' here? You might be standin' in your kitchen one mornin' and he'll pick you off like a bird settin' on a fencepost. Just like that—" He snapped his dirty fingers. "Just like he did my poor Wes. And with no more feelin', either."

Althea backed up, truly terrified not only by the malevolence she saw in his face, but by the picture he painted.

Jeff grabbed the back of Matthews' collar. He steered the man down the steps and over to the gate. Though she shivered with terror, once again Althea sensed a ghost of Jeff's old authority. He seemed like one of the steely eyed lawmen Ned Buntline wrote about in his famous dime novels—confident and in command.

And just as cold.

"You get back on your horse, Matthews, and don't ever come around here again." Jeff gave the man a light shove toward his horse, but what he really wanted to do was throttle him.

Cooper Matthews adjusted one of the straps on his overalls and glared at Jeff. "You don't tell me what to do, Hicks, no mor'n that female or anybody else does. I ain't forgot what you did to Wes—"

"I haven't forgotten what *you* did to him, either."

"I ain't the one who put that bullet in his chest." He leaned in closer to Jeff and poked him in the shoulder with an index finger. It took everything Jeff could muster to keep from snapping that finger off. "I'll tell you something, though. I'm gonna get even with you, for Wes and for those times you threw me in that stinkin' hole of a jail. And I'm gonna get even for today."

"Just get out of here, Matthews." Jeff didn't want to stand here in the road and argue with him. He felt that anger coming to life in his heart again, a sleeping giant that he didn't want disturbed.

"I ain't sayin' when or how . . ." Cooper glanced back at Althea where she stood watching from the porch, her hands clasped tightly at her waist. "And it might not even be you I get my revenge on." He untied his bony nag from the fence and swung a leg over its slatted sides. "This ain't finished yet between us." He gave the horse a kick and it shambled down the road back toward town.

Jeff watched him to make sure he didn't turn around and come back. No, it wasn't finished, and now Althea might be in danger, too. Matthews had a grudge against him that he wasn't going to give up. And it wouldn't be satisfied until one of them was dead.

Worried about Olivia, Althea went upstairs to see if the noisy scene on the porch had upset her. But when she reached her sister's room she found her propped up against her pillows, reading and looking very much like the blond doll sitting on Olivia's chest of drawers.

"What on earth was that racket outside?" Olivia asked. "It woke me up."

"It's all over now, dear, don't worry. Cooper Matthews and Mr. Hicks had a little—altercation—but Cooper has gone."

Olivia sat up a little straighter. "Didn't you say it was his son that Mr. Jefferson shot?"

"Hicks, Olivia. It's Mr. *Hicks*. Yes, I guess there's bad blood between them."

"Yes, I'm sure there would be, wouldn't there? I imagine that Mr. Matthews might even want revenge. At least that's what I heard him say." She paused for a moment, as if lost in thought. "Oh, well . . ." Olivia shrugged her narrow shoulders and went back to her book.

For her part, Althea's legs felt so rubbery and unsteady, she feared she might fall headfirst down the stairs. She gripped the railing more tightly and descended with careful steps. Cooper Matthews—oh, God, he was more horrible and despicable than she'd realized. She was so glad that she hadn't had to hire him after all. And yet . . .

And yet something he'd said stuck in her mind. She shouldn't give it credence, or even think about it. She tried to push it away, but it sat there in her thoughts whispering to her. *Murderer*. The best thing—right thing—to do would be to dismiss what Matthews had said. Doubt nagged at her, though, and she realized the doubt had been there from the first moment Jeff Hicks had arrived at her door.

She went to the window in the parlor and peered through the lace curtain at Jeff. He stood next to the fence, one hand gripping the top of a picket, while he stared at something far down the road.

Was it her imagination, or was he beginning to look healthier already? The sun fell across his nicked face, turning his eyes the color of pale jade. She wouldn't have thought that a couple of decent meals and a day without alcohol could make a man look so good.

One thing was certain—the attractive man she remembered seeing on the street in town was beginning to emerge again. And while Sheriff Mason had said there was nothing to fear from Jeff Hicks, doubt nibbled at her confidence.

What did she know about him, really? He'd been the sheriff in Decker Prairie, he'd killed a boy, and he'd started drinking. That was *all* she knew, but was there more to those events? The fact that Will Mason had assured her of Jeff's trustworthiness didn't answer the questions in her mind. The only way to do that was to ask the man himself. She thought he owed her that much, anyway, given that she and her sister were here alone.

Althea crossed the parlor and went to the front door, determined to talk to Jeff before her courage deserted her. On the front porch, a pile of rose clippings lay where he'd left them.

"Mr. Hicks?" Althea approached Jeff where he stood next to the fence, watching. Just watching.

After a moment, he faced her, and she saw something piercing and direct in his eyes that made her back up a step. "I suppose you want to know what Matthews was talking about. I mean about me killing his son."

His bluntness caught her off guard; it was as if he'd read her mind. "I heard something about it."

"What did you hear?"

Almost sorry that she had come out here, Althea stopped herself from twisting her apron around her fingers. She felt as uncomfortable discussing this as she would talking about her mother's death. "That you caught the boy breaking into a store in town and you shot him." What more could there be to a story like that? she wondered.

Jeff nodded and let his gaze wander to the mountains on the distant east edge of the valley. "Wickwire's. He broke into Wickwire's." The afternoon sun highlighted the fine, strong bones of his face, his broad brow, his mouth that was generous without being too full. "I always felt a little sorry for Wes. Cooper had been walloping the hell of out him ever since the boy's ma, Elly, died. Sometimes I think death was the only way she could escape the beatings Cooper gave *her*."

"Dear God," Althea interjected softly. She could well imagine that with his low regard for all women, Cooper Matthews would think nothing of hitting his wife.

Jeff kicked at a grass tussock by a fence post. "After Wesley came to the jailhouse a couple of times looking for his father, he took to hanging around. Nobody saw to it that he went to school or learned anything, and I realized that there was a pretty smart kid hiding under the bruised face and dirty hair. He just needed someone to give him more encouragement and less punishment. Since his father wasn't doing that, I sort of fell into the job."

"You did?" A very dark picture was beginning to form in Althea's mind, one of heartache and cruel regret.

"Yeah, I guess I started to think of him as *my* son. I talked to the schoolmarm about helping Wes. She had to work with him after regular class hours because he was so far behind most of her other students. She didn't have any other twelve-year-olds who couldn't read. But like I said, he was bright and he wanted to learn, so he caught on pretty fast."

He went on in a soft voice, telling her how the boy would sometimes come by the office in the afternoon. Jeff would listen to Wesley read or cipher. "I was proud of him. But Cooper didn't give a damn about what the kid had accomplished, and he didn't like him going to school. He told Wes he didn't want a son who knew more than he did. Cooper still knocked him around when he got drunk and the boy couldn't duck fast enough, or hide soon enough.

"One evening, I had one foot in the stirrup, just about to ride home for the night. Sally—I had dinner waiting for me, and I didn't want to be late. But I heard the sound of glass breaking down the street and I had to see about it. That's what the town paid me for.

"The streets were quiet. Dusk had fallen and everyone had gone home. I checked the storefronts and offices along the street, looking through each window. When I got to Wickwire's, I saw that the door glass had been broken near the lock. The door itself was ajar and I knew someone was in there. I drew my revolver, and slowly, quietly, I went in and found a man rifling the cash box.

"He had his back to me and it was dark, so I didn't recognize him right away. Wes had grown a lot in the past couple of years, too, so I didn't realize that it was just a fourteen-year-old boy standing there."

Now Althea did twist her apron in her fingers, and the lump in her throat felt as if she'd swallowed a rock.

In a quiet voice Jeff told the intruder to turn around, slowly, and no one would get hurt. When Wes turned, Jeff saw the gun in his hand, but he barely recognized his face. Both eyes were black and the left side of his face was so swollen and bruised, he looked as if he wore a grotesque mask.

"He dared me to stop him. Cooper had beaten him again—this time bad enough to break some bones in his face."

Althea lowered her eyes. She felt scalding tears gather behind her lids and she couldn't bear to look at Jeff's impassive expression while he told her this awful story. Her heart ached for the battered child she'd never even known.

"He said he was leaving then, that night, and he needed money to get away. He couldn't stay with his father another minute. If I tried to stop him, he'd shoot me. I did everything I could think of to get him to put down that gun and surrender. I promised to get him another place to stay, to protect him from Cooper—"

Glancing up at him, Althea broke in, "Why didn't you just arrest his father?" How could Jeff let the man continue his torment of his own son?

Jeff's eyes held a peculiar, dead expression. "If a man mistreats an animal—a horse, a mule, whatever—there's a law on the books against that, and he can be arrested for it. But he can beat his wife or children, and no law can touch him. Not around here anyway, and not in a lot of other jurisdictions. The idea is that a man's possessions, including his wife and kids, are beyond the reach of the law and he can discipline them as he sees fit."

"But that's horrible! What kind of law is that?"

Jeff shrugged. "A common one. The world is a hard place."

"And that's that? Couldn't you save that young man?" Althea was dumbfounded. But then, she'd lived a life isolated from many of the daily events of Decker Prairie, much less the world.

He smiled, but there was no warmth in it. "Well, ma'am, I tried. Wes refused all of my offers. He wanted to go far away, some place where his father wouldn't find him. He said he'd kill me if I tried to stop him, and he raised his gun even higher. I'd seen that trapped, desperate look in a man's eyes before—I should have known he meant what he said. But I still thought I could reason with him, and I tried again. He pulled the trigger and the bullet grazed my chin."

"Oh, no!" Althea realized that a narrow, bright pink scar crossed the side of his chin; his beard had hidden it until this morning, and he had so many razor nicks on his face she hadn't noticed it until this moment.

"He cocked the pistol again and kept it aimed at me. That's when I figured he was going to kill me and I guess my instinct to survive took over. It all happened so fast . . . so damned fast. I fired once and hit that boy square in the heart. He was dead before he hit the floor. It was self-defense, plain and simple." He shook his head in wonder, then he met her eyes straight on and Althea thought she saw a glitter of tears before he looked away. "But if you think it was murder, I guess that's all right. I've thought so, too, every day and night since."

She started to reach out to touch Jeff's arm, but held back, uncertain. "Mr. Hicks, I'm so sorry." Her voice was tight and whispery with remorse for him. "You didn't murder that poor boy."

He turned his head and quickly swiped the back of his broad hand across his eyes. "It's in the past now, ma'am. At least for Wes it is, and there's no changing it. Believe me, I wish I could. I'd trade places with him in a heartbeat."

Later that afternoon, Althea stood in the kitchen getting a chicken ready for the oven. She sprinkled a touch of pepper over the bird and the little potatoes surrounding it in a blue enamel pot. The weather had turned hot, and she paused to touch the back of her wrist to her damp forehead. It had been a hellish day, long and emotionally trying. In the parlor, Olivia played a slow, mournful rendition of "Greensleeves," and it seemed to fit Althea's mood.

Althea had always believed that life was either black or white. There were no shades of gray, and no room for compromise. A man was either good or bad, guilty or innocent. Those had been her father's unyielding views, and by her upbringing he'd made them hers, too. If a person was guilty of a deed, that was the end of it. Extenuating circumstances or explanations didn't improve matters—they were only excuses.

But Jeff hadn't made excuses for himself. He'd simply told her what had ultimately led him to Wickwire's the night Wes had chosen to break in. Although she still didn't approve of him squandering his life, now she had a little better understanding of why Jeff had started drinking. Sometimes Althea believed that if she had been a man, she might have taken to drinking, too. She'd once heard there was temporary oblivion to be found in alcohol.

In her mind's eye, she could still see him standing there in the road as he told her about the death of Wesley Matthews. He was dressed little better than a beggar, and though his voice had been devoid of emotion, he'd moved her to tears. Althea knew she shouldn't care one way or the other about Jeff Hicks. He was here to do a job—he *worked* for her.

But in listening to his story, she realized that perhaps not everything was black and white.

Maybe life had some gray places, too.

Chapter Seven

JEFF SAT ON THE CORN–HUSK–STUFFED TICK IN THE LEAN-to and poked a roast potato around his plate. It wasn't that the potato didn't taste good. It most likely did, and the chicken it had been cooked with was probably good, too. It was seasoned with just the right touch—he smelled a little sage and some pepper. No one could say that Althea Ford wasn't a good cook. And although he should have been hungry enough to eat two chickens, he hadn't taken one bite. His mind wasn't on his stomach or his plate.

His scratched arms felt like they were on fire, but he wasn't even thinking about them.

Jeff wanted a drink.

Well, no, if he was going to be honest with himself, one drink wouldn't do it. He wanted a whole goddamned bottle, wanted it the way he'd yearned for Sally, back when their love was strong and whole. He closed his eyes for a moment, the fork in his loosened grip clacking on the edge of the plate he balanced on his lap.

There was the smell of the whiskey, sharp and full, as he lifted the glass to his mouth. The first swallow would roll to the back of his throat where it would burn with a kindly fire and fill his head with its vapor. The drinks that followed would burn less, but would bring a merciful gray blur that would draw a curtain between himself and the image of Cooper Matthews, rabid and yelling *murderer* at him on the Fords' front porch. More importantly, the whiskey would blunt the picture in his mind of Althea's chalky, stunned face when she'd heard Matthews' ranting.

It had bothered her enough to come outside and question Jeff. Then he'd felt compelled to tell her most of the story, at least the worst part of it. And it had bothered *him* to have to tell her about it. Not just the telling of it and the remembering, although that had been hard.

What he'd worried about most was losing Althea's respect. He chuckled wryly to himself. Hell, he didn't even have it to begin with, and he had no idea why it mattered to him, one way or the other. But it did.

Funny, though—she hadn't reacted as he'd thought she would. Allie Ford didn't strike him as the flexible type. In fact, he guessed that what little he'd heard about her was probably true, that she was unyielding and hidebound. He'd seen traces of those qualities himself. But when she stood next to him at the fence this afternoon, he'd also seen compassion in her.

After he told her about Wes, he'd figured that she'd send him packing back to Will Mason. She could yet.

Jeff hoped that wouldn't happen.

He opened his eyes and glanced at the kitchen window through the lean-to's open door. Even though he didn't fit in here with the stiff-backed woman and her feeble-minded sister, he was beginning to like getting regular meals and having something to do every day.

Sighing, Jeff picked up his fork and took another stab at the potato on his plate. He still wished he had that drink.

*   *   *

After dinner, while Olivia read *Jane Eyre* to herself, Althea stole up the back stairs to the attic. She usually worked on her needlepoint in the evening, but now she planned to turn her needle to another task.

A rush of heat, like that from a stove, rolled out of the small airless space under the roof when Althea opened the door. A pair of tiny flyspecked windows draped with cobwebs provided the only light, but the sunset on this side of the house cast bright yellow beams across the floor. Fortunately, this part of the roof hadn't leaked during the rains.

Up here was a dusty clutter of trunks, tea crates, and a few long, cedar-lined clothes boxes. Toys mingled with the chests and barrels, but the only remnant of Althea's childhood was the wicker doll carriage pushed against the back wall. She pulled a tattered footstool close to the little carriage and sat down.

Putting out a tentative hand, Althea let her fingertips trace the bumpy texture of the woven strips of willow. As a little girl, she had promenaded her doll up and down the road in the buggy, pretending that she was walking to town. When they got to Decker Prairie, she would have tea with toast and jam, while her faceless, make-believe husband—her doll's father—worked on their farm. It all seemed so long ago now.

Althea's childhood had ended in her seventh year, the day Olivia was born. She had acquired adult obligations then. Her mother was never really the same after the birth of her second daughter; that was when her strangeness began.

Althea took over the house, just like a grown person. And grown people didn't play with toys, did they? According to Amos Ford, they didn't. Then she had a real-life doll named Olivia to take care of.

She sat forward, her elbows on her knees, and let her gaze drift. If she were the type to feel sorry for herself, she might think that with all the responsibility laid on her shoulders she had been cheated out of her girlhood and the opportunity to do the things other young women enjoyed. If she were a dreamer it would be very easy for her to envision that life she'd pretended as a child. And she'd have made herself crazy with yearning by now.

Crazy.

Althea shook her head and stood up. She had come up here for a purpose, not to think about the past and what could have been.

Avoiding the trunk that she knew contained her mother's belongings, she went straight to a large cardboard box that sat next to a bushel basket. She lifted the lid and carefully pulled away layers of tissue to uncover a length of gray chambray. Althea smoothed the close-woven material with her hand and nodded decisively.

It would be perfect for what she had in mind.

"Mr. Hicks, could you spare a moment of your time?"

Surprised to hear Allie's clear voice outside the lean-to, Jeff sprang up from the bed. The door was already open, and he saw her standing a good four feet back. "Yes, ma'am."

Her auburn hair glittered with red, brown, and gold lights in the setting sun. Had a man ever touched that hair? he wondered. Had anyone pulled out the pins and had the pleasure of watching the dark fire of it unwind down her bare back? He could imagine it very easily. He'd bet with that coloring of hers, her skin was like white velvet— smooth and soft, every fold, every curve, every warm cleft under his hands.

"Mr. Hicks . . . please." Her cheeks turned pink and she averted her eyes.

He glanced down. Damn, no shirt. "Um, sorry—your rosebush pretty much ripped up the shirt you gave me."

"I know it didn't fit very well and I thought—" She cast a sidelong gaze at him, obviously trying to avoid looking at his bare upper torso, and her eyes flew open. "Good Lord, what happened to your arms?" Crossing the distance between them, she leaned closer and looked at the scratches crisscrossing his hands and forearms.

He shrugged, feeling a little self-conscious under her scrutiny. "That rose ripped into me, too. It had thorns as long as bear claws and it didn't give in without a fight." He had washed before dinner but some of the deeper wounds had seeped for a while and were crusted with dried blood.

"Oh, dear," she said, her fingers resting at the base of her throat. "You should have told me about it."

"We both had other things on our minds today."

She nodded. "Yes, well . . . but this needs to be cleaned up or the wounds will fester."

Jeff wasn't accustomed to having someone fuss over him. "Naw, it's nothing. I'll be all right."

But she was already hurrying to the house, and it seemed to him that she was gone no longer than a second. She waded back through the tall grass, her skirts swishing against the green, serrated blades. Struggling to carry the stool from the porch, she also juggled a dark brown glass bottle and some cotton wool.

Jeff stepped forward and took the stool, and she shooed him into the lean-to.

"Go on, now. You sit there on the bed and let me tend these scratches."

Jesus, two minutes ago, she'd been afraid to even get

close to his door. Now she was pushing him into the room, all busyness and in charge.

Jeff felt the edge of the bedframe against the back of his knees and sat down. Althea pulled the stool close and uncorked the bottle she'd carried with her.

"My soul and body, I've never seen the like," she said, shaking her head.

"It looks worse than it is."

She gazed up at him with those soul-searching eyes, and Jeff felt another emotion stirring, one he couldn't even identify. "I doubt that," she said. "I would think all these scratches would sting something terrible."

"It's not so bad," he lied. In truth, his arms burned like hellfire, but he wasn't about to tell her that.

"Well, this will fix things up." Using her lap for a work space, she made a pad of the cotton wool, then tipped the bottle opening against it, letting the potion flow.

Jeff pulled back and eyed it warily. In his experience, liquids that came from dark bottles also burned like hellfire, whether a man drank them or put them on an open wound. "What is that stuff?"

"It's just a decoction of comfrey and lavender, mixed with witch hazel." She took his left hand and held it on her open palm. "This might sting a bit, but only for a while." With great gentleness she touched the cotton pad to the back of his hand and dabbed at the angry, red marks.

Jeff sucked in a breath between his clenched teeth, but didn't snap out the oath that leaped to mind.

Althea kept her eyes on her task. Sitting this close to her, he could see the graceful arch to her russet brows, and the way her lashes curled at the ends. "I want to thank you for stepping in with Cooper Matthews today. Dealing with him was—it was horrible. When he didn't show up yesterday morning, I didn't expect him to come out at all."

"Matthews has a temper like a mad dog. Seeing me here just made him worse." Jeff decided not to worry her with Cooper's implied threat to her. It shouldn't matter to him whether Althea worried. He'd stopped caring about everything long ago. But those feelings, the emotions that he'd suppressed, were rumbling to life, and it scared him.

"I wish I'd never spoken to him to begin with." She frowned slightly, bringing those russet brows together as she worked her way up his arm with the decoction. Her hands were small and cool. "There just wasn't anyone else to ask."

"Have you been alone here for a long time?"

She leaned closer to reach a long scratch on the tender underside of his arm. When he looked down to watch, it brought his nose within inches of her hair. It smelled faintly of honeysuckle. "My father died three years ago. He was poorly for months before that. But I'm not really alone—I have Olivia."

Jeff didn't know how much company or help a feeble-minded girl could be, but he kept that to himself. "Oh, right—your sister."

"Do you have family in Decker Prairie, Mr. Hicks?" He felt her gaze touching him, feeling for the dark places that hurt, probing gently, seeking to expose them to the light.

"No, ma'am." He let his gaze stray no farther than the lower half of her face. Her pink mouth looked soft, like the petals of the roses on her porch. "They're in Klamath Falls. I haven't seen them since the day I married—" Of all the things that had happened to Jeff, talking about Sally was the hardest. "Well, it's been a long time."

Althea waited for him to volunteer more about his wife, but he didn't. He had been married and he wasn't now. What had happened? Though she knew it was none of her business, her curiosity about Jeff had her speculating over the mystery.

Apparently, though, their conversation had reached its end. Silence stretched between them while she finished treating his scratches. She struggled to keep her mind on her work and away from the thought that she'd never been this close to a man before, and under such intimate circumstances. Fate, it seemed, found all kinds of reasons to put her together with Jeff Hicks. And he was usually without a shirt.

"There now," she said finally. "That's better, I hope."

"Yes, ma'am. Thank you."

"All right, then." She set the bottle on the floor and reached into her pocket for her tape measure. "I need to take your measurements."

"What for? My coffin?"

Startled by the question, Althea looked up into Jeff's serious face. He wasn't joking. "Of course not. Why would you ask that?"

He shrugged. "I just don't expect to live very long. I could fall off your roof or a horse could kick me in the head. Maybe even get shot. I don't know what could happen, so awhile back I gave Cyrus Cheney some money to put in an account for me at his bank. It's enough to bury me and pay a preacher to say a few words over me. Just in case, ma'am. Cyrus will handle everything."

His words squeezed her heart, but she ignored the feeling. "Working here isn't going to kill you, Mr. Hicks," she replied dryly.

He smiled, and this time it reached his eyes. "No, ma'am."

Ma'am. Even "Allie" was beginning to sound preferable to that. "I'm going to make some shirts for you. You can't very well go around here in rags. Or—or like that." She gestured at his naked upper torso. "It isn't decent." It wasn't much good for her peace of mind, either. Seeing him like this made her feel hot and shivery at the same time, due to embarrassment she was sure.

"I can't pay you for them. Not yet anyway," he said.

"We won't worry about that. I already had the cloth so there's no extra expense. Now stand up so I can take the measurements."

Jeff stood, and what remained of Althea's forthright composure withered away. The room was suddenly too small, and Jeff too close. He seemed as tall as an aspen, and all sinew and long bone. Although he was a little too lean, his broad chest was braced with muscle and dusted with a V-shaped pattern of sandy hair that began between his nipples and reached to his abdomen. His old jeans hung on his hipbones, giving her a clear view of a narrow strip of dark blond hair that stretched from his navel down to his low waistband and beyond to a place she couldn't see—

Althea dragged her gaze back up to his face, and realized that he'd caught her studying him. Hot blood rushed to her face, scalding her from chin to scalp. "Well, um, if you'll turn around . . ."

He held her gaze a moment longer with a look that was so potent and elemental, it made her suck in a breath. It wasn't a broken-down drunk who stared at her, or an ex-sheriff who had fallen from grace. She saw the bare essence of the man who lurked beneath both faces.

The very air around them grew heavy and charged, like a summer night before a thunderstorm.

After what seemed like an eternity, he turned his back to her. Awed by the solid wall of it, she wished she could run her hands over its planes and angles, to touch what she realized was one of the most beautiful forms she had ever seen. That a man's back could be beautiful baffled her, and yet, it somehow made perfect sense. Althea felt a most distressing urge to put her arms around his waist and rest her cheek against its strength.

Unraveling but trying to hide it, Althea fumbled with her tape measure and even dropped it once. Finally she got it smoothed out, and with hands that had suddenly lost all their dexterity, she reached up to hold the end of the tape up to the prominent bone at the base of his neck to measure the length of his back. His skin was warm, but her fingers were ice-cold, and goose bumps appeared on his flesh. From the same starting point, she measured the length of his arms.

To do a proper job, she should have determined the circumference of his neck and chest, but both would require putting her arms around him to encircle him with the tape.

No! Althea could not make herself do that, especially given the chaotic feelings churning through her mind and body. She would have to work from memory when she cut the fabric. Looking at Jeff now, she didn't think that would be difficult.

"That—that should do, Mr. Hicks," she said, and stuffed the tape back into her pocket. He turned and faced her again, and her heart began pounding so hard from the nearness of him she thought she might faint.

"Jeff . . . my name is Jeff."

She stared up into his green eyes, feeling like a deer hypnotized by lantern light, as if she dared not look away. Although he wasn't touching her, he held her fast. "What?"

"Say it."

She could feel waves of heat pouring off his body. Dear God, what was he going to do to her? "J-J-J—Mr. Hicks— really, I should be go—"

"*Say it*, Allie." He commanded her with a whisper that caressed her name. "Say 'Jeff.' "

"J-Jeff."

"Again."

"Jeff."

"No more 'Mr. Hicks.' No more 'ma'am' or 'Miss Ford.' "

She shook her head slightly, her gaze still fixed on his weary, handsome face. She saw loneliness and fear in his green eyes that pierced her heart. But she saw fire, too.

"Jeff. Allie."

"Jeff," she repeated, beginning to tremble. All she wanted at that moment was to lean closer and feel his arms enfold her. He brushed her jaw with his fingertips, then let his hand slide down her shoulder and around to her back. With a little pressure, he pulled her toward him as though they were dancing.

Her breath came faster, as her heart demanded. She'd never been held by a man, and had never thought she would be. Until now.

Slowly, Jeff tipped his head toward hers, filling her field of vision with his eyes and handsome face, bringing his lips within scant inches of her own—

"*Althee-ah!* Where *are* you?"

They jumped apart. The sound of Olivia's voice cut between them like a cold, sharp blade, dragging her back to the present, and to everything else.

She glanced over her shoulder toward the house. "Oh—I shouldn't have stayed so—my sister—I'll start work on your shirts as soon as I can." Then she turned and fled the tiny room where a man she hardly knew had made her feel, for a breathless, dizzying instant, that they were the only two people in the world.

The only two people who mattered.

*   *   *

"Althea, I was so worried when I couldn't find you. I didn't know where you went. One moment you were in the kitchen, the next you had disappeared." Indeed, Olivia looked pale and distraught as she tagged after her sister. Althea could only hope that her own face was not as red as it felt. "I looked in every room for you. For all I knew, you could have had an accident outside somewhere or been hurt by that—that handyman—"

Althea clutched the length of gray chambray that she'd fetched from the attic in her arms. Olivia had become so uncertain and clinging since Jeff Hicks had come to stay. But Olivia had nothing to fear from him—only Althea did, and that was the loss of her own good sense. If her sister hadn't interrupted, Jeff would have kissed her. And she would have let him.

She carried the fabric to the dining room table. "I had to measure Jeff—Mr. Hicks, that is—for the shirt I need to make him."

Olivia lifted her brows delicately. "You're going to sew for him? Whatever for?"

"He doesn't have any shirts of his own and we don't have any here that he can wear." Althea hoped she sounded brisk and businesslike. In truth, her jaw still tingled where Jeff's fingers had touched it. She unfurled the chambray down the length of the table. "I have this perfectly good cloth going unused. It's the least we can do—the man can't go around without a shirt."

Olivia stood with her hands resting on the back of her father's chair at the head of the table. "I suppose not . . . how can he have no shirts? I never heard of a grown person not having clothes."

Althea regarded her, dressed in sea-green muslin with frothy billows of ruffles edging the hem. Though they both lived a simple, isolated existence, Olivia had never been

denied anything in her life, and from her childlike viewpoint, she couldn't imagine anyone else's bad luck or bad
choices. "Some people aren't as fortunate as we are."

"Because Daddy always took good care of us."

Althea couldn't respond to that. Yes, though farming
wasn't a wealthy man's occupation, Amos Ford had given
his family a comfortable life. They'd never starved, and
he'd kept a roof over their heads and put clothes on their
backs. But to Olivia he'd also given his regard and approval. If only there had been something left for his eldest
daughter—

"Now it's our turn to help someone else," Althea replied,
smoothing the fabric with her hands, fabric that would
eventually curve around Jeff Hicks' shoulders.

Olivia watched her for a moment, then turned to leave
the room. "I believe I'll go up to bed. I've been feeling
weak and tired today."

Althea, trying to decide the best cutting layout, turned
her attention back to the chambray. "Oh? Well, that's fine,
dear. You go on."

"I hope I feel better tomorrow," her sister ventured from
the doorway.

"I'm sure you will." Her mind racing with pictures of
Jeff, his lips, the heat in his eyes, Althea didn't look up.

"Oh, I thought you'd like to know—when I looked out
my window this afternoon, I noticed quite a few weeds on
the graves."

Althea's head snapped up, her full attention on Olivia.
"Weeds?"

Olivia nodded, making her long, silky curls bounce.
"They seem to be *thriving*. And I know how particular you
are about tending the graves. Well, good night." She glided
away then, her taffeta petticoats rustling against the doorframe as she passed.

*   *   *

Jeff sat outside the lean-to on an old crate, looking at the velvet night. From the nearby creek he heard the faint sound of croaking frogs, and a lone night bird sent a high-pitched call across the fields.

The moon was just a scrap of silver-white in the black sky, a hint of what it had been in the past and would grow into again. As he watched it, for the first time in many months Jeff found himself wondering about the man he had become.

Over the course of all this time, he'd allowed his feelings—his *heart*—to die. It was funny how a man's spirit could wither, yet his body still worked and his legs still walked. But while he'd had nothing else to be proud of, he had actually begun to take pride in the fact that he cared about nothing and no one, not even himself.

Then he'd met Althea Ford and in a matter of days, for no reasons he could understand, his silent, withered heart had begun to beat again. He'd felt anger. He'd felt satisfaction. A few hours earlier, he'd felt desire for a woman.

But most of all, he felt lonely. That was new to him, and he couldn't say he liked it much. Whiskey was a reasonable cure for a man's emptiness, and up to now he'd cured it every day.

He still saw Allie as she'd looked, with her tape measure and no-nonsense manner. Beneath that exterior, though, he sensed a softer woman with her own desires and hopes left unfulfilled. When her fingers touched him—lightly, so lightly—he'd hoped she wouldn't notice the goose bumps she raised on his skin. Or the hard, swift arousal that strained against the front of his jeans. He had been just seconds away from claiming her soft, coral-pink mouth with his own.

After she ran back into the house, he'd found his appetite again and wolfed down the cold chicken and potatoes that had been his dinner. He could have eaten a whole coop of chickens, he'd been so hungry.

But Jeff knew that food wasn't what he really craved.

He turned his gaze to the dark house on his right. The only light came from a window upstairs. He didn't know if it was Allie's window, but he knew that whether or not he wanted to think about her face and soft form, they would be in his mind when sleep finally took him.

Althea lay in her narrow bed, tense and restless. The night was unusually hot and still, and sleep would not come to her. When she closed her eyes she saw Olivia, looking lost and anxious as she'd stood on the porch. Or she envisioned her parents' graves, overrun with weeds, and her father's stern, dark expression.

But sometimes she saw Jeff Hicks standing before her without a shirt, long and lean and warm to the touch.

Guilt and yearning tore at her in equal measures.

Don't let me down again, girl.

Jeff. Allie.

The guilt won out.

There was no Allie and Jeff. She rolled over to her side, dragging the sheet with her and binding her body in its length. She'd hired the man to do some work around the farm and that was all. She had no right to begin daydreaming just because he'd touched her cheek and *might* have kissed her while she measured him for a shirt. She couldn't.

Besides, Althea supposed she didn't deserve any dreams at all. And even if she did, her responsibility to Olivia came before anything else.

Jeff Hicks was not part of her life and he could not be. That was a certainty.

Some women were meant to be wives and mothers. Althea knew that she was meant to be her sister's companion.

Chapter Eight

THE SUN HAD BARELY CREPT OVER THE HORIZON WHEN Jeff pulled himself out of bed in the lean-to and jammed his arms into his shirtsleeves. The shirt was one of the ones Allie had brought to him, and it fit no better than the first one had. But if she'd meant what she said last night, he'd soon have a new shirt that would be the right size.

He stood in the doorway with his hands braced against the frame. It was a clean, dewy morning, touched with mist. The kind of morning that only May could bring. He hadn't seen one like this for years. It surprised him to realize how much he'd missed it.

Grabbing his towel and the tin washbasin he used for shaving, he headed off for the trough. His hands were steadier this morning, and so was his stomach. In fact, they seemed to be getting a little better every day. Today he had to start clearing the field for Allie's garden. Given the tangle of weeds and grass choking it, he knew he had a hell of a job in front of him.

As he crossed the yard he glanced off to his right toward the pair of headstones that marked the graves of Allie's parents under the limbs of a stately oak. A short, white wrought-iron fence surrounded the area, and unlike the rest of the property it was freshly painted. Looking closer, Jeff realized that Allie was kneeling inside the enclosure. With her head lowered that way, the thick braid that fell over her shoulder swung back and forth with her movements, and made him think of a dark garnet caught in a ray of sun.

At first he thought that maybe she was having a personal moment at her parents' graves. He would respect her privacy and go on about his business. But then he realized she was working at something, and working with a vengeance as if the devil were driving her. Her flushed face was smudged with dirt, and strands of hair straggled around her temples. She wore a faded, plum-colored skirt, and her snug-fitting white blouse clung to the roundness of her full breasts. She was not as neat and tidy as usual, but that made her look even more appealing than she had last night.

Jeff stepped up to the short fence and saw Allie clawing at the soil with a pronged weeder, grim determination creasing her forehead.

"Isn't that something you'd like me to take care of, Allie?" he asked quietly. It seemed like a fair trade for the shirt she was going to make him.

She jumped, obviously startled, and looked up at him. "Oh, Mr. Hicks—I'm sorry, what did you say?"

Back to "Mr. Hicks." He stepped inside the fence but kept a respectful distance from the margins of the graves. "I can do this for you. You probably have better things to see after in the house."

She rose on her knees and clutched the weeder to her breast as if it were a sacred object. "Dear God, no! I mean, thank you, but I have to do this. It's my responsibility. Besides, I know how he—how I want it."

Jeff thought he saw fear in Allie's eyes. He glanced around and it looked as though she'd just gotten started;

not much of the dirt had been disturbed. The burying ground, though, was a complete contrast to the rest of the farm. Sure, a few weeds had popped up, but he could see that it was well tended. Some kind of small-bloomed flowers—pansies maybe—were planted in neat half-circle beds that had been cut out in front of each granite headstone. The rest of the ground was planted with grass. Tiny daisies dotted its rough green plane.

Amos Ford's headstone was plain and spare, carved only with the dates of his birth and death. Her mother's, though, had been engraved with birds and flowers, and a peculiar inscription: HAPPIER IN DEATH THAN IN LIFE.

"It looks nice here—your hard work shows," he said, tucking the basin against his side.

"My father wouldn't tolerate a weed on his grave or on my mother's." She talked as if Amos was still alive, and the fear he saw in her eyes grew when she mentioned him.

Nodding at Lucinda Ford's marker, he added, "Your mother has been gone a long time."

Allie turned her weeder back to clawing at some chickweed trying to take root in one of the flower beds. "Yes."

Jeff sighed. She was all stiff and formal again, and he was sorry that side of her had returned. She had softness in her—he'd seen it.

"I want you to start working on the garden today," she said, not looking up.

"Yes, ma'am. That's what I thought I'd do."

"Fine. We don't have a horse to pull the plow, but old Mr. Smithfield will let us use his mule. You just have to go borrow it and tell him that you're working for me."

Jeff rubbed the back of his neck, and suddenly felt awkward. "I don't know if that's such a good idea."

Allie stopped clawing and looked up at him. "Why not? What's the matter?"

Jeff's memory didn't always work very well. The past months had blurred together and run over each other until the passage of time had become nothing but a featureless gray mist. But he still remembered the morning a few months ago when Elisha Smithfield had encountered him asleep in a doorway on a side street in town and called him a lazy, drunken bum. Even if it was partly true, his pride has felt the sting of the old man's accusation. And Smithfield wasn't likely to let Jeff borrow anything. "I'm not one of his favorite citizens."

Allie waved off his thin protest. "Bosh—I'll give you a note to take to him. Now let me finish here so I can start your breakfast."

Knowing that he'd been dismissed, Jeff stared at the top of her downturned head for a moment. Then he turned and walked toward the trough.

Suddenly the morning didn't seem so fine, after all.

The next seven days amounted to nothing more than backbreaking work for Jeff. Old man Smithfield loaned him his mule but not until he presented Allie's note. Even then he showed so much reluctance that Jeff wished he could pull the damned plow himself and tell Elisha to keep the braying beast.

The only person he saw come and go was Seth Wickwire, Eli's son, who brought out the Fords' grocery order. The farm wasn't far from town, but it might as well have been at the edge of the earth, as isolated as it was. Althea continued to keep her distance, never again showing the vulnerable softness he'd seen that one time. The hint of optimism that he'd felt early on in his stay at the Fords' fizzled out, and his memories leaped forward into his thoughts. At night, he crawled into the bed in the lean-to, stiff and aching from physical labor he wasn't used to. But sleep eluded him. He lay on the tick, staring at the low ceiling overhead, seeing Wesley's surprised expression the instant he'd been shot. The scene had worn a deep groove in Jeff's tired mind. Or he'd remember the letter that Sally had left him as if he had it in his hands once more.

. . . can't take the loneliness . . .

A drink or two would send those private demons back to their hiding places. After all, Althea had said that she didn't want him drinking on her property or her time. That didn't mean he couldn't go to town at night. The only thing stopping him was the lack of money. He even considered asking her for an advance on his pay but abandoned the idea—she didn't think much of him as it was. Short of trying to get credit at the Liberal Saloon, or cadging drinks from customers, Jeff could only endure.

One evening he came back to his room to find a gray shirt on his bed. It was neatly folded and crisply ironed, and it had all of its buttons, unlike what he wore now. The inside of its plain band collar and yoke were lined with a gray-checked material that made the work shirt seem very fancy, indeed. He picked it up to feel the new fabric. Lifting it to his face, he pressed his cheek against it and drew a deep, ragged breath over the knot in his throat. He smelled starch and the faint scent he recognized as Allie's. It was the first new possession he'd had in years and he longed to try it on. But he was afraid to—he'd just get it dirty. He had no idea when something so nice would come to him again. So Jeff pulled open a drawer in the bureau and carefully laid the shirt inside.

Althea, having promised herself that she would stay away from Jeff Hicks, still found a dozen reasons to go to the kitchen window to watch him work. A few times she even ventured outdoors, lured by the spectacle of the tall, powerful man sweating under the June sun as he guided the plow. She'd seen plowing every year of her life, but now it fascinated her—the large, shiny blade that cleaved the soil, making it ready to receive the seed that Jeff would scatter there.

But she was keenly disappointed that he didn't wear the shirt she'd made for him—it had been one thing she could do for him and yet keep her distance. Obviously, he didn't like it. All the times she looked for him, she saw him either wearing one of her father's old shirts, or worse, no shirt at all. Maybe it was because she'd run out of the chambray and had had to use a piece of gray gingham to finish the inside. Granted, it wasn't perfect but the gingham couldn't be seen. It seemed to her that a man with no other decent shirt wouldn't be so choosy about linings that didn't show. And her pride wouldn't let her ask him about it.

Finally, late one morning the earth was ready, and Althea knew that a moment she had worried about was upon her. While Olivia played "In the Gloaming" on the piano, Althea pushed open the back screen door and went down the steps in search of Jeff. In one hand she clutched a list and a ten-dollar gold piece. In the other she carried a pie tin of lard mixed with raisins and sunflower seeds.

The rich smell of turned dirt reached Althea's nose before the field came into view. It was a smell that was rooted in her earliest memories, before Olivia was born, before her mother's real strangeness began. It meant spring and new beginnings, although in this case, summer was almost upon them.

Althea scanned the yard and the fields for Jeff, and finally saw him at the end of the fence, driving a nail into a loose picket. Even though he wore one of those old, ill-fitting shirts she'd given him, he looked better than he had any day since he arrived. Hours under the sun had put blond streaks in his hair, and three big meals a day had taken the gaunt look from his face. He swung the hammer with sure, powerful strokes that landed squarely on the nailhead.

He glanced up as she approached and gave her a hesitant smile. "I noticed a couple of these were loose." He nodded at the pie plate in her hand. "I hope that isn't for me."

Allie glanced at the beef fat and almost laughed. "Oh— my, no. I put this out for the birds. I suppose I spoil them, feeding them at this time of year—they really don't need my help now. But they're pretty little things, giving pleasure to the world. I like to give them a treat in return."

Jeff studied her with a look that for the briefest instant reflected such tenderness, her breath caught in her chest. She had to turn her eyes from his. "They're lucky," he said finally.

Unraveling like an old sweater, she tried to stick to her purpose. "Yes, well—I've made up a list of the seeds we need to plant." She handed the paper to him. "Just the usual vegetables—corn, potatoes, green beans, squash, and so on. You can find everything at the feed store."

He nodded. "Yeah, I know. I used to buy from there, too."

"You did?"

"Sure. I didn't want to be the sheriff of Decker Prairie forever. I planned to quit eventually and farm full-time. I had a couple dozen head of cattle, a few acres planted, a house that I'd built—"

Allie stared at him open-mouthed. "I didn't know that! I guess I thought—well, I suppose I never gave it any thought at all. Didn't you live in town?"

He shook his head. "The home place was just about a mile southeast of town. Close enough to do my job, but out far enough to have some breathing room and quiet." He closed his eyes for a second and smiled, as if to himself. "I loved the quiet."

Althea knew she shouldn't ask, but she couldn't help herself. "What happened to it?"

"It's still there. Land never goes away."

"No, but . . . who owns it now?"

"I do."

"Then why don't you live there? It would certainly be better than sleeping in a different place every night." The comment was out before she realized how rude it sounded.

A shadow of pain crossed his face. "The house is gone. Allie, did you want to talk about this list?"

Good Lord, she'd been prying, a fault that Althea herself disliked. She fumbled for words. "Oh—yes, well, I think I've included everything. Please go to Wickwire's, too, and buy yourself some dungarees . . . and a new shirt if you like. You can pay with—" Gripping it in her fist a moment longer, she finally opened the hand that held the gold coin. "Here's ten dollars. It should be more than enough."

Jeff gazed upon the money in Allie's palm like a starving man would view a banquet table. He let his eyes connect with hers, and an unspoken question hung between them. Would Jefferson Hicks do as she'd asked and return from town with the goods and change left from the coin? Or would he take the money, stop at the Liberal Saloon, and disappear back into the bottle that she and Will Mason had fished him from? He saw worry written in the depths of her eyes. But he saw trust, too.

He took the money from her and folded it inside the list, then put it in his pocket. "Maybe I'll just wash up a little, and then I'll hitch Smithfield's mule to your wagon and be on my way."

"All right, then." She turned to walk toward the pear tree in the corner of the yard, carrying her suet bird treat. Jeff admired her form as she went—her long, slender neck and narrow back, her rounded hips that swayed softly with the rhythm of her pace. She stopped suddenly and called over her shoulder, "I'll see you when you get back."

That lonely, scared feeling came over him again, stronger than ever.

"Come on, Kansas, keep moving," Jeff muttered to the mule. He thought Kansas was a stupid name for a mule, but he didn't own the bad-tempered animal. The old wagon beneath him rattled and lurched along the rutted, potholed road, and he hoped it would hold together long enough to get him to Decker Prairie.

If he could only make himself relax and enjoy the ride, there were lots of things to see and appreciate. The afternoon was so sharp and blue, the trees on the far side of the valley seemed close enough to hit with a rock. The stream that ran across the Ford property paralleled the road, and the water looked clear and icy, like liquid glass, as it gurgled over the rocks in its bed.

He noticed things that had always existed around him, but until recently had been hidden by the blurry curtain that he'd drawn over his mind.

The turmoil galloping through Jeff's thoughts prevented him from taking any pleasure in his surroundings, though. He'd seen Allie watching him from the kitchen window as he pulled away, and then he'd felt her eyes boring into his back. That she trusted him enough to send him to town with money gave his self-respect a considerable boost. But terror sluiced through his veins with every beat of his heart.

He hadn't been to town since Will Mason sentenced him to the country hush of the Ford farm. After being away from the jangling piano and the smell of whiskey at the Liberal, Jeff's head had begun to clear. The ground he'd gained was shaky, though, and as the gray outline of Decker Prairie's buildings emerged in the distance, he knew it could crumble beneath him by a single moment of temptation.

He didn't want to be in town.

He didn't know if he could make himself leave after he got there.

The town loomed closer, and he let Kansas slow to a moseying dawdle. Why had Allie put her trust in him and sent him into Decker Prairie, and with a ten-dollar gold piece, when she knew it would be so easy for him to backslide and disappoint her?

Then a treacherous thought occurred to him. Maybe Althea expected Jeff to fail. That way she could send him back to Will Mason and be rid of him. She'd been so cool and distant since that one evening in the lean-to, when he'd merely *thought* about kissing her, this might be just the opportunity she'd been looking for.

The very notion made Jeff sit up straight on the wagon seat, boiling anger and cold fear tightening the muscles in his back.

"Damn her!" he snapped at the mule's rump. "That's just what she'd like, fussy Miss Althea Ford—to see me knocked on my ass again." Well then, by God, if he started drinking again it would be her fault, not his.

He rode along, nursing the idea of blame-shifting. He'd done it often enough before. It wasn't even his fault that he'd started drinking in the first place. It had been Cooper Matthews' fault—if he'd done right by his own boy, Wes never would have broken into Wickwire's. Sally, with her complaints about loneliness—a married widow, she'd called herself once—had only helped to keep him on the bottle. Decker Prairie had done its part, too, he rationalized, by whispering about him. The notions all worked for a moment, filling him with a kind of righteous indignation. Those people had all wanted him to fail, to see him flat on his back, so they could dispense their pity and disapproval and moralizing. Oh, it made them feel so superior.

But in his heart Jeff knew better. He'd always known better.

And whether he failed or succeeded today would be his responsibility.

Once he reached Decker Prairie proper, Jeff's foreboding was overshadowed by a sense of amazement. He'd only been gone for a couple of weeks, but the town looked different somehow. A new sign hung over the café, except it didn't really look new. Judging by the way it had weathered, it must have seen at least one winter. Why hadn't he noticed it till now? And the bakery—hadn't it been white before? Today the storefront was pale green with cream-colored trim.

He was so busy taking in the changes around him as Kansas pulled him farther into town, it was several moments before he realized that the people on the street were watching him. He heard his name as heads bent to discuss him. Jeff did his best to ignore the curious stares—hell, he knew they'd talked about him all along, there was no reason it should bother him now. It had just never seemed so obvious to him.

As he neared the Liberal Saloon, he let Kansas slow down again, and the reins grew slack in his hands.

Don't look at it, don't listen to the sound of it.

Don't even smell it.

But it was all there, as unmistakable to him as a stock tank would be to a thirsty horse. From those open doors he smelled stale cigar smoke, and the rich, yeasty scent of warm beer. The piano clanked out the heartrending "Rose Connelly." All of it familiar, inviting. It wasn't the camaraderie that drew him. Jeff was not a sociable drinker; he liked to sit alone in a corner or on a back porch somewhere.

No, what pulled at him now was the simple promise of forgetfulness. One drink, maybe. What could just one drink hurt? His heart thudded in his chest. If he didn't buy the whole bottle he wouldn't be able to take it back to the farm with him—

"Thinking about going inside?"

Snapped out of his reverie, Jeff looked around and saw Will Mason on the sidewalk on the opposite side of the street, sitting in front of the barbershop.

"No, I'm not," he snapped impatiently. Yes, that was exactly what he'd been thinking.

Will pushed himself out of his chair and walked over to meet him in the street. "Well, you're stopped dead in front of the saloon, Jeff."

"I'm just here to buy seed and a couple of other things for the farm."

"That's good." Will pushed his hat off his brow and considered him for a moment. "You know, you're beginning to look like the man I used to know. Life out there must agree with you."

"It isn't like you gave me much choice." Jeff resented what he saw as Will's high-and-mighty attitude. He felt like a kid having to answer to a schoolmaster.

Will scanned him up and down. "It doesn't seem to have hurt you."

Jeff chuckled but not with humor. "Well, don't get your hopes up. No matter what happens, I'm never going to be the man you used to know. Never again. That man is dead."

Will shrugged. "Maybe. Maybe not. Someday down the line, you might even be glad I sent you to the Ford farm."

The tension of being in town and sparring with Will burned Jeff's fuse down to the last inch. "Look, Will, you got your way. Don't expect to be thanked, too."

The sheriff pushed his hat down again. "I didn't do it for you. I was helping out Miss Althea."

"Uh-huh."

"Just remember, Jeff. For you, one drink is too many, and a hundred wouldn't be enough."

Jeff slapped the reins on the mule's back and the wagon lurched forward. Then he turned down the side street that ran between the Liberal Saloon and the feed store. He set the wagon brake and jumped down, raising a cloud of dust when his boots hit the dirt.

Sheriff or not, friend or not, Will Mason wasn't his keeper. Jeff had seen too much and lived too many years to let anyone, including Althea Ford, treat him like a naughty boy. They could tell him to jump, but he'd be damned if he'd ask how high. Reaching into his back pocket for the ten dollars she'd given him, he closed his fist around the coin and set off to prove that.

"By God—by *God*, ain't that Hicks over there?" Cooper Matthews pushed himself away from the doorframe and pointed a dirty finger at a man jumping down from a wagon. From his vantage point near the back door of Kincade's Livery, Cooper could see the town's main street and most of the side street next to the saloon, including all who came and went there.

"I won't bother gettin' up to look at that son of a bitch, if you don't mind," Floyd Endicott groused, and aimed a stream of tobacco juice at a sand bucket. He sat on an old milking stool by a back stall, alternately gnawing on a piece of jerky and a tobacco chaw. Between bites he used the blade of a pocketknife to dig at the festering wound in his hand caused by a splinter. The same hand was missing its index finger, lost when an angry madam had slammed his hand in the door of her safe for pilfering her cash. "I wouldn't even waste a fart on the effort," he added primly, as if such conservation were noble.

"What the hell is he doin' in town?" Cooper muttered. "I figured he was cozying up with those two crazy Ford women."

"Who cares what he does?" Floyd asked, screwing up his face when the point of the knife went too deep.

"I b'lieve we ought to keep an eye on him, watch what he's up to. I got old scores to settle with him. Didn't you say you wanted to get even with him, too? For that time he put you in the pokey overnight?"

"Watchin' ain't gettin' even."

Cooper, whose overalls made him look like a bag of soup bones, folded his arms across his chest and continued to watch Hicks with a ruminant expression and narrowed eyes. "No, but he's givin' me an idea. And I got a plan comin' up. A big one."

"I got a big one comin' up myself," Floyd said, scratching his crotch. His grin was mostly toothless and wet. "Why don't we wander over to New Era and find them gals again? They ain't beauties, but they don't charge much."

"Get your head out of your pants, Floyd," Cooper snapped. "This is more important."

"Aw, shit, what's more important than gettin' a leg over a female?"

"*This is* . . . yup, I'll start slow-like. And I'll fix that Ford bitch in the bargain. She'll learn what it means to double-cross Cooper Matthews." He turned to look at Floyd. "I'll bet you'd like to get even with her, too, especially after she wouldn't pay you. Are you comin' with me?"

The other man tossed aside the remainder of the jerky and folded his knife. "Hell, I guess so. If we ain't goin' to New Era, I got nothin' better to do."

*   *   *

"Just the shirt and the pants, then, Jeff?" Eli Wickwire peered at Jeff over the top of his spectacles and gestured at the shirt and two pairs of dungarees on his counter. He literally had the biggest mouth Jeff had ever seen. He guessed that the shop owner could push a whole apple between his jaws and still be able to close them. "There are lots of other things to choose from here—you remember my motto: 'A Wealth of Goods for Man and Beast.' " He pointed at the sign hanging behind him that said the same thing. It seemed to be true—Jeff had only to look around to see all the merchandise Eli had for sale.

"Yeah, I remember, but this stuff will do, Eli. I have to be getting along." Jeff shifted from one foot to the other. He either had to get to the Liberal Saloon before his conscience changed his mind, or he had to leave while he still had the will to do so.

Eli, however, was in no hurry at all.

"It's good to see you out and about, Jeff. You're looking more like an upright, breathing human again. How's it going out there at the Ford farm?" He tore a length of brown paper from the roll at the end of the counter and began wrapping the clothes. "You going to get the planting done and fix things up a little?"

Jeff tried not to sigh too loudly. "Something like that."

"The place has sure gone downhill since Amos died. But then his daughters wouldn't be able to handle it, just the two of them. Althea's had her hands full since she was just a girl. And I doubt that Olivia would be much help to her. Pity about the younger sister—she has those fits, and Althea won't leave her."

Jeff's spinning impatience slowed to accommodate his curiosity. "Fits? I thought maybe she was addled."

Eli shook his head. "Nope, she's all right in the head—

well, I s'pose that might be stretching it. The whole family was never quite right, you know."

Jeff did know, or at least he'd heard it, but he didn't feel comfortable trading gossip with Eli as if they were a pair of meddling old ladies. Anyway, except for a couple of eccentricities, like the business about the barn door, Althea seemed fine. Very fine. He reached into his pocket and took out the money for the clothes, hoping that cash would distract the man. "Here, Eli—"

But he simply kept talking as he wrote up the sale. " 'Course, the girls' mother strung herself up when Althea was, oh, seven-eight years old and her sister was still in diapers. I guess that might make anyone a little odd."

Stunned, Jeff snapped his gaze to Eli's round face. "God—she hanged herself?"

"Yes—well, I guess that's what happened. Amos never said a peep about it. I guess he didn't want everyone in town to know, but it's pretty hard to keep something like that quiet. Word got out that the preacher wouldn't say even word one over Lucinda's grave—suicide was an abomination in the eyes of God, he said. So there wasn't any funeral, but I remember Amos bringing his wife to the undertaker's with Althea on the wagon seat next to him." Eli looked up and gazed across the store, obviously remembering the scene. "Olivia wasn't more than a few months old, I don't think. I can still see Althea holding the baby in her arms, her little face pale and blank. I'd never seen a kid look like that before. She had old eyes, like she'd lived fifty years instead of eight." He shook his head and then chuckled. "It made quite a fuss around here, I can tell you. It was a long time before something else came along to cause a stir like that. I don't think it was until that Matthews boy—" Eli broke off then, his face crimson and the great cavern of his mouth hanging open, obviously realizing who he was talking to. Jeff's own jaw clenched, but he simply stared back at Eli and said nothing. "W-well, it was a shame, of course, the Ford girls losing their mother and all."

The transaction came to a swift end after that, and Jeff found himself back out on the sidewalk with the paper-wrapped package under this arm. The afternoon sun was heading down the sky and he knew he should get back to the farm. The Liberal Saloon was just a few paces across the street, closer than he wished now.

Somehow, learning about Althea's mother put a different face on things. Jesus—suicide. A chill rippled through him. As desperate as he'd felt at times, he'd never thought of putting a gun to his head. Or a rope around his neck. When he died, he expected something else—or someone else—to do the deed. What a hell of a thing to happen to a kid, to lose her mother that way.

Jeff walked down the plank sidewalk toward the side street, kicking up dust as he went, and the wagon and Smithfield's mule came into view. Kansas turned a baleful look on him, but he barely noticed. He was looking at the wagon.

It was an *old* wagon, he realized. Old enough to have served as Lucinda Ford's hearse. Drawing closer, he looked at the seed sacks on the rough-planked bed and could easily imagine a woman lying there instead, wrapped in a quilt. And up there on the sprung seat, a scared little girl had sat who now bore the responsibility of a sister who would never really grow up. Suddenly his heart ached for Allie— Jeff's own life had taken a seriously wrong turn in the last few years, but at least he'd had the chance to be a kid. The chance to grow up and know love, and the soul-deep satisfaction of physical closeness with another person, even if it hadn't lasted. Allie had known none of that, he was certain. Her innocence and almost-fearful modesty were so obvious.

The ache in his chest made Jeff realize that more of his feelings were coming to life again. Damn it all, he didn't want that. All feelings ended up being the same one eventually: pain. And God knew he'd had enough of that to last the rest of his life. It had flowed over him like a swift-running river rushed over rocks, wearing away, wearing away. He didn't think he could stand any more.

Only one thing had made him forget that pain. Sighing, he reached into his pocket and fingered the change left from the seed and his clothes. He looked at the side of the building next to him. Painted in yard-high yellow-and-black letters, THE LIBERAL SALOON.

Just one drink—what could one drink hurt?

Just one and then he'd go back to the farm.

His hand closed around the money in his pocket. Just one—

"Well, Floyd, look who we got here. I do believe it's our old sheriff." Jeff didn't need to see who was behind him to recognize Cooper Matthews' voice.

Jeff's spine stiffened and every defensive instinct came alive in him. He glared at both of them but kept moving, hoping to walk away from them without another confrontation. He knew neither man was very smart, but how far would they push him right here on the street in broad daylight?

"I guess he ain't so brave when he don't have a gun strapped to his leg, huh?" Floyd taunted, dogging Jeff's steps.

"Or when he's got some woman's skirts to hide behind," Matthews added with hooting derision.

Jeff turned to face them, anger throbbing through his limbs, but he bit back the fury. Despite everything that had happened, he never forgot that he'd cut short the life of this man's son. That knowledge and the guilt that went with it had saved Cooper Matthews from Jeff's wrath more than once, if he only knew it. The shotgun Matthews carried gleamed dully under the afternoon sun.

"I got a bone to pick with you, Hicks. More than one bone, in fact, and my list keeps growing. So you'd better watch your back. I aim to get satisfaction one of these days." He hefted the shotgun once, a short, light bounce in his hand, as if to bring the weapon to Jeff's notice.

Weariness, heavy as a millstone, descended upon Jeff. Cooper Matthews was a mean son of a bitch, mean to the core. Jeff wasn't about to let him think he could be pushed around, but he just wanted to walk away and be left in what little peace he had.

He gave Cooper a wry grin, then stared into the man's small, cruel eyes. "Hell, Matthews, you can't kill a man who's already dead. Even you and your dimwit pard, here"—he gestured at Floyd—"ought to be smart enough to know that. You can threaten me all you want—it just doesn't matter to me."

Plainly spoiling for a fight, Jeff's indifference made the man even angrier. While Floyd gaped at Jeff, his companion sputtered for a snappy retort, choler twisting his face. People on the street were turning to stare at them.

Jeff turned and walked on toward the Liberal. Then he heard Cooper yell an extremely crude remark about Althea Ford, one that sent another surge of anger through his veins. Jeff knew he did it to goad him, and oh, damn it, he shouldn't care. He should just let it go. But Althea had no part of this fight, not really. It had started long before the day she talked to Cooper about working for her, and she didn't deserve to have anyone call her a filthy name. He turned and strode back to the two men, his boot heels pounding on the boards in the sidewalk. It felt as if there were a face at every window up and down the street watching and listening.

Floyd let out a short *yip* and jumped aside. Jeff grabbed Cooper by the suspenders on his baggy overalls and pulled him up to his face. Although Jeff done nothing with his life in the past two years, he didn't feel that he was as completely worthless as the man who faced him now. Stealing an egg was nothing compared to Matthews' history of bullying and inflicting years of physical and mental abuse on his wife and child. Jeff thought Elly Matthews died simply to escape her life with Cooper.

"Say it again, Matthews. Call Miss Ford that name again, this time to my *face*."

The other man only grinned at Jeff, showing off his stained, peglike teeth. "What're you gonna do, Hicks? Kill me? You two think you're better than everyone else, you and that cu—"

Jeff's fist smashed against Cooper's mouth, cutting off the end of the word. The man's head snapped back and he landed on his backside in the street. He wiped his dirty hand across his mouth and looked at the blood there. He sent Jeff a look of pure, undiluted hatred.

"You're gonna pay for that, Hicks."

Jeff stood over him and pointed a finger at him. "That's fine. I don't give a damn. You just leave the lady out of it." He turned and walked away again, past goggle-eyed bystanders and counter boys who'd come out of the stores and saloon to have a look.

He didn't think Cooper and Floyd were following him. He'd barked louder than they had. This time. But just as he'd recognized the other day, this thing between Matthews and him wasn't finished, and Jeff truly didn't know which of them would die in ending it. But all of it had come about because he'd gone to Wickwire's that night and seen Wes, instead of riding home to have dinner with Sally.

Guilt, fury, and the frightening novelty of dealing with trouble sober had his insides shaking. More determined than ever to get that drink, he reached the saloon and gripped the top of the batwing doors. From within, the noise and smells and voices, all so familiar to him, drew him with an unspoken promise to kill the pain in his soul. He pushed on the doors—he thought he heard someone inside call him by name. This was where he belonged, even if he'd once had other dreams . . .

Then a pair of blue-gray eyes rose in his memory. The effect was so sudden, so unexpected, that Jeff stopped as if someone had pulled him back by his shirttail.

"Hey, Jeff, are you coming in or not, son?" A ripple of laughter rolled through the place.

He released his grip on the doors. No, he wasn't. Althea had put her trust in him, and it sat on his shoulders with his weariness, a burden that he knew he couldn't put down. Not even for a minute.

Not even for one drink.

Jeff turned around and walked back to the wagon that had borne a child into adulthood. He climbed up to the same sprung seat that had held her, and unwrapped the reins from the brake handle.

"We'd better get back, Kansas. Allie's waiting."

Chapter Nine

CALLING HERSELF EVERY KIND OF GOD'S FOOL, ALTHEA had watched Jeff leave with a leaden feeling in the pit of her stomach. He'd been gone for what seemed like hours, and though she tried to keep her mind on her ironing and hide her concern from Olivia, she wasn't having much luck with either.

"I don't know if I would have given him *money*, Althea. After all, a man like him might just take it and never come back." Olivia sat at the kitchen table sipping tea and stitching on a doll's dress. Her nose wrinkled delicately as she spoke, as if she discussed a very disagreeable smell.

Althea had been surprised to see her downstairs—lately her sister had begun looking wan again and taking to her bed. Today, distracted though Althea was, she noticed that Olivia positively bloomed. Her cheeks had color and her eyes were bright, even though she pursed her mouth slightly with obvious disapproval.

Trying to change the subject, Althea gave her sister a fond smile and said, "You look so fresh and pretty today, dear. I'm glad to see you up and about again."

"Well, when I looked out my window and saw your Mr.

Hicks leave, I knew you'd be needing company. It's so disappointing when someone you've counted on lets you down. I hope the sheriff puts him back in jail if he catches him." Olivia shook her head and tsk-tsked while she tacked a narrow strip of lace onto the little skirt. "You probably should have told him to have the supplies put on account."

The same thought had already occurred to Althea. But if he bought clothes for himself, he might feel uncomfortable about getting them on what might look like charity, and a woman's charity at that. With cash, no one was the wiser. She tried to sound unconcerned when she replied. "I'm not worried. Besides, he'll probably show up starving for his dinner."

Olivia peered closely at the fine stitches she took in the doll's dress and shook her head again. "No, I think we've seen the last of him. But when he doesn't come back you won't have to worry about cooking for another person, or sewing for him, or doing his wash. Next time, you can hire someone who'll go home at night."

Her sister's pessimistic certainty made her head begin to ache. "Of course he'll be back. We still have lots of work to do around here." But Althea looked out the kitchen window even more often than she had when Jeff was plowing in the field without a shirt. That was a dangerous thing to do when working with fire-hot flatirons. With her gaze fixed on the road outside, she groped blindly for the iron and her hand came to rest on the bare metal.

Letting out a cry that launched Olivia from her chair, Althea jerked her hand away and ran to the sink to pump cold water over it.

"Let me see," Olivia demanded. She made passing swipes to grab her wrist, but Althea refused, afraid to see the burn herself.

"No! I'll be all right! Please," she begged, huddled over

the sink, "please just leave me alone." Her voice shook with suppressed tears and frayed nerves. She didn't mean to be short with Olivia. But a sense of defeat sat on her heart like a rock, and searing her hand on the iron stole the shreds of her brave front.

With a pointed show of hurt feelings, Olivia dropped her hand and backed up. "Certainly, Althea. I'll run along to the parlor, if that's the way you want it." Allie could tell from her tone that her sister was thinking of herself again.

With a shaky sigh, Althea forced herself to look at the burn. A big triangular blister was forming on her palm, its angry red shape conforming with the top end of the iron. Butter—that's what people put on burns. She pulled out the butter crock and spooned some onto the blister. Then she cradled her hand to her chest and tried to fight the tears rising in her eyes, while Olivia played the piano, battering the keys like an asylum inmate.

What if he didn't come back? What if Jeff took the mule and the wagon and never came back? It wasn't losing the money that worried her, although that wasn't a happy prospect. And she'd have to pay Mr. Smithfield for the loss of Kansas. She looked out the window at the plowed field. But who would plant that garden out there? Who would help her? Her gaze drifted to the lean-to.

Who would stir in her those frightening, fascinating feelings that he did? a tiny voice whispered. Althea practically jumped away from the window, guilt adding its burden to her anxiety.

In the parlor Olivia continued to pound out a song, and Althea felt that she must escape or completely lose her composure. Grabbing a small meal sack from the corner, she pushed on the screen door and went outside, away from the pouting and the angry piano notes. There was a stiff breeze blowing, but the afternoon was hot, so she crossed the yard to the leafy shade of the old oak that towered in the meadow next to the barn. It was always cooler under here, and even in the hottest part of summer, the grass and wildflowers under the tree's limbs stayed green and tender.

Opening the meal sack with her uninjured hand she reached inside and took out a small handful of shelled sun-flower seeds. Then with her hand open and slightly out-stretched, she stood perfectly still and waited. In the peaceful hush of the countryside, she could hear her own breathing, and her heartbeat beneath her breastbone, but the only other sound was the whisper of her skirts against the high grass. Still she waited.

It didn't take long. First she heard curious chirps coming from the higher branches above her, and the sound of wings fluttering against the leaves. An instant later she felt an airy tap on her shoulder, and then a black-capped chickadee jumped from her shoulder and settled on her fingers.

"Ohh, there you are," she murmured softly. "I came to see how you're getting along. Did you bring your wife?"

As if answering her question, another bird with plainer feathers fluttered down to her hand from a low branch, and Althea's heart warmed as the little black-and-white birds plucked the sunflower hearts from her palm. Watching them, she could almost her forget the pain in her other hand, and the very real possibility that Jefferson Hicks had taken her money, her wagon, and Mr. Smithfield's mule, and now was long gone.

After his encounter with Cooper and Floyd, Jeff spent the ride home in moody reflection. There was no telling how Cooper would decide to strike next, and Floyd Endicott was his toadying tagalong. Floyd didn't have as dark a mean streak as Cooper, but he'd do anything his friend told him, so that was just as bad.

When the Fords' peeling yellow house came into view, Jeff was surprised by the vague sense of relief that settled over him. Not because of the house—although the roof looked better, overall the thing was an eyesore that might never be right again. But there was refuge here, and a kind of peace where the Cooper Matthewses of the world wouldn't bother him, and the pull of the Liberal Saloon wasn't as strong.

As he and Kansas passed the house on the way to the barn, he noticed Allie standing stock-still in the fruit or-chard with her hand extended. The breeze whipped at the hem of her skirt and her apron ties, and strands of her dark-red hair pulled loose from its knot. What the hell was she doing? She looked like a statue in a town square, or a pho-tographer's notion of a forest nymph, posed and captured on a camera's glass plate.

He let the reins grow slack in his hands and Kansas took that as a signal to stop. Jeff heard the tortured piano notes coming from the house, but his attention was on the mahogany-haired woman in the grass.

The whole family had never been quite right, Eli Wick-wire had said. Was he was seeing an active of example of Allie being not "quite right?"

Then suddenly, a bird landed on Allie's shoulder and hopped down to her open palm to eat something right out of her hand.

Jeff hunched forward and put his elbows on his knees. "Well, I'll be damned . . ." He'd never seen anything like it. Most birds were as skittish as horses, flying off with little or no provocation, never letting anyone get close. Yet here was Allie, feeding them as if she were one of them. The sight of it lifted some of the darkness from his heart.

It suited her, he decided. She was small and delicate like those birds. She had graceful little ways, like when she pushed her hair back with her hand. It reminded him of a bird preening its feathers.

He wondered if she knew about the bird's nest in the barn, the one with the family of new swallows. He'd seen it when he'd gone in search of the shingles. She'd like to see that little family, he'd bet. Watching her now, he knew it would be just the kind of thing to make her smile.

The birds on her hand flew away to the higher branches above, and Allie's head came up. Apparently sensing his presence, slowly she turned toward him, and a spontaneous smile lit her face.

"Jeff! You came back!" She sounded surprised. Surprised enough to forget to call him Mr. Hicks. She waded through the tall grass and wildflowers, her skirts swishing like a wheat field in the wind. When she reached the wagon, he noticed the meal bag in her hand.

He pointed at the bag. "I've never seen anyone hand-feed birds before. At least not those little ones."

She tipped her face up to his. "They're shy, but they'll come once they realize they aren't in danger. It took some time and patience to prove that to them, and for them to get used to me." She smiled again and extended the bag. "And I think the sunflower hearts were too tempting for them to resist."

Maybe it was more than the seeds, Jeff thought, looking at her. It wouldn't take much to have *him* eating out of her hand. She was so beautiful, her face and her slender softness, he got a lump in his throat just looking at her. Sally had been pretty, too, but in a different way. His wife had been younger, and yet there had been a spark of undisguised lust in her eyes that she'd carried to their bed.

Allie's was a quiet, simple beauty, like that of a clear mountain morning, or wild filly running across a stretch of grassland. She was probably wary of a man's touch, but maybe her trust could be earned, just as she'd tamed the birds enough to eat from her hand. A man could almost forget his foolish past and begin to think about tomorrow if he had a woman like her beside him.

"You got everything, then?" She searched the wagon box behind him. "The seed and all?

"Yeah. Oh, here—" He leaned back on the wagon seat and dug two fingers into his front pocket. "I've got your change." And a damned good thing he did, too. How could he have come back here with part of the money missing, or worse, with no money at all? He would have run off to hide rather than face her with the proof that she'd been a fool to trust him.

When she held out her free hand to take the coins, he saw an ugly burn on her palm. He gripped her wrist. "Jesus, what happened to your hand?"

Althea had put out her hand without thinking, and she saw the blister at the same time that Jeff did. Self-consciously she struggled to pull her hand away, but his grip was firm and warm. "I burned it on the iron. It was my fault—I wasn't watching what I was doing."

"It must hurt like hell," he said, studying it with a frown that laid furrows on his smooth forehead. But she wasn't looking at her hand. She was looking at Jeff. Faint lines fanned out from the outer corners of his eyes, the badge of a man who'd spent time laboring under the sun. His dark lashes were golden at their roots, like corn silk. So were his brows, and the sight fascinated her.

He had come back, she thought. He'd come back even though Olivia had told her he wouldn't. Even though she herself had doubted it. Althea didn't think she'd ever been so glad to see someone.

His gaze, as green and deep as a bottomless lake, shifted from her hand to her eyes, and Allie's thoughts were occupied with nothing but their hold on her. "Doesn't it?"

"W-what?" She rather wished he wouldn't look at her like that. How could she think straight if he did?

"Doesn't your hand hurt?"

"Um, yes, I guess so." His touch made her completely forget about the burn on her palm.

He continued to cradle her hand in his own. "You should see to it. Did you do anything for it?"

"A little butter. I'll put some baking soda on it when I go back inside." Her insides felt like the butter that had melted on her hand, and she hoped he wouldn't notice the goose bumps that rushed down her bare forearm. "Things went all right in town?"

Jeff released her wrist and shrugged, obviously uncomfortable. "Yeah. Fine." Althea wasn't convinced. He jumped down from the wagon, all long legs and grace, and walked around to lead the mule to the barn. "I'd better get Kansas here unhitched and these sacks put away."

She took a couple of steps to follow him. He was so tall that her head just reached his shoulder, and he moved with a loose, easy gait that she found curiously stirring. But something was bothering him. "Did someone in town make a comment about you working here?"

He turned to look at her. "What do you mean?"

She smiled slightly. "It's funny—people talk about Olivia and me and they think we don't know. Well, I suppose Olivia doesn't. But I do. I know what they say—I've known it for years. So I thought that maybe someone asked you about working for the crazy Ford sisters."

He frowned. "They'd better not call you that in front of me. Anyway, that didn't happen." Since it didn't seem that he was going to say more, she was about to let the subject drop when he said, "I saw Cooper Matthews in town, that's all. We tangled a little. You know how he is."

Yes, she certainly did. He'd been no better as a boy, but as a man he was more menacing. Cooper made trouble wherever he went. "Do you think he'll come here again?"

He shook his head. "I doubt it. He'll wait until I'm in town again, or some other time when he can sneak up on me."

She looked up at his clean profile again, and took a breath. "I-I know it's none of my business—and I know you were only doing your job at the time and had no choice. But maybe—if he's carrying such a grudge about Wesley, do you think it might help if you apologized to Cooper for killing his son?"

He came to such an abrupt stop, Kansas bumped his nose against Jeff's shoulder. His face full of anger and raw pain, he spun toward her with a violence that made her shrink from him.

"Apologize!" The mule's ears went flat and Althea jumped. "Good God, woman, don't you think I did that? I was the one who went to Matthews to tell him I'd killed Wes. I could barely string my words together for the guilt I felt and the anger. For the senselessness of it all. But I told him I was sorry—that it was the sorriest day of my whole goddamned life. All he said was that I hadn't seen that day yet, but he'd make sure I did. I even paid the undertaker for the boy's burial expenses and I went to his funeral. Cooper didn't. As far as I know, he's never visited his own son's grave. I'm not apologizing to him again."

"No, of course not—" Althea fumbled, her heart beating double-time in her throat. She was unaccustomed to raised voices. In the Ford house, anger had always been expressed with austere disapproval and a dour cold shoulder.

"And anyway, to Cooper's way of thinking, a man who shows pity or remorse or mercy is weak, and I'm not going to be the one to change his narrow little mind. I don't *have* to."

"Then maybe it isn't important that Cooper forgives you. It might be that you need to forgive yourself." Althea couldn't believe she'd given voice to the suggestion.

His sandy brows went up. "Myself! That's what Sally— What the hell is that supposed to mean?"

She didn't want to make him angrier. Besides, it was really none of her business. She retreated another step and shook her head. "I spoke out of turn. I'm sorry."

He glared at her with eyes that looked like green ice. "Everyone is great at giving advice. Well, I'll tell you something, Miss Ford. Until you've walked in my boots— Oh, hell, just forget it!" he snapped.

Turning, he wrapped his hand in the mule's bridle and pulled him forward again, drawing closer to the barn doors than Althea wanted to go. Why she cared she wasn't sure, but she didn't want him mad at her.

She stood on the path and called after him. "Mr. Hicks— Jeff—wait." He didn't respond and she called again. "Please stop?"

He stopped and faced her, his expression suddenly weary, as if the outburst had cost him all of his newly gained strength. The sight of it struck her heart.

She closed the distance between them and tried not to twist her hands together like an awkward girl. "I really am sorry."

His hard expression melted. "Well, I guess I shouldn't have gotten so hot under the collar," he muttered.

"I'm glad you—I want to thank you for coming back," she said, fiddling with the meal sack. She didn't know why, but she felt it was important to tell him that.

"You didn't believe I would, huh?"

She opened her hands. "I know you don't really want to

be here. And I gave you the perfect chance to run off."

He turned his attention to a bloom of Queen Anne's lace near his boot, avoiding her gaze. "I didn't plan to do that. I have to confess that once I got into town, with money in my pocket I had some trouble staying out of the Liberal Saloon. But I did." He lifted his eyes to hers and took a step toward her. "You're wrong about one thing, though, Allie. I do want to be here."

There was something about the way he said it that made Allie's breath come a little faster. "You do?"

He moved closer, keeping his grip on the mule's lines but letting them out a little, the way a cowboy might give some slack to a yearling after a hard day. "Well, not at first, I admit that. But it's good to have a tie to the land again, to sink my hands into it and grow things. To watch the season turn. I haven't felt like that for a long time. Anyway, you need someone around here to fix things up."

His reaction was so different from that of the other men she'd hired to work here. Jeff didn't treat her like a crackpot, watching her with rude, sidelong gazes, or talking down to her as if she were an idiot who couldn't understand. But maybe he didn't because he knew what it meant to be treated that way himself. And it might be why she didn't want him angry with her.

So relieved that he'd gotten over his temper, Allie said, "For dinner I thought that you might want—that is—you're welcome to have dinner with my sister and me. If you like." She extended the invitation, feeling so awkward and shy, she knew she was blushing.

"You're eating on the porch again?"

"Well, no, we'll sit at the dining room table inside. Maybe it might be a nice change from eating from a tray in the lean-to, or in the yard. You know . . . not so lonely."

Absently he stroked the mule's neck and finally he nodded. "Thanks, Allie. I'd like that very much."

He was so handsome standing there, she thought. The late afternoon sun glimmered on the blond streaks in his hair and his lean-muscled height called to her. She was loath to leave his presence. In fact, just looking at him flooded her with a torrent of feelings and emotions that pulled her to him in a way she felt powerless to resist. *Was* he ever lonely, she wondered, lonely to the marrow of his bones as she sometimes was?

"We're having roast beef," she noted inanely.

Allie could have told Jeff she was serving boiled goat hide for all he cared right now. She had invited him to her table and that was good enough for him. At this moment he felt just a little taller than the man who had robbed Farley Wright's henhouse.

His eyes never left hers—they were the color of a sunset sky in winter—and he watched her hesitant approach. Sometimes when he looked at her he saw loss and a loneliness that he couldn't define. It was there in those eyes.

But right now, all he saw was the woman. Her breasts swelled beneath the plain bodice of her serviceable dress, and her waist cut in sharply to flare gently at her hips. He imagined running his hands over her bare skin, following the flowing line of her body. A curling tendril of auburn hair resting on her pale forehead hair fluttered in the breeze, as delicate as a flower petal.

She stopped not more than a pace before him, and Jeff dropped the reins. A surge of desire bolted through him, not unlike what he'd felt the day Allie measured him for his shirt. But it was even stronger now.

His instinct driving him, he knew what he must do, what everything male in him demanded that he do.

He leaned forward, his lips just inches from her face.

Closer—closer until he touched his mouth to hers,

softly, gently, with a kiss that was little more than a shadow.

Jeff hadn't kissed a woman sober since Sally left. The sensation was so moving, so sweet, he felt his emotions rise even as his body responded with hardness.

Resisting the urge to crush her to him, he allowed himself only to bracket her chin with his fingertips. But God, it was a trial to keep his hand on her jaw. He heard her swift intake of breath. *Please don't pull away, Allie ... please, no*, he thought. But she didn't.

"Allie," he whispered, breaking the kiss. "Thank you." He was so damned grateful to her, it was all he could manage to say. Her hand, at least he could take her hand—

"Ouch!" She jumped back and snatched her fingers from his.

"Damn, I'm sorry, I forgot about your burn—"

She backed away, then, her eyes still wide, her fingers pressed lightly to her lips. "It's all right. Um—I'd better see to dinner if we're going to eat." She turned and hurried through the grass to the back porch.

When she reached it, she looked at him over her shoulder, then ran inside.

"Do you mean he came back?" Olivia, ashen-faced, stared at her sister across the lid of the grand piano. Althea thought she looked crestfallen, as though she'd suffered some grave disappointment, but she couldn't imagine why. Olivia got her way on nearly everything.

"Yes, isn't it wond—I mean, of course he did. I've asked him to have dinner with us." Althea had dashed upstairs to her room to put on a clean dress and tidy her hair. Now she fussed with a bud vase on the side table next to the settee and straightened a needlepoint pillow. She felt excited and lighthearted, terrified and rather womanly, all at the same time. Jeff had kissed her! A proper lady would not have permitted such a liberty. In fact, she should probably be very angry. But she wasn't and at this moment, she didn't care.

Womanly. Yes, that was how Jeff Hicks made her feel.

Her sister scowled, wrinkling up her delicate face like a Danish squash. "Dinner! Althea, you can't mean you're going to invite that man, that derelict, into the house."

"He's really tried hard to get back on his feet since he got here, and he's made progress. Anyway, I think it will do us both good."

Olivia traced the ivory keys with her fingertips. "But you know I get tired so easily."

"But that's all right. You won't have to do anything special except help me set the table, and maybe slice the bread. The roast is almost finished—it's been in the oven for more than an hour." Distracted, she added, "I wish we had a dessert."

"But you can't cook with your hand burned like that," her sister continued, a faint panicky sound in her sweet voice that Althea chose to overlook.

"I've already cooked dinner, Olivia," she pointed out again. "Just as I always have." With her teeth gritted, she had applied a cooling paste of baking soda to her burn and bandaged it.

"I don't want some stranger sitting at the table with me, watching me eat."

Althea had spent most of her life catering to her sister's wishes and had never asked anything for herself. Just this once, she would. She walked to the piano bench and put her uninjured hand on Olivia's shoulder. The blond hair under her palm was as silky as a child's. "Heavens, dear, he's not going to watch you eat. Please, Olivia—I think it would be a nice change. It's Saturday evening—a lot of people entertain on Saturday evenings. We can do it just this once. Besides, I've already asked him. I can't take back the invitation now."

Olivia pursed her mouth into a white line. "All right, Althea." She looked up at her with a sidelong gaze. "If that's what you want."

Chapter Ten

JEFF STOOD OUTSIDE THE LEAN-TO AND STARED AT THE back door across the yard. He had washed, shaved, and washed again, as nervous as a moonstruck boy calling on a girl for the first time. He wasn't really calling on Allie— she had only invited him to dinner after all, a mere courtesy extended by a woman to her employee. Just the same, he'd stood before his shaving mirror, trying to see all of himself by ducking and stretching, although it had been no use. A little bay rum would have been a nice touch, too, but he'd settled for slicking down his clean hair with water.

He hadn't sat down at anyone's table for a long time, and the prospect had him so edgy he almost wished he'd declined the invitation. He'd spent so much time alone in his blur of endless days and nights, he didn't remember how to make small talk and was worried that he might forget his table manners. Maybe if he just concentrated on his plate— But he wasn't really going there to eat. He was going because he wanted to be close to Allie.

He couldn't believe he'd kissed her like that, in the middle of the yard with a damned mule looking on. Wasn't *that* romantic as hell? He hadn't planned to do it, but with her standing so close and looking so good, he'd settled his mouth over hers before he knew quite how it happened. With all the other women he'd ever kissed, he'd considered each move before he made it, but with Allie, it had been a spontaneous act, as natural and essential as breathing.

And it had more than made up for Cooper Matthews' bedevilment.

After ducking back inside the lean-to for a last glance in his shaving mirror, Jeff decided he looked as good as he was going to. He struck off for the house. Stiff as celluloid, his new jeans sang like a pair of crickets with every step he took. He cringed at the noise. Hell if he didn't look and sound like a new-made Christian, fresh from the river of salvation and all spruced up in his new clothes, ready to shout *hallelujah*. Remembering the feel of Allie's soft lips beneath his and picturing her smooth, creamy skin, though, his thoughts were anything but pious.

When he reached the porch, the aroma of food drifted to him, rich and savory, and he paused with his knuckles hovering over the door. What would he say? What would Allie and her sister say? Maybe they'd ask a lot of questions that he didn't want to answer. They might want to know about Sally and why she'd left him. People loved to hear about the miseries of others. It made their own mundane lives seem more tolerable.

He glanced back at the lean-to, as weathered and gray as the barn it was attached to. He could still turn around and go back. Make up some excuse to avoid hurting Allie's feelings and escape this—

Suddenly the door opened and Jeff found himself face-to-face with Allie Ford, his upraised knuckles perilously close to tapping on her nicely formed nose. He dropped his arm and backed up a step. Damn, wasn't she pretty? Her pink dress was complemented by a pink satin ribbon that she'd wound through her curls, and her smooth skin looked as velvety and delicately colored as a rose. All thoughts of begging off fled from his mind.

"Mister—I mean, Jeff—please—come in." Her gaze swept over him and his clothes, and she smiled. "You wore the shirt I made for you. I haven't seen it since the afternoon I left it in the lean-to." She tipped her face down in a gesture of shyness that touched him. "I was worried that you didn't like it."

He fingered one of his cuffs. "No, ma'am, it's a fine shirt. I was saving it for a special occasion." He looked up again. "I guess this qualifies."

Her cheeks colored a bit as her eyes slid away from his. He couldn't help but smile. "We're just about ready to sit down. Come on this way."

"Thanks." He followed her inside, noting that at the nape of her neck, wispy little curls had escaped the hairpins to lay in shimmering red ringlets against her pale skin, making him think of swirls of raspberry juice on cream.

She moved ahead of him with precise, fluid grace, the rosy folds of her skirts whipping the doorjambs as she passed. Jeff couldn't decide which smelled better—Allie or dinner.

Inside, the house looked better than it did from the yard. As he passed through the kitchen, he saw it was big and bright. In the dining room, curtains graced every window with a definite feminine touch that, surprisingly, didn't seem so bad to him. Jeff would prefer more rugged surroundings himself, but the lace tablecloth and flowered upholstery on the seat cushions in the dining room made him think of the house he'd grown up in.

Except for the pale specter of Olivia Ford.

She sat at her place at the table and studied him with a careful, assessing look from beneath long lashes.

Not addle-minded, Eli Wickwire had told him. No, up this close Jeff could see that his original assumption had been wrong. He had the feeling that this young woman missed nothing. There was also something that lurked behind those hazel eyes, something Jeff had seen somewhere before, but couldn't quite—

"Olivia, won't you say hello to Mr. Hicks?"

"Hello, Mr. Hicks," she parroted and gave him a flat smile.

"Ma'am."

Allie directed him to the place across the table from her own. "This is a real treat, isn't it, Olivia? We don't have company very often."

"I'm so sorry about that, Althea," Olivia said in a soft voice that struck Jeff as too sincere to be real.

"Sorry?" Althea echoed. "Whatever for?"

"Well, it's my fault that you never get to entertain," Olivia replied earnestly. "Because I haven't been well for the longest time." She took a biscuit from the plate that Allie handed to her. "I don't know if Althea told you that, Mr. Hicks. I worry about being a burden to her, but she's an angel to have put up with me all this time. I have no idea what I'd do without her—a person couldn't ask for a better sister."

Surprised by the younger sister's sudden talkativeness, Jeff looked at Allie as she served a slice of meat to Olivia. "I'm sure that's true, ma'am."

Allie smiled and shrugged. "I only do what anyone else would. But tell us about the garden, Jeff. You'll start planting tomorrow? It's already so late, I hope we'll have enough time to get a decent harvest."

He spooned mashed potatoes onto his dish. "I'll get the corn in first. It needs the longest growing time, but it shouldn't take too long to sow, providing that Kansas is still agreeable—"

"Excuse me, Mr. Hicks," Olivia broke in and turned to her sister. "I forgot to bring out your blackberry jam, dear. Would you mind? It's so good."

Althea paused, her fork suspended on its path to her mouth, holding the first bite from her plate. "No, Olivia . . . of course I don't mind. I'll get it. Please excuse me, Jeff." She smiled apologetically at Jeff and abandoned her un-touched meal, pushing herself away from the table to go to the kitchen.

During Althea's short absence, Jeff considered Olivia Ford, but she gave him another bland smile and put a tea-spoon of peas on her plate.

"I really think you'll like Althea's blackberry jam. My father used to say it was the best he'd ever tasted."

Allie reappeared with a small bowl of jam and put it on the table.

"Now then," she said, and put her napkin back in her lap and turned her attention back to Jeff. "What about the corn? We usually plant ten rows, and I'd also like to put in a few pumpkins this year. I think I have some seed in a jar in the kitchen."

"Althea," Olivia interrupted. "Isn't that the shirt you made for Mr. Hicks?"

"Yes, that's right."

She studied both Jeff and his shirt with an appraising stare. "Hmm, it looks very nice, like you put in a lot of work on it. Maybe even days."

"Heavens, no, it didn't take that long." Althea added to Jeff, "I had years of practice making shirts for my father."

"It fits just right," he said, feeling like a fly under a magnifying glass.

"Yes," Althea agreed with a faint smile, "it does."

She returned the topic of conversation to the garden, and Jeff was satisfied. No personal questions came up, and he asked none, either. The food was good and as Allie had pointed out, having dinner in the house was less lonely than eating from a tray in the lean-to.

The one thing he would have changed, though, was Olivia's presence.

They made an awkward triumvirate, the three of them, with Allie sitting across the table from him, and her sister at the end. He felt Olivia's eyes on him through most of the meal, and she had her sister hopping up and down, waiting on her as if she were a queen.

Her tea had grown cold. Would Althea bring more hot water?

Was there another piece of meat in the roasting pot that wasn't quite so fatty?

The breeze was blowing dust through the open window behind Althea and it was falling into Olivia's dinner. Would she mind closing it?

This last time Jeff got up. He wasn't sure what Olivia's game was—the wind wasn't even wafting the curtains, and the ground outside had barely dried from the spring rains. But he thought Althea ought to have the chance to finish her meal. It was probably already cold as it was. "I'll get it, Allie. You go ahead and enjoy your dinner." He nodded to Olivia. "You, too, ma'am."

Olivia giggled a bit nervously, her hazel eyes darting between her sister and Jeff. "*Allie!* Why, I've never heard anyone outside the family call you something so personal. Isn't it—clever? A person would almost think you two have spent some time together."

Althea, who had been watching Jeff's shoulders flex as he pushed down on the window frame, snapped her attention back to the cold food on her plate. She wished he hadn't called her by that name, especially in front of her sister. "Won't you try to eat something? You're just picking at your dinner."

Olivia put her hand to her throat, as though something were caught in it, and her delicate features faded to paper-white. "I-I guess I'm not really very hungry. I'll just try to finish my tea." She reached for her cup with a hand that shook.

A chill rolled over Althea, a sudden sense of dread that made her think of being trapped on a railroad tie with the train approaching.

Jeff, obviously unaware, returned to the table and took up his fork again.

Olivia leaned back in her chair and began rubbing her temples with her fingertips.

Not again, Althea thought desperately, not now. "Olivia? Are you all right?"

Her sister's hazel eyes welled up and her voice shook. "No, I'm not. I don't think I want—"

Jeff looked up, and as soon as his gaze connected with Olivia's, her eyes rolled back and closed. A deep wail, rising from the depths of torment, worked its way up her throat and escaped her with a sound that would have brought chills to the dead.

"Jesus Christ . . ."

"Olivia!" Althea sprang from her chair, her napkin tumbling down her lap, and she hurried to Olivia's side.

With her arms extended rigidly on the table, her sister gripped bunches of the tablecloth in her fists, then snapped both hands to her chest with maniacal strength. The plates and serving dishes flew from the tabletop, landing on the floor and in Olivia's lap. A river of warm gravy drizzled over Althea's arm as she tried to grasp her sister's flailing wrists. Olivia's body stiffened and she rose from her sitting position so that only her shoulders and thighs rested against the chair, as though she were a wooden plank that had been leaned against it.

All the while she kept up that bloodcurdling wail.

His shirt covered with the contents of his plate, Jeff dropped his fork and with some trepidation, approached Olivia from the other side to help Allie control her. His boots crunched on broken glass and china. He felt as if he were putting his hands into the spinning blades of a windmill during a hurricane. This seemed a hell of a lot more dangerous than breaking up a saloon brawl, even when the brawlers had been armed.

Allie's hair flew loose from its pins and ribbon, and long, dark-red strands hung next to her pale, set face while she struggled with her sister's considerable strength. Olivia anchored her hand on Allie's sleeve and hung on with the strength of the insane, twice nearly pulling her off her feet.

Jeff grabbed Olivia's arm and tried to untangle her hand. At his touch, Olivia's eyes flew open and she snarled, *"No! Don't you touch me!"* She pulled against his hold on her arm and tried to shake him off. When that didn't work, she began pounding her heels on the floor, and finally with a look of lucid, calculating rage in her eyes, she bent down and sank her teeth into his index finger.

"Ow, goddamn it!" he snapped. He jerked his hand away and clamped it between his arm and his ribs. Never in all his life had he wanted so badly to turn a grown person over his knee and paddle her backside.

"Make him go away!" Olivia screamed between the breathless sobs that had overtaken her. With the dripping tablecloth drawn up to her shoulders like a blanket and her flaxen hair tangled around her shoulders, she buried her face, now crimson with exertion, against Allie's breasts.

Althea's right shoulder was covered with blackberry

jam, but she rocked her and crooned to her as if the woman were a five-year-old child. "It's all right, Olivia, it's all right."

"No! Make him go away!" she demanded and slid her gaze to Jeff. She pointed at him as though he were the devil himself. "I don't want him in here!"

Allie looked over her sister's head at Jeff and sent him a helpless, apologetic expression, one that he had no trouble reading. "I'm sorry," she whispered, and nodded toward the back door. "Please."

Jeff glanced down at his new shirt, splattered with peas and gravy, and at Allie's distraught face. Then he fixed the sobbing, hysterical woman in Allie's arms with a steady, unflinching look. She merely went on howling, and hid her face against her sister's bodice.

Tossing his napkin on the table, Jeff walked through the kitchen and out the back door. As his footsteps fell heavily on the porch stairs and he crossed the yard to the lean-to, he could still hear Olivia Ford's shrill wailing.

The prospect of eating his future meals from a tray in the yard was no longer a lonely one. After tonight, it struck him as a wish come true.

It was well past ten o'clock when Althea stepped out to the back porch and lowered herself into the rocking chair. She felt stiff and old. Her joints creaked audibly, like groaning hinges in need of oiling.

The hush and peace of nightfall surrounded her, enfolded her. The air smelled fresh and from the darkness came soft, familiar sounds of crickets and frogs down at the creek. Leaning her head against the high-backed rocker, she looked at the stars overhead. How much easier their existence must be. They simply lay on their bed of black velvet sky and sparkled. They had no worries about planting or hired hands or lifelong responsibilities.

Olivia was upstairs, bathed, combed, and tucked into bed. The convulsion had sapped her of all her strength, and once it passed she became her same docile self, apparently with little memory of what had happened.

Althea remembered, though. After she'd seen to Olivia, she returned to the dining room and was stunned by the full extent of the damage done. It looked as if a terrible battle had been waged there. Broken dishes and glasses littered the floor. The remains of the roast had skidded under the table, leaving a wide, greasy trail on the hardwood. Gravy, water, and jam glued the surviving dishes to the tabletop, and mashed peas formed dime-size green dots on everything they'd touched. Her needlepoint seat cushions might never come completely clean.

It had taken her two hours of careful mopping, sweeping, and scrubbing on her hands and knees to clean it up. In the middle of it all, her burned palm had begun to sting unbearably, screaming with pain whenever she tried to use it. Working with just one hand had slowed things considerably. As it was, a blackberry jam stain on the wall would probably remain until it was painted over. Althea's pale pink dress bore a similar stain on the shoulder and sleeve, and now lay at the bottom of a heap of laundry that must be done tomorrow. The dress would probably be a loss, though.

She closed her eyes and set the chair in motion, rocking slowly. At least Olivia hadn't wet herself this time. That was generally the way her convulsions ended, with everything soaked in an astounding quantity of urine.

Olivia couldn't help it, Althea insisted to herself, massaging her forehead with her fingertips. It wasn't Olivia's fault, it wasn't, wasn't, wasn't.

If anything, tonight had been her own fault for having

a weak moment, for craving Jeff's company at dinner.

Poor Olivia. *Yes, poor, sick Olivia.* Motherless Olivia.

She had to remind herself of Olivia's frailty every time one of her convulsions occurred in order to stamp out the spark of resentment that flared in her heart. She had given most of her life to her sister's care, and chances were excellent that the rest of her years would be sacrificed to the same.

When Althea realized where her thoughts had turned, involuntarily she glanced in the direction of her parents' graves. The dark night hid their detail, but the moon was bright enough to reveal the outline of the low fence and the shape of the headstones. She pressed her fist to her mouth.

No, she hadn't meant it—she wasn't sacrificing her life. It was her duty to care for Olivia; what would happen to her if Althea failed in that duty?

Don't let me down again, girl.

No, she wouldn't—she'd promised on her father's deathbed, and even now she knew he must be watching her . . .

"How are you, Allie?"

Althea gasped and nearly jumped from her chair as the tall, rangy form of Jeff Hicks emerged from the darkness. Lantern light from the kitchen gleamed softly through the open door and highlighted the angles and planes of his handsome face.

"Good Lord, you took a year off my life sneaking up on me like that!" she whispered impatiently. She made a supreme effort to avoid thinking that it would be one year less that she'd be bound to her duty.

"Sorry." He'd changed his shirt, and now he wore one of the old ones she'd given him, unbuttoned, with its sleeves rolled up on his powerful forearms. Althea tried not to stare at the expanse of bare, muscled flesh revealed by

the open shirtfront, but it was nearly impossible. His maleness was not easy to overlook.

Without waiting to be invited, he pulled up the stool and
sat down next to her. He twirled a long stalk of grass between his fingers, wagging its seed top like a tiny mop.

"What are you doing up at this hour anyway? Dawn will
come early enough, and you'll need to be out in that field."
After everything that had happened, the brief kiss Jeff had
given her seemed like a long-ago dream that faded in the
reality of Althea's life. It was just as well.

In the shadows she saw his shoulders lift in a shrug. "I
couldn't sleep. It took a long time for my heart to slow
down." His voice was rich and close, familiar.

"Oh, well, yes—I imagine that's true." Althea fiddled
with a piece of old twine that was tied to the chair arm.
Olivia's spells were startling—someone who hadn't seen
one before would be understandably rattled. "I'm sorry
about— Well, I'm sorry I had to ask you to leave. The
sooner poor Olivia recovers from one of her convulsions,
the better. For some reason, having a stranger in the house
made her worse. Thank heavens she seems to not remember
them."

"Does she have these fits very often?"

"She used to when she was younger, and then when my
father died three years ago. But she's only had one other
since then."

"Yeah? And do you know what caused it?"

"It's not a matter of 'cause.' " No, it couldn't be. It had
been only a coincidence that the last one happened the day
Lane Smithfield had dinner with them. "They just come
over her."

He shook his head, Althea assumed in pity for Olivia.
"It was more than my being a stranger." He looked at her,
half of his face hidden in shadow, the other half revealed

in the kitchen lamplight. "I know what upset your sister. And I think you do, too."

She brought her chair to a stop and stared at his cleanly hewn profile. "Whatever do you mean?"

"It was when she heard me call you Allie. She didn't like it, and I've got the teeth marks on my finger to show it."

"She shouldn't have—I'm sorry that she bit you. Anyway, I don't know why you want to call me Allie. My name is Althea."

"But it doesn't suit you. Althea sounds the way the moon looks on a clear winter night. Beautiful, but as cold and hard as a diamond, and far away. That's not you. You're more like that—" He pointed to the low-slung, pale-butter orb in the eastern sky. "Warm and close enough to touch. That's your moon up there tonight, Allie, full of promise. And beautiful in the bargain."

Althea squeezed the chair arm under her uninjured palm. Despite her frayed nerves and bone-deep weariness, a quiver of joy ran through her that made her forget them both. The pleasure of hearing his words was almost excruciating, like rain falling upon a drought-stricken flower. No one had ever told her something like that before. Certainly no man had.

And for a single irrational, selfish, immodest moment, she wished she could put her head on his shoulder and rest, to feel his arms around her, and hear his heartbeat under her ear. In the tableau she envisioned, there were no worries, no responsibilities . . . no Olivia. Just her and Jeff and the night.

Then her gaze wandered to the two graves again. Her spine tensed against the spindle-backed rocker.

"That's not the kind of thing we should be talking about."

"I think it is."

"And I don't think this is a proper topic of discussion. Besides," she added, and turned her gaze to her lap, "you don't know anything about me."

He put the end of the grass stalk in the corner of his mouth. "Maybe I do, more than you think."

She froze. It sounded like a threat, a secret that he'd discovered about her. He couldn't know about *that*. Hardly anyone did, except for Dr. Brewster and Father and Olivia. Father was dead, Olivia never talked to anyone, and surely Dr. Brewster wouldn't have told Jeff. Doctors took a vow of silence, or something like—

"What do you know?" she asked, struggling to keep the tremor out of her voice.

He put his elbows on his knees and hunched forward, studying the dark, featureless planking between his boots. "I know that you weren't close to your father, that you might have even been afraid of him."

Althea's spine grew rigid as she sat upright in her chair. "What gave you such an idea?"

"You did, Allie. I've noticed how you tend those two graves over there. It isn't out of respect as much as fear. You let the rest of this place go, but the area inside that fence—it's as tidy as a park."

"That's ridiculous—"

Jeff didn't know how far he should push Allie. Her sister's display at dinner had been very revealing. "Is it?"

"Please, if you want to discuss tomorrow's work, fine. If not, I'll say good night." She gathered her skirts in preparation to rise from the rocker.

Jeff couldn't explain to himself why he pressed this. Time and again he told himself he shouldn't give a damn about this woman beyond their arrangement, but he couldn't get her off his mind. He'd ended up working here because Will Mason sentenced him to this job. Yet he sensed that Althea was just as much a prisoner as he was. More so, in fact.

"Stay in your chair, Allie. We'll talk about something else."

She looked at him and then settled back into the rocker with a sigh. He could see the weariness in her pretty face. "All right."

They sat in silence for a few moments, the quiet broken only by familiar night sounds and the soft creak of Allie's rocker. In another time and place, Jeff wouldn't be wondering what to say to this beautiful woman on a shadowed porch on a soft summer night. He'd take her hand in his own and press his lips into her palm. Then, to overcome her shyness—Allie Ford would be shy, he knew—he'd dust her temples and cheeks with soft kisses before he took her mouth with his own.

But he was here and this was now, with years of experience and disappointment behind him. And Jeff was a different man than he'd once been. So instead he said, "You must know this land pretty well, watching your father work it year after year. Ties like that run deep."

"I guess so. But sometimes I've thought I could leave this place without even a glance over my shoulder." Astounded, Althea blinked at Jeff with her mouth open slightly, as if someone instead of her had said those words. "I mean, it's been so hard the last few—of course, I would never leave."

"Never?"

"Well, no. I was born here and my parents are buried here and—"

"What if a man asked to marry you?" His voice was lulling, warm.

Althea felt a flush of confusion, then almost laughed. In

her mind, the very idea had become as far-fetched as a man walking on that yellow moon in the sky. "I can't leave Olivia. I'm all she has. Besides," she added in a moment of tart candidness, "not too many men would be interested in making a home for both of the crazy Ford sisters." She shifted in the rocker. Heavens, what personal thought would pop out of her mouth next? And what was it about this man that made her admit things she'd never said aloud to anyone else?

He wasn't the handsomest man Althea had ever seen—he still had the proportions of a scarecrow. Even so, she felt a low, humming vibration jitter through her whenever he was around. It was a sensation like none other she'd ever experienced. His powerful physical presence went beyond his long, rawboned body and clear green eyes. And the pull she felt, something she barely understood, was so strong it frightened her. The memory of measuring him for his shirts had never left her. If he called her it would be so easy to go to him—and yet so difficult.

"Olivia is a grown woman. Don't you think she'd learn to manage on her own?"

She turned and stared at him. "Why, she's hardly more than a girl. And you saw yourself that she *cannot* manage on her own." So undone by his suggestion and all it implied, she began to sputter. "It—it would be like abandoning a child."

Jeff had looked straight into Olivia Ford's eyes when she'd demanded that he leave. What he saw was a woman who knew exactly what she was doing, one who'd been spoiled and coddled all of her life. "Maybe it's time you let her grow up."

"You make it sound as though my sister chose the life she has, and that I'm forcing her to keep it."

"No, I don't mean that." Jeff sighed. Olivia wasn't the

one he was concerned about. There were old ghosts and secret hurts hiding in Allie's heart; he could sense it and everything pointed to it. A mother who'd committed suicide, a cold, humorless father, a sickly, clinging sister.

But what did he care, anyway? It was none of his business—how many times did he have to remind himself of that? And he was in no position to give advice, that was certain. He leaned against the porch upright and hooked one boot over his knee. "I wonder if anyone's life turns out they way they expect it to when they're young. I sure as hell never thought I'd be where I am now."

"Do you mean working off a sentence for breaking into a henhouse? Or are you referring to the damage you've done to yourself?"

She could be painfully direct—there was no beating around the bush with Althea Ford. But she spoke without malice or an underpinning of sarcasm. Obviously, she expected an answer to her straightforward question. Hunching forward, he rested his elbows on his thighs and stared at the dark shape of the barn.

"I guess I have that coming."

"You have the chance to walk away from the last two years and start over. When you leave here, will you go back to filching eggs or will you go home?"

He threaded his fingers through his hair. "I don't make plans anymore. I found out the hard way that planning can set a man up for a big fall."

"But it doesn't have to be that way. That's a notion you can change."

She made it sound so simple. But it wasn't simple at all. Without intending to, Jeff began talking about the shadows that lay on his soul. "I had big plans once. Decker Prairie is usually a quiet, peaceful little town, so I figured I'd be the sheriff for a few years. But what I really wanted to do after that was farm full-time. I was going to grow the best crops in the valley with my hundred acres. I'd stand at the end of the rows and burst with pride every time I looked at the tall, green corn, and the carrots and beans and squash. I'd have a wife who carried my child in her belly just as I carried them both in my heart. There were going to be kids underfoot and dogs in the yard. The seasons would come around like the hands on a clock, and I'd go to bed every night thanking God and fate for giving me a good life. A man couldn't ask for more than that."

"No, I suppose not. Except that isn't what you got."

"Nope. I came close, then I lost it all." Funny—he'd never talked to anyone about this. Not even to Len Deardorf, the barkeep at the Liberal Saloon, and that man had heard just about every customer's troubles. Jeff felt the need to tell it now, though, as if the story were a rotten tooth that had to be pulled.

"Sally and me—I guess we were married for about four years. We hoped for children, but I figured we had lots of time. Or at least I thought we did. After I shot Wes, everything started to change between us. I wanted to go to her, to talk about what I'd done. But when I tried, she didn't understand how I felt. She thought that shooting people was part of a lawman's job, and that I'd have to accept it. I couldn't talk to her—I couldn't talk to anyone. The people in town, well, they just stared and whispered every time I walked by. So I crawled inside of myself and stayed there."

Jeff knew he shouldn't tell the prim woman sitting next to him about his nights back then. That when sleep wouldn't come, he had turned to Sally, looking for the solace in her arms and in their bed that eluded him everywhere else. He shouldn't discuss something so personal with this virginal tabby, yet, despite her innocence he sensed that she would understand.

He'd sought his wife with a need that he couldn't define. It had been something beyond desire, that need. Maybe he'd hoped that by burying himself in her soft body, he'd be able to pour out his grief and bury it as well.

"But Sally turned me away. Night after night."

"Oh." The word came as softly as a dandelion puff pushed along by the breeze. He glanced at Althea. She sat with her hands clasped tightly on her lap and her eyes downcast. He couldn't see her scarlet cheeks, but he practically felt them through the darkness.

"I'm sorry. I shouldn't tell you—"

She looked up quickly. "No. No, please go on. I'm listening."

I'm listening. Those two words were a balm to his spirit.

He nodded and took a deep breath. "I started drinking. Just a little. I wanted to try and kill the guilt and loneliness I carried around with me. Sometimes I'd go to the saloon, order a bottle of whiskey, and sit at a back table."

"Why didn't you just go home?"

Home. When was the last time he'd imagined himself at home? "By then, I felt more empty with my wife than I did when I was alone. I don't think there's a lonelier feeling than being with someone who has stopped caring. So I started spending some nights in one of the cells in the office. I still loved Sally, but I just didn't know how to show it anymore. And I didn't know how to fix that."

"I think I know what you mean. About being lonely with someone else, that is."

"You do?"

Althea nodded, her earlier irritation with him gone. She had never been married, or ever really been courted by a man. But she knew that hollow feeling, the emptiness that could not be filled with work, or responsibility, or dedication to duty. It made itself felt in a hundred little ways, but in the dark valley of night its pang was most acute.

Jeff sat with his chin in his hand, absently running his thumb over his jaw as he considered her in the low light. She heard the rasp of his beard, saw the dark green fire in his eyes. "Yeah, I think you probably do." He straightened on the stool and took up his story again. "Finally, one night I decided that if things would ever be right again between Sally and me, I'd have to go to her, on my knees if I had to, and talk to her. I mean really talk." He chuckled and shook his head. "When I got there, the place was dark and all of her clothes were gone. She'd left me a note on the kitchen table. 'I can't take the loneliness anymore.' That's all it said. Not a word of regret for what she was doing, not a word of hope or love, even if it was dead. That was it. She was gone." He sat staring at the darkness for so long, Althea began to grow uncomfortable with the silence. It was full of the memories of heartache.

"Do you know where she went?" she whispered at last.

"I'm surprised *you* don't. Everyone in Decker Prairie was blabbing about it. Someone saw her leave with a feed salesman who passed through town. I kept hoping she might come back, but a few months later I received a divorce decree from a law office in San Francisco."

"Divorce!" Not one of Althea's limited acquaintances was divorced. She didn't even know anyone who knew someone else who had been divorced. Humiliation and betrayal must have torn deep slashes through his heart.

"It doesn't take much account of the 'for better or for worse' part, does it? When I saw that decree, I yanked the sheriff's badge off my shirt and threw it on the desk. Then I went out to the homestead with a bottle of whiskey, and after I was good and drunk, I burned the house to the ground."

"Oh, my God—"

He tossed the grass stalk aside. "Hell, I don't blame her anymore. It was as if all my anger and every other feeling I had went up in flames with that house."

"Except your guilt over Wes Cooper." Althea mourned the loss of the man Jefferson Hicks had once been, and seemed determined to never be again.

He stood and stretched his long back as he regarded the starlit sky. His drawn expression revealed a wealth of pain—a kind of pain that Althea knew all too well. Guilt. It was like a cancer that ate away at the heart instead of the flesh, but it was no less hurtful, for all that. She yearned to reach out and touch his arm, to offer him whatever comfort she could. But after the kiss they had shared, she couldn't trust herself to pull away again.

After a long moment, he glanced down at her again and flashed her a mocking grin that she knew was directed more at himself than at her. "Yeah, well, I guess a man has to do something with the time he has left on this earth, worthwhile or not. Guilt doesn't accomplish a whole lot, but at least it gives me—" He broke off, as if his train of thought had momentarily deserted him. "A reason, I guess," he finished in a hollow voice that conveyed just how empty he felt. "We all need a reason for being, and that's all I really have left, Allie. Deep regret."

That was the saddest thing she'd ever heard anyone say. If he'd been any other man, she might have suspected him of trying to play on her sympathy. But the ache in Jeff's eyes told her he truly meant it. His life had been stripped. He was just marking time with no hopes or dreams to sustain him.

Althea understood exactly how that felt and wished with all her heart that she didn't. To look at the endless road that lay ahead of you . . . knowing that you would never escape the deep rut in which you walked . . . and even worse, that there was no end in sight. Just day after day after day of putting one foot in front of the other, moving relentlessly ahead to go nowhere, your only companion a deep, soul-searing regret over events you could never change. Oh, yes . . . she understood very well.

"Good night, Allie," he said softly. Then he bounded down the stairs and into the darkness toward the lean-to.

For a long while, Althea stared into the blackness that swallowed him and wished she had the courage to call him back. Only for what purpose? To tell him that she understood? To offer him the solace his wife had refused him? Her own pain ran too deep for her to hope to heal his.

Althea sighed and rose stiffly from the rocker, her gaze locked forlornly on the buttery sphere that hovered on the western horizon. *That's your moon, Allie.* If it was hers, why did it remain so far beyond her reach? That was a question for which there was no answer, so why torment herself by asking it? Some things simply weren't meant to be.

Turning her back on the moonlight, she went into the kitchen and blew out the lamp.

Chapter Eleven

OLIVIA REMAINED IN BED ALL NIGHT AND PART OF THE following day. Althea slept occasionally, sitting up in a chair next to her. The rest of the time, she read to her sister, spooned soup into her mouth, and brushed her hair. She left Olivia's side only to cook, and Jeff found his trays on the back porch once again. She gave him plain fare—luke-warm oatmeal for breakfast and sandwiches for lunch and dinner, made from the roast beef he hadn't gotten to taste the night before.

Though he looked toward the house for Allie so many times he'd lost count, he never saw her, and the day seemed lonely somehow. He spent it sweating in the sun and curs-ing a seed drill he was trying to resurrect from near-death. It had been left out in the weather for several years.

A month ago he couldn't have cared less about Althea Ford. In fact, he would have been hard-pressed to recognize her name or remember anything about her. He'd been lost in a haze of whiskey and reliving the past, and that was where he'd wanted to stay. Now, though, he more often found himself thinking about the here and now, and looking forward to tomorrow. And he realized that whenever he did so, Allie was part of both.

Allie, with her sister bound to her as surely as a ball and chain bound a prisoner.

Finally Jeff wrenched open the screeching barn door to look for an oil can. The damned seeder was rusted solid. He'd had to hack a path through the brambles and tall weeds just to reach it. If he couldn't make the thing work, he had a big job ahead of him, seeding the field by hand.

He rummaged through the items on the shelves, squinting in the cool semi-gloom to make out the contents of various dusty cans and bottles. His finger, the one Olivia had bitten, ached a little. She hadn't broken the skin but she'd left her teeth marks on him. He still couldn't get the scene at dinner out of his mind—those blood-freezing shrieks, the plates and bowls flying off the table, Allie, gravy dripping from her hair and blackberry jam smeared on her dress, trying to comfort her sister. But by far, his most disturbing recollection of last night was Olivia's lucid, calculating hazel eyes glaring up at him when he'd tried to restrain her.

He'd seen manipulation in his time, but Olivia Ford took the prize. The reasons for her behavior and how she'd gotten to be that way were mysteries to him. Her intentions were pretty clear, though.

Allie didn't seem to have a clue that her sister was anything but a helpless, childlike invalid. In *her* face he'd seen only worry, sympathy, and tenderness as she'd clutched Olivia to her shoulder. The "helpless invalid" was controlling her strong, good-hearted nursemaid with a tyranny that Jeff knew would eventually break Allie's spirit like a dry twig.

He put down a dusty bottle of old liniment with a thud.

Damn it, he knew life wasn't fair, but sometimes it seemed that fate deliberately stepped in to crush people. To turn their lives upside down, to keep happiness just beyond their grasp, to prevent them from having any life at all.

Forget it, Hicks, just forget it, he grumbled to himself, resuming his search for oil. He'd do well to stay out of the Ford family's problems. He had plenty of his own troubles to ponder if he wanted to give himself sleepless nights. He didn't want to think about a smart, pretty woman shriveling up out here on this tumbledown farm, her life spent in servitude to a sister who knew exactly how to get her own way. Even if a body could get past thinking of Althea as one of the peculiar Ford sisters, it was a certainty that not one man in the whole valley would be willing to take Olivia Ford as the booby prize for marrying Allie. He sure as hell wouldn't.

It didn't matter that sometimes when he looked into Allie's bottomless blue-gray eyes, he swore he saw the chance to heal his soul in their depths. And if he had just half the tenderness she gave to Olivia, he might even be able to stop thinking about Wes Matthews every single day. It wouldn't take much encouragement from Allie to make him give up drinking for good and settle down again. If he had someone like her to come home to— He sighed and stared unseeing at the cobweb-draped shelf in front of him. If . . . if . . . Not much could be accomplished with "if."

A glaring truth shot through his mind then and stopped him cold in his tracks. He didn't want to be saddled with Olivia—what made him think that Allie would want anything to do with *him*, a broken-down drunk without a penny to his name, save whatever she was going to pay him? Even his own wife had given up on him.

Until that night at Wickwire's, he'd never thought of himself as a bad person. His mother had instilled right and wrong in all her sons; she'd stressed the value of goodness. But after he'd killed Wes, all that might have been good in him drained away, as sure as that boy's lifeblood had drained from his gunshot heart.

Jefferson Hicks didn't *deserve* a woman like Allie Ford, and realizing that made the hope for tomorrow wither in the pit of his stomach. At one time, he would have been worthy of her but not now, and probably not ever.

He touched his shirt pocket where a keepsake lay furled. Giving in to the urge, he withdrew it. Sometime during the fracas of Olivia's tantrum, amid the flying peas and gobbets of jam, Allie's ribbon had come loose from her hair. He hadn't even realized he'd taken it until he was back in the lean-to and found it wound in his fingers. It was such a simple thing, a bit of delicate femininity in a world that had been hard and unforgiving of him. He lifted it to his nose to inhale the faint scent of her hair. Soon the pink satin would take on the smell of his sweat and his own body, but he would savor her fragrance while he could.

After harvest time, he'd go back to his old way of life, his whiskey and its blessed forgetfulness. If Will Mason harassed him, he'd move on to another town. But somehow, the idea of sleeping in doorways and haystacks wasn't as tolerable as it had been just a month ago. He'd gotten used to his little arrangement in the lean-to next to the barn. Well, he would just have to give it up when the time came. He stuffed the ribbon back into his pocket. There were some things a man couldn't change no matter how much he wished for them.

When Jeff at last put his hand on an old oil can, he carried it to the barn door and oiled the thing so it didn't screech anymore. Allie hadn't wanted him to bother fixing it, but that high-pitched scraping of metal against metal set his teeth on edge. He slid it back and forth on its wheels until the lubricant coated the mechanism and it ran smoothly.

Satisfied, he held a faint hope that the farm tool outside would be as easy to fix, but it was in far worse shape. He'd turned to go back to it when he became aware of an insistent cheeping. Looking up, he saw the mud-and-feather nest of the barn swallows anchored to a corner formed by a beam and the wall. A doting parent, dressed in steel blue and chestnut plumage, flew through the open barn door and clung to the side of the nest. Eager babies bobbed up in unison with beaks open wide to receive their breakfast. Jeff chuckled.

He wondered again if Allie knew these birds were out here. Remembering how she loved to feed the birds in the orchard, he thought she'd probably get a kick out of seeing them. And like it or not, he knew he'd get a kick out of showing them to her. It might be a nice change for her, a chance to get away from her sister.

"Will you just forget about it?" he muttered to himself again, making a disgusted noise. Allie was no princess who needed rescuing.

And he sure as hell didn't own a white horse.

Despite acting as his own Dutch uncle, Jeff looked up eagerly the next time he heard the screen door open. But instead of Allie, as he expected, it was Olivia Ford who stood on the back porch. She moved to the rocker and sat down, watching him as though he were a most fascinating subject.

He was still wary. He saw nothing of the wild harpy who had pitched a tantrum at the dinner table and sunk her teeth into his finger. In fact, with her pale hair secured by a cherry-colored ribbon, she looked rested and very tidy, like someone expecting visitors or going to a tea party. But there was a smug, knowing glint in her expression.

The swallows flitted back and forth, while a silent, awkward moment stretched between them as they studied each other. Eli Wickwire had said that Olivia's only problem was her fits, but Jeff wasn't so sure. Hell, the whole town referred to Allie and her sister as crazy. Allie seemed perfectly normal, but what if Olivia really was deranged? She couldn't very well be blamed for her behavior. When he'd looked into her eyes last night at dinner she'd seemed sane enough to him, just spoiled and willful. But he didn't have much experience with lunatics. Drunks and belligerent cowboys, yes—mean bastards and cranky bitches, some.

So which was it? Was she touched in the head, or merely a conniving, coddled, overgrown brat, determined to keep Allie under her thumb?

"Afternoon, Miss Olivia," he ventured, since she seemed not inclined to speak first. "How are you today?"

"Me? Why, I'm fine, Mr. Hicks. In fact, it's such a pretty day, I thought I'd come outside for awhile and take some air while Althea is napping. She seems to be rather tired today." A shadow of concern crossed her delicate features.

Jeff dropped his gaze to the gear he was oiling. "Is she? Do you think it's because of last night?" It wasn't a very subtle question, but he was doing his best.

Olivia leaned back in the rocker and gave it a slight push to put it into motion. "Last night? Oh, you mean all the preparations for dinner? I'm sure it's possible. She takes such good care of me, just like a mother cat with one kitten. She really doesn't have much energy left for company. One person can only do so much, you know."

Kitten. Jeff glanced at the teeth marks on his hand. More like a cougar with a burr up its ass. But he stifled a smart remark. Allie had said her sister had no memory of her fits. Well, damn, maybe it was true. How else could she carry on this conversation with him as though nothing had happened? Maybe he'd been too harsh in his judgment of Olivia—he knew how it felt to be on the receiving end of that kind of thinking. God knew the display he'd seen at dinner yesterday wasn't the everyday act of a rational person. His curiosity demanded an answer to this riddle and the only way he could think of learning that answer was to spend a little time with Olivia Ford. But how? She wasn't the type a person could engage in conversation. She seemed so immature. Then an idea struck him.

"You know, I found a family of barn swallows in there." He gestured at the rickety structure behind him. "They're just babies—would you like to see them?"

She clapped her hands together girlishly and left the rocker in an eddy of long curls and flowing skirts. "Oh, yes, how wonderful!"

Jeff put down the screwdriver he was holding and wiped his hands on the rag he'd stuffed in his back pocket. "Come on this way, ma'am, and watch your step. It takes a minute for your eyes to adjust to the dim light in here."

Olivia giggled as they stepped into the barn. "*Ma'am*. No one has ever called me *that*. It makes me sound all grown up."

Jeff made no comment, but wondered if this little-girl act was just that, an act. Or was there really the mind of a child in this adult's form? He led the way over the hard-packed mud floor to the corner where the swallows were nesting. "There, see?" He pointed up at the nest. "One of the parents is feeding them."

Olivia looked up, following the direction of Jeff's arm. "Ohh, aren't they precious?" She stood with her hands clasped to her chest, and delight made her face glow. This innocence and sweetness were not what he'd seen when she'd eyed him from the porch.

"They're sure growing fast. The first time I saw them, they didn't have any feathers at all. Now they've got that baby fuzz. I suppose they'll be learning to fly pretty soon. I was hoping your sister could see them before they're gone."

She turned to him with gratitude in her voice. "Oh, Mr. Hicks, I know Althea would like to see this! She just loves birds—she can even make them come to her and eat from her hand." A scowl flashed across her features as she muttered, "I could never get them to do that for me."

"Well, maybe when Allie—I mean, when Miss Althea wakes up from her nap you can send her out here to have a look."

Olivia tapped her chin with her fingertip. "Hmm, I don't think today would be good. She's so tired. I know! Let's make it a surprise. Althea is always doing little things for me, and I never really get to pay her back. Tomorrow would be better. Say, in the morning, when she brings you your breakfast. Tell her to close her eyes so that she won't have a clue about what you're doing, then lead her in here to have a look. I probably won't be up in time—you two are such early risers and I guess I've always been a slug-abed. But I know she'll be thrilled. I wish I could see her face!"

The sincerity of Olivia's wish to please her sister surprised Jeff. Maybe she recognized that Allie got so few small pleasures in her life. Doubt niggled at the back of his mind, but he dismissed it. Those years as a sheriff still made him second-guess people.

"Sounds like a good idea to me." ·

"Yes, doesn't it?"

Olivia left him then and went back into the house. The next time Jeff saw her was later that afternoon when Seth Wickwire came out with a grocery delivery from his father's general store. She came down the back porch steps, smiled at Seth, and handed him what looked to be a letter to mail.

Just before she turned to climb the steps again, she waved at Jeff and gave him a smile, too.

"Got any more swell ideas to get even with Hicks?" Floyd Endicott took a long pull from a whiskey bottle and wiped his mouth on his shirtsleeve.

"I got him lookin' over his shoulder, don't you worry," Cooper Matthews replied and took the bottle. The two men occupied their usual post, the back doorway of Kincade's Livery. Floyd sat on the milking stool and Cooper leaned against the doorframe with his arms folded over his chest. This late at night, even the clanging piano at the Liberal Saloon was silent. "He'll think twice before he even goes to the outhouse. Didn't you see how scared he looked the other day?"

Floyd shifted uncomfortably on the milking stool. "I dunno, Cooper, he just looked riled up to me. An' you heard him yourself—he don't care what happens to him. Anyways, what if he don't come back to town? It's nigh on to impossible to get even with a man when you don't meet up with him."

Cooper gave him a poisonous look. "It's a good thing I've got the brains in this outfit, Floyd, or we'd be like bogged heifers. You don't need to come face-to-face with him to get revenge. Anyway, maybe he doesn't care what happens to him, but I think he cares about that Ford woman. That son of a bitch," he continued bitterly, talking to the empty street outside, "*still* actin'. like he's better'n everyone else, after all that's happened. He killed my boy but tried to make *me* look bad, like I pulled the trigger. Folks around here blame me almost as much as they blame Hicks." He turned to Floyd, worked up into an angry rant. "I expected that boy to be a comfort to me in my old age. Who's goin' to do that now?"

Floyd shrugged. "Hell, Cooper, you could just get married again."

"You got anything else on your mind besides females?"

"Well, they're soft and some of 'em smell nice and are pretty to look at. A woman is even better than a dog for keepin' a man warm on a cold night."

"Yeah, and they're more trouble than any dog ever thought of being. At least if a dog pisses you off, you can throw it outside or shoot the damned thing. Do that with a female and folks who got nothin' better to do take it into their heads to complain. That's how I landed in jail one time." Cooper waved a hand in disgust. "Damn it, Hicks even turned that crazy Ford woman against me. Well, by God, he's got to pay for insultin' me. Her, too. But I'm going to fix 'em both, startin' tonight."

Floyd shrugged and passed the whiskey bottle to him. "Maybe we just ought to leave well enough alone. He don't bother us, and we don't bother him. Anyway, there's something not right about someone who talks like a dead man."

"He called you a dimwit," Cooper reminded him.

A faint light of realization crossed Floyd's slack features. "Hey, that's *right*."

"He thinks you're stupid, Floyd. As stupid as an old cow."

"That bastard!"

"How do you like that, Jeff Hicks thinkin' you're so damned dumb while he's better than anyone else?"

Floyd was clearly insulted. "Well, by God, I don't like it a-tall."

Satisfied, Cooper smiled. He drank from the whiskey bottle and turned to head back to his shack. "Then grab that lantern and come on. We ain't the only ones who want to get the upper hand with Hicks, and I know about a woman who's even willin' to pay us to do it. A right smart sum she's offering, too. We got us some work to do."

The next morning Althea rose early. Though she'd heard Olivia stirring several times before dawn and had made a couple of trips to her sister's door to check on her, at least she'd been able to sleep in her own bed. Or rather, lie in her own bed. At any rate, it was more restful than sitting up in a chair as she'd done the previous night. But with Olivia rattling around in her room, sleep had come to Althea in fits and starts. Most of the night she lay staring at the ceiling and thinking of Jeff. What he'd told her about himself, and how he looked, and the way that *Allie* sounded on his tongue.

Now she padded to the window, gritty-eyed and tired, and looked out at the clean new day. Ribbons of mist lingered in the cottonwoods down by the creek bottom, and above them dawned a sky that was pink and blue and yellow-white with a rising sun. A pair of mallards skimmed the treetops toward the water, quacking as they flew. Dew sparkled like crystals on the overgrown lawn, making it seem more magical than unkempt. It was a beautiful pastoral scene.

A movement caught her eye. She dropped her gaze to the yard where she saw Jeff tinkering with the old seed drill. He looked so much better than he had the first day she met him. Now his back was straight and he stood a little taller. Working in the sun had erased his unhealthy pallor, and his hands were strong and steady. She had kissed that man—God, had it been just two days ago? After what had happened at dinner that night, it seemed like ten years ago.

She gripped the windowsill. What if that were her husband down there, starting his day, heading off to the fields? They would build a life together, just the two of them. She would be like the other farmwives around the valley— she'd cook big, hearty meals to feed her hungry man and their sturdy, healthy children. There would be chickens and cows to tend. In the summer the whole family would pile into the wagon to go to the grange dance on Saturday nights, and she would save all the waltzes for Jeff. No one would stare at her and whisper behind their hands about the peculiar Ford sisters, because she would not be Althea Ford. She'd be Mrs. Allie Hicks.

At harvesttime she would put up preserves and fruit and vegetables to fill the pantry, saving the prettiest and best samples to enter in the state fair. On cold winter nights they would burrow beneath down-filled quilts and she would confess her love to him again and again. Jeff would whisper her name and tell her that he loved her, too, while he pulled her into his arms and kissed her . . .

Girl, stop that lollygagging and do your chores. They won't get done by themselves.

Althea released her hold on the sill and left the window. Turning to her washstand, she poured some water into the bowl and caught her own reflection in the mirror hanging over it. Crimson-cheeked Althea Ford stared back at her, not Allie Hicks. But it was Amos Ford's voice she heard in her memory, stern and cold.

When Allie went downstairs she was surprised to find that all of yesterday's dishes had been washed and put away. The teacups were placed right-side up in the china hutch, as Olivia stored them, rather than upside down, as Allie preferred. But she was touched by her sister's effort, just the same. Olivia seemed to know instinctively when Allie had been pushed to the end of her rope, and would do something nice for her, like wash the dishes or offer to brush her hair. The little gestures always made Allie feel small and selfish for those moments when she would wish she were someplace far away.

Or with someone else far away. She glanced out the window at Jeff.

Better that she keep her mind focused on the resolution she had come to during the hours she'd spent at Olivia's bedside. That dreams and wishes were luxuries she couldn't afford. They only tore at her heart and had no possibility of coming true. She had her duty and responsibility, and Jeff Hicks had his job to do around the farm. Nothing more. And come harvesttime, he'd be gone. Yes, best that she remember that, best all the way around, no matter how it made her heart ache.

Not only for her sake, but for Olivia's, too.

Jeff had started in on the seeder again at first light. He had to fix it today or give up—time was slipping away and that field had to be planted. He was engrossed with the farm implement and calling it every filthy name he knew when he heard the screen door open on the back porch. Althea stood there with his tray. He straightened to look at her and realized with a sense of hopelessness that just seeing her lightened his heart. He'd missed her yesterday. She had a way of making him feel better about himself. A smart, sensible woman, she had demanded a lot from him since he got here—his best work. More often than not, he'd been able to deliver his best. And she had never once judged him. When the time came to leave . . .

She was as tidy as always, with every hair in place, and her lavender dress was crisp with starch. But even from here he could see that her shoulders drooped a bit and her pretty face was drawn.

"I brought you a big breakfast since I wasn't able to fix you much yesterday," she said, lifting the tray as if to show him. She put it down on a little table on the porch beside the rocker. "I'm sorry about—" She broke off awkwardly, then turned to go back inside. He wanted to tell her to stop apologizing. She was always apologizing, and for things that weren't her fault. "Well, I'd better get back to my chores."

No, don't leave. Please, not yet— He dropped the oilcan and took a couple of running steps toward her. "Allie, wait."

She paused with her hand on the door pull.

He pushed aside the warnings he'd given himself yesterday. He just wanted to spend a minute or two with her, and the plan that Olivia had devised would do the trick. "I want to show you something. A surprise."

A shadow of distrust crossed her face. "A surprise?"

Jeff wiped his hands on the seat of his pants and closed the distance between them. Hopping up the steps, he touched her arm. "Yeah, something I found the other day. I guarantee you'll like it. Come on." Lightly, he tugged her sleeve.

"But you should eat this food while it's hot."

He glanced down at what looked like a pound of bacon and four fried eggs, and felt his stomach rumble appreciatively. He could put it off a little while, though, for the chance to smell her hair again, to stand close to her. "It looks like a real good breakfast. I promise it'll only take a minute. Then I'll come right back and eat."

She looked at the kitchen behind her, as if searching for watchful eyes. "Well, I guess . . ." she replied, and released the door, letting him pull her across the porch to the steps.

He grinned at her. He felt a little silly about what he meant to say next. It seemed childish to make such a fuss about something as ordinary as a bird's nest. Only to Allie, it wouldn't seem ordinary, and for reasons he didn't want to examine too closely, he wanted to make the moment as special as possible for her. He suspected there had very little foolishness, or joy, in Althea Ford's life. "Great! Come on—" Then he remembered Olivia's advice. "But close your eyes."

"What?"

"Yeah, close 'em."

She folded her arms and pulled back. "Jefferson Hicks, this had better not be some kind of joke—"

"No, I swear it's not. When I saw this thing, the first person I thought of was you."

She smiled then, and almost looked pleased. "All right." She closed her eyes.

Putting his hands on her waist, he walked behind her to guide her slowly across the yard and over the path of grass that had been flattened by use. He was ashamed to find himself bending his head just slightly to catch the scent of her hair. She smelled faintly of lavender, and a sudden, sharp hunger made him wonder how that silken spot behind her ear might taste if he were to press his lips to her flesh there. He was also acutely aware of the slender waist he held and the way her hips moved under the heels of his hands. He resisted an almost overpowering urge to stop her in her tracks, forget the bird's nest, and gather her into his arms. He took a breath and forced a casual note into his voice. "No peeking, now."

"I won't," she agreed, allowing him to push her along. "Is it far?"

"Nope, in fact we're here. But don't look until I say so."

Jeff reached over Allie's shoulder and pushed open the newly greased barn door, which slid almost silently on its wheels. Then, still behind her, he directed her inside and positioned her at the best place to view the birds' nest. His eyes were still adjusting to the interior gloom and he hoped he'd stood her at the right place.

"Jesus Christ!"

Allie's eyes snapped open when she heard Jeff's exclamation and the timbre of his voice. She saw a beam and a high, dark, cavernous space above it. The smell here was so familiar—old straw and mustiness. She whipped her head around and saw the walls, the rafters, the stalls, darkness . . . darkness.

The barn! *She was in the barn.* The place that she didn't even like to look at from her kitchen window.

Suddenly she felt seven years old again. This was the spot—the very same spot where she'd stood all those years ago. And, oh, God, her mother. She was up there, just as before, swinging ever so slowly back and forth, like the sluggish pendulum on a case clock that needed rewinding. Shock gripped her throat with a tight iron fist. Her lungs struggled for air but only a puff slipped through. Chills raced over her scalp and body, making the base of every hair stand erect.

The horror that had intruded upon her sleep so often over the years had come to vivid life, only this time she was awake and it was broad daylight. Not a nightmare. It was real again—just like before—her mother, hanging by her neck from a length of rope thrown over a beam, turning slowly at the end of the tether, her head resting on her shoulder, her face the color of an eggplant.

It couldn't be! How could it happen again?

It was Althea's fault. *Your fault, girl! You hear me? All your fault!*

Allie's hands flew to her mouth and her heart began pounding in her chest like a sledgehammer on granite. Her breath shortened to suffocated gasps.

She wanted to run but her feet were fixed in place.

She wanted to scream but no sound issued from her open mouth.

"*Jesus Christ!*" Jeff snapped out again as he looked up at the dangling figure. "What in hell—?"

Allie gaped at him, consumed by the panic sluicing through her veins like icy water. "Oh, God! Dear God!" she finally managed to squeak out, her wind coming in panting whistles. Then she filled both lungs. "*Mama!*" she screamed.

Jeff clutched her arm again. "Allie, no—"

"Mama!"

"Allie, honey, it's not your mother! Look, see?" He grabbed the apron on the form and turned it toward her. The face, she realized, wasn't purple, but blue-and-white striped, like a pillow tick.

"No!" She backed away.

"Allie, it's just a dummy, not a real person! Not your mother!"

A dummy—*a dummy!* His voice seemed to come to her from far off, the words making no sense. No, no, no! The barn began to spin around her. The walls leaned inward. The very air seemed to pulsate—or was that her heart pounding? A joke. A heartless joke. He thought this was funny? *There goes Althea, one of those crazy Ford sisters. You know what they say about them.* People talking and snickering behind cupped hands as she walked along the street in town. Their laughter had always filled her with rage that she dared not express. But it erupted within her now.

"How *could* you?" She tore her arm from his grip. "How could you be so cruel?" She found enough locomotion in her rubbery legs to run for the door, but Jeff was right behind her and closed his hand on the back of her skirt.

"Allie! I don't know anything about this!"

"Althea! Althea, what's wrong?" Suddenly, Olivia was in the barn, too, dressed in only her nightgown and frilly wrapper, her feet bare. She looked up at the effigy. "Dear God above! You horrible man! You did this!" she accused Jeff.

"The hell I did!"

"Let me go!" Allie wailed, trying to free her skirt from his bunched fist. Her hair tumbled around her shoulders and in her face, further obscuring her vision.

He uttered some obscenity, and then stretched out one hand to yank viciously on the dummy. Its pillow-tick head came off, releasing a blizzard of feathers, and Allie screamed again. The rest of the body fell to the barn floor in a heap of more feathers and the old dress it wore, leaving the noose swinging from the rafter.

Allie brushed at the down that stuck to her clothing, beating at it as if it were fire. *Out. Please, God.* She had to get *out.* Only a few feet away, sunlight beckoned. Just a few more steps. She'd be safe out there. Separated from the barn and this monstrosity, separated from the screaming and the chaos and the horror.

Your fault, girl! You killed your mama, God damn you to hell. You killed your mama. I don't ask much of you, and just look what you've done! Off lollygagging when I told you to watch after her. You look at her now, damn you! See the fruit of your laziness and remember it well. I pray it haunts you all the days of your life. All your doing! You murdered my wife, robbed your sister of a mother—

Jeff's hands had latched onto her skirt like demon claws, pulling her back into a nightmare she'd spent her whole life trying to escape.

"Allie, it's all right." His voice seemed to come to her

from far so away. *"Allie? Allie, honey, look—it's down now. It's not real."*

"Let go of my sister! What have you done to her?" Olivia's shrill voice was distant as well. *"Althea, I told you he'd give us nothing but trouble! How could you bring my sister out here to the barn when she's terrified—"*

Unable to see clearly in her panic, Althea flailed frantically with her fists, trying to knock Jeff away, trying to free herself. Her right hand connected with his face somewhere, but still he wouldn't release her.

"Damn it! Stop it, Althea, right now! Do you hear me?"

The next instant, she felt like a child's top spinning on a freshly waxed floor. She fell against something rock-solid. His chest. Relentless, hard arms clamped around her. A broad hand cradled the back of her head, strong, calloused fingers locking over her hair to hold her. *Jeff.* She struggled to get out of his embrace, but even though terror doubled her strength, it was no match for his. "Let me go! I have to get out of here!"

"Everything is all right, Allie. It's all right."

Her head began to swim then, and black spots appeared in her field of vision. She was going to die—her pounding heart had burst and she was dying.

Blackness washed over her and engulfed her like a wave, pulling her down with it.

Jeff could remember only one other time when he'd been as scared as he was now. That night in Wickwire's, facing an angry, hurting boy with a loaded gun in his hand.

Trembling himself, he'd carried Allie's limp body outside and now she lay half in his arms and half in the dew-damp grass where he'd put her down. Olivia had followed, and she stood over them, raining accusations upon him like a she-devil spitting fire, her nightclothes flapping around her in a stiff morning breeze. All traces of her childlike facade were missing. But if she pitched a fit now, as far as Jeff was concerned she could twitch herself to death before he'd leave Allie's side.

Allie's face was drained of all color and her eyes remained closed. She lay so still, so silent, at first he thought she was dead. She sure looked it. Then he saw a vein throbbing along the column of her pale throat, and his heart slowed from a runaway gallop to a fast canter.

Jeff had practically no experience with fainting women. Oh, he knew that some females pretended to get giddy and would fall into the most convenient chair while fanning themselves with a hanky. Olivia Ford was probably that type. But that wasn't what had happened with Allie. She'd fainted away and would have fallen hard if he hadn't been holding her.

Not that it had been easy to maintain his grip. She'd thrashed around like a wet bobcat in a pillowcase. His left eye throbbed and he realized that it was beginning to swell, the result of being hit with one of Allie's flying fists. He'd probably have a first-rate shiner before long.

He couldn't blame her, though. The sight of that dummy hanging from the rafter had unnerved him, too, and he wasn't dragging around the kind of memories that Allie probably had stored in her mind.

Who the hell had hung that gruesome effigy in the barn? And when could they have done it? He was always nearby, patching the house or working in the field. At the moment, the wild-haired sister standing over him was his chief suspect.

But Allie believed *he* was guilty, and it would be hard for him to prove otherwise with Olivia screeching her lies. If only he'd bothered to look in there this morning before subjecting Allie to a living nightmare.

He looked down at her as she lay in his arms, watching her the way a man might study an angel who'd suddenly tumbled into his embrace, her wing broken. He was worried, yet captivated. She was a beautiful, delicate woman, but strong, he thought, like finely tempered steel. Her dark lashes threw shadows on her cheeks which were just now regaining the merest tint of pink. The angle of her body in his arms gave him a direct view down the front of her dress where the fabric gaped away from her bosom. He didn't mean to look—it was a lowdown thing to do, especially given her helplessness. He dragged his gaze away, only to find it straying back to the soft, white flesh no more than a foot from the end of his nose. Well, damn it, he was only a man, and not a good one at that, by anyone's reckoning. And women had been a rarity in his life since Sally left.

Finally, after what seemed like a lifetime, Allie's eyes fluttered open. He saw her confusion in them, along with a terror that was a tangible thing.

"What—what—" When her gaze focused on him, she sent him a hurt, accusing look. Then more vigorously, "Where are we?"

She struggled to sit up, but Jeff held her fast, savoring the feel of her in his arms. The wet grass was soaking through his jeans but he didn't care. "Hold on, now. We're outside. But give yourself a minute—you won't have your pins back under you yet."

"Let me go. I don't need your help." She tried again to sit up but he wouldn't release her. Olivia grabbed Allie's arm and tried to pull her to her feet, but Jeff held on just as hard.

"Take your hands off her, you wicked, wicked man," Olivia demanded. Allie tried to get up again but she fell back, too weak to fight Jeff.

He felt as if he were wading through a mist, trying to

make himself heard. "Allie, you've got to believe me—I swear to God I didn't hang that thing in the barn."

She turned her face away and her voice, sounding tired and old, sent chills down his arms and back. "No? Then why did you take me in there? Who else but you has been around here? Olivia?" Again Jeff clutched at the possibility of her sister's involvement, but Allie's next words stopped him in his tracks. "What have I done to you to deserve such a heartless trick? Did you get a good laugh from it?"

Stung, he pulled back. "God, Allie, no! I didn't know that thing was in there—it wasn't yesterday. I just wanted to show you the nest of barn swallows." He looked at Olivia and stared. "Your sister said you'd love to see it."

Olivia clutched her wrapper to herself and pointed an accusing finger at Jeff. "He's lying, Althea! Why would I tell him to take you into the barn when I know better? I said no such thing. I barely spoke with him at all."

If Jeff needed an answer to his puzzle over Olivia's sanity, he had it now, and in spades. There was nothing wrong with her mind. She was simply a manipulative and possessive bitch. And she had trapped him very neatly in this scheme, her obvious motive to be rid of him because she saw him as a threat.

Allie cried, "I never go into the b-barn. Never!"

No matter which way he turned, thanks to Olivia, he'd hurt her. Not purposely, but clearly she believed that he had, and almost had him convinced of it, too. He felt about two feet tall. "Well, hell, I didn't know that. And no one told me."

Olivia made a noise of disgusted impatience. "Oh, nearly everyone in Decker Prairie knows, Althea."

Jeff ignored the remark. He hadn't encountered a smoother liar in all his life. "Anyway, Allie, I just wanted to show you those birds. I found that nest of barn swallows in there and I thought you'd like to see them." He felt like a kid, trying to explain an intended good deed that had turned into a disastrous blunder.

She turned her head to look at him again. "Birds?"

"Yeah, I remembered that you liked to feed the ones in the orchard. You *like* birds, don't you?" He hadn't gotten that wrong, had he?

"Yes, but I wouldn't go into the barn to look at them. Anyway, I didn't see anything except that—that— And if you didn't put it there, who did?"

"If I knew we wouldn't be sitting here talking about it. I'd be kicking that bastard's ass all the way to the county line." Allie said nothing, but the hurt he saw written on her face hit him like a punch in the stomach. "I guess you don't have any reason to believe me. But I'm telling you the truth."

"Don't listen to him, Althea!" her sister harangued, towering over them like one of the Furies calling down the wind. "After what he did, you should order him off the property now, this minute!" She narrowed her eyes. "Whatever would Daddy say?"

Allie felt pummeled by the events and the quarrelsome voices yammering around her. "Olivia, please, just go back into the house. There's no point in both of us being upset."

"But—"

"*Please.* We'll talk about this—later."

"Very well, Althea." Straight-backed and her nose in the air, Olivia flounced off through the wet grass to the back porch.

Allie and Jeff both watched in silence until she slammed the door.

Jeff sat across from her, cross-legged and facing the barn. He gestured in its direction. "Allie, this might not be the time to talk about it, but Olivia *did* tell me to take you in there. She said you'd want to see that bird's nest."

Allie gazed at her lap for a moment, so long that Jeff began to fidget. "You might be telling the truth, Mr. Hicks." She said it with a halfhearted whisper, stealing a glance at him and then looking away again. "But everyone in town knows my mother hung herself. Are you telling me you didn't?"

"I never said that!" Jeff protested. "I knew. But I swear to you, Allie, I didn't know she hung herself in the barn!"

With great effort Allie managed to draw herself to her knees, making him think of a wounded doe, caught in the open and frantic to find shelter in the woods. Plainly too weak to run, she struggled to her feet with her shoulders hunched and her arms wrapped around herself, as if waiting for the hunter's second, and fatal, shot. The image made his heart twist in his chest. Her chin lifted a notch. Even as she made the effort, the wind whipped at her heavy skirts, and she swayed slightly. "How could you not know? I told you never to leave the barn door open. That day I made you come down from the roof to close it—" She lifted a hand to her throat, her eyes shining with tears. "Why else would I have done that? Why else would I care? I would have closed it myself."

Jeff couldn't think of an argument to that. She *had* insisted that he climb down from the roof to closed the damned barn door. At the time, he'd thought she was just being a fussy old maid who wanted her own way. He hadn't known about her mother then, but in retrospect, she'd made her revulsion for the barn very plain. A clear-thinking man would have figured out that she was afraid of something in there, but his only concern had been getting his next drink.

Now he realized that her mother had hung herself from that very rafter. Well, Jeff Hicks didn't need a house to fall on him before he understood a point—no, sirree, it took a whole damned barn. He kept remembering the look on Allie's face when she'd found herself in there, how she'd stared at the dummy and then flown into a panic. Her mother. He may not have engineered the prank, but he'd been the one to lead her in there, like a lamb to the slaughter. The realization made him feel sick.

"I won't ask you to leave because I need your help," she said hollowly, "and because I want to be fair to you. But I won't hear you say anything bad about my sister."

She walked away then, unsteady but clearly determined to get to the safety of her kitchen. Climbing the stairs, she never once looked back at him or the barn.

Jeff watched her go, that gut-punched feeling back on him, stronger than ever.

Chapter Twelve

OVER THE NEXT·FEW DAYS, ALLIE MAINTAINED HER DIS-
tance from Jeff. She still left his meals on the back porch,
but she had no encounters with him. At least he seemed to
realize that she wanted nothing to do with him and he
stayed away from the house. In fact, sometimes the only
evidence of his presence was the empty dishes she collected
after he ate.

Her initial anger at him faded to disappointment. Whenever she thought about what he'd done to her—intentional
or not—her eyes burned with tears. Not only had he given
her the second biggest scare of her life, he had dredged up
unbearable memories that she had tried hard to keep in the
back of her mind.

Could she have been wrong about the man? The tenderness she'd detected in him, the compassion—if what
Olivia told her was true, he'd been very good at deceiving
her. Olivia was after her night and day, reminding Allie
that she hadn't trusted him from the first day. Allie was not
as quick to judge, but she felt like a fool for believing in
him, trusting him, falling in love with him. Love—it had
crept up and taken her heart, foolish spinster that she was,

she thought bitterly. But what did she really know about men or love, anyway? Nothing.

Within an hour of the barn incident, Olivia, who'd stunned Allie with a strength she had never suspected, returned to her girlish, doll-like self. She had been tight-lipped and disapproving when Allie explained that she couldn't run Jeff off. Her sister had reminded her—in vivid and exacting detail—of the terrible deed Jeff had committed. But they still needed his help, and as she'd told him, there was no one else to ask. When Allie had promised to have as little to do with him as possible, Olivia seemed satisfied.

Now she played her piano every afternoon and often wore a complacent smile. But the image of her sister charging out to the barn, dressed only in her nightgown and wrapper to avenge Allie, gave her new insight into the person she always thought of as a child.

Allie had almost quit thinking about the heart-stopping terror of that morning every moment of the day. Almost. There was something familiar about the dummy, more than what it represented, that nagged at her waking hours but she could never put her finger on what it was.

The gruesome *thing* still visited her dreams, though, sometimes with a pillow-ticking face, sometimes with her mother's. It would reach out to her with the arms of a skeleton and point a bony finger at her in mute accusation. No matter how she tried, she couldn't get out of that barn. No matter how loud she called and cried, or how hard she pushed on the door. She was trapped, the door locked from the outside. Just the way it had happened so long ago. In her dream, though, always, *always*, someone would come to rescue her, a kind, courageous champion who feared nothing and released her into the sunlight, but whose face remained in the shadows. She'd jerk to wakefulness without learning her protector's identity, shivering in cold perspiration and wishing that someone was with her to chase away the demons that plagued her sleep. To her distress, the someone she imagined usually took the form of Jefferson Hicks.

Though Allie had no direct contact with Jeff, she kept her eye on him and the progress of his work. Once, on his way to the lean-to, he'd turned suddenly, as though he felt her watching him from the kitchen window. He'd stared back at her with a steady, unflinching gaze, like a man who had nothing to be ashamed of. She thought that he looked nearly as haggard as he had when he first came to the farm, and it seemed as if he even wore a wistful, troubled expression on his drawn features. Hearing footsteps that signaled Olivia's approach, she had jumped away from the window, as guilt-stricken as a child stealing a piece of candy.

At least the kitchen garden, the source of her other great worry, had been planted. She'd stood at her bedroom window upstairs, watching as Jeff sowed the field with the restored seeder. The rows were as straight and orderly as she could have asked, and the under the warm sun of late June, seedlings were beginning to pop up.

Eager for a closer look, one bright afternoon while Olivia was napping and bread dough was rising in the warm kitchen, Allie slipped out the back door to inspect the garden. It gave her the perfect opportunity to learn for herself exactly what work Jeff had done. He was in the front yard, cutting the high, fast-growing grass with a scythe. She saw him from the parlor window, swinging the blade with long, smooth strokes that made her pause to watch, peeping at him from the shelter of the curtains. The muscles in his raw-boned arms swelled with the effort, and when he turned to face the house, she saw that his ill-fitting shirt was completely unbuttoned. Apparently, he still wouldn't wear the shirt she'd made for him, and now she felt like an idiot for having taken the time to do it. But that thought faded as she looked at his torso gleaming with sweat. A breeze came up to catch the loose tails of his shirt, revealing the smooth, hypnotic motion of flesh and rib and sinew. The damp waistband of his jeans hung low on a belly that looked as firm and ridged as her washboard.

Allie's breathing sped up to keep time with the tireless to-and-fro swing of the scythe while she watched the grass surrender to the blade. Back and forth, rhythmic, powerful. She gripped the curtain in her fist and swallowed. It was not a particularly hot day, but she felt restless and edgy in the parlor, which had suddenly grown too warm and close. Her high collar seemed too tight, and her hair too heavy at the back of her head. When she realized that she was staring, she tore herself away from the window. Imagine, gawking at that dreadful man who was responsible for her latest round of nightmares! He was beneath contempt, and he certainly did not warrant the kind of attention she'd paid him.

Allie struggled to force her mind back to the task at hand. The task at hand—what was it? Of course, the garden. With a last backward glance at Jeff, she left the parlor and went to the back door. She was reasonably certain that she would be able to avoid him if she circled around the other side of the house.

As she walked along the path between the house and the fields, she heard the birds twittering in the orchard but it was the grounds that held her attention. Although a lot of work had yet to be done, here and there the farm was actually beginning to look better. True, shrubbery and blackberry brambles grew wild over the springhouse and toolshed, and the house still needed painting. But the shutters, which had bracketed the windows at precarious angles, were now straight and secure again. The wire fence that ran along one side of the road, the one that had become as bowed as a canvas sail in a hard wind, now stood upright and taut. The bushes growing around the house had been trimmed so that Allie no longer had to stand on tiptoe to see out windows. They hadn't merely been hacked down, either. Jeff had followed the natural line of the plants so that they really looked nice. She was a capable woman, but these were tasks that she could not have accomplished alone.

When she reached the field, she breathed in the scent of newly turned earth as she inspected each row. Spinach and cabbage were already sending tender green shoots toward the summer sun, a fact for which Allie was profoundly glad. They'd gotten a late start but now she had real hope that there would be a decent harvest to can in the fall. She walked between the rows that bore onions and garlic, stooping to pluck the occasional weed as she went. When she reached the top edge of the field she found an orderly line of plants that bore no resemblance to any vegetable she was familiar with. As she examined them more closely, she saw a rich purple bloom emerging from the dark green foliage. She reached down to touch its velvety petals.

Violets. They grew wild all over the farm. Jeff had transplanted violets and put them here. Violets, with their soft, velvety petals and delicate hue, had stolen her attention that day so many years ago.

Allie lifted her head and looked across the field again. She could find no fault in Jeff's work, but she found plenty in the man. What kind of person would plant a border of violets in a garden just for their beauty, and then arrange to scare ten years off a woman's life? It didn't make any sense.

She chided herself for asking the question, but despite every common-sense reason her mind could conceive, it lurked in her heart. She gripped her arms as if the summer breeze had turned suddenly chill. In time, the horror of that morning would probably fade a bit, but she felt as if the hurt never would.

Walking back along the path, she reached the low fence that enclosed her parents' graves. As she passed, she spied a bright yellow dandelion in full bloom right in front of her mother's headstone. Its foliage spread wide and audacious on the otherwise manicured spot. Hurrying inside the enclosure, she dropped to her knees to get a firm grip on the weed. Dandelions had long roots and if she couldn't get the whole of this one, the plant would keep coming back. But she succeeded in only stripping off the leaves and breaking the stem of the flower, staining her hand green in the bargain. The thing was securely fixed, almost as if something held its other end in a tug of war. She glanced up at the headstone.

Happier in death . . .

Panicky desperation growing in her chest, Allie clawed at the weed with her bare fingers, trying to dislodge it, driving earth and grass under her nails. She wanted to run away from this place and this moment, but she had to pull out the weed. Perspiration beaded at her temples and between her breasts. Her hair worked loose from its pins and the breeze picked up the freed tendrils around her shoulders. Suddenly a shadow fell across her and Lucinda Ford's headstone.

"I'll dig that out if you want, Allie. It'll take a shovel."

Allie's head snapped up and she found Jeff Hicks looming over her, holding a burlap sack. Behind his head, the afternoon sun gave him a blinding halo so that she couldn't see his face. "Dig *what*?"

"That weed."

"N-no, I can manage fine, thank you." She couldn't reveal how unnerving it was to have him so close, how confusing. "You just go back to your chores," she ordered in her best brisk voice. "God knows there's plenty to do."

He dropped to a crouch across the grave from her, his elbow resting loosely on his knee. His black eye had faded from purple to green and yellow, but it did nothing to detract from his good looks, damn him. The sleeves of his old shirt were rolled up and she glanced at his forearms, dusted with hair that sparkled golden in the sun. The front of the garment still gaped open, and she couldn't help but shift her gaze to the expanse of bare chest and belly just three feet away from her. When he put the sack between them, though, she stared at it, terrified of what might be inside.

"Allie, I need to talk to you."

No, *no*, she didn't want to talk to him. Didn't he realize that she wanted to avoid him? That he shouldn't even be on this side of the fence, talking to her across her mother's grave? What would her father say? She stuffed the torn leaves and stem into her apron pocket. "Have you finished the front yard?"

He nodded. "Listen, the other morning in the barn—"

"Well, the fence along the road isn't right yet." She knew it was a lie.

He straightened his shoulders. "That fence is as even as it was the day it was put in!"

"It needs fixing. Some of the posts wobble."

"No they don't. I reset the loose ones."

"They all need painting."

Jeff let out a gusty sigh. He knew what Allie was doing, dancing him around like this. She might blame him for that morning in the barn, but she couldn't pick his work apart.

He'd be damned before he'd let her. "Those posts have never been painted. Give me one reason why in hell they need it now."

"Because I want you to do it. That's the only reason you need. Don't compound your mounting sins by adding disobedience to the list."

"Disobedience!" he barked. "Allie, I'm not a boy and I'm not your slave. I'm a grown man, goddamn it, and I want you to treat me like one!"

She kept up her frantic digging, reminding him of a dog trying to bury a bone. "You *work* for me, Mr. Hicks. Sheriff Mason brought you here to do as I say. And so you shall." She looked as starched and self-righteous as a minister's collar, and she made it plain that the conversation had ended. But he had the proof of his innocence in the burlap sack, and he was determined that she would hear him out.

"I finally figured out why you're so goddamned picky!" he stormed.

A rosy stain spread across her cheeks and nose. "That's no great mystery! I pay a fair wage, I expect an honest job."

He shook his head. "Oh, no, that isn't it. This"—he gestured at the house and the yard—"is the only part of your life that you can control. The rest of the time your sister has you dancing to her fiddle." There. It was out.

Allie looked as indignant as if he'd slapped her hand. "How dare you say such a thing? Olivia is frail and sickly—I have to take care of her."

"Bullshit! Let's talk about frail, sickly Olivia." He grabbed the sack and pulled out the shirt she had made for him and a wadded length of fabric. He unfurled the latter like a bedroll to reveal the gray gingham dress the dummy had been wearing that morning in the barn. Feathers and bits of the straw it had been stuffed with still stuck to it here and there. "Whose dress is this?"

Allie made a strangled noise. "Wh-what—"

The color drained from her face, but Jeff knew he must plunge ahead. Being guilty of his own bad deed gave him enough sleepless nights—he refused to carry the blame for this one, too. "Is this Olivia's dress?"

She didn't answer right away. The breeze sighing through the trees seemed almost deafening while he waited for her response. "No," she whispered, finally. Her mouth looked soft and vulnerable. "It was my mother's."

As he suspected. "Do you know where it's been all these years?"

"In a trunk in the attic. All of Mama's things are up there. My father couldn't bear to look at them after she— He made me take them up there."

Jeff's suspicions were nearly confirmed. Just one more piece to the puzzle . . . "So then, what do you know about this?" He opened the chambray work shirt and displayed its collar and yoke, lined with the same gray gingham.

Allie's gaze switched back and forth between the shirt and the dress, obviously trying to comprehend what they showed her. She stretched out a shaking hand to touch the shirt, then withdrew it, pressing it to her mouth. "Oh, dear God."

"You made this shirt, right?"

She touched the garment again, plainly rattled. "I-I didn't have enough chambray to finish— I used a couple of scraps I found in the trunk—"

"Did you hang that dummy in the barn, Allie?"

"Of course not! God in heaven, why would I do something like that?"

"A good question. Here's another one—if you didn't do it, and I didn't do it, who does that leave?"

She looked up at him with such profound bewilderment and hurt in her eyes, for the space of a heartbeat he wished he could take back all of this. What did it matter if he had another black deed against his name? Compared to his real crime, this would be nothing. But then he realized that this went beyond clearing himself. Allie had the right to know the truth.

Still on her knees, she backed away from him a pace or two, grinding the turf into her skirt. "No, it can't be. I don't believe it."

He reached out to take her wrist, trying to soften the blow of his words. She didn't shake him off, but stayed there on her knees, as rigid as a statue. "Allie, honey, you know it's true. Olivia put that thing in the barn, and then arranged for me to show it to you, telling me you'd love to see the swallows' nest. She even told me to have you close your eyes before I took you in there so I wouldn't give away the 'surprise.' She knew you wouldn't go in there any other way." He went on to repeat the events leading up to that god-awful morning.

"She probably forgot that I won't go in there. I'm sure she did."

"She didn't forget."

Allie regarded him and pressed her mouth into a tight line. "She *must* have."

He shook his head. "She can't have forgotten if she made the dummy. And it looks like she did—she's the only one besides you who knows where to find your mother's dresses."

"Maybe she just wanted to scare *you*, and she didn't remember that I won't go in—there."

"How long has it been since you were last in the barn?" He asked gently, but the question felt like a saber slicing through her.

"Not since my father—" Even after all these years, she shrank from the memory. Those black nights, alone in the darkness, the musty smell of hay and dampness . . . She shuddered. "Not for years."

Lightly, he reached out and gripped her upper arms. She felt his warmth through her thin sleeves. "Do you think Olivia would forget something like that?"

She pulled away from his hands. "Yes!" She couldn't endure the thought of any other reason.

But Jeff wasn't pushed away so easily. "Not likely."

"Oh, sweet Jesus," she moaned, her breath coming in short bursts. Of course he was right. She knew he was right and it all fit together to make sense. Whatever kind of man Jeff might be, whatever sins he had committed in his life, he was not really a cruel person. She had sensed that all along. This dress was what had made the dummy seem even more familiar than the memory, and had nagged at the back of her mind. Contrition swamped Allie. She'd said harsh things to him that morning, and accused him of a terrible deed. "Jeff, I'm sorry. I apologize for Olivia, and I'm sorry I didn't believe you that morning."

His green eyes looked as deep as a mountain lake. "Don't apologize for your sister. She *isn't* a child, Allie."

"I can't understand why she would do such a thing."

"It seems pretty obvious to me. She wants me out of here."

"But Olivia knows we need help to get the home place fixed up. I've told her that so many times."

"It doesn't matter. I'm guessing she thinks I somehow threaten her way of life." He shifted his weight. "That maybe I'll steal you away from her."

"Steal me away— But that's ridiculous!"

Jeff looked at her kneeling there, the afternoon breeze ruffling wispy copper curls that framed her face and trailed along her white throat. She had no idea how pretty she was—like a rosebud that had never been allowed to bloom. Jeff could only guess at the beauty that would emerge if Allie were given the chance to blossom. He rubbed the back of his neck. "Yeah, I guess it does sound ridiculous. I don't have a thing in the world to offer a woman." A bitter pang shivered through him. "But someday another man, a more worthy man, is going to come along who will want you. I think your sister knows it better than you do."

Allie shot to her feet so quickly it startled him, and fairly jumped over the low fence surrounding the graves. "If Olivia thinks that, I have to do everything in my power to reassure her." She glanced back at the house. "It will never happen! Never. I promised I'd stay with Olivia always. Anyway, I can't talk about that, especially not in—in there." She gestured at the headstones and plunged into the tall grass and strode toward the house, stumbling over tussocks as she went.

Jeff stuffed his evidence back into the burlap sack and stepped over the fence to catch up with her. "Allie, wait." He gripped her slim arm and turned her around. "Why would you make a promise like that? You're not doing your sister a favor by letting her get away with this. She has to be made accountable for her actions, just like everyone else in the world. What if you *weren't* here tomorrow? How do you think she'd manage? You're sacrificing your whole life to take care of someone who should be making a life of her own."

Allie wrenched her arm from his hand. "You don't know what you're talking about! You don't know what I did—how bad I am! Olivia needs me, and what I took from her I can never make up." Her face crumpled, mirroring a soul that was perhaps even more tortured than his own.

Dropping the sack, instinctively Jeff pulled her into his

arms, to somehow shelter her from whatever devils beset her. "Allie, honey," he murmured against her ear, "don't be so hard on yourself. What could you have done that's so terrible?"

"Don't do that. Don't touch me that way," she demanded.

"Why not?"

"Because I'm afraid."

"Afraid?" He released her. "Of me?"

She took a deep breath. "No! Of myself. Of how you make me feel and how often I think about you." She yielded for a moment then, leaning against him as if she had no strength left to stand on her own. He closed his arms around her again. "You don't know how bad I am," she repeated, her voice breaking. "I can't begin to tell you."

She was soft and lithe in his embrace, and faintly fragrant of lavender. The swell of her breasts against him brought blood pounding to his groin. The effect almost startled him—hell, except for his dealings with Allie, it had been longer than he realized since he'd been close to a woman. The wind blew over the grass in waves, flattening the blades to reveal their silvery undersides. It tugged at the loose curls around her face and the afternoon sun caught glints of ruby fire in the strands. Her lips—he'd kissed them and he knew they were as soft and as inviting as they looked now. Jeff felt a balm on his own injured spirit just to touch her. A man might have half a chance to turn his life around with Allie Ford standing beside him.

"I don't think you're bad," he murmured against her hair. "Maybe you're just tired. You've hauled a lot of responsibility for a long time, I think." The last few years had been lousy for him, but of his own making. Despite Allie's protests, though, he suspected that her troubles were a legacy she'd inherited. He took her face between his

hands and looked into her eyes. "If I had my way, if I could
change everything that happened in the years that came
before now, I'd do it, and take the burden off your shoulders."

She gazed up at him, and her bossy, self-reliant mask
slipped. "You would?" He saw a wistful innocence that
made his heart ache for her.

Somewhere in the trees a song sparrow called *sweet-
sweet-sweet*.

"Yes." Before reason or the hard hand of fate had the
chance to stop him, he lowered his head and took her mouth
with his own. It was a real kiss this time—he plied her with
his lips and tongue—not just a tentative brush. And for a
moment, all of their troubles did fall away. It was a young
summer day—nothing existed but the wind and a man with
a woman in his arms. Her ripe mouth was warm and slick
and yielding, and her breath fanned his cheek. With his
hands he searched the length of her rib cage, seeking her
full, soft breast. Her nipple pushed against the thin fabric
of her summer dress and hardened beneath his fingertips.
When a whimper sounded in her throat, the fire that licked
through Jeff's body burned higher and he tightened his
arms around her, pulling her off her feet and up against the
length of his torso. She fit perfectly in his arms, and he
would bet good money that they'd be a perfect fit in every
way. With his pulse pounding in his head, he drew back
for a moment and muttered hoarsely, "God, Allie, if I
could, I'd lay you down in this tall grass right now and
make you forget all the bad things that ever happened to
you, whatever they were."

At his words, she straightened away from him. He
reached for her, but she put out an unsteady hand, as if to
hold him back, and he cursed himself for scaring her. Her
face was flushed and she sucked in a deep breath.

"No one can change the bad things, Jeff. I-I'm sorry that Olivia blamed you for the trick she played on me. It was very wrong of her, very wrong. But I'm sure she didn't mean to hurt you."

Frustrated to find his arms empty and Olivia Ford the topic of conversation again, Jeff snapped, "Who did she mean to hurt, then? You?" As soon as the words were out of his mouth, he could have bitten off his tongue for asking the sarcastic question.

Allie gave him a look that made his heart thump against his ribs. "I guess she did."

For only the second time in his life, Jeff felt compelled to right a wrong. The first time he'd been powerless to undo the damage—he could not have called back the bullet to his revolver, or healed the wound it made in Wesley Matthews' chest. This was different, though. He would save Allie Ford, if he could, if he knew how . . .

"Are you going to face your sister? Tell her what you know now?"

She shook her head. "It might upset her. I don't want to risk that."

Oh, no, we wouldn't want to upset the fragile flower. Never mind that the woman had framed him and terrorized Allie. This time Jeff did bite back the smart remark that popped into his head. Allie didn't need any more trouble than she already had. Instead he suggested mildly, "Honey, maybe if you tell me about your mother, it won't seem so terrible anymore."

She gave him a fearful, doubting look.

"Come on—it can't be as bad as what I told you about Wes and my wife and all."

Her look turned hard and ice-blue. "It's worse. You acted out of self-defense when you shot Wesley Matthews."

"For God's sake, Allie, you didn't *kill* your mother."

"Yes, I did." She turned on her heel and retraced her steps back to the house.

Jeff stared at her narrow back as she went. Then he headed off to the barn to get a shovel to dig out the dandelion.

Allie walked back to the house to discover that Seth Wickwire had left her grocery order in a crate on the back porch. Between learning about Olivia's deception and partaking of Jeff's heated kiss, by the time Allie reached the bright kitchen, she was almost wringing her hands. Hoping that to occupy those hands would also occupy her mind, she washed the dirt off them, and put the provisions away. Then she greased her hands with lard and went to work shaping the bread dough into loaves.

The warm, yeasty smell in the kitchen was nice, but the distractions didn't help. Her thoughts raced around in her brain like a bee trapped in a glass jar.

This kitchen, this *house* seemed so confining to her. More often lately, Allie had caught herself daydreaming about putting on her shawl and walking away. Away from the farm, from her responsibilities, just leaving without a backward glance.

She hadn't wanted to hear whatever Jeff was suggesting about her sister.

She hadn't wanted to believe that Olivia, her own flesh and blood, had so cruelly and deliberately hurt her. But that she was responsible for the horrible prank with the dummy was glaringly clear, and Allie couldn't deny the facts presented to her. Jeff wouldn't have known where to find her mother's clothes, or in fact, that the gray gingham dress had belonged to Lucinda Ford.

Did her sister truly see Jeff Hicks as such a threat that she would stop at nothing to be rid of him? Did she really believe that anything could make Allie forget her duty?

The question in her mind faded before the memory of Jeff's hands on her, urgent and seeking, lifting her off her feet. The kiss and the hot sensation of his intimate touch *had* made her forget everything else—just for a minute. No one had ever touched her like that. Every fiber in her body had come alive, and it surprised her to feel so intensely. She knew it was probably wrong, but nothing in her life had ever seemed so right. She'd felt transported, and pulling herself away from him was one of the most difficult things she'd ever done.

Glancing down at her hand, she realized that she'd squeezed a lump of dough until it ran out between her fingers. With an impatient "tsk" she shook off the dough and reshaped it. Allie had done everything she could to protect Olivia, defer to her, dote on her. And now, just because a hired hand was working around here . . .

Except Allie couldn't think of Jeff Hicks that way anymore. Maybe she never really had. Something about him had challenged her from the beginning. Not the way that Cooper Matthews had challenged her—that man was simply rude and overbearing. Jeff had roused her curiosity.

But regardless of what she'd told Jeff about reassuring her sister, she realized that Olivia's deed was simply too much to bear in silence.

Allie would have to speak to her. Even children had to be corrected from time to time. Their father had certainly corrected Althea.

Then there was Jeff, innocent of the ghastly deed he'd been accused of. It was horrible, distressing. But oddly enough, the moment she'd permitted herself to be enfolded in his arms had been both calming and stunning. Allie stared at the greased loaf pans on the kitchen table, not really seeing them. She had pulled away, not because she feared him, but because she was afraid of the flood of sensations and crystallized emotion that rushed through her veins when he touched her. Afraid that if she didn't pull away, she would never want to again—

"Althea, where are you?"

Her sister's voice cut into her reverie like a piece of broken glass. "Here, Olivia. In the kitchen."

Olivia swept in, her pink dimity skirts rustling. She looked very upset. "Althea, that horrible man is digging up our mother's grave! I saw him from the upstairs window."

Allie immediately dropped her gaze, hoping that Olivia had seen nothing else from that window. She knew Jeff must have gotten a shovel to dig out the dandelion after she left him. "No, he isn't. He's just getting a weed."

"But aren't you going to at least go see?"

"I don't need to, Olivia. I know what he's doing, and so does he."

Her sister huffed out an impatient sigh. "After that awful trick he played, how can you trust him to do anything?"

Allie looked up again and gave her an even gaze. "I trust him."

Olivia laced her fingers together. "You seem out of sorts, Althea. Maybe you need a cup of tea. I know—scurry over and put the kettle on, and we can both have one. And make us some toast with butter and jam, too, for a treat. Wouldn't that be nice?"

Force of habit strong within her, Allie began to wipe her hands on her apron to carry out Olivia's request. Then she stopped. Jeff was right. Her sister should be made to answer for what she had done, regardless of her motive. Allie stared at the woman who was as overdressed as a fashion plate from *Godey's Lady's Book*, a lifetime of sisterly devotion in her heart at odds with inescapable fact. She drew a bracing breath. "Olivia, Jeff showed me something this afternoon from that day in the b-barn."

Olivia's expression turned sour. "I thought we'd agreed that you wouldn't have anything to do with him." Allie quailed. Had Olivia seen her in Jeff's arms, seen them kissing?

Recovering, she reminded her, "I still have to talk to him, you know. Olivia, he showed me the dress that dummy had on. It was Mother's dress."

Olivia leaned against the edge of the kitchen table. "Dear God, Althea, hasn't that man put us through enough? Why in the world would he drag out that thing again?"

Allie stressed the obvious. "If he's guilty, how would he have gotten the dress?"

She waited for an answer, her pulse drumming in her throat, her fingers sunk into the bread dough. Hope struggled in her chest, hope that Olivia would give her some reason other than the one Jeff had. A reason that wouldn't be a lie, but one that would exonerate her. Even that pixies or leprechauns had gone to the trunk in the attic, she thought desperately. *Please, God, please let Jeff be wrong about this,* she prayed. But one look at her sister's face told Allie that Jeff was right. Olivia had hung that hideous effigy in the barn.

"W-well, he probably found it in a shed someplace, or maybe in the lean-to," Olivia said. "He's had lots of time to look through all the old junk stored out there." Her evasion of the truth hurt Allie even more.

"All of Mother's things are in a trunk in the attic. I put them up there myself, and I've never moved them. You know that—we even spent an afternoon going through them. And Jeff told me about the bird's nest he showed you." Her voice dropped to a choked cry. "Why did you do it, Olivia? Why?"

Hot color suffused her face. "You—you believe him over me? Your own family?"

Allie held out her greased hands like a supplicant. "Oh, dear Lord, I don't want to, but I can't ignore the truth when it's shown to me!"

"I guess I know where your loyalty lies. And after you promised Daddy!"

At the mention of Amos Ford, an icy sensation gripped Allie's insides but she remained adamant. "Loyalty—Olivia, you *used* me. I've stayed by your side all these years, but you're so anxious to be rid of Jeff that you used me to play that dirty trick. You didn't care how much it hurt me!"

Olivia's face blanched and her voice grew distant and cool. She clutched the edge of the kitchen table with one hand and rubbed her temple with the other. "Please, Althea, I would really like to have that tea now. I guess I'm not as strong as I thought."

Allie made no move to comply, and after a lifetime of waiting on her sister it was difficult to resist. She closed her hands into fists. But perhaps Jeff was right, maybe it was time that Olivia started to take care of herself. "You know how to boil water, Olivia. You can put the kettle on."

"The room is beginning to sp-spin."

"It won't hurt you to make your own tea."

Olivia's eyes rolled upward, and acting out of sheer instinct, Allie whipped around to the other side of the table and pushed a chair under her sister just as her knees buckled. "It's all right, now. Just take a few deep breaths—"

Allie put an arm around Olivia's shoulders to keep her upright. At her touch, Olivia began rocking back and forth, howling like a banshee, her body as rigid as a plank. The howls gave way to deep, rough sobs that tore from her throat.

Her flying hands fell to the bowl of flour on the table,

and she grabbed handfuls, flinging it everywhere. A choking white cloud enveloped them both. With her free arm, Allie tried to keep Olivia's grasping fingers from reaching the pans and other utensils on the table. But before she could push them away, Olivia gripped a heavy cast-iron pan and flung it across the kitchen as though it weighed no more than an empty matchbox. The next one Allie made a grab for, but it struck her cheekbone before sailing toward the kitchen window.

White-hot pain flashed through her head and she tasted the salty tang of blood where she bit the inside of her cheek. Tears sprang to her eyes and she saw bright flashes of stars. Olivia's spells had never made her fear for more than her sister's safety.

Now she feared for her own.

Jeff was taking the shovel back to the barn when the sound of shattering glass brought him up short. God, what the hell was that? he wondered. Fear for Allie's safety propelled him across the yard and he flew up the back porch steps in one leap. Through the screen door he saw Olivia pounding the table with a big cooking spoon, and he heard her ululating like an old Cree chief he'd once seen in a medicine show.

Allie was trying to restrain her sister but it looked like she was losing the battle. The top half of her apron had been torn from around her neck and an angry-looking bruise was forming on her cheek. Allie's strength was no match for Olivia's—when she looked up and he caught her gaze, he saw genuine fear in her eyes.

Fury, complete and consuming, radiated from the pit of his stomach. But no matter how much he wanted to, he knew he couldn't run in there and slap Olivia to snap her out of this temper tantrum. There was no good excuse for hitting a woman. And he didn't want to risk another bite if he could avoid it.

Short of hog-tying her what could he do? Scanning the porch around him and hoping for an idea, Jeff spotted the three-gallon water bucket that always sat next to the top step. Inspired, he picked it up, flung open the screen door, and charged into the kitchen where Olivia's howling was even louder.

"Jeff, no—" Allie protested when she saw him. Ignoring her objection, he upended the bucket over Olivia's head, feeling as desperate as a man putting out a fire in a dynamite factory. Water sluiced over both her and Allie and flooded the floor. Olivia's sobbing stopped abruptly on a shocked, high-pitched gasp, and she sprang from her chair, spitting like a cat.

"*How dare you?*" she demanded, quivering with indignation and, Jeff noted, in sudden and complete possession of her faculties. Water soaked her elaborately curled hair and fancy dress, but her eyes were as focused as they had been the day she bit him. She looked down at her pink dimity, positively stunned. "You have ruined my dress, you—you vagrant!"

If Jeff had been in a better mood, he might have been amused by Olivia's waterlogged appearance. But the purpling bruise on Allie's cheek and Olivia's unmasked deceitfulness with which she had controlled her sister for so many years gave him nothing to laugh about.

Marshaling all the authority he'd used to break up saloon fights, Jeff put his hand on her shoulder and pushed her back into the chair. "Lady, you'd better sit down, shut up, and behave like an adult, or I'll tie you to that chair! You've done a lot of damage of your own."

Apparently not defiant enough to challenge Jeff, Olivia sat down, as sullen as a twelve-year-old. But she raked him with a look that might have withered a weaker man. A monster of selfishness and hatred lurked under her sweet face and artful curls. She hadn't fooled Jeff, but her sister had been taken in.

Allie, her skirts and shoes also drenched, gaped first at Olivia, then Jeff, then Olivia again. She could barely grasp what she'd just witnessed. Oh, God. Realization knifed through her mind like a blinding pain. Squeezing her eyes closed, she clamped her hands over her face. It couldn't be true. It simply couldn't. She refused to believe it. Olivia hadn't faked her illness all these years. To even entertain such a notion for a moment would be despicable.

No . . . Allie drew a deep breath and struggled for calm. There was another explanation, she assured herself. There had to be. The water in the bucket had been cold. Quite simply, the shock had ended Olivia's hysterical convulsion, much as a hard slap to the face would snap someone out of a panic. It was shock. Yes, that had to be it.

Regaining her composure, Allie shoved all other possibilities from her mind. To believe another reason was just too horrible to contemplate. She clutched her sister's wet forearm. "Olivia, you're better! How do you feel?"

"How do you think I feel?" Olivia snapped impatiently. "I'm soaked to the skin, thanks to your hired hand."

"Tell her, Olivia," Jeff prodded. "Tell your sister that you've been faking these attacks just to run her around in circles."

"I will do no such thing. I don't have to answer to you!"

"*Tell her.*"

Allie's heart felt as if it had stopped in her chest. No, it couldn't be true, she told herself again. It was bad enough that Olivia had tricked her and Jeff with the episode in the barn. But her illness—*that* had to be real. She truly was sick. Otherwise Dr. Brewster would have been right. *Lane*

Smithfield would have been right. "Olivia—my God—"

Jeff put his foot on the overturned bucket and leaned closer to Olivia, fixing her with a hard look that made her shift in her seat. "Tell Allie how you double-crossed me and that you're the one who hung that dummy in the barn for her to see."

"He's lying!" Olivia shrieked, twisting toward Allie. Her face was contorted, pulling her mouth into an ugly pink slash. "I have not been faking! And I didn't put that horrid thing out there. I swear on Daddy's grave. On Daddy's grave! Oh, God, I wish he was here. He wouldn't have let this awful man set one foot on our property so he could say these dreadful things and turn you against me! I was his little princess, and I deserved to be treated like one because you cheated me out of my mother's love. Daddy said it was all your fault and you know it!"

"Yes, he did," Allie agreed woodenly, staggered by the terrible realization that had dawned upon her. "He always did."

"I got word from that crazy Olivia Ford about another job for us, Floyd. Seth Wickwire brought me another letter from her. So you be ready a couple of hours after midnight. There'll be a half moon, enough to see by, but not so much to give us away." Cooper Matthews spoke to his companion over his beer glass in a hushed voice. Nobody in the Liberal Saloon appeared to be paying any mind to them as they stood at the far end of the bar. The barkeep had his nose buried in a green-backed ledger, and since it was the dinner hour, business was slow. But a man couldn't be too careful.

Floyd Endicott upended his mug to drain the last dribble of beer into his mouth. "I'll be ready. I hope she's payin' a little more this time." He dragged his grimy sleeve across his foamy lip and smiled, revealing tobacco-stained teeth.

"But I'd almost have been willin' to string up that scarecrow for free if we coulda seen their faces when they found it danglin' there in the barn. Hoo-ee, I'll bet they went whiter than a glass of milk in a snowbank." He straightened. "Still, a man's gotta earn a livin', and I need beer and tobaccy money."

Cooper closed his hand around the fragrant stationary in his overalls pocket. It bore Olivia Ford's message, including the promise of twenty dollars for a job well done. He let his gaze make another sweep of the saloon's patrons and kept his voice down. "She's payin' the same as before—ten dollars. You get four after the job's done, just like last time. Then there's all that satisfaction from gettin' even with Hicks and the Ford woman."

"I dunno, Cooper. Satisfaction won't buy me another beer." He shrugged. "If I'm going to take the risk I want it to be worth my while. Besides, why should you get more than me?"

Cooper signaled the barkeep to bring another round of beers, which he paid for himself. "There. Happy now?" he asked as Floyd slurped down his drink with the noisy enthusiasm of a thirsty dog. "Why do I have to keep remindin' you, Floyd, that I'm the brains of this outfit? This ain't like the first time, when the woman left us everything we needed out by the road. There were supplies to buy for this job—am I supposed to pay for them myself and you pay nothin'? That wouldn't be right."

"I guess not," Floyd replied, but sounded unconvinced. "But if we get caught, we'll *both* go to jail, and I don't think Will Mason is gonna care who paid for what."

Cooper slammed his glass down on the bar and, with no little difficulty, defeated the urge to yell at Endicott. "Goddamn it, Floyd, quit bellyachin' and take what I'm offering you. Now, I got the wagon loaded and tied up out back of the livery. I'm goin' out to the Ford place tonight, and I expect you to come with me. If you don't, you won't even get four dollars. You'll get no dollars."

Floyd looked up at Cooper from under the brim of his greasy, gnarled hat. Pulling a small chaw of tobacco from his pocket, he bit off a hunk and grumbled around it, "Yeah, I'll come. But I'm not sure I much like it."

Chapter Thirteen

Numb and yet beset with a strange kind of grief, Allie stood at the back screen door, staring at Jeff's lean-to across the yard. A variety of emotions assailed her—betrayal, astonishment, and a bone-deep hurt that she could barely comprehend. The night was still warm, but her hands were icy with a cold that seemed to radiate from deep within her. She reached for her shawl where it hung on a hook by the door and drew it around her shoulders.

In the wake of the intense drama with Olivia, she had asked Jeff to leave them alone, and he had done so. But once he'd gone outside, Allie realized that she had nothing to say to her sister. Olivia had followed her around the kitchen, weeping and pleading, protesting her innocence and Jeff's guilt. She had even fallen to her knees and tried to soak up the water on the floor with her skirt.

For reasons she still couldn't define, Allie had felt nothing. She'd simply stood there, staring down at her sister with a sense of detachment that was with her even now. That place within her chest where she normally felt pain or gladness had turned oddly empty, leaving an awful, hollow nothingness. Unable to bring herself to speak one word, she'd gone about the business of mopping the kitchen floor.

Olivia, who was unaccustomed to being ignored, had finally flown to her bedroom and slammed the door, sobbing at the top of her lungs. Her wails could be heard downstairs and out in the yard, reminding Allie of nothing more than a spoiled, thwarted child having a tantrum. She had quieted down as dusk gathered, and Allie thanked God for the peace.

Afterward, she'd gone to her own room to wash and change into her nightgown, hoping to escape her terrible loneliness in sleep. But sleep would not come to her. Her cheekbone ached where the pan had struck it, and it had positively throbbed whenever she lay down. That pain, though, was nothing compared to her sense of betrayal. All these years she'd devoted to Olivia, defending her, deferring to her, believing that she herself deserved no life beyond this house and the farm upon which it was built. The thoughts had kept spinning through her tired mind, and she'd left her bed again to come downstairs.

Now that full night had fallen, Allie was certain she'd never felt more alone in her life. As she remained at the door, her fingertips resting on the nubby texture of the screen, she considered the fact that she had no family from whom to draw comfort. She never had. Her father and Olivia had always been their own family, shutting Allie out in subtle but obvious ways, both of them blaming her for a moment of inattention, a single heartbeat of time upon which four lives had turned and irrevocably changed. Father and Olivia had had each other. And after Amos Ford died, Olivia had Allie.

But Allie had no one.

There was no familiar shoulder where she could rest her head or her ice-bound heart, no one to help her pass this night of terrible emptiness and disillusionment.

She glanced up at the cloudless, blue-black sky and saw the moon, a buttery half-round, with stars flung around it like jewels.

That's your moon up there tonight, Allie . . .

Jeff had given her a summer moon one night when she had still believed she knew her world and everything in it. One night a lifetime ago.

There was no light coming from the window in the lean-to, so he was probably asleep.

In bed.

He was hardly more than an acquaintance.

She touched the tucks on the bodice of her nightgown, letting her fingers trail over her breasts. To go to a man dressed only in a nightgown and shawl was so inappropriate she supposed it was downright immoral. And it seemed doubly so, given the kiss they'd shared this afternoon and the thoughts she'd had about him, hot and disconcerting. She had watched him all these weeks gaining strength and rugged confidence. He was not the broken-down drunk he'd been when she met him, dirty and needing nourishment and a haircut. Now he was almost fully restored to the tall, vital, lean-muscled man she'd once admired as he'd walked down the street in Decker Prairie.

But he'd known pain and disappointment, and the shock of a life turned suddenly upside down. It was almost as if he called her, urging her to come to him.

Perhaps in the company of a stranger she would find the understanding and consolation that her own kin had denied her.

Allie tightened her wrap and pushed open the screen door.

Jeff lay naked in his bed, a restless drifter through the night, not awake yet not asleep. The sun had pounded down on the lean-to all day, and the tiny room was still like an oven. His rough sheet seemed to brush the nerves raging just beneath his bare skin, rousing him whenever he dozed. As he tossed and turned, images of a red-haired woman floated through his dreams. She was sweetly curved, with skin like honeyed cream and a soft body that had never known a man's touch.

In this twilight place, he imagined that she came to his bed to lie beside him, her hair flowing over the pillow like tongues of flame. His body responded, hard and keen, to the feel of her smooth thigh against his. He could not move to embrace her. Instead, he lay paralyzed in a helpless fever-pitch as she caressed him and ran her hands over his chest and belly.

Jeff, I've been waiting for you . . . waiting all my life . . .
Her fingers trailed lower, and he heard himself groan.
I need you, Allie, to give me back my soul again.
I love you, Jeff, more than you can know . . .

The distant sound of an owl woke him, making him aware of the sheet on his skin once again. Jeff lurched to consciousness. He was alone in the hot darkness, slick with sweat, uncertain of his surroundings. It had been just a dream, he realized, a sweet, unattainable dream. A feeling of profound disappointment settled on him like a stone.

Allie wasn't with him. She hadn't touched him or called his name or said she loved him. Just this afternoon, hadn't she told him that she thought about him? Hadn't he held her and kissed her and fought the urge to take her right there, in the tall grass? Yes. But the other events of the afternoon came flooding back over him—Olivia, the bitchy, spoiled brat, and Allie, confused and disillusioned by what she'd learned. For his own part, Jeff sometimes thought of the hero in the old fairy tale about Briar Rose, trying to hack his way through a wall of thornbushes to reach the princess. The Fords had a whole briar patch of problems, both literally and figuratively, and Allie stood at the center of them. Jeff was certainly no hero—his saber was nothing more than a history of loss and a future of uncertainty.

He rolled over on his side and looked at the empty place beside him lighted by a wedge of moonbeam pouring through the open door. But as he watched, a long, feminine shadow fell across the bed. No figure appeared in the entry, and all his muscles tensed. Jesus, maybe it was Olivia Ford, here to exact some kind of revenge for exposing her charade.

"Jeff?" The voice was so tentative it could have been a breath of night breeze through the willows. But he recognized it immediately.

Allie came to the doorway dressed in only a nightgown and her shawl, her hair falling around her like a girl's. Jeff was acutely conscious of his nakedness and his state of arousal that was obvious beneath the sheet. He wasn't a man given to personal modesty, and being undressed in front of a woman had never bothered him. But Allie Ford wasn't just any woman. He sat up, hoping the darkness would hide his desire.

"Allie—are you all right?"

She advanced a step. "Well, I was wondering if—that is, would it be all right if I sat with you for a while?"

He couldn't see her face in the shadows, but the moonlight gleamed through her thin gown, revealing the shape of her legs. He wanted to tell her that she shouldn't have come, that seeing her like this after his dream, after thinking about her all day and craving her every night, could very well make him forget what few manners he still possessed. But how could he send her away? She sounded so vulnerable, so defeated.

"Uh, sure, Allie. I'm sorry I'm not dressed for callers."

He rearranged the sheet around him and put his pillow behind his back. Then he lit the kerosene lantern that sat on
the windowsill next to him. The small room sprang to light
and shadow.

Allie stepped inside and perched on an old chair he'd
taken from the barn and put next to the bed. The faint,
sweet fragrance of lavender seemed to rise from the folds
of her gown as it would rise from a field planted with the
flowers.

"It's a long night for you, isn't it?"

She sighed, folding and unfolding her hands in her lap.
"Yes, and it's not even ten o'clock yet. I feel as if . . . as if
someone pulled the floor out from under me. Everything is
topsy-turvy. Do you know what I mean?"

Oh, how he knew. "I've had some experience with that,
yes."

"Of course, I suppose you have." She dipped her head
in a way that revealed the angry bruise on her face. Jeff
sucked in his breath.

"Jesus Christ!" Instinctively he reached out to take her
chin and turned her injured cheek toward the lantern. Even
her eye was a bit swollen. "Did your sister hit you?"

"No. You know . . . Olivia throws things during her
spells. This afternoon she threw a pan and it glanced off
my cheek before she flung it through the window. I'm sure
she didn't mean—I don't think she meant to hit me with
it."

"Is the bone broken?"

She touched her fingertips to the bruise and pressed gingerly. "I-I don't think so."

It looked so painful, and just the knowledge that she was
hurting turned up the fire under his boiling kettle about
Olivia. "I've seen men beat up like this after a bar fight."

He released her chin and it began to quiver. She dropped her gaze to her lap.

Damn it, could he be any more tactless? he wondered. Allie had had a lousy life, he concluded, and he knew only the very thin top layer of it. Deeper than that were years of loneliness and servitude to a sister who knew exactly how to get what she wanted. He wanted to pull her off that chair and into bed with him, just to cuddle her and protect her. "Hell, honey, I didn't mean to say that. I'm sorry," he murmured and took her icy hand. "This'll heal, and you'll be as pretty as ever."

She jerked her hand away and a sob rose in her throat. "Pretty! I don't care about that! What does pretty matter? I took care of my father and I took care of Olivia. I did everything I was ever asked, except that one time. And that one time, just that one horrible, single mistake, led me to this." She gestured at her cheek. "It was all my fault, but if not for that, why, I would have left here years ago! I had dreams once, about a home and family of my own, far away from here."

She looked at him with her mouth slightly open, obviously as surprised as he was by her statement.

He reached for her hand again. "Allie, tell me about it. I think you need to tell someone, and I want to hear it. What mistake did you make that was so bad?"

"I killed my mother!"

She'd said it earlier that day, too, but he didn't believe it. It had to be something else. Something that had haunted Allie every day of her life since it happened. But she obviously believed what she'd told him, so he went along with her.

"How? What did you do?"

Tears welled in her eyes but she remained mute.

"Allie, honey, how did you kill your mother?"

She dropped her gaze to her lap again, as if looking at him were too painful to bear. When she finally spoke, her voice trembled, like an old woman's. "From the day that Olivia was born, my mother wasn't quite—well, she wasn't quite right. Dr. Brewster said she had melancholia, that it was a common ailment following childbirth, and that women usually come out of it. Except Mama never did. It dragged on for months, and if anything, she seemed to get worse. She'd sit by the window all day long and stare at nothing. Or she'd stay in bed. She rejected Olivia. She wouldn't even n-nurse her, so I had to feed her with a bottle. Father didn't have much patience with Mama's strangeness. He expected her to get better, and right away." She fixed her gaze on the wall, a curiously distant look entering her eyes. " 'No more of this nonsense!' he'd say. 'You snap of this, woman. Right now, I say, or by God, I'll know the reason why.' " Her gaze flicked to Jeff, then back to her lap. "Only she didn't seem to hear him. Not really. So he took me out of school to see to things around the house."

"All the chores fell to you? God, Allie, how old were you, eight or nine?"

"Yes. He was busy with the farm, and I was the only one who could help. I did the cleaning and cooking and washing. I took care of Olivia and Mama."

"Your father didn't want to hire someone to help?"

She looked up at him then. "Dr. Brewster suggested it. But Father said it was *my* job. The Fords took care of their own, he said. So I was responsible for running the house. I did everything I was told to, or I'd get a licking."

The picture forming in Jeff's mind was of a flinty, bitter man who enslaved his own child and probably browbeat his wife. Hell, no wonder she didn't come out of her melancholia.

"One day, I convinced Mama to get dressed and come for a walk with me. I'd fed Olivia and put her down for a nap, so I had a little time before I had to start dinner. It was spring and I thought that getting out on a nice April day would be good for her."

Jeff listened as Allie went on, telling the story of how she walked her mother across a fallow field down to the creek. The cottonwoods were leafing out and wildflowers were blooming along the edge of the clear, gurgling stream.

Allie stared at the lantern flame on the windowsill, lost in another time. "I sat my mother down on a blanket I'd brought with us. I can still see her hair, sparkling in the sun. It was the same color as mine, I think. She didn't talk much, so it was almost like being alone. Then I saw the wildflowers. Violets—they were violets. They were so pretty, I wanted to pick some for her. I hoped they'd cheer her up and make her smile again. The flowers were scattered up and down the banks, and they were so small it took me a while to gather enough to make a nice bouquet."

The tears that had been gathering in Allie's eyes began to flow in earnest now, falling in droplets on her tightly folded hands. "When I turned around to look for her she was gone. I didn't realize how much time had passed since I'd last checked on her. I still don't know, but it didn't seem like much. One minute she was sitting on the blanket, the next— Oh, God, I searched everywhere along that creek. I was afraid that maybe she'd fallen in. But there was no sign of her. Nothing." She tipped her head down and closed her eyes.

Jeff stared at Allie, her head bowed and her hands folded like a penitent's, and his heart squeezed in his chest. She looked like a damned soul sitting in that chair, waiting for God's hand to strike her down. He didn't even care if he heard the rest of her story. He wanted to tell her it didn't matter what she had done, she had paid for it many times over. But he'd asked her to tell him about it, and he had to make himself listen.

"What did you do?"

"I ran to the house, hoping she'd gone back inside. But I checked every room, even the closets. She wasn't there. Then I remembered that sometimes, before Olivia came, she'd liked to feed the barn cats. They never let her get close, but she'd leave kitchen scraps for them." She wadded up the tails of her shawl in her fists, and recounted to Jeff the ghastly discovery she'd made in the barn, so like the day with the dummy, but a thousand times more horrific. Listening to her, Jeff felt the hair on the back of his neck rise, and despite the heat, shivers flew down his back and arms.

"F-Father said it was my fault. He screamed at me—it was the only time—and he damned me to hell for lolly-gagging. He said I killed his wife and Olivia's mother. I should have been watching her instead of frittering away my time and attention looking for flowers. We took Mama to the undertaker in town. Then when we got back, h-he locked me in the barn. He'd make sure he taught me a lesson, one I wouldn't forget, by God. I begged and cried to get out and pounded on the door—I was s-so scared, so scared— But he left me in there until morning. And after that, every time he thought I was bad, he locked me in the barn! Oh, God, I *hated* him for it!" She appealed to Jeff, as if seeking answers or some explanation from him so that she might understand. "Why did he do that to me? I was only eight years old!"

She wept bitter tears and wore such a wild expression that even now Jeff feared for her sanity in dredging up these old memories. It was all too clear to him now, her fear of the barn, her zealous attention to her parents' graves, her slavish devotion to her sister. He gripped her clenched hands in his, thinking that if Amos Ford weren't already dead, he'd take great pleasure in seeing the man horsewhipped. And Jeff, fool that he was, had planted a row of violets in the garden, hoping to please her. "Allie, it's all right now. All right. And I'm sorry about the violets in the garden—I didn't know. I just wanted to make you happy." God, he was babbling like she was. "It wasn't your fault. You didn't kill your mother—you see that now, don't you?"

She went on, though, as if Jeff hadn't spoken, purging anger and demons that had plagued her since she was a child. "On his deathbed he made me promise to take care of Olivia, his darling Olivia. I've stayed by her, believing she was sick and helpless, that she needed me. It was the least I could do to atone for the terrible wrong I'd committed. To find out that she has tricked me all this time, pretending to be sick, that she was the one who hung that dummy in the barn—" She looked at him with such anguish and bewilderment in her eyes, Jeff felt his own throat grow tight with emotion. "I know my father hated me. He always made me feel like an outsider, and he never forgave me, not even at the last moment of his life. But Olivia must hate me, too, to do those things!"

Jeff needed to hold her, to comfort her and himself. Shy about letting her see the tears gathering behind his own eyelids, he grabbed her shoulders and pulled her off the chair into his embrace. The corn-husk mattress rustled as Allie fell against him on the bed and sobbed as if her heart were broken. He swallowed the hard knot in his throat and rocked her, pressing her head to his chest while he stroked her silky hair. Silently, he cursed both Amos and Olivia Ford. God, Allie had had no love in her life at all.

"No, honey, it's not hate, exactly. Olivia isn't capable

of considering anyone else's feelings but her own. She's spoiled and used to getting her own way. Like I said, I think she's trying to make sure you won't leave her. But what she's done is wrong. And you did not kill your mother." Jeff lifted his head and stared through the window at the moon crossing the midsummer night sky. Wes Matthews' young, battered face appeared in his memory, bringing with it a dim realization. "Some people can't be saved no matter how we try."

"You don't think it was my fault?" Her words were muffled with her cheek pressed to his chest.

"Hell no! Allie, your father did a lousy thing, punishing you for your mother's death—a child can't be held responsible for the actions of an adult. I guess when it comes down to it, we're not really responsible for anyone's actions but our own."

"But I was supposed to watch after her and—"

"Yes, and you said yourself that you were just eight years old. It sounds like she was so lost and unhappy, she would have found the opportunity no matter what. If not then, maybe later. Who knows, your love and attention might have prevented it from happening sooner."

She sat up and looked at him, a desperate gleam of hope for absolution in her teary eyes. Ironic that she should seek it from him, of all people. "Oh—do you really think so?" She turned her face to the doorway and her brow wrinkled. "I missed her very much. I think it started long before she died. The mother I knew disappeared and had been replaced by a silent, despondent stranger."

Jeff felt such remorse for Allie, he pulled her back into his arms, barely aware that only a sheet separated his nakedness from her. He couldn't think of a plausible, comforting comment to make, so he did the only thing he could think of and held her close.

No one—certainly not Amos or Olivia Ford—had apparently given any thought to the fact that Allie had lost her mother, too, and the nurturing that any child should have had. But it occurred to Jeff. "If I had the power, Allie, I swear I'd turn back the clock and make it all different."

He held her and stroked her back. She was fine-boned and delicate under his touch.

At this moment, it felt as if he were doing a very important job, taking care of Allie. She was independent and capable, but she had a tender vulnerability that made him want to protect her. What a hell of a tangle their lives were in, though. Even after everything that Olivia had done, he doubted that Allie was likely to abandon her charge. Her sense of responsibility was lifelong and too ingrained to turn her back on. He'd move on at the end of summer and always wonder what could have been if they had met at a different time and place. Allie and her kindness would be just a memory he could warm himself with on empty nights.

But for now, time seemed to stop here in this little room, and it was safe to let himself realize that he'd fallen in love with her.

She began to quiet in his arms. Either his words gave her comfort, or more likely, she'd simply worn herself out. It felt so good to hold her, though, almost tantalizing. He had to remind himself that she had come to him as a friend, and that she had no one else to turn to. But hell, he was just a man, and as she shifted a bit, he was again painfully aware that only a couple flimsy layers of fabric separated their bodies and bare skin.

His thoughts returned to his dream of Allie's smooth, pale skin and long, slender thigh lying along his, and for the first time in years, he thought he might find his own soul again in Allie Ford's warmth. But what right did he have to seek it? Hadn't she given him more than he deserved? Because of her he was able to stand tall again. His hands were steady, and he knew the satisfaction of doing a day's hard work and doing it well. She didn't owe him more than that, and she deserved a better man than him. But if time had truly stopped and tomorrow were not coming, he'd tell her she'd stolen his heart. He'd get down on his knees and beg her . . .

Allie rested against Jeff, and her sobs slowed to sniffles as a kind of relief stole over her. Just the sound of his voice was comforting to her. How strange and yet how right it felt to be in this man's arms. And despite all that had happened, the weight on her shoulders seemed a bit lighter. Maybe it was just because she'd finally gotten to tell somebody the secrets she'd carried in her heart for years, ones that she had hidden even from herself. And not only had Jeff not judged her, he had defended her. No one had ever done that. No one before had even asked what she thought.

But now that the storm raging within her had quieted, she felt a little awkward. What must he think of her, a hysterical woman who'd barged in on his privacy? His handsome face was blank, as if his thoughts had traveled beyond their conversation, and his eyes were dark and unfathomable in the shadows. The two of them were scarcely decent, he with no shirt and in bed, for heaven's sake, and she wearing only a shawl and a nightgown.

She pulled away from him and sat up, wiping her eyes on the handkerchief she pulled from her nightgown pocket. "I'm sorry. I didn't mean to wake you up from a sound sleep and cry all over you. Thank you for listening and, well, everything." She stood and adjusted her shawl. It was really too hot in here now to wear it, but it was all that covered her gown. "I'd better go back to the house."

"Allie, stop apologizing. You have nothing to be sorry

for. Nothing. Anyway, I wasn't sleeping soundly." He
glanced up at her from under sandy brows, and the heat in
his eyes said a hundred things that his husky voice did not.
"Stay . . . please . . . I don't want you to go."

Allie swallowed. She had no knowledge of men or the
mysteries that existed between a man and a woman. But
without being told, she knew what he wanted. It both
thrilled and frightened her.

"N-no?"

Keeping his eyes on her, he shook his head slightly.
"No."

She didn't take the hand he held out to her but word-
lessly she groped behind her for the chair and sat down
again. Her knees bumped the edge of the corn-husk mattress where he sat with his back propped against the pillow.
Her mind and heart were galloping neck and neck, at top
speed; the first asked if she knew what she was doing, the
other urged her to ignore the question.

Though she'd been in this room for the better part of an
hour already, she just now really noticed Jeff's appearance.
In fact, she noticed everything. Could this possibly be the
same man who'd appeared at her doorstep in May, dishev-
eled and derelict? He'd regained the natural grace she'd
noticed long ago. His sun-streaked hair was sleep-tousled,
and his shoulders were wider than she had realized. The
faint shadow of his beard outlined his firm jaw and chin.
Lean, hard muscle defined the breadth of his chest and the
strength in his arms. His flat belly bore a narrow strip of
hair down its center that disappeared beneath the sheet that
barely topped his hipbones. Dear God, but he was a beautiful man, the most handsome one she had ever seen. Not
that she had seen all that many.

Her attention moved downward, over his pelvis, over the
shape of his long legs beneath the sheet, and back to his

hips again. When Allie realized where her eyes had strayed to, her face burned and her heart thudded in her rib cage. His very maleness drew her, and she felt womanly in a way that she had known only in his presence. She realized that they had been moving toward this moment since the day she met him.

Jeff swung his legs over the side of the bed, the sheet still wound around his middle. "Allie," he whispered, and took her hand to press a kiss into her palm. "I owe you a lot, and I've got nothing in this world to give you. I used to be a man of some standing. Now, well, you know what happened to me. A lot of it was my fault, and some of it was just fate and bad luck. I don't know what's coming tomorrow, honey. But there's tonight—there's still tonight. If you'll have me."

Modesty tugged at her. She should refuse. She should demand an apology and when she had it, storm back to the house in a huff of outraged female virtue. Society's conventions of decency would require that she do so.

But society's conventions had been cold comfort to her all her life. Far stronger than modesty was the yearning she had to share a closeness with Jeff that allowed nothing else to get in the way. No bad memories or silent indictments haunting her from the burying ground, no Olivia, no blame for past deeds or failures. She didn't need to be the mother or the servant. Instead, she would be a woman. Looking into his lean, handsome face, she saw sincerity. He was offering her the chance to feel close to someone for the first time in her life, perhaps for the only time.

"Your past doesn't matter to me, Jeff. I think you're a good man, with a good heart, and I can't ask for more than that." Meeting his searing green eyes, she returned the kiss on the work-roughened hand that held hers. "I'll have you."

Jeff closed his eyes and sighed, the way a condemned

man might if he was granted a last wish. Then he gazed at her for a long moment. "Come to me, then." He pulled her out of the chair to sit beside him on the bed, and her shawl fell away. Touching gentle fingertips to her bruised cheek, he followed them with soft kisses that brushed her ear and hairline. Pleasurable shivers flew down her arms and over her scalp, and shyly, she turned her lips to his.

His kiss was more demanding than it had been this afternoon. She had been unwilling to stop him then—now, with the exquisite feeling of his lips on hers, she put her arms around his neck and gave herself up like a wanton. Fiercely he took her mouth as he plunged his hands into her hair and held her, threading his fingers through the strands. When she felt his tongue tease her lips apart, her breath came faster as if trying to keep pace with her thundering heart.

He smelled of the wind-dried bedding and of sun and an essence that was his alone, making Allie think of the bare elements of earth and sky. Pulling back, he ran his hands up and down her bare arms while his gaze touched her lightly. Then he reached for the kerosene lamp and turned down its wick, plunging the little room into darkness and the dim, gray-white light of the moon.

He threw back the sheet and pulled her onto the bed with him. In the feeble light she glimpsed a dark, imposing shadow low on his torso at the juncture of his long legs. With detached surprise she realized that he had nothing on at all. He was naked.

Jeff propped himself up on one elbow and looked down into her face. "Allie, you're as pretty as a red rose in the snow."

Her emotions choked off any reply she might have made. No one had ever said something so nice to her. Prim Althea Ford, one of "those crazy Ford sisters," lay in the arms of a beautiful, naked man who found beauty in her as well, and she reveled in it. He followed his compliment with another deep kiss. Hot and slick and insistent, it shook her to the very core. She reached up to touch his ribs and her hand brushed his bare hip. Growing more daring, she caressed his hard-muscled buttock and he groaned faintly.

His fingers whispered over her breast, stopping at the row of tiny buttons closing her nightgown. With poorly concealed impatience, he unfastened them, all the while laying a line of kisses up her throat and over her jaw. His warm breath in her ear raised goose bumps on her arms, and when he ran his tongue over her lobe, she shuddered.

At last her nightgown lay open to Jeff's touch and she froze, waiting, hoping that he would touch her again the way he had that afternoon. Instead, he leaned over her and caught her nipple in his mouth, lightly suckling at her breast. Allie gasped at the intense sensation and sank her fingers into his hair. Bolts of electricity seemed to shoot directly from her breast to her womb, and an aching hunger that she had never known before began to simmer in her.

After he treated her other nipple to the same attention, she arched against him, a small moan rising from her throat. He smoothed his hands over her legs, pushing her nightgown higher with each pass. Finally, with a muttered curse, he gripped the hem and pulled the garment off over her head and flung it to the end of the bed. Allie lay as naked as Jeff. He pulled her up against the length of his warm body, and they embraced skin to skin, their limbs tangling.

"Allie, God, you feel so good—like cream, like velvet. I've lain here every night imagining you with me, in my arms. But I never knew it would feel this good."

She'd had no idea he'd given her any such thought at all. "Jeff . . ." She could say nothing more, but she didn't need to. With some of her shyness stripped away by the desire he kindled in her, she reached out to touch him, to feel the silky hair scattered across his chest, the smooth, hard muscle in his arms, the ladders of his ribs. His erection, pulsing and hot, pressed insistently against her thigh.

At the same time, Jeff pushed her to her back and moved the flat of his hand down over her belly, lower and lower, until his hand covered the warm apex of her thighs. Every nerve in her body arced beneath her skin and the longing that had begun to grow in her now escalated. With a careful, deliberate touch, he grazed that most sensitive part of her, inexplicably wet. She jumped, accidentally nipping his shoulder with her teeth.

"God, woman, you're a she-cat," he said with a low huff of laughter.

"I'm sorry—"

"Don't be." He lowered his head and tugged on her nipple again with his mouth.

Her sudden movement had bumped his hand away, but he came back again, seeking the slick folds and delicate, innermost flesh, massaging her with light, rapid strokes.

Allie thought her heart would surely burst in her chest, it beat so hard. Though she had a virgin's inexperience, her shameless body seemed to have a will of its own, and did as it wanted. She heard herself moan in response to Jeff's touch. Her hips thrust upward to meet his hand, giving him complete access to continue the sweet torment he inflicted upon her.

"Jeff, please. Oh, please—"

She believed she might lose her mind if he didn't stop, and that she most certainly would if he did. All the while he muttered encouragement and endearments against her ear, urging her to do something, but just what she didn't know. Perspiration drenched her as she pushed against his hand again and again. When she believed that she could take no more of this tender torture, her body climbed to a knife-sharp precipice and teetered there for a breathless, dizzying instant. Then it flung itself into wave upon wave of contractions that racked her, releasing the pent-up yearning. She sobbed Jeff's name and he answered her with some wordless sound in the darkness.

Nearly limp from the chaos of emotions and feelings that had gripped her, Allie couldn't speak. All she could do was hold out welcoming arms to him.

Jeff answered her summons, covering her swiftly and showering her face and temples with quick, warm kisses. "I'll be careful, Allie, I swear," he whispered roughly.

Maybe at another time, Jeff would have taken a moment to soothe Allie and let her catch her breath. But her feverish release and the temptation of her sweetness had driven him to the point of near climax. Now she lay open and ripe before him with her hair spilling around her like a medieval bride, compelling him to ease the demanding ache that dragged at his belly.

Mindful of her virginity, he pushed forward to join her moist, heated flesh and met resistance. Allie froze beneath him and her pliant limbs tensed. A whimper of pain sounded in her throat.

"Jeff—"

"It's all right," he intoned, "it'll be all right." Steadily, he pressed past the seal on her femininity that had stood like a sentinel, waiting for this night, waiting for him. She squirmed, as if to pull away.

Jeff sheathed himself, then he gripped her hips to hold her still. "Wait, Allie—it'll pass." It took every ounce of willpower he had to lie within her tight warmth and not move. Fire licked through him—Allie felt like a glove of molten honey surrounding him. Staring down into her beautiful face, he lowered his head to kiss her. When he could stand it no longer, he deepened the kiss and completed their joining with a long, slow stroke.

Allie relaxed as the discomfort subsided, relishing the feel of Jeff inside her. He was part of her now, and always would be no matter what happened. Running her hands over his back, she felt the hollow of his spine, and the powerful flex of tendon and muscle.

"God, Allie," he groaned, his breathing rough and ragged. He thrust again and again, faster now. As he did, she felt a restless urgency building again. It grew with each push and pull that Jeff plied her with, and she gripped the edge of the mattress. Could it happen again, that sensation so pleasurable that it verged upon pain? That loss of self that transcended the body—almost as if their very souls touched?

Faster and more powerful was each stroke, carrying Allie ever closer to that exquisite conflagration. She lifted her hips, and Jeff pushed himself up to the full length of his arms. Gazing up at him, she found him beautiful and masterful, bathed in sweat and moonlight. He drove her on, advancing, ebbing, until Allie felt as if her earthly body were stripped away, leaving only her soul. Her muscles contracted fiercely, pulling Jeff into her with surging spasms that left her weeping and calling him.

Jeff plunged forward, harder, more urgent, more desperate for his own release. He seemed to tower over her, and she saw the tendons in his neck defined by the moonlight. At last, with one final thrust he strained hard against her body while a low, anguished groan escaped him and white-hot pulsations shook him. Lowering himself to his elbows, he buried his face against her neck.

Finally, their breathing slowed and Jeff sighed with a sound of replete contentment. He rolled them over slowly, and they lay in the darkness with the sheets tangled around them, listening to the soft night. From its quiet came the faint croak of the frogs down at the creek.

"Are you comfortable?" he asked, pressing a kiss to her forehead.

"Yes, I'm fine. Jeff . . . did—did I do it right?"

She felt him chuckle. "You did it better than right."

"I guess you have lots of experience, being a man and—"

"Allie, there has been no other woman since my wife. Just you."

That pleased her enormously, although she couldn't say why.

This communion, the giving as well as taking—this was what it meant to love someone completely, Allie realized, with heart and mind and body. Putting her hand on his chest, she felt his heart beating beneath her palm, strong and steady. Her own emotions lay so close to the surface, she wished she could tell Jeff about the love she held for him. But shyness and fear of rejection held her back. What would he think—that one of those Ford sisters, and the spinster of the pair to boot, fancied herself to be in love with him? No, she had this night, just as he'd said, and she would live on its memory for the rest of her life.

But what kind of life would it be? Would she be able to forgive Olivia for her duplicity? Her options were just about nonexistent, as they often were for women.

"I don't know how I'll go on now," she said, her words muffled against his shoulder. "Things will never be the same between my sister and me, and I can't act as if they are. But I can't really imagine leaving her, either. I'm not sure she would survive."

If God or Fate had ever handed a man a golden opportunity, Jeff knew he was getting one now. With Althea Ford he felt whole again. He could not forget Wesley Matthews or the night at Wickwire's—the event had worn a groove in his mind that would never go away. But drowning himself in whiskey had not brought the boy back, either. Nothing would. For the first time in two years, Jeff thought there might be hope for the future.

Before he had time to overthink it, he lifted Allie's chin so that he could look into her eyes. He spoke with the urgent desperation of a captive who saw a chance to escape his prison. "Come away with me, Allie. We'll go away from this place, even leave Decker Prairie. There's nothing for us here."

Allie clutched the sheet to her breasts and stared at him, plainly amazed by his suggestion. "You mean leave Olivia?" Even now, after everything that had happened, he knew her ties to her duty were strong.

"Yes, that's exactly what I mean." He spoke in earnest, hushed tones, and brushed her injured cheek with a tender touch. "Allie, do you—maybe you feel—" The words came hard to Jeff. He wanted to tell her how he felt about her, that some nights he dreamed of holding her in his arms and dancing with her until sunrise. But sometimes those dreams ended with him clutching nothing except the wind to his chest. Trust was something he'd lost—Sally had stolen most of it, and the past years had taken the rest. God, he wanted to tell her that he loved her, but it scared him spitless when he thought of taking that risk again. Her moonlit expression was expectant, as if she waited to hear more from him than he could tell her. He smoothed her hair back from her forehead. "I don't want to promise something I can't deliver. So I guess I'm asking a lot without offering much." The missing pieces of his suggestion were obvious, and by their very absence, lay between them like a third entity in the bed. "But a life with me will be better than what you've had here, I promise that."

Allie continued to watch him in the darkness. Leave Olivia? He knew it was an earthshaking suggestion, even though she'd admitted to wishing she were gone from here. But Jeff had said nothing of marriage. In fact, he had not spoken of love, and he felt like a coward for it. He knew the feeling he had for her, though, as strong and vital as a living thing. Maybe it would be enough to heal them both eventually. Maybe.

"I—I'll have to think about it, Jeff."

Pulling her into his arms, he was filled with an aching tenderness he'd not felt in such a long time, it was almost a stranger to him. Jeff couldn't remember the last time he'd felt so much emotion that wasn't tinged with guilt or regret. "I understand, Allie. You think it over. But I really believe there's a future for us now. A reason to keep looking forward."

Allie turned her face against his neck and Jeff sighed, knowing that sleep would come to him more easily tonight.

Just then, over the top of Allie's head he caught sight of another feminine shadow lurking just outside the door. Olivia. The shadow vanished then, and he heard the faintest sound of bare feet retreating. He opened his mouth to tell Allie, and then changed his mind. He guessed that this was one of the few happy moments in Allie's life thus far, and he didn't want it tarnished by any talk of Olivia.

If her sister had stood outside listening, he didn't like it, but so be it. Maybe she would realize that there was more to life than living like a mannequin in a store window, with a servant to do her bidding.

Chapter Fourteen

A HORSE NICKERED OUTSIDE.

A fine, sleek filly kicked up her heels in a new corral that Jeff had built with his own hands, on the land that he owned. He should go out there and give her a ration of oats, but another filly, his beautiful, flame-haired wife, was commanding all of his attention right now. She stood before him in their bedroom, her slim fingers slowly and deliberately unbuttoning each button on his shirt, one at a time. He saw desire, warm and smoky, in her eyes. Then she slipped her warm hands inside to caress his ribs and back, and she pressed damp kisses to his chest. She smelled of lavender and rainwater, and he knew the promise of intense pleasure waited in her lips and soft curves.

Jeff stirred and realized he'd been dreaming again. He was still in the lean-to. But this time, Allie was with him. He pulled her closer, pressing his cheek against her silky hair. She lay on her side within his embrace, with her soft bottom nestled against his groin. He could spend ten thousand nights like this, a million. With Allie at his side the future, which had recently looked so bleak, now seemed full of possibilities.

The most beautiful part was, they had all the time in the world to plan for it. He smiled in groggy contentment before he began to drift off again.

Then he heard another nicker. He was instantly alert. It was real, not part of a dream. He waited, not breathing, not moving, just listening. His heart pounded in his chest.

There was no horse on the Ford farm. Even Kansas, Elisha Smithfield's old mule, had been returned to its rightful owner. Someone was out there. He heard a drone of low male voices, rising and falling as if buffeted by the wind, too indistinct for him to understand over the blood rushing through his head.

After tucking Allie in more securely, he eased himself from the bed, silently cursing the corn-husk mattress for crackling like a crate of burning tissue paper.

"Jeff?"

"It's all right, honey, you go back to sleep."

She lifted herself up to one elbow. "What's the matter?"

"I just want to check on something outside. I thought I heard a noise. It's probably nothing." Closing his hand over his belt buckle to keep it from clanking, he grabbed his pants and put them on.

"Oh, well, come back soon."

He stepped over to the bed and dropped a kiss on her forehead. "I will." Then he groped in the shadows for his boots, but couldn't find them. He couldn't go tearing out into possible danger barefoot, but neither could he risk lighting a lantern. Damn it, he needed to get out there, now, to see what was going on.

Just as he was about to give up and take his chances in the thistles and blackberries outside, his hand fell upon leather. Forgoing socks, he jerked on the boots, then crept out of the lean-to, quiet as a cat and keeping to the shadows. He wasn't sure what time it was, but a glance at the low-slung moon and the eastern sky told him it must be just moments before dawn. Next to the barn stood an axe that he'd sharpened just the day before, and he wrapped his fingers around the handle.

By the eerie light of the coming dawn, he saw a distant feminine figure running along the path that led from the field to the house. Stripped of any discernible color by the ethereal gloom, her dress seemed to almost glow against the backdrop of darkness, the full skirts drifting around her like a ghostly shroud. Olivia. What the hell was she up to out here? She stopped to look at him, like a deer in flight, then shot off again and scurried to the shelter of the back porch. He didn't bother to talk to her; she was close enough to safety if she needed it.

Barely breathing so he could hear, he took to the same path she had used. Careful. Twigs, parched weeds, and last autumn's withered leaves carpeted the earth. Each time he stepped, the debris snapped and rustled beneath his boots. He hunched low and crept forward cautiously. Probing the shadows with eyes that burned with the strain, he felt the muscles in his shoulders and back knot up with tension.

Again he heard men's voices, louder now, as if in argument. Ahead of him, a parked wagon loomed in stark silhouette next to the field he'd planted. Instinct honed by his years as a lawman made him extremely wary, and for the first time since he'd shot Wes, he wished he had a gun strapped to his hip. God. Even if he had one, could he hold a steady bead on a target? Thoughts galloped through his mind—he wished he had a gun, he wished he had a drink, he wished he had more courage so his insides would stop shaking.

He felt the smooth axe handle beneath his rough palm. It was no match for a shotgun, but if he was lucky, the intruders wouldn't be armed. He almost laughed. Who besides Jeff himself would trespass on another's property in the middle of the night without a gun?

Still crouching low to the ground, he crept up to the small wagon, raising his head only high enough to scan the field on its opposite side. At his approach, the horse danced restlessly in its harness and gave a nervous snort. Jeff could only hope the sound didn't alert the intruders to his presence. Since he was without a firearm to defend himself, he needed the element of surprise to even out the odds. On the tailgate of the wagon box he saw a large sack. Running his free hand over its contours, he gave it a quick jostle and determined by touch that it held something heavy. The light was too poor for him to read the print on the cloth. What the hell was going on here? He stole another quick glance over the wagon box and tightened his grip on the axe.

Revealed in dim outlines, two men stood at the edge of the field. He moved a bit closer, never forgetting that he was basically unarmed. A flurry of obscenities erupted from the pair, and he recognized the voice of Cooper Matthews.

"You'll get paid! Now do like I told you and let's get the hell away before Hicks catches us. We're almost done."

"You were gonna cheat me, Cooper. And after I stuck by you through thick and thin! You told me she only paid you ten dollars. Not twenty, like she just said! It's been hard work drivin' that wagon all over this field in the dark, not to mention spreadin' this stuff over a plot this size. The sacks weigh fifty pounds apiece! I want my fair share of the take."

Sacks, Jeff puzzled, fury racing through his veins.

"Goddamn it, Floyd, I'm sick of your whinin'!"

"Well, you won't have to listen to me anymore! I've had a bellyful of you." One of the pair—Floyd, Jeff thought—broke away and ran to the wagon.

Jeff stepped forward. "Just stop right there, Floyd!"

The man gaped at Jeff. "Talk to Cooper. This was all his idea!" Throwing a pick into the wagon bed, he pulled himself up to the seat and unwrapped the reins. He flapped them on the horse's back so suddenly the animal whinnied in surprise and took off running across the field, narrowly missing Cooper in the bargain. Floyd yelled, slapped the reins on the horse's back again, and then jerked hard to the left to steer the conveyance toward the road. The wagon squeaked and rattled as it bumped over the plowed earth.

Cooper stood motionless, and then flung his hat down and stomped it. "God*damn* it all to hell! Just wait'll I get my hands on you again, you simpleminded bastard! Your own mama won't recognize you!" he yelled after the wagon.

"It won't be anything compared to what you'll look like when I'm finished putting my hands on *you*, Matthews." Jeff approached Cooper, filled with so much rage that he'd forced himself to leave the axe behind in the blackberries. In his state of mind, it seemed the smart thing to do.

Cooper whirled around and faced Jeff. "Hicks! You ain't the sheriff no more. You can't arrest me for trespassin'."

"Arrest you!" Jeff's laugh was grim. "I'm not interested in anything as formal as all that. I just want to beat the shit out of you. Who the hell do you think you are, you piss-ant, white-livered son of a bitch? You sneaked out here in the dead of night and salted this field!"

"You hold on there with your name-callin', Hicks. Miss *O*-livia Ford paid us twenty dollars to do just that. If you don't believe me, you can ask her yourself."

"She never sets foot off this property. I'm supposed to believe she went searching for you two?"

"I don't give a damn what you believe. I'll tell you something else," Cooper said, chortling, "she paid us to

hang that spook in the barn, too. She said she was playin'
a joke, and by God, I guess it was a good one! Oh, damn,
but I wish I coulda been here to see your faces!" He
laughed outright.

Jeff clenched his back teeth. "Really—you haven't explained how she arranged all this without leaving the
house."

"I don't owe you no kind of explanation, Hicks. But just
so's you'll know, she sent me letters. Seth Wickwire, that
tall, big-eared kid with the rabbit teeth who delivers groceries out here once a week? He brought them to me at the
livery stable."

"Yeah? Where are those letters now?"

"I did like she said—I threw 'em away. But Floyd'll
vouch for me."

As if Floyd Endicott were an upstanding citizen whose
word was his honor. Jeff clenched his jaw so tightly his
head ached. He wanted to call Cooper a liar and shove his
words back down his throat. But, even though the man had
never given Jeff a single reason to trust anything he said,
in this case, he believed him. God, was there no end to
Olivia's hatred of him? She was willing to do anything,
hurt anybody, including her sister, to either get rid of Jeff
or get even with him. He'd worked his ass off, preparing
and planting this stupid field. Now, just to spite him, Olivia
had destroyed the whole crop. To make matters worse,
while Allie pinched and saved every penny she possibly
could, Olivia had pissed away twenty dollars, no small sum.
Obviously it didn't matter if it meant taking the food out
of her own mouth—if she'd thought that far ahead. It was
just so damned senseless—and maybe that was what en-
raged him most of all, the sheer stupidity of it.

Jeff took a deep breath. His anger made his hands shake,
but his voice was steady and dead calm. He leaned forward

to look down into Cooper's bony face. "You get off this land right now, Matthews, and don't ever come here again. Go fast, like the devil was after you. And don't look back, not even once—if you do, I swear to God you might find me behind you."

Nothing Jeff ever said or done seemed to have made much of an impression on Cooper. He was stupid and mean, a bully and a blowhard who enjoyed watching other people squirm. But like all bullies, he was also a coward. Jeff's anger rolled out of him, as palpable in the air as the charged feeling right before a lightning storm. He no longer felt any regret for taking Cooper's son—he still grieved for the boy, but not for his father. All he felt was white-hot rage. Cooper must have sensed it, too, because Jeff smelled his fear now. It came to him in a sickening green wave, from beneath the stench of the man's sweat and body odor.

It felt good—freeing—to watch Cooper grow pale with fear, his face suddenly pasty white in the thin light of the breaking day. It was Cooper's turn to squirm. Maybe a better man would have risen above that kind of pettiness. If Jeff wasn't that kind of man, he didn't care.

"I a-ain't afraid of you."

"The hell you aren't. Go—before I take you apart with my bare hands, you no-account, weasely bastard."

As though spurred by a rowel, Cooper wheeled and lurched into a run across the plowed rows, taking the same general route that the wagon had. When the freshly turned earth gave way under his plodding boots, making him stagger and nearly fall, he didn't slow, and he didn't look back. Not even once.

Allie tried to go back to sleep, but she kept listening for Jeff's return. He was back in only a few minutes.

She saw his silhouette in the dim room and watched as

he shucked his clothes. When he climbed into bed with her, tension radiated from him. He smelled of the night air and, not unpleasantly, sweat.

"Is everything all right?" she asked.

He pulled her into his arms and sighed. "It is now."

She smiled and let sleep take her once more.

Allie awoke to find herself alone in Jeff's bed. A sleepy-eyed glance around the room told her that the sun was already up. Everything was bathed in the bright, yellow-pink light of a summer dawn.

Oh, had last night really happened? Had she given herself to Jeff in that frenzy of heart-pounding passion and tender intimacy? She rolled over and looked at the low ceiling and smiled. Yes, she had and it had been wonderful. She'd given him her heart and body, and in exchange, he'd offered her sanctuary.

It might be the chance to change her life that she'd dreamed of. Could she go with Jeff? Just the idea of escaping from this place made her heart feel lighter. They'd go someplace where no one knew either of them. No longer would she be one of the crazy Ford sisters. He wouldn't be the sheriff who had fallen from grace. Maybe they could put all of the grim days behind them now.

Then her happiness dimmed, and doubt crept in. What if Jeff never opened his heart to her? The scars on his spirit might be so great that no amount of love she gave him could change that. Could she bear living with a man who not only wasn't her husband, but who didn't even love her?

And even if she decided that she could accept such a life, she would have to tell Olivia she was leaving, and Allie didn't think her sister would receive the news with grace or gladness. The promise that Allie had made to her father would demand that she bring Olivia with her to her new home, wherever it might be. It was her duty, regardless of whatever Olivia had done. Dear God, Allie didn't want to. She couldn't. She didn't believe that Jeff or Olivia would want it, either.

She *loved* Olivia, she assured herself feverishly. She *had* to love her, she was her sister. Olivia wouldn't be destitute. There wasn't much of their father's money in the bank in town, but she would have the farm. And although she gave every impression of not knowing how to care for herself, she'd watched Allie for years. Surely she'd learned *something*.

First things first. Clutching the sheet to her chest, Allie swung her legs over the side of the bed. She had to get back to the house and get dressed. Jeff was already up and around, and he'd be wanting his breakfast. She was famished herself this morning. And she didn't want to risk having her sister catch her out here. She threw back the sheet and pulled her nightgown from the footboard where Jeff had thrown it. Wiggling into the garment, she plucked her shawl from the floor and tidied the bed.

Standing in the doorway, she took a last look at the place where Jefferson Hicks had given her hope, and his body and soul to hold, even for just a little while. Then, with a secret smile tucked in her woman's heart, she sped across the yard to the house.

Allie hummed through her chores and created a special breakfast consisting of cornbread, bacon, and fried potatoes. Their redolence filled the kitchen. She decided that she and Jeff would eat together here in the kitchen this morning, so she set the table for two with nice napkins and the good china. It might be a rehearsal for all the mornings to come when they would do this every day. Well, maybe not with good china and table linen, she thought as she poured the coffee. But she would make certain that Jeff had a hearty breakfast to start his days.

It was a beautiful morning, warm but not too hot yet. Outside the birds in the orchard were calling back and forth, and a light breeze rustled the trees. Had there ever been a more spectacular day? she wondered, her heart as light as swan's-down. She knew it was possible for one day to make a huge difference in a person's life—she simply had never considered the possibility that the difference could be positive.

Expecting Jeff to come to the back door any second, she served the food so that it would look welcoming. Except for the one disastrous dinner, he'd never eaten in the house.

But the minutes ticked by and Jeff did not appear. She put the bacon and potatoes back on the stove. When a half hour had passed, an odd sense of foreboding crowded in on her, and she decided to look for him. He wasn't in the yard and the barn door was closed, thank God. She walked the perimeter of the house, in case he was working on some task, but still she couldn't find him.

At last she decided to check the field. As she walked past her parents' graves, she purposely averted her gaze. If some weed had invaded again, or if the flowers planted there needed water, she didn't want to know. Not now, not today.

When the garden came into view, she saw Jeff standing at its edge, tall and broad-shouldered, staring at it as if he'd never seen it before. She was pleased to see that he wore the shirt she'd made for him. Dear God, but he was a handsome man.

"Jeff?" she called.

He didn't acknowledge her.

Well, what on earth— Her sense of uneasiness grew as she approached him. "Jeff, didn't you hear—" And then she saw, and her light heart felt as if it had fallen to her knees. "Oh, dear God—"

He continued to stare at the ruined garden, an empty sack clutched in one hand at his side. "I've looked at every inch of it, Allie. Nothing can be saved."

It was obvious why not. All the rows, so carefully plowed and seeded and well on their way with established plants, were mangled and ground into the earth, and the soil was as churned up as if an army had marched through here. Scraps of dirty sacking lay here and there, and what was that white frost coating everything and the peculiar briny smell?

"What—what—?" She couldn't even get the question out.

"Cooper Matthews and Floyd Endicott came out here with a wagon during the night. They drove it back and forth over the vegetables, and then for good measure they finished off the job with bags of salt." He held the white cotton sack out to her. It had been torn down the middle, maybe with a knife or some other pointed tool. When she held the two halves together, she read DIAMOND SALT.

"Salt!"

He just stared at the field, his arms crossed over his chest. "Yup. Nothing is going to grow in this ground for a long time."

"How do you know it was them?"

"I saw them both. I woke up when I heard their horse and I came out here with the axe to chase them off. I was so angry when I realized what they'd done, I figured I'd better leave it in the blackberries—I honestly didn't know what I'd do if I had it in my hands. They had an argument before I could talk to them, and Floyd left by himself in the wagon. I threw Cooper off the property and told him to never come back."

"But—but, why would they do such a thing?" She couldn't control the quiver in her voice. "Do they hate us so much?"

"Well, I know they hate *me*, but that's never been a secret. There's more." He sighed once, as if trying to decide how to tell her.

"M-more?"

"Cooper told me that Olivia paid him twenty dollars to come out here and do this."

She stared at Jeff. "And you believe him?"

He turned and looked directly into her eyes. "Yes, I do. I think she did it to get even with me for throwing a bucket of water on her. And probably just for being here. She sent him a letter that she asked Seth Wickwire to carry back to town for her."

Allie sputtered for air and words, having trouble finding either. The accusation was preposterous, and her automatic defense of her sister jumped into play. "I agree that Olivia has behaved badly, but I can't believe she'd do something like this! Jeff, she's never even seen Cooper Matthews."

"I'll bet she did the day he came out here and raised hell because you'd given 'his' job to me, his boy's murderer. She's even talked to him by now. I saw her running back to the house last night while those two men were out here, and she saw me. She waited on the porch."

Allie opened her mouth to dispute his theory, then closed it again. She remembered that Olivia *had* seen Cooper that day, and heard him, too. She'd even overheard him promise revenge against Jeff. Allie wished it wasn't true, but she realized it was.

"Oh, God, oh, God. I'm sorry, Jeff. I'm so sorry." She lowered her head for a moment and gazed blankly at the salt sack in her hand, ashamed of her sister and feeling as if she bore part of that shame as well, simply by being

related. Then she looked at the garden again. Jeff had
worked so hard out here with Kansas, that balky mule, and
the plow. He'd labored with pure grit and determination to
fix the seed drill. He'd planted each row so carefully
to satisfy her exacting demands. He'd planted the border of
violets to appeal to her heart. "All that work. For nothing."

He glared at her with rock-hard eyes. "I'm not going to
take this, Allie. Not for another goddamned minute. I just
can't. I won't be able to look at myself in the mirror if I
do. And if I let it go now, it will only get worse and worse."

She turned away from his set face. Her heart clenched,
then sank from her knees to her feet. Of course he wouldn't
take it. Why would a man want to tie himself to a woman
who'd brought as much trouble to him as she had? She
tried to swallow the knot forming in her throat, but it remained there, aching enough to bring tears to her eyes. She
would let him go without railing at him about broken prom-
ises. She'd been a fool to think that she could escape to
that life she'd envisioned for herself.

Her throat was as dry as powder. "I-I understand, Jeff.
I'll pay you for the whole season, just as if you'd stayed
till harvesttime. If Sheriff Mason objects, I'll explain everything to him. You should get on with your life."

He put a finger under her chin to draw her face back to
his. "What are you talking about?"

God, did she have to go into excruciating detail and
lacerate her heart even further? She gripped the salt sack
in her fist. "You want to go, so go. You're right—this is
too much for anyone to take. You certainly have every reason to leave. I won't stand in your way."

His expression melted and comprehension softened the
look in his eyes. "Oh, Allie." He took her into a fierce
embrace and pressed her head to his shoulder. "Allie,
honey, no. I don't want to leave. I *can't* leave you." He

held her back at arm's length and peered into her wet eyes. His own voice was rough with emotion. "Did you forget what I told you last night? I need you beside me, Althea Ford. You made me remember what it means to be a man. In every possible way." He kissed her and pulled her back into his arms.

"Ohhhh . . ." Her relief was so great, her knees so watery, she would have fallen if he hadn't held her upright. She wrapped her arms around his slim waist and gripped the back of his shirt in both hands.

"What I meant was I'm not going to let Cooper push me around anymore. Ever since Wes got killed, he's egged me on, trying to provoke a showdown. I've mostly let him get away with it because I figured I was on borrowed time anyway, and I felt so damned bad about his son. I still do, but I know I felt a hundred times worse about Wesley than his own father did. I'm not going to let him get away with it this time. Even if Olivia did pay him to do this, you own half of this farm and you can press charges against him and Floyd."

"Will I have to accuse Olivia, too? I won't be able to do that, Jeff."

"No. They were trespassing. If they bring her into it, no one is going to believe them. And if Will asked her if she ordered this, what do you think she'd say?"

Allie nodded, understanding his implication. "She would deny it." How had her sister gone so wrong? Worse yet, how could Allie have been so blind not to see her true self? Amos Ford may not have been much of a father to Allie, but he'd doted on Olivia, and he'd set a good example by being forthright and hardworking. Since he'd been gone, Allie had taken his place. She'd tried to do her best by Olivia, to remind her to be respectful, loving, and honest.

She seemed to have learned nothing but selfishness and treachery.

"Come to town with me, then, and we'll talk to Will Mason," Jeff said, looking down at her. "At least you've got a good witness—me."

"We'll go. But we might as well eat the breakfast I cooked. The sheriff probably won't be in his office for another hour or so."

Jeff turned her back toward the house with his arm looped over her shoulders, leaving the garden that would never see another harvest until the soil recovered from Olivia's latest shenanigan. The woman he would soon call sister-in-law was filled with poisonous obsessions, Jeff realized, and to such a frightening degree that it was impossible to predict what she might do next.

The idea filled him with an icy dread, not for himself—Olivia couldn't hurt him. But Allie . . . he wanted to protect her from any more hurtful ugliness. The best way he could do that was to get Allie away from here.

Just as Allie finished washing the breakfast dishes, she heard Olivia come down the stairs. She slumped into the kitchen, cool and pouting, and acting as though she'd been wronged. She wore a dove-gray dress with a berry-colored sash and her hair was tied up in a matching ribbon, but her face looked as though she hadn't slept at all. Well, if she'd been up and around in the night conspiring with those terrible men, perhaps she hadn't.

Out of habit long ingrained, Allie nearly asked, "Do you want some toast?" But then the absurdity struck her. Life couldn't continue as it always had, with her constantly scurrying and scraping to keep everything aright in her sister's cloistered little world. Olivia had done a terrible thing—an unconscionable deed that could never be justified or explained, and Allie was finished mollycoddling her like a spoiled child.

In a stern voice she couldn't quite believe came from her, Allie said, "You and I are going to have a long talk, Olivia."

Her sister gave her a startled, wary look. "About what?"

Allie clenched her fists, scoring her palms with her fingernails. "I can scarcely believe you have the gall to ask."

Just then, a knock sounded at the back door. Expecting to see Jeff, Allie was surprised when she found Will Mason standing on the porch.

"Sheriff Mason, what a coincidence. Jeff, that is, Mr. Hicks and I were about to come to town to talk to you. We had some trouble out here last night." She couldn't help but spare a glance at Olivia. Then she pushed open the screen door. "Won't you come in?"

"Only for a minute, Miss Althea." The sheriff stepped inside, advancing no farther than the hooked rug in front of the door. He peered at Althea so intently that she wondered what he could be staring at. Then she remembered her bruised cheek. Self-conscious, she put her hand over the bruise. What on earth would he think?

Fortunately he shifted his gaze to Olivia and dragged his hat off his head. He began rolling and unrolling its brim. "Ma'am," he intoned to Olivia. "I'm afraid this isn't a social call. I'm here to talk to Jeff Hicks. I heard about what happened here. Floyd Endicott got me out of bed at daybreak to tell me."

His tone and manner made Allie think of a man who'd come to deliver horrible news, and she was immediately uneasy. "Do you mean he actually turned himself in?"

"Um, not exactly, ma'am. He admitted that he and Cooper were here and did some damage to your property."

"Indeed they did! They destroyed all our crops and cov-

ered them with salt so that nothing will grow in that field
for who knows how long!" She cast another sidelong look
at her sister, but she didn't even seem to be listening to the
conversation.

"Yes, well, I haven't had the chance to talk to him about
it much."

Just then, Jeff bounded up the back steps. "Allie, are
you ready to—" He saw Will Mason then. "Will, we were
just about to come see you."

The sheriff looked as uncomfortable as he had the day
Allie visited him in his office, looking for Cooper. "So I
heard. Jeff, I need to talk to you about the murder of Cooper Matthews."

"What!"

"Murder?" Allie whispered in shocked dismay.

"Right now you're the prime suspect," Will said, inclin-
ing his head at Jeff. "Floyd Endicott came to my door this
morning with Cooper's body in the back of a wagon. He
said that the two of them were out here last night making
mischief—"

" 'Mischief' hardly describes it!" Jeff barked.

"He said you and Cooper scuffled and then you split his
head open with a pick. He showed me that pick, Jeff. It's
all bloody. And Cooper's head looks like a melon that
someone dropped."

"He's dead?" What color remained in Jeff's face drained
away.

"That's not the kind of injury a man usually survives.
Doc Brewster confirmed the cause of death."

"Jesus Christ, Will, you must know Floyd is lying! How
the hell can you take his word against mine?"

"Maybe he *is* lying. But it's no secret that there has been
bad blood between you and Matthews for a long time. What
were you doing last night?"

"Sleeping, goddamnit! What does everyone else do in the middle of the night?"

"Do you deny you confronted Floyd and Cooper?"

"No, I talked to them, but only for a minute." He went on to explain overhearing the two men argue, and seeing Floyd take off with the wagon, leaving Cooper behind. "The last time I saw Cooper Matthews, he was running across the field he'd just destroyed, very *much* alive."

"So you spent only a minute with them. And the rest of the night?"

"I was in bed!"

"I don't suppose someone can verify your story."

"No, Will, you'll just have to take my word for it," Jeff snapped with sarcasm.

Allie opened her mouth to speak, but Jeff sent her a look that froze the words in her throat. *Don't you dare tell him you were with me*, his eyes said.

Like a conjurer, Will produced a pair of wrist manacles. "Well, it's your word against Floyd's. So we're going back to town to get this all straightened out. And until we do, you're going to sit in my jail where I can keep an eye on you. Jeff, you're under arrest."

"Arrest!" Allie cried.

"Floyd is lying!" Jeff repeated.

"Mr. Endicott is not lying! I saw him do it, plain as day." All gazes turned to Olivia. Her eyes glittered with sudden excitement, and she leveled an accusing finger at Jeff. "I saw Mr. Jefferson murder that man."

Allie had never seen the ocean, but she'd read about it, and irrelevantly, she thought it must sound like the blood rushing through her head at that moment, pounding at her ears. She felt as if she'd been punched in the stomach, and her heart thumped so hard she thought it might burst from her chest.

She stared at her sister in utter horror. With each passing day, Allie felt she knew less and less about her. "My God, Olivia, how can you make such—"

"Miss Olivia," Will said, "I'll need you to come to my office and tell me what you saw."

Allie struggled to subdue the panic rising in her. "Sheriff, my sister is not well, as you know. I'm sure she's made some kind of mistake. Jeff was in the lean-to all night. He could hardly have been in two places at once."

"I know what I saw, Althea! I saw this man go out to the garden carrying a pick!" Olivia's face was flushed with color.

"She's lying, too!" Jeff barked.

"We're not going to discuss this here," Will interrupted. His tone of authority silenced all other protests. He put the manacles on Jeff, and, watching, Allie felt her heart squeeze painfully, and only with supreme effort was she able to stifle the sobs threatening to erupt from her throat.

Jeff glared at Will, but the man remained detached and emotionless. He ushered Jeff outside and down the steps to two horses waiting in the yard.

Allie followed behind, watching as Jeff struggled to climb into the saddle with his hands bound in front of him. The sun reflected off the silver star on Will's vest, making it gleam like a mirror. A sheriff's badge was supposed to represent order and safety—defense against chaos and men like Cooper Matthews. Allie looked at the blinding symbol and only knew that the individual wearing it had the authority to take an innocent man to jail for a murder he didn't commit. Suddenly she thought she had never seen anything more terrifying in her life.

Not even that dummy she'd found in the barn.

Chapter Fifteen

NEVER TRUST HAPPINESS.

An old cowboy, who'd broken more bones than Jeff had years, had told him that once. Jeff had been standing at the far end of the bar at the Liberal Saloon, doing his best to find the bottom of his whiskey bottle, when the graying, old guy came in, limping slightly. Jeff had never seen him before, and never did again. He'd had a wise dignity about him, though, that made him seem taller than he really was. He'd looked at Jeff briefly, but long enough to make it seem as if he'd seen into his head and read his troubles. Standing a respectful distance down the bar, he'd asked no questions, but ordered a beer and told Jeff about a cowboy's existence. It was a good one, but lonely. To stave off the loneliness, the cowboy had married a beautiful woman and fathered three fine children. Life had never been better or more sublime. He'd loved them more than he thought it possible to love. A man couldn't have asked for more. Then one winter when the snows were deep, influenza had taken them all.

Never trust happiness. It'll double-cross a man every time.

It had been a good lesson.

Wishing he'd remembered it sooner, Jeff lay on the stinking mattress in the jail cell and stared at the water-stained ceiling. It all smelled and looked much worse now that he was sober, but he didn't care. He wasn't sure how many hours he'd been here, but he'd watched a rectangle of sunlight cross the floor and climb the wall.

Happiness, sweet and poignant, had been just within his reach. He'd closed his fingers around it briefly, held it to his heart, and sighed with profound relief upon finding it.

And now . . .

Murder. He'd been arrested for Cooper Matthews' murder, and Olivia Ford had arranged it merely by pointing her finger at Jeff. It had been so simple, so much easier than all the other stunts she'd pulled up to now. He certainly didn't think she'd killed Cooper, but hadn't it worked out nicely for her?

Will Mason had told Jeff that Judge Cavanaugh would come to town in a few days for the trial. Would a jury of Jeff's peers believe Olivia? A crazy Ford sister? Yes, possibly, because it was socially unacceptable to question a lady's veracity, even if that lady was spiteful and vindictive. Besides, Jeff had no allies in Decker Prairie anymore. It had been a long tumble from his days as sheriff to his status of the town drunk who'd been prone to sleep in upstanding citizens' doorways and barns. No one knew or would care that he'd managed to climb back out of that dark pit he'd wallowed in for over two years.

Jeff could view it all with a detached indifference, even a sense of the inevitable, until he thought of Allie. And he thought of her every other minute. Oh, damn, but she didn't deserve this. He'd promised her so much more—hell, he'd even promised her the moon one night. A man who had nothing to give could afford to give away the moon, couldn't he? But stuck in this cell, his only gift to her now would be heartache.

Just then, he heard the key turn in the main lock. Will Mason walked in and spoke to him from the other side of the bars.

"You have a visitor, Jeff. Althea Ford wants to see you."

Jeff didn't look up, but he closed his hand into a tight fist on his thigh. He wanted to see her so damned bad, he had to stop himself from flying to the cell door. But as much as he yearned for Allie, to touch her hands and look at her beautiful face, his pride wouldn't permit it. He didn't want her to see him this way. It was a hell of a time for him to develop self-respect. If it hadn't been so pathetic, he would have laughed—for years he hadn't cared what anyone thought of him or how they saw him.

"No visitors." His reply sounded gruff and low, but it was the only sound he could make with his throat so tight with emotion.

He felt Will move closer. "You're in a high holy mess this time," he said quietly.

Jeff's head came up sharply. "It sounds like you've got me tried and convicted already."

"No, I don't. I'm glad to see you sober and cleaned up. It'll help you in court. But two eyewitnesses are going to be hard to dispute. You need a lawyer."

Jeff made a disgusted noise. Standing up, he paced around the small enclosure with his hands jammed in his back pockets. "Right, a lawyer. And how will I pay him? With my sterling reputation in Decker Prairie?" He came to a stop in front of Will.

The sheriff idly turned the big iron key ring he held. "I might be able come up with someone who'll help."

"Do you think I killed Cooper?"

"It doesn't matter what I think."

"It matters to me!"

A gaping moment of silence engulfed the small room before Will answered. "I don't think you *meant* to kill him."

"Great," Jeff snapped sourly. "I guess I can count on you to give the judge a character reference."

"I don't suppose you'd believe me if I said I wish to God I wasn't the sheriff right now."

"Sure, I believe you, Will. Go home to Caroline tonight and tell her what a lousy day you had! Things look a lot different from this side of the cage—you should shut yourself in here sometime and enjoy the view. And while you're at it, try picturing old Charlie Acton and his son closing their carpentry shop for a couple of days to build you a custom-made gallows at the end of the street."

Will sighed. "Are you sure about not wanting to see Miss Althea?" He gave Jeff a speculating look. "She seems pretty concerned about you."

Jeff heard the question in Will's comment, but he wasn't willing to reveal personal information. They'd been friends at one time, he and Will, but things were different now, about as different as they could get. He shook his head and went back to the bunk.

"Do you want me to give her a message for you?"

"No, goddamnit! Will, just leave me be."

Will nodded, apparently taking no offense, and turned to leave. With his hand on the big oak door separating his office from the cell, he said, "Jeff, you might think you're alone in this. But you're not—I promise you that."

Then he was gone and Jeff flopped down on the stained mattress, with only his thoughts for company. He might not want to let Allie see him in jail, but that didn't stop Jeff from seeing her. She was vivid in his mind's eye, as delicate as a bird, as strong as tempered steel. He pictured her red hair, curling in tendrils over her creamy skin, like cherries on porcelain, her blue-gray eyes that seemed to find all the hurting places hiding inside him and ease the pain. Just to look at her made a day brighter. Holding her in his arms had brought peace to his spirit, and a happiness he'd not expected to know again.

The last of the daylight hours passed with her in his heart, and sunset gave way to purple-shadowed twilight. He could imagine sitting on a front porch swing, watching the dusk with a single glass of whiskey on his knee. Allie sat next to him, holding their baby to her breast. Before them spread acres of planted fields, tilled with his sweat and love of the land, sowed with seed and his love for his wife and child.

Jeff rolled over on the on the creaking bunk to face the wall, and a single sob worked its way up from his chest. He wished to God that Allie were with him now.

Allie trudged along the final, dusty quarter mile to the farm, her feet like lead. Even her skirts felt heavy as she dragged them with her. She had to pass the ruined field on the way, still white with salt and dotted with sacking. The crushed and mangled plants had already begun to dry up. Jeff had been right—not a single one could be saved.

What a living nightmare this day had been. How could she have flown to such heights in Jeff's arms last night, only to be plunged to the depths of despair today?

Of course, she knew the answer, and it could be summed up in a single name: Olivia.

Olivia—her sister, her own kin—had sat in Will Mason's office and told him that she'd seen Jeff murder Cooper Matthews with a pick. She'd told the lie with such wide-eyed innocence, Allie realized how she had been duped all these years. Olivia was a very accomplished actress. Allie, tight-lipped and quietly furious, had sent her home while she stayed behind at the sheriff's office to visit Jeff.

But then, oh, then, worst of all—Jeff had refused to see her and her heart had broken. Of course he would want nothing more to do with her. The Ford family was responsible for his latest round of torment, from Olivia's fit at the dinner table to her accusation of murder.

As Allie approached the house she could hear Olivia's piano. The notes were high and sweet and true, as if the woman playing them had not a care in the world. And no conscience.

Anger, righteous and throbbing, bubbled to the surface in Allie. Remembering what Jeff had said this morning, she repeated it to herself—she couldn't take this anymore, not for a minute. Some things were too monstrous to be endured, and Allie had reached her limit. She would have it out with Olivia as she'd planned this morning.

Determination gave her new energy and drove her stride like the pistons in a steam engine. Lifting her skirts slightly, she marched over the path to the back door, up the steps and into the kitchen. She reached up to unpin her navy straw hat.

"Olivia!"

The melody of Stephen Foster's "Beautiful Dreamer" trailed off and the piano fell silent.

"Olivia, come into the kitchen right now!"

The swish of taffeta announced her sister's approach. She entered the room wearing the same open, innocent look she'd shown to Will Mason. "Althea—I'm so glad you're home! Look, I've started our supper." She pointed to the stove where a pot of unpeeled, finely chopped potatoes had boiled down to an inedible brown mush.

Allie now recognized this ruse. Olivia had used this kind

of maneuver over the years, anytime she believed she'd overstepped her bounds. Exasperated, Allie demanded, "Do you realize what you have done? The damage you've caused?"

"Oh, dear, I know I'm not very good in the kitchen. I can start over. I'll just toss that—"

Allie crushed the straw hat she still held in her hands, her knuckles white. "Just stop it, Olivia! Stop it right now! I'm not talking about potatoes or your deliberate incompetence. Why did you tell Sheriff Mason that horrible lie about Jeff?"

"It's not a lie! I did see him outside last night, and he was carrying a pick. He went straight to the field, and he argued with those men."

"Those men you *paid* to salt our land?"

Olivia lifted her chin. "I did no such thing! The argument got worse and then he hit one of them in the head with that pick. I saw it!"

"Why have you done these horrible things to me and to Jeff? You've lied to me, tricked me, and practically put a noose around Jeff Hicks' neck! I want to know why you would condemn an innocent man."

"He killed once, he could do it again. Anyway, how do you know he's innocent? Were you with him?"

The question took Allie aback. "N-no! Of course not. I just know what kind of man he is."

Olivia's childlike face hardened into a shrewd expression. "Now who's lying? I saw you last night—you and him. Together in his bed, all sweaty and breathing hard."

Allie stared at her sister, overwhelmed by a vague nauseous feeling. Olivia had always kept odd hours and Allie had never really known what she did at night. But now, the idea that she had watched her and Jeff while they— Oh, God, it sickened her to think about.

Allie finally found enough breath to speak. "*How dare you*? That was none of your business!"

"I even heard him ask you to go away with him. Everything was fine until *he* came here, and he wouldn't leave. But he's gone now, and I know he won't be coming back. So everything will be fine again, and our lives will go back to the way they were before."

Allie could scarcely credit the twisted way her sister's mind worked. To think that she actually believed Allie would be content to return to the prison of catering to her whims, to have no happiness or contentment or companionship—it staggered the imagination.

"Olivia, know this—no matter what happens, our lives will never be the same as they were before. I will leave this farm regardless of what happens to Jeff. But if he's convicted, God forbid, I'll leave Decker Prairie and I will never speak to you again. If you think I'm joking, I swear to you that I am not."

"You would put that—that farmhand ahead of me?" Olivia put special emphasis on the word, as if it described the lowest form of life on earth.

"I love Jeff Hicks, with my whole heart." Allie blurted this out, hating that Jeff had not heard it from her first, and that she'd had to reveal something so personal to a woman who could not understand any emotion that didn't involve her. "He gives me *joy*."

"You promised Daddy you'd take care of me!"

How that statement had once struck fear in Allie's heart. During his years on this earth and then from his grave, Amos Ford had ruled her with iron edicts. Now, perhaps because the love of her life was in mortal danger, she realized that there were more frightening threats than a dying man's admonition, and greater sins than abandoning a pledge made under duress. She felt as if the shackles with which her father had bound her all those years ago now fell away.

"I *have* taken care of you, all of your life and nearly all of mine. I've seen you through those hysterical tantrums you faked, and I've doted on you and tried in every way to please you and keep you happy. I spoiled you. I'm finished now. For God's sake, Olivia, you're twenty years old! It's time you grew up." As unaccustomed as Allie was to losing control, it felt wonderful to speak her mind after a lifetime of keeping everything inside for fear of upsetting her sister, or angering her father. The blinders had been stripped from her eyes—Allie realized that Olivia was much stronger that she'd ever guessed.

"You can't leave me here!"

"I can, and I will."

As Allie started to step around her sister, Olivia suddenly sank to the floor and her limbs stiffened in the beginning throes of a spell. For just an instant, Allie's feet froze to the boards, and that old sense of panic washed through her. But then, sanity returned. This wasn't a spell; it was merely another attempt on Olivia's part to bring her to heel.

The anger that had begun simmering in Allie on the way home now erupted into a full rage in the wake of her quickly evaporating panic. Uncertain of what possessed her, but glorying in the heat of it, she snatched up a towel that Olivia had left lying on the kitchen table. She bent to shove it into her sister's clutching fingers.

"While you're thrashing around down there, make yourself useful and dust the bottom of the wainscoting. Your servant has just quit."

Olivia's eyes stopped rolling and she gaped at Allie in startled amazement. "But I—*Altheeah!* Come back!" Miraculously recovered, she twisted onto her knees and made a frantic grab for Allie's skirt. "Don't go! I'm sick. You can't just walk off when I'm having a spell!"

Allie jerked her hem from her sister's clinging grasp. "I am doing exactly that."

It was all so clear to her now. She walked through the kitchen to the hall and climbed the stairs with Olivia thundering up the treads behind her on legs as sound and sure as Allie's own. When Allie reached her room, she pulled an old carpetbag from beneath her bed. It smelled musty inside. Of course, it would—when had she ever used it? Musty or not, it would have to do. She plucked her silver brush and comb from the dresser and shoved them into the bag. Then, resolutely, she began emptying the drawers.

"What are you doing?" Olivia demanded, wild-haired and pale. She took the underwear that Allie put on the bed and carried it back to the dresser.

"I told you. I'm going."

"But where? I want to come with you!" Briefly, the two women struggled over a camisole—Allie tried to pull it away from Olivia, and Olivia worked to put it back in its drawer.

With a final yank, Allie captured it and stuffed it into her bag. "Why?"

Olivia wrung her hands and began crying. "I don't want to be alone. I don't know how to do anything." She narrowed her eyes. "You would never teach me about cooking or sewing."

"That isn't true, and you know it isn't. I tried to show you lots of things. You didn't want to learn. For heaven's sake, you won't even make your own tea. All you wanted to make were doll clothes."

Olivia attacked from a different position. "You stole my mother from me. I never even knew her. Daddy always said you were supposed to be watching her, but you were off wasting time while she went to the barn! It's only right that you take her place."

Allie didn't bother to reply. She couldn't respond to that accusation, and nothing she said would make any difference to her sister. Allie had lost her mother, too, that day, and there had been no one who even tried to fill the void. She packed as much as she could carry and closed the clasp on the bag while her sister stared at her, goggle-eyed.

"Take me with you!"

"For the last time, Olivia, no! Don't you see I can't be with you anymore? I *can't*. Not after everything you've done, the dummy in the barn, spying on me, bearing false witness against Jeff—"

Desperately, Olivia smoothed back her hair and dragged her sleeve across her streaming eyes. "I'm sorry about everything, Althea, truly I am."

Allie wanted to believe her. Oh, how she wanted to. But her abrupt switch was so obviously meant to sway her, Allie resisted. "You're not sorry. Olivia, you need to find out what it means to be a responsible adult. A lot of women your age are already wives and mothers. You can't go on pretending that you're twelve years old. At least, I'm not going to help you pretend any longer." She looked around her bedroom, the one she had slept in since her girlhood, making sure she'd taken everything she would need. "I'm going to get a room at the hotel and wait for Jeff's trial. You can have the farm and everything on it." She added, "I'm sure Father would want it that way."

Olivia's face crumpled again. "I think you're just being hateful!"

"No, I'm saving myself. And I'll do whatever I can to save Jeff."

Allie turned and walked out to the hallway and down the stairs, wondering what it would be like to have a grown-up relationship with her sister. She supposed that she'd never know.

As she crossed through the parlor and the kitchen again, she glanced at the rooms where she had spent her entire life. Again, Olivia was fast on her heels.

"I'll fix it so that Jefferson man never sees daylight again," she shouted after Allie. "They'll hang him and you'll be back here. You'll see!"

Allie tugged on the hem of her light jacket and adjusted her grip on the carpetbag. She was filled with uncertainty and fear for the future. Like Olivia, she'd never been on her own. But she walked away from the house in the waning daylight without once looking back.

Chapter Sixteen

"It's true that Floyd Endicott's involvement in the vandalism potentially weakens his testimony. But I have spoken with Olivia Ford and I found her to be a charming young lady. Her sweet innocence will make her a credible, sympathetic witness. I think a jury would believe her."

Jeff stared at Royal Purdy, the nervous, pencil-necked lawyer on the other side of the bars, who spoke so dryly of what would be a life-or-death event for him. Purdy was a shirttail relative of Will Mason's wife and he looked as if he'd never seen a day of physical labor in his life, or spent more than a minute in the sun. Hardly more than a wet-nosed kid in a boiled shirt, he was pale and slight, with light hair and eyes. Jeff got the impression that this was the lawyer's first case. He'd agreed to let the young man represent him because his price was right—free. But every minute spent in his company convinced Jeff that he might be better off defending himself.

He took to pacing the limited floor space of his cell. "Olivia Ford could make some people believe that the sun rises in the west, but that wouldn't make it true."

"Hmm, well, I'm afraid, Mr. Hicks, that your case

doesn't look very good. There are two people who don't know each other, both claiming to have seen you sink a pick into Mr. Matthews' head. Miss Ford even says she saw you carry it to the field."

"I *didn't* kill Cooper Matthews. Hell, I never even saw a pick on that farm. There must be some way to prove that she's lying."

Plainly, Royal Purdy believed Olivia Ford as well. "It would be extremely difficult."

"What are you saying, then, Mr. Purdy? That you've changed your mind about representing me?"

"Oh, my, no. Every accused man deserves legal representation, and I'll do the best I can considering the adverse circumstances. I'll come to court with you and intercede if the prosecution steps beyond the bounds of its rightful authority."

Such as organizing a lynching, Jeff thought darkly. Purdy gathered up his papers, none of which appeared to pertain to Jeff's case, and called for Will to let him out.

Left alone with his thoughts again, Jeff stopped his pacing and rested his forehead on one of the cold iron bars while he considered his situation. He'd been in jail for three days and with each sunset, his hope for deliverance dwindled a little more.

Allie—God, it hurt just to think her name, much less to envision her beautiful face. But he did it anyway, the way a person might keep touching his tongue to an aching tooth.

He closed his eyes. If he were very careful, if he thought only of Allie, he could imagine her without the interference of her bitchy sister, and before the awful morning that had landed him in here. He could see her lying in his arms in the moonlight, her lips trembling slightly just as he bent his head to touch them with his own. He could feel her warm body, smooth and finely made, writhing beneath him, joining his very spirit to hers.

Like it had happened yesterday, he saw her standing in the orchard that afternoon he'd come back from town, the breeze tugging at the strands of her hair while she fed those little birds from her hand. She'd had her back to him and the wind had molded her skirts to her shape, revealing a nicely rounded bottom and slender legs.

He remembered her tending the scratches on his arms when he'd crossed paths with her climbing rose on the front porch. Her touch had been infinitely tender and soothing— he'd wished he could lay his head in her lap while she stroked his hair.

He still wished that.

Allie had tried to visit him every day, and every day he'd refused to see her. Originally, he'd thought that he'd get out of here after the details of the murder had been sorted out, and they could go on about their lives as they'd planned.

Now, he wasn't nearly as certain. In fact, left alone with this much time on his hands, there was nothing to do but think. And in the thinking, he was reaching some conclusions.

One such conclusion was that he would see Allie the next time she came to visit, if there was a next time. He'd turned her away so often, he wouldn't blame her for not coming back. But he'd like to look at her one more time.

He had the feeling it might be the last time.

Allie looked out the window of her hotel room, twisting the corners of her handkerchief into points. Dark clouds gathered in the southern sky. The air was heavy and threatening—rain was coming. It matched her mood.

What a curious experience it had been, staying in the

hotel. While checking in, she'd spoken very quietly to draw less attention to herself. Allie was not unaware that a lone woman renting a hotel room might set tongues to wagging. And if the woman was a Ford sister, it was guaranteed. The clerk, however, apparently had no sense of discretion, and had bugled her name in a voice loud enough to carry through the lobby. Every neck in the vicinity had craned in her direction. And when the clerk had turned the register around for her to sign, there had been a space on the page that asked for an address—she'd almost laughed. After all, she really had no address, did she?

The room was surprisingly homey, with pleasing, flowered wallpaper and a desk and chair by the window. She ordered her meals sent up to her room, to avoid the curious stares of other diners at Elmira's Café, and also because it seemed so very lonely to eat in a restaurant by herself. Up here, Allie had a view of the street below, which bustled with more activity than she was used to in the pastoral quiet of the farm.

At night, she'd lie in bed and listen to the rowdy voices and clanking piano coming from the Liberal Saloon down the street. The sounds, though muted by distance and walls, carried easily in the summer darkness. In the morning, shortly after sunup, shopkeepers up and down both sides of the thoroughfare emerged to sweep their stoops and wash the dust from their sidewalks to get ready for the day's business. It was all much different from the country hush and solitude.

She wasn't sorry about her decision to leave Olivia and the farm. But the novelties of having no one to answer to, no chores to do, no meals to cook, were luxuries she could scarcely enjoy when the circumstances were so dire. With nothing to do but think and worry, she spent most of her time staving off tears.

Oh, dear God, how she longed for Jeff. She missed him more than she thought it possible to miss another human being.

He had still refused to see her when she went to the sheriff's office. Although she hadn't told Will Mason any personal details, she suspected that he knew her interest in Jeff was more than that of a concerned employer. He'd considered her with a searching, empathetic gaze every time he returned from the cell holding Jeff. Oh, Lord, he probably thought she was an unwanted female admirer Jeff wished would just quit pestering him. And maybe that's how Jeff really felt.

Allie's stomach clenched at the idea. She didn't want to flog herself with self-doubts but what else could she think?

I can't *leave you . . . You made me remember what it means to be a man.*

Had it really been just a few days ago that he'd held her in his arms and told her that? It had been one thing for him to ignore Olivia's previous attempts to run him off, but this—God in heaven, this robbed him of his freedom and threatened his very life.

Well, Allie wouldn't give up. Jeff's trial was tomorrow—the Constitution guaranteed a speedy trial, didn't it? Judge Cavanaugh and a prosecutor would be here and set up their courtroom in the Liberal Saloon.

She would see him before then. She *must.*

Testing her fledgling resolve, she turned from the window and went to the washstand to rinse her face. Crying and moping accomplished nothing. Staring at her reflection in the mirror, she repinned her hair and pinched a little color into her cheeks. The ugly bruise on her cheekbone had finally faded, and now she just looked white and scared.

Well, she had lived like a victim most of her life, letting

herself be carried along by what others thought and said. That was the old Althea Ford. This new woman, Allie Ford, the one who'd left the only home she'd ever known to strike out for an unknown future, wasn't going to take "no" for an answer again. Until he told her otherwise, Jeff Hicks was still the man who had promised her a better life somewhere else. If he wanted to withdraw his offer, then he would have to tell her so to her face. She put on her jacket and picked up her reticule.

Crossing the room to the door, she gripped the knob and took a deep breath. Then she stepped into the hallway and closed the door behind her.

"Good afternoon, Sheriff Mason. I would like to see Jeff Hicks, please." Allie made every effort to keep her eyes off the silver badge on the sheriff's vest. She made certain her back was straight and her chin parallel with the floor. She would be firm. She would not be denied again.

Will Mason sat at his desk. Until she had so rudely interrupted him, he had apparently been drinking coffee and studying a dog-eared copy of the *Oregon Statesman*. "Yes, ma'am. You come on with me." He folded the newspaper with a snap and pulled his big iron key ring from the side drawer of his desk.

Allie felt her jaw drop before she quickly closed her mouth again. Goodness, being firm had worked the first time she tried it. She hadn't even had to make the carefully worded, polite demand she'd rehearsed in her mind on the walk over here from the hotel. She followed Will to the heavy oak door that separated her from Jeff, thinking that the sheriff's tall, wide-shouldered stature resembled the hardwood itself. He unlocked the door, and without bothering to announce her, he stood back to let her pass.

The first thing that struck her was the profusion of

closely set, vertical bars. Her eyes madly sought Jeff in the small enclosure—he was a big man, he should be easy to spot. But when she saw him sitting on a bunk against the wall, he looked smaller than she remembered, as if he'd physically withdrawn into himself.

She rushed to the cell door. "Jeff!"

He looked up, unfolding his tall form, and came to his side of the bars. Reaching between them, he took her face in his hands. "Oh, God, Allie, honey— Let me look at you." His fingertips brushed over her mouth and nose and brows, as if he were a blind man. He reached for her hands and held them to his lips, pressing kisses on her knuckles.

This horrible place couldn't diminish his handsomeness, but he looked as if he rarely slept. Obviously he hadn't shaved since he'd been here, and Allie made passing note of the blond and brown stubble of his beard. Dark smudges beneath his green eyes gave him a hollow look, and his face seemed thinner. To see him this way, caged and vulnerable, was more painful than she'd expected. She wished this iron barrier were not between them so that she could pull his head down to rest on her shoulder and stroke his hair.

"I've been here every day. Did you know that? Will Mason told me you wouldn't see me."

He laced his fingers with hers. "I know. I wanted to, but—" He gestured at his wretched prison with his free hand. "How could I let you see me in here? Hell, I'm even wearing the same clothes I had on my back when Will brought me in. At least he's going to loan me a suit for the trial." Lifting her palm to his cheek, he closed his eyes for an instant. "God, I've missed you, Allie. I've had a lot of time to think these past few days. There hasn't been anything else to do. I had to see you one more time, so I told Will to let you in if you came to visit again."

"*If*! Of course I came!" She searched his lean face. "Are you eating? Is the sheriff treating you well?"

"I'm all right, honey, I'm all right." She found no comfort in his words. He didn't look all right.

There was so much to tell him, her words tumbled out one after the other. "I'm staying at the hotel. I left Olivia and the farm. For good."

"You did?"

She told him everything, about Olivia spying on them in Jeff's bed, and the selfish reason for her treachery.

He told her he knew Olivia had watched them. He told her of Royal Purdy, the man's favorable impression of Olivia, and his obvious pessimism about Jeff's case.

"She insists she saw me with the murder weapon, that damned pick of Floyd's." His smile was rueful. "We almost made it, didn't we, Allie? We were going to have a new start on a good life." His voice trembled ever so slightly. "I even imagined holding our newborn son in my arms."

An icy shiver of foreboding washed through Allie's veins. "Jeff, what do you mean, 'almost made it'? You're not giving up—you can't give up. As long as we're alive there's still hope."

"I can't fight the whole world. And I'm beginning to think that this is the way things were supposed to happen."

"What? Please, Jeff—I love you." God, but she wished she had told him sooner, under better circumstances. "I have to tell Sheriff Mason I was with you that night. I am your alibi."

"No. If you do, you won't be able to hold your head up in Decker Prairie ever again. Besides, I already admitted that I talked to Matthews and Endicott. Your sister saw me, Floyd saw me."

Frightened, angry, determined, she stared at his green eyes. "But you were only there for a minute. I was with you the rest of the night, and I'll tell anyone who asks where you were."

"No. I won't let you do that."

"You really can't stop me."

He fixed her with a hard look. "If you go through with this, I'll swear that you're lying. In this case, I know everyone will believe me. This town thinks little enough of me already—they probably wouldn't put it past me to try and hide behind a woman's skirts. And they'll never forget your part in it."

"I don't care what Decker Prairie thinks of me! Remember? I'm already one of the crazy Ford sisters. They've always talked about me."

"But I do care. If I can't be here to look out for you, I want to know that you'll be all right." His expression gentled again. "I love you, too, Allie. A lot more than my own life."

Allie knew she should find joy in his declaration, but there was none to be found right now. She struggled to blink back the tears gathering in her eyes but she failed, her chaotic thoughts snagging on something he'd said earlier. "What do you mean, this is the way it's supposed to be? You didn't kill Cooper Matthews."

He sighed. "No. I didn't. But I killed Wesley. That boy's spirit has haunted me every day since. This is like a reckoning. It's my atonement, I guess."

"That's ridiculous! You shot him in self-defense. Letting yourself be convicted for Cooper's murder doesn't solve anything!"

He went on as if she hadn't voiced this objection. "My mother did well by us boys. She was a widow with five sons to raise, but she did a good job. When I think about it, it makes me feel small. She gave me the best start she could. If she could see me now—this complete ruination of her son—well, I'm grateful that she can't." He let out a puff of humorless laughter. "Maybe she thinks I'm already dead."

Allie didn't try to stem the tears flowing down her face. "W-why?"

"She hasn't heard from me in years, and she doesn't know about . . . anything that happened to me. I just couldn't bring myself to write and tell her. After I shot Wes, well, that was when I realized that everything I'd believed in, been taught, held as truth, was wrong. I *couldn't* fix a problem just because I knew how. Some things can't be fixed. Marriage *doesn't* last for better and for worse. If you give some people a hand up, they'll take your whole arm." He talked like a man who had learned hard lessons, and now, seeing Death lurking in the shadows, he accepted its presence as inevitable.

It scared Allie. If she could hold him, just hold him and keep the world away from him. "Jeff, please—don't give up. You can't. I *love* you, and I need you. We'll work this out yet."

He gave her another wistful smile. "Sweetheart, please, don't get your hopes up. According to Purdy, I don't have the chance of a snowball in July. Olivia and Floyd are complete strangers to each other, yet both of them swear they saw me bury a pick in Cooper's skull. And Olivia is—" His mouth twisted bitterly. "Well, according to the lawyer, she comes off as sweet and angelic, the kind who wouldn't lie to save her soul. Purdy doesn't think it's going to go well for me at the trial, and I . . . I'm inclined to agree. You have to face that."

Allie felt an awful pressure building in her chest. She wanted to scream and pound her fists on the bars, to cling to Jeff and sob. She needed for him to tell her everything would be all right.

But no—she wasn't the one facing a noose. Not the one locked up in this dank cell. He was the one who needed comforting, not her. And if that was all God had seen fit to let her give this man, it was little enough. "Oh, Jeff . . . please," she whispered, framing his face between her hands. "Even in the worst storm, you can find patches of sunlight shining through the gloom if you really search."

His gaze trailed slowly over her face. In a thick voice, he said, "You're my sunlight, Allie—and my moonlight."

Tears filled her eyes, nearly blinding her. "We're going to be strong and get through this. Together."

He nodded and pressed close to the bars to kiss her tears away. "All right, honey. Strong. We'll be strong. And we won't give up hope."

Even as he parroted the words, Allie heard the ring of hopelessness in his voice.

"But if it all goes wrong," he went on, "I have to ask a favor of you."

She gripped his hands and took a deep breath. "I'll do anything you want."

"Write to my mother and tell her what happened to me. Mrs. Kate Hicks in Klamath Falls. You can tell her that Sally left me, but leave out the really bad things, like how I turned into a drunk and was arrested for stealing an egg. That would just hurt her. If I'm convicted and they hang me, don't tell her that, either. Maybe you can just say I died to protect someone else? I know you'll find the right way to put it. Will you do it for me?"

Allie had heard of heartache and she thought she'd known it. But what she felt now was a thousand times worse. It made her voice shake as if she stood in a high wind. "Yes, if it comes to that. I'll tell your mother that her son is the finest man I've ever known."

He nodded. "Thanks, Allie." Then he pulled her closer

and reached to place a tender kiss on her lips. She heard an anguished sound in his throat when his mouth touched hers. "You go on now. Are you coming to the trial?" His eyes were wet.

She pressed her hand to his face. "Yes, of course I'll be there! I won't leave you alone in this."

"Okay, then. I'll see you tomorrow. And Allie? Thanks. For everything."

Allie turned and stumbled out of the back room, tears blinding her. Will Mason asked some question of her as she hurried through his office, but she didn't hear it, and she didn't stop until she was outside on the street.

She looked around her, at a town in a world that rolled on despite the tragedy about to occur to the man locked up in the office behind her. Her sense of helplessness infuriated her to the point of overriding her heartbreak. She clutched her reticule in tight hands. There had to be something she could do to help Jeff.

Her head came up then as an idea occurred to her. A possible way out. It was a slim chance, and it might mean a final and complete schism between her and Olivia. But to save Jeff, Allie was willing to sacrifice anything.

Turning on her heel, she walked back into Will Mason's office. He was back at his desk, reading his newspaper, and looked up at her with a surprised expression.

"Ma'am?"

"Sheriff Mason, where might I find Royal Purdy?"

Chapter Seventeen

"I DON'T KNOW, MISS FORD. IT'S NOT MUCH TO GO ON."
Royal Purdy sat at his gouged pine desk and leaned back
in his chair.

Allie sat across from the lawyer, her back to the wall
and with barely enough room for her knees. Her chair was
so rough and splintered that she was sure it would catch
her skirt. "I know it seems that way, but we could at least
go out to the farm and have a look."

No wonder Jeff had sounded so bereft of hope when
Allie had talked to him. She'd been here for the better part
of an hour, trying to convince Royal Purdy that Jeff was
innocent, and must be defended in court. His interest in the
case was, at best, lukewarm. Dear God, wouldn't this man
make any attempt to save his client? Did he care nothing
at all for the plight of a man who might hang despite his
innocence? Her efforts to remain calm were failing, and
desperation crept in. "The real evidence might provide just
enough discrepancy to befuddle the two witnesses."

Purdy put his hands together and tented his fingers. "But
the trial begins tomorrow morning. Judge John Cavanaugh

and Marshall Hastings, the prosecutor, have already arrived. At this point, I don't know what—"

Allie thumped her fist on the arm of her chair. "Mr. Purdy, if you are going to represent Mr. Hicks, you cannot stand by and make no effort to spare him from conviction for a crime he didn't commit!"

"I'm curious, Miss Ford, why are you so concerned with the fate of Jeff Hicks?"

Allie sat back, unprepared for the question. "Well, h-he worked for me, and I believe he's a good man."

"Forgive me for saying so, but when I spoke with your sister she indicated that your interest goes somewhat deeper. She even went so far as to reveal that you can, shall we say, *account* for Mr. Hicks' whereabouts most of the night before the murder took place."

Allie felt hot blood rush to her cheeks, and silently cursed disloyal, loose-tongued Olivia. She could barely meet Purdy's pale gaze. What was he suggesting? That some other kind of inducement from Allie would inspire him to help Jeff? Gathering her tattered dignity to her, she lifted her chin and met his eyes squarely, ready to confront whatever she found there. "Would it help him if I testified to that in court?"

The silence that hung between her question and his answer told her that they were both thinking of her offer. "It might. But I wouldn't dream of calling a lady to the stand to make such a statement."

"I believe that's my decision to make."

He shook his head in a paternalistic sort of way. "It is not your decision at all. It leaps the bounds of decency to even consider it."

She let out a quiet sigh of relief. "Then you must make use of the evidence I already told you about."

"Miss Ford, I think it's pointless to spend any more time discussing this." He gathered a stack of papers and tapped their edges on the desk, plainly dismissing both her and the subject.

She would not be told *no*, she vowed to herself again. She would do whatever it took to exonerate Jeff. But what? What could breathe life into this languid, prosaic man? What was it he wanted? Looking around, it suddenly occurred to her.

"If it's a matter of money, I can pay you." She had a little in the bank, and if it meant that there would be less for Olivia, well, that was too bad. Her sister would have to help pay to undo the horrible wrong she'd committed. "I understand that you've agreed to represent Mr. Hicks for free. It's a noble, humanitarian thing you're doing. Surely, though, you must have expenses to meet." She gestured at the office around her, a grubby little closet on a side street behind the barbershop, barely large enough to accommodate his rummage-sale furniture and the chair where Allie sat. The walls were painted a dirty tan, and the plaster upon them was cracked like a dry riverbed during a drought. In her opinion, if he paid more than two dollars a month rent for this place, he was being robbed.

Purdy straightened and sat forward, his eyes sharply focused on her face. "Yes, well, my practice is very new and I haven't had the chance yet to establish myself."

Although Allie's life had been fairly sheltered, she was not so unworldly that she didn't understand what power the lure of a dollar had. Despairing, but not wanting to appear so, she threw Purdy another tempting morsel. "I'm sure you have a bright future ahead of you, especially if you display your legal talents and help clear Mr. Hicks."

He drummed his fingers on the arm of his chair and studied her while he mulled over her suggestion. Pushing himself away from his desk, he said, "You could very well be right, Miss Ford. I think we understand each other better than I first believed. We should make the trip to your farm, right now, while we still have good daylight."

Jeff lay in the darkness counting his heartbeats between the flashes of lightning and the claps of thunder. Funny, he couldn't usually feel his heart unless he'd been working hard in the sun, or as he had the other night, when he'd made love with Allie.

But he felt it now thudding in his chest, just lying here with the storm raging outside. He knew it was because he was scared. Despite what he'd told Allie about atonement and a reckoning, he was so scared of tomorrow he wished he could curl up and hide beneath his bunk.

Royal Purdy had reminded him that Judge John Cavanaugh usually preferred to dispense with a jury, as was within his authority, and decide cases himself. He was a fair man, but stern, with no patience for the follies of humanity. So tomorrow, the judge would listen to Floyd Endicott and Olivia Ford spin their lies, and with a stroke of his gavel, he'd find Jefferson Walker Hicks guilty of murder. And by doing so, he'd bring Jeff to the end of a long, directionless road he'd set his foot upon two years ago. The hope for the future that Allie had given him would be thrown back in his face, because he had no future.

But he was so damned grateful for the time they'd had, and that he'd known love one more time. Any man in his right mind would consider himself lucky to have the chance to hold Allie in his arms, and to have that again was worth facing a whole courtroom full of Judge Cavanaughs.

Will had told him that no matter what happened, Jeff had to make a good showing in court, so he'd accompanied him to the barbershop for a bath and a shave. At least he'd arranged for it all to take place after closing, but the walk down there had been torture for Jeff. Decker Prairie had whispered about him before, but he'd always been too drunk to care. As he'd followed Will on the sidewalk, he'd been painfully aware of every pair of eyes on him and his bound wrists, every murmuring voice, even if he hadn't been able to hear what was said.

Old Pete Gerard, the barber, had gone to great lengths to tell Jeff that Floyd was going around town, telling anyone who'd listen how Jeff had cracked Cooper's noggin with that pick and taken from him the best friend a man ever had. Oh, it was such a sorry tale, and good for lots of free beers at the Liberal.

For the briefest moment, Jeff had considered bolting and trying to escape. Even though his hands were shackled, if he could get away he could worry about freeing them later. But he'd abandoned the idea almost as soon as it crossed his mind. Will, the man he'd once called a friend, would have been forced to shoot him down in the street, right there in front of everyone. Maybe in front of Allie.

Somehow that had seemed worse than hanging. Meeting his fate like a man, with his head up, had more dignity than running away. He owed Allie and his family that much.

So now he lay here, listening to the rain, counting his heartbeats, and counting the minutes until morning.

At last, when he couldn't do that anymore, and because he could do nothing else, he slowly rolled over on the bunk, buried his face against his arm, and wept.

Allie chose her best dress, a French-blue cambric wrapper, and was carefully dressed and ready to leave her hotel room by seven-thirty the next morning. But court would not convene at the Liberal Saloon until nine. There was nothing to do except wait, so she perched on the desk chair and tried to keep her insides from shaking.

She'd slept little the night before. Most of her time had been spent pacing in a circle in her room at the hotel. Flashes of lightning occasionally accompanied the thunder that seemed to roll in waves from one side of the valley to the other. Rain, when it came, had fallen in angry, wind-blown torrents. The lace curtains billowed into the room like the remains of a ragged death shroud.

Allie must have gone to the window a hundred times to look down the darkened street toward the sheriff's office. Now she stood and went to the window to look again. Last night's storm had passed and the morning had dawned a tender blue. The day promised to be a warm one. It was too fine a day to ruin a man's life, she thought.

Would it work, the plan that she and Royal Purdy had devised? Could he ask questions that would unravel Olivia's seemingly calm self-assurance, and break down Floyd's web of lies? He thought he could. She left the window and recommenced pacing the circle she'd traveled over last night.

As Allie had guessed, the lawyer's interest and level of energy directed toward Jeff's behalf took a giant leap forward when, upon returning to Decker Prairie from the farm, she'd stopped at the bank and withdrawn one hundred dollars to pay him.

After treading her well-worn circuit on the carpet, Allie glanced at the clock on the nightstand one last time. Eight-forty-five. Thank God. As she collected her reticule and took one final look in the mirror, she thought that there was almost nothing worse than waiting for fate.

Except perhaps meeting it.

* * *

The Liberal Saloon, now temporarily transformed into a makeshift courtroom, was packed with what seemed to be every citizen in town. People had come from miles around to see this grand spectacle of justice. Borrowed chairs and benches had been pressed into service, and still there were people who stood along the walls and in the back. Although the doors were left open, heat was already beginning to build within the saloon's confines. Those who couldn't get a place to sit or stand lingered on the steps outside. The air was thick with whispering, throat clearings, the occasional laugh, and murmuring. This was probably the biggest event in the town's history and no one wanted to miss out on it.

Allie was fortunate enough to have secured a spot just behind Royal Purdy's table, which she recognized as having come from the library. The judge's bench and the rest of the furniture, according to discreet signs attached to them, were provided courtesy of the furniture display at Wickwire's. She saw Olivia on the other side of the room, sitting behind the prosecutor's table. She was dressed as impeccably as ever in a beautiful mint-green walking dress, but her face was the color of plaster. Allie knew she was completely unaccustomed to being in a crowd this size— certainly Allie was. But Olivia had no one to keep her company, no one familiar to sit next to or chat with. Allie caught herself beginning to feel sorry for her before she put a stop to the idea. Olivia, with her own lies, had put herself in this position.

Farley Wright, whose henhouse Jeff had been arrested for raiding, leaned against the bar, in deep discussion with another farmer. Even Lane Smithfield and his father, Elisha, had taken the time to come into town for this big event.

Floyd Endicott sat on a bench along the wall, unshaven and in overalls—essentially, looking no different than he did on any other day.

Allie frequently intercepted curious stares from people in the crowd. That was to be expected, she supposed, but it was still unnerving. And if Olivia had told Royal Purdy about the night Allie spent with Jeff, there was no reason to believe that others didn't know about it now, as well.

There was not one person in this room that Allie could count as a friend, she realized. Her life had been so empty and narrow. The one person who had changed that was going on trial for his life.

Sending up a silent prayer for Jeff's deliverance, she laced her fingers tightly in her lap and waited—her stomach was knotted just as tightly.

Finally, after what seemed like an interminable delay, Jeff was ushered in through the Liberal's back door, accompanied by Will Mason. Low, wordless murmuring rolled through the crowd like the wind moaning through treetops. Allie's heart climbed to her throat. Dear God, he looked almost as pale as Allie felt herself, and yet she'd never seen him so handsome. The suit that Will had loaned him fit fairly well, showing off his wide, lean-muscled shoulders. Underneath, he wore a clean white shirt, and a dark tie was knotted at his collar. He stood straight with his head up and his shoulders back, looking neither right nor left. He had the appearance of a soldier going into battle—scared but determined to hide it. Oh, gallant Jeff, she thought, pride lifting her own chin slightly as she gazed at him.

Will seated him at the table next to Royal Purdy, and only then did Jeff catch her eye. He sent her a brief, private smile that she knew was meant for her alone.

"All rise for the Honorable John Cavanaugh," Will said.

A general shuffling of chair legs and light stamping of shoes on the plank flooring brought everyone to their feet. The judge, a dignified, white-haired man, entered, followed by his clerk. All were seated again, and the proceedings commenced.

The charges against Jeff were read, and sitting behind him, Allie saw his shoulders rise and fall as they would if he took a deep breath. Beside him, Royal Purdy, appeared unconcerned as he scribbled notes on a piece of paper.

Following opening statements, the first witness was called.

"Yes, indeed," Dr. Brewster said, "I examined the body of Cooper Matthews. I'd say the blow to his head killed him. The wound appeared to have been made by a slender, pointed object."

"Such as the point of a pick?" Marshall Hastings asked, taking up a big pick and holding it up for the physician to examine.

"Yes, exactly like that."

"Let the record show that Dr. Brewster has indicated the murder weapon. Your witness," Hastings said to Purdy.

The pale young lawyer stood, his voice infused with more authority than Allie had heard yet. "Doctor, in your learned opinion, could the wound have been caused by another kind of tool? Say an axe?"

Allie held her breath.

The doctor shook his head. "No, not in my opinion. The weapon pierced the brain, the sphenoid bone that forms the bottom of the brain box, and continued all the way through the roof of the man's mouth. An axe would have left a bigger hole and created a much messier injury." A few distressed moans rippled through the spectators. "The configuration of the wound indicated it was inflicted by that kind of weapon, there." He pointed to the pick on the evidence table.

"Again, let the record show that Dr. Brewster is referring to the pick. Thank you, Doctor. No more questions."

The doctor was excused.

Next, Floyd Endicott was called to testify. Allie stared

at him while he swore on the Bible to tell the truth, and felt such a wave of anger and revulsion for the man, she grew lightheaded. She had disliked him ever since the day he'd demanded payment for painting her fence, when he'd spent the afternoon napping under her pear tree. Now, for telling this outrageous lie about Jeff, she despised him with every ounce of her being. He lounged negligently in the chair next to the bench until Judge Cavanaugh barked at him to sit up and pay proper respect to the court. Floyd, wearing the idiotic grin of one so chastised, straightened up.

Hastings began his questioning. "Mr. Endicott, will you tell the court how you and Cooper Matthews came to be on the Ford property the night of the murder?"

"Miss *O*-livia Ford sent Cooper a letter. She asked him to come out and do another little job for her. Cooper wanted me to come with him to help, so I did."

"And when did you encounter Mr. Hicks?"

Allie noted that the prosecutor neatly avoided the issue of the trespassing and vandalism committed by the two men.

Floyd sat up. "Oh, he come runnin' out of the darkness, madder'n hell, cussin' and callin' us all kind of names like bastards an'—

Squeaks of offended feminine sensibility sounded here and there.

"That will do, Mr. Endicott," Judge Cavanaugh interrupted. "A recitation of any profanities won't be necessary."

Floyd shrugged, and Hastings prompted, "Go on, please."

"He was carryin' that there pick with him, and he told us we were trespassin'. Well, everyone knows there's been bad blood 'tween him and Cooper for a long time, even before Hicks killed Cooper's boy. There was lots more more yellin' and"—Floyd glanced at the judge—"bad words, and before I knew it, he swung that pick down on Cooper's head with all his might. God a'mighty, it was horrible! It made an awful sucking noise when he pulled it out. And blood squirted out of pore Cooper's skull."

"What did you do then?"

"Well, hoo-ee, boy, I figured I was next. I managed to pick up Cooper and dump him into the back of the wagon we come in, and I made tracks outta there."

"How did you come into possession of the pick?"

"I decided I'd better take the thing along with us so's Hicks couldn't poke it into my head next!"

"You drove the wagon back to town?"

"Yessiree, I didn't stop until I got to Sheriff Mason's office. Cooper, he—he was dead by then." Here Floyd worked up a few crocodile tears and his voice quavered. "He was the best friend I ever had—you can ask anybody. And that son of a bitch"—he pointed at Jeff—"he killed him! If there's any justice, he'll hang for crow bait!"

Allie bit back a gasp, and general murmuring broke out among the onlookers.

Royal Purdy stood. "Objection!"

"Sustained, and quiet in the court!" the judge ordered, and banged his gavel. "Mr. Endicott, you will confine your remarks to questions put to you."

"I have no further questions," Hastings said, looking rather smug. "Your witness, Mr. Purdy."

Purdy paced slowly in front of Floyd, with his hands clasped behind his back. First one circuit, then another. Finally, he said, "You say that you and Mr. Matthews were on the Ford property because Miss Olivia Ford asked you to come out."

"Yessir."

"To do *another* job for her, I believe you said."

"Yessir, that's right."

"Did you ever see a letter that Mr. Matthews received from her?"

"No, Cooper said he tore 'em up, just like she wanted."

"What previous chores had you performed at her request?"

"Well, just one other. She had us come out one night and hang a spook in the barn."

"A spook."

"Yeah, it was a dummy she made up, stuffed with feathers and wearin' a dress. Said she wanted to play a joke on someone but she couldn't reach the rafter. So me and Cooper came out and strung it up for her."

This time Allie did gasp. So that's how it had come about. Olivia swore she hadn't put that horrible thing in the barn, and in her mind, she probably believed it was close enough to the truth. She glared at her sister across the room. Olivia, keeping her eyes on the proceedings, blanched a bit, but otherwise showed no emotion.

Purdy nodded and kept pacing. "Miss Olivia paid you to do this."

"She paid Cooper ten dollars. He gave me four."

Allie swallowed and swallowed, but her throat was as dry as chalk.

"And what job were you doing out there the night Mr. Matthews was killed?"

"We were salting the field that Hicks had planted."

"Destroying the Ford vegetable garden, wasn't it?"

"Uh, yeah." Then more emphatically, he added, "That's what Cooper said she wanted!"

"And how much did she pay you to do this?"

"At first Cooper told me it was ten dollars, and that I'd get four, same as the other time. But then when we were working, she came out to pay us and I found out she was givin' him twenty, and he was still gonna give me four."

Sitting behind him, Allie couldn't see Jeff's face. She could only judge his reactions by the way his back stiffened or relaxed. Right now, he sat bolt upright.

"So Mr. Matthews—your best friend—lied to you. He knew it was twenty dollars all along."

"Yeah—"

Marshall Hastings came to his feet, plainly displeased with the direction of Purdy's questioning. "Your Honor, I fail to see what any of this has to do with the matter in question. None of it pertains to the crime or the charges."

"*I* would like to hear this, Mr. Hastings." Judge Cavanaugh fixed the prosecutor with a hard look, and Hastings sat down.

"How big would you say that field is, Mr. Endicott?" Purdy continued.

" 'Bout an acre, I guess."

"An acre—that's a lot of salt to spread in the dead of night when most people are sleeping. Especially for four dollars. Did you consider that?"

Floyd shifted in his chair. "It crossed my mind."

"I imagine it did." Purdy gazed at him for a long moment, as if considering something the man had said. Then, "I have no other questions."

"Does that mean I can go?" Floyd asked the judge. From where she sat, Allie could see a thin sheen of perspiration on Floyd's face.

"It does not. It means you can return to your seat."

He shambled back to his chair, looking none too pleased.

Next, Olivia was called to the stand. Allie stared at her, feeling as if she were watching a stranger.

Marshall Hastings was especially solicitous to her, and led her through a testimony in which she repeated the same story she'd told Will Mason. It differed somewhat from Floyd's version. She didn't look nearly as confident as she had before, though.

When Royal Purdy was called to cross-examine, he was every bit as polite and mild.

"I understand that you are of delicate health, Miss Ford, so we'll try to move things along as quickly as possible."

"Thank you. I appreciate that."

Allie gritted her teeth.

"You testified, under oath, that you never sent any letters to Cooper Matthews?"

"Oh, my, no. I'd never seen him or Mr. Endicott until this whole sorry business came about."

"So you didn't pay either one of them to perform chores on your property."

"No, my sister, Althea, has been in charge of those things since our father died."

"How is it that you happened to see Mr. Hicks out in the field the night of the murder?"

"Well, sometimes I have trouble sleeping, and I sit on our back porch. The night air helps clear my head. There was a half-moon that night and I saw Mr. Hicks leave the shed—that's where my sister had given him a place to sleep. He was carrying a pick."

"Did he see you?"

"No, he never looked at me. He didn't know I was there."

"Where did he go?"

"He headed off toward the field he'd planted. I couldn't imagine what he'd be doing outside in the middle of the night with a tool like that. And he was gone for the longest time. Finally, I decided I'd better go and have a look myself." She turned wide, innocent eyes on Purdy. "After all, a person wandering around in the dark by himself could get hurt. I had to check."

Allie heard a faint snort come from Jeff. She herself closed her hands into fists in her lap.

"You said he was gone for a long time. How long would you say?"

"Oh, it must have been an hour or better. You can see why I was worried."

"Do you know what time it was?"

"I think—yes, I'm sure it was about two o'clock. I heard the clock chime on the mantle in the house. It wasn't until after three that I went looking for him."

Liar, liar, liar! Allie screamed in her heart. Jeff wasn't outside at two o'clock, and he wasn't gone for over an hour. He wasn't! The muscles in her back and legs began to flex, as if fighting her will to remain seated. She clenched her back teeth, every muscle in her body as tight as an overwound mainspring.

"And you're sure he was carrying that pick over there when you saw him." Again, Purdy indicated the murder weapon on the evidence table.

"Yes, definitely."

"You don't think the moonlight could have played tricks on your eyes."

Olivia lifted her chin a bit haughtily. "I know what I saw, Mr. Purdy. There is nothing wrong with my eyesight."

Royal Purdy stepped over to the bar and reached behind it, producing an axe. "You didn't see this axe in his hands?"

Olivia couldn't hide the surprise on her face upon seeing the axe. "N-no! He had a pick."

As Purdy turned he caught Allie's eye and shrugged slightly. They'd gone out to the farm yesterday and after some searching, they'd found the axe exactly where Jeff had told her he'd left it—in the blackberries.

"And he was gone a long time," Olivia re-emphasized. "Long enough to have killed Cooper Matthews!"

Allie had sat quivering in her chair, listening to the lies Floyd and Olivia told. Fear and anger raged within her. She would not stand by and let them convict Jeff of this horrible crime in order save their own worthless hides. She had a furious desire to run up to the front and knock everyone's heads together. Couldn't they see what Olivia and Floyd were doing? Then, as if some power other than her own had willed it, she found herself shooting to her feet. "She's lying!"

The room erupted in a buzz of murmurs, and Judge Cavanaugh pounded his gavel. "Order!"

All eyes were turned on Allie, but she felt Jeff's flinty look boring into her like a physical thing.

"Allie! For God's sake, don't do this."

But she continued, heedless of the judge's command or Jeff's appeal.

"I was with Jeff Hicks that night, all night, and I will swear to it under oath."

"Dámn it, Allie, I told you I wouldn't let you say—"

"Order in this courtroom!"

Jeff jumped up as well. "I was *not* with her. Miss Ford is lying to protect me."

Yes, she was, and even though it was a small lie, it didn't come easily to her. But Allie had vowed to do whatever it took to protect Jeff. And if lying under oath and in the face of God would help, she'd do it. She knew Jeff was innocent. God knew it, too.

Judge Cavanaugh continued to pound his gavel.

Eli Wickwire's discreet furniture advertisement fell off the desk and was trampled by the clerk.

Chatter swirled through the crowd.

"What did she say?"

"Jesus, those Ford sisters really *are* crazy."

"This is an outrage. Do young people have no decency at all anymore?"

"I will have order in this courtroom or find everyone here in contempt!" the judge said, now on his feet as well, his face the color of a rooster's comb. He pointed his gavel handle at Allie. "Young woman, who are you?"

Though Allie's insides were shaking like her best raspberry jelly, she forced herself to speak up. "I am Althea Ford, Olivia's sister." She glared at Olivia. "I can vouch for Mr. Hicks' whereabouts, and I will."

"Allie, honey, no," Jeff whispered, his feelings for her plain on his face. But she would not heed him. Her love for him was stronger than any lie, stronger than her fear. She wouldn't sacrifice Jeff without a fight.

"I was . . . I kept company with him the night that Cooper Matthews was killed. The *whole* night."

Judge Cavanaugh commented sourly, "Two witnesses have been sworn in this morning, and I have the feeling that no one has told the truth yet. Mr. Hicks, you sit down right now. This isn't a free-for-all, it's a court of law. We'll get to the bottom of this if it takes us till kingdom come!" Then turning to Allie, he ordered, "Miss Ford, you come up here and be sworn in."

He excused Olivia, who left the stand without sparing her a glance. Terror made Allie feel as if she were running a gauntlet to reach the chair next to the judge. All eyes in the room were turned upon her, assessing her. They stared at her as if they would stone her for fornication, but she also sensed their hunger for salacious detail. Shame flooded her cheeks with hot blood. She felt no shame for what had passed between her and Jeff. But it had been private, to be shared with only him, not a roomful of people.

After she raised her right hand and promised to tell the

truth, prosecutor Marshall Hastings sauntered up to her. He wore a faint, smug sneer.

"Miss Ford, please tell the court how the defendant came to be on your property in the first place."

"I hired him to make repairs around the farm, and to plant my kitchen garden."

"Isn't it true that Mr. Hicks, who has a reputation for chronic public drunkenness, was arrested for robbing"— here he consulted his papers—"one Farley Wright, and the sheriff sentenced him to work for you?" His tone was so insulting and self-satisfied, she wanted to smack him.

"He took one *egg*. And he's not a drunkard anymore."

"Yes or no, Miss Ford."

She sighed. "Yes."

"Apparently he did improve, working for you. So much so, that you developed, shall we say, a fondness for Mr. Hicks?"

"I respect him, yes."

"Oh, come now, Miss Ford. That would seem to be an understatement, in light of your earlier proclamation. Don't your feelings run somewhat deeper than respect?"

Allie looked at Jeff as she spoke, connecting her gaze with his bottomless green eyes. "I love him. He is a worthy, honorable man."

"And isn't it safe to assume that those feelings prejudice your testimony? Are you really willing to throw away your reputation for a condemned man? Would you brand yourself as a woman of loose morals, a veritable whore of Babylon, in a doomed attempt to exonerate him?"

Rapt silence blanketed the saloon. If circumstances had not been so grave, Allie might have even laughed at Hastings' ridiculous attempt to give the small, backward town of Decker Prairie Babylonian proportions. But nothing about this was the least bit amusing.

Allie looked at Jeff again and saw love and emotion brimming in his eyes. Then she leveled a direct, even gaze on Hastings and lifted her chin. She spoke to the prosecutor but raised her voice to carry to every ear in the place. "I would much rather be known as Jeff Hicks' whore from this day forward than to live with the knowledge that I allowed a gentle, good man, an innocent man, to be convicted of a murder he didn't commit. Yes, I was in his company the night of Cooper Matthews' murder. And when Mr. Hicks heard trespassers and went to investigate, he took the axe with him."

"How can you be so certain of that?" Hastings demanded.

"I've been responsible for our farm and everything on it since my father became ill years ago. I know which tools we own and those we don't. We don't own a pick. When Sheriff Mason brought Mr. Hicks out to work for us, he didn't carry a pick with him. Not only that, last winter I had Seth Wickwire check the shovels, the axe, and the rake in the barn for faulty handles. He took all of them into his father's store for replacements. Seth would testify to that, I'm sure. If every merchant we've ever done business with produced our sales records for farm tools, they would not find one for a pick."

"Where, then, did the pick come from that pierced Cooper Matthew's skull?" Hastings asked.

"I saw the empty salt sacks that Floyd and Cooper left in our destroyed field. I'd say they were split open with the pick they brought with them."

"By God, that's a dirty lie!" Floyd exclaimed, jumping up from the bench where he sat. "Hicks had that pick in his hands when he come out to the field."

"I saw it, too!" Olivia agreed, her eyes wild. The insane glint she saw there reminded Allie of the morning they discovered the dummy. She had charged out of the house like a she-devil, not the delicate flower she had always pretended to be. With a blinding flash of insight, Allie suddenly realized that the taunts might have been true—perhaps there *was* a crazy Ford sister. Olivia. But regardless of that, she could not allow Olivia to condemn Jeff.

Allie looked directly at Floyd first, and then her sister. "The pick that killed Cooper Matthews belonged either to Floyd Endicott or to Cooper himself." Eyeing Floyd again, she said, "I'm willing to bet my life that Jeff Hicks didn't kill Cooper. And if he didn't do it, who does that leave? Who had the motive? Wouldn't he have been so furious when he learned that Cooper had cheated him, that he flew into a killing rage?"

In the midst of her nervous righteousness, a fragment of a memory popped up in Allie's mind—never look a threatening animal in the eyes. It will only provoke—

Floyd's jaw flopped open, revealing gums that were missing several teeth. "You can't hang that on me, you goddamned meddlin' female!" He lunged across the saloon and launched himself at Allie. She fell backward, still in the chair, with Floyd sitting on her chest, and his hands around her throat. The man's face twisted into an angry, frustrated mask. "Cooper was always sayin' how stupid I was, an' how he had all the brains. He called me names and cheated me out of the money I was supposed to get—*me*, the only friend he had. I wasn't gonna put up with it anymore—no, sir! He cussed me out again that night for takin' the wagon out to the road and leavin' him to face Hicks. Called me stupid, *again*. I seen that pick in the wagon bed—I was just gonna knock him on his ass. It was just a tap, a little tap! But it went right through his brain and finished him off! I guess he won't be callin' me stupid no more!"

Panic filled Allie, a gnawing mortal fear that she would die. Floyd's filthy hands around her neck were like iron vises cutting off her air. She couldn't breathe—God, couldn't they see she was suffocating? She struggled and tried to lift her own hands to claw at his, but her arms were trapped under his knees. In her chest, her heart was screaming for air. Faces. There were faces behind Floyd's, fading in and out—there was Jeff with his arm around the man's neck, and Will Mason was on the other side. No air . . . no air. Everyone was talking at once and yelling, but the sounds began to fade away as if disappearing into a dark mist. The faces dissolved behind a grainy black curtain that materialized before Allie's eyes. Jeff—dear God, where was he? She couldn't see him.

She couldn't see anything.

As tense as a buggy spring, Jeff sat beside Althea's inert form where she lay on Doc Brewster's examination table. It smelled of carbolic in here, and, faintly, of ether. His elbows on his knees, he rested his chin on his folded hands and never took his eyes from her face. He was afraid that if he did, even for a second, she'd be gone. Jesus, she was so pale and fragile-looking; except for the wine-colored bruises on her neck, she looked, well, he dared not let himself even think the word.

He'd carried her in his arms here to the doctor's office once they were able to pry Floyd's hands off her. Jeff had taken a swing at him, connecting solidly with the man's unshaven jaw, and Will Mason had immediately taken Floyd into custody. Amid the chaos, Judge Cavanaugh had found Jeff not guilty, and then ordered Will to return after locking up Floyd to charge Olivia with perjury and obstruction of justice.

Jeff had been keeping vigil by Allie's side ever since,

and it seemed as if hours had passed. Before going back to the saloon, the doctor had said she'd be fine, but he also said she was in shock. Jeff took one of her hands and pressed her fingers to his lips, terrified by their iciness. He'd never known a finer, stronger woman, or seen a braver deed than when she strode through the disapproving crowd at the Liberal Saloon, saying that she had spent the night with him. He hadn't wanted her to say that. He'd wanted to spare her from the ostracism that must surely follow her admission, especially with that bastard, Marshall Hastings, roasting her over the open flame of the witness stand. But she hadn't faltered or hesitated.

Allie Ford had saved his life, in every possible way a man's life could be saved. She'd given him back his dignity and self-respect, she had faith in him, and in front of the town of Decker Prairie, had declared her love for him.

"Allie, honey, please wake up," he murmured, trying to swallow the knot of emotion closing his throat. "I want to tell you how much I love you. Do you know that? I love you more than I do my own life."

The long, slender fingers he held in his hand twitched then. Jeff jumped up and stared into her still face. "Allie?"

She moaned and turned her head slightly.

"Allie, it's Jeff. I'm right here." He squeezed her hand. "Can you feel that?"

She squeezed back, and her eyes fluttered open. She looked puzzled and disoriented, but Jeff grinned with relief and said a silent prayer of thanks that she'd been restored to him.

"What happened?" she asked muzzily. Her voice was a bit hoarse, no doubt from the way that son of a bitch, Endicott, had bruised her neck. Slowly she looked around and a slight frown creased her brow. "Where is this?"

"Everything is fine now, honey, just fine." He reminded

her about Floyd's attack. "You passed out and I brought you down here to Doc Brewster's. How do you feel?"

"Kind of achy, like I fell or something." Her eyes widened as they cleared. "What about the trial?"

"I'm free, Allie. Because you were brave enough to speak up."

"Oh, Jeff, really?" She lifted heavy arms to hug his neck. They fell back to the table. He scooped her into his embrace. "But what about Floyd?"

"Floyd's in jail and he'll stand trial for murdering Cooper. After all, he confessed in front of a couple of hundred witnesses."

Her smile was radiant, then it dimmed. "I wonder what will happen to Olivia."

Jeff sighed. "It's time that you stopped worrying about her. You did more than anyone could expect of you. Now it's time for your to live your own life. You have that *right*. You have the right to be happy. And, hell, I guess I do, too." He pressed his forehead to hers briefly, his eyes closed. "God, when I think about how close I came to losing everything—we'll go make a new start. We can leave, or there's my land. I've still got that. We could go there." He kissed her, savoring the feel of her tender lips beneath his. "What do you say, Allie? Will you be my wife?"

With a sound that was something between a giggle and a sob, she threw her arms around his neck. "Yes, Jeff, yes. I will!"

"How about a quiet little ceremony before Judge Cavanaugh leaves town?"

She looked at him, and Jeff saw the love and devotion on her pretty face. "It sounds perfect!" She hugged him tighter.

Allie was so happy, she wanted to share it with the whole world. She would climb to the roof of Wickwire's and shout that Jeff Hicks loved her and she loved him. Everyone in town would gather in the street below and give her gracious applause, glad that two of Decker Prairie's least popular citizens had found joy at last. She almost giggled at the fantasy, as implausible as it was.

Just then, Doctor Brewster walked into the examination room. "Well, young lady, I'm glad to see you back among us again, You gave us quite a scare."

He looked into Allie's eyes and had her stand up to make sure her balance and strength had returned. "Good girl," he said, nodding in approval. "In case you didn't hear, your sister is in a peck of trouble with the judge."

Allie gazed up at the doctor. "Is—is he going to send her to jail?"

"Bah, no! John Cavanaugh wouldn't put a woman in jail for something like perjury. She might wish he had, though, before long. He sentenced her to work for Mary and Louise Pratt, for five years. They'll having her hopping night and day. And Will Mason has to make sure she serves her time. They might be old, but as their doctor I can tell you they're in perfect health, and I imagine they'll both outlive that sentence."

Allie sighed. Five years. Now her sister would learn what it meant to fetch and carry and wait on someone to the extreme. As angry as she was with her sister, Allie was glad that Olivia wouldn't be going to jail. But she couldn't muster one spark of sympathy over the punishment that had been imposed upon her.

"Doc, do you know if the judge is still down at the Liberal?" Jeff asked, putting his arm around Allie's waist.

"As far as I know. But I wouldn't think you'd want to have any more dealings him for a long time."

"Just the opposite—I need to talk to him right away, before he leaves." Jeff smiled and pulled Allie a bit closer. "I need to see the man about a wedding."

Epilogue

CARRYING TWO BLUE ENAMEL MUGS OF COFFEE, ALLIE stepped out to the porch swing to enjoy the last peachy fingers of the August sunset, and the view of a good-looking horseman riding up to the front step.

"How did you know that's one of the things I'm craving?" Jeff asked, climbing down from a sleek, bay gelding that matched the color of Allie's hair. He tied its reins to a railing post.

She laughed. "I'm getting the hang of you, I think. How did your meeting with Eli go?"

"Good. He'll take corn and potatoes for the store."

A year after their ordeal, he was more breathtakingly handsome than she would have ever dreamed the day he appeared at her door with Will Mason. He had filled out with lean muscle and sinew. His sandy hair was sun-bleached from his days outdoors, and his green eyes sparkled with joy and health. He pulled off his leather gloves and took a mug from her.

Settling beside her, he patted her thigh with his free hand. Intimacy and understanding, to be able to touch and be touched, seemed like never-ending miracles to her. They renewed her spirit daily, and she felt like the luckiest woman on earth to be loved by Jeff Hicks.

They sat in easy, companionable silence, looking out at the rolling acres surrounding their new home. This was Jeff's land, which had stood empty and untended for years. Some acres were under cultivation now, and the coming harvest would be a good one. The house still smelled of fresh paint and wood, flowers grew in wild profusion in the beds surrounding the foundation, and it was just another symbol of their new beginning, separately and together.

That new beginning had started the day immediately following the trial. Judge Cavanaugh had performed a simple but heartfelt ceremony for them in Will Mason's office.

As if he now read her thoughts, he commented, "It's hard to believe that a year has passed since the trial. And everything else. No more bad dreams?"

She smiled and squeezed his broad wrist where it lay on her thigh. "No, not anymore. Not since the fire."

Despite her happiness with Jeff, Allie had been plagued by nightmares that made sleep a time of terror rather than rest. Images of her mother had still haunted her.

Finally, after one especially difficult night, Jeff had put Allie on the wagon seat next to him and driven her to the Ford farm. With no one living on the property, it had looked worse than ever. While she had watched, Jeff splashed two five-gallon cans of kerosene around the barn walls. Then he'd handed her a match.

"Go ahead, Allie." She'd climbed down from the wagon, walked up to the barn, and struck the match on a rock. Then she threw it onto a puddle of the fuel. Within minutes, the entire structure had been engulfed in towering sheets of white-edged flames. They had stayed and watched until the roof and walls crashed in, and nothing was left but a huge pile of red embers and blackened timbers.

With the burning of the barn, Allie was finally at peace with her ghosts. She and Jeff later sold the property to a newly arrived Swedish family from Minnesota, who didn't mind building a new barn, or the fact that two graves occupied a fenced space on the land.

With her foot on the porch flooring, Allie gave a gentle push and set the swing into motion. "I've had a lot of time to think about, well, everything. My mother was never right again after Olivia was born, but I think that was only made worse by my father. He really was an unsympathetic tyrant. And even though Olivia was his favorite, he filled her head with poison and resentment all her life, and encouraged her to depend solely on me. She was as much a prisoner in that life as I was. In the end, she got caught up in her own web of deceit. There was no one to step in and smooth everything over, as I'd always done for her. Now she's paying for that."

Jeff took a sip of coffee and nodded. "Maybe she's finally growing up."

"I hope so." Allie gazed out at the darkening blue sky, and noted a pair of swallows, winging their way home in the twilight.

She'd seen Olivia just once in the past year. It had been at Wickwire's while Allie was shopping for curtain material. Louise Pratt had tottered into the store, with Olivia trailing behind and the old harpy barking orders at her. Allie hadn't spoken to Olivia, and her sister had stared through her as if she weren't there. She didn't know if their breach would ever be healed, but it didn't matter now.

"You know, I'm glad I built this house with the front porch facing south," he said, changing the subject, and the timbre of his voice. "That way we can enjoy the sun and the moon. It's very romantic, don't you think?" He set his coffee down and put an arm around her shoulders to pull her closer.

"Hmm, yes, it is. That reminds me—you said the coffee was one of the things you'd been craving. What else did you have in mind?"

Jeff lowered his head to sprinkle soft, slow kisses along her neck. "I'll bet you can guess." He worked his way up to her ear and ran his tongue along its outer edge. Delicious shivers made goose bumps bloom all over her body. Turning her lips toward his, she eagerly accepted his full, lush kiss. His tongue moved slowly over the inside of her mouth, making her moan softly. His warm hand crept up her ribs, and he brushed the backs of his fingers over her erect nipple where it pushed against the bodice of her blouse. Emboldened, her own hand sought the hard, full length of him straining against his fly buttons.

"I think we've sat out here long enough, don't you?" he asked, taking tender little nips at her mouth. "Unless, of course, you'd like to try it in the swing."

She laughed. "No, I don't think so. It's not really long enough."

He chuckled, too. "I guess you're right." He stood up and held out his hand to help her to her feet. Glancing at the sky, he said, "Look Allie, there's your moon coming up over there."

She followed his gaze to the eastern sky and saw a huge moon climbing into the firmament, brighter than a lamp. "Allie's Moon? I like that better than Corn Moon, like the *Farmer's Almanac* calls it."

"All right, then. From now on, it'll be Allie's Moon."

Taking Jeff's hand, she followed him into the house, believing with all her heart that perhaps it truly was her moon, after all.